T0148432

DARK WORKS

THE UNTRUE

SUE KELLER

IUNIVERSE, INC.
NEW YORK   BLOOMINGTON

Dark Works
The Untrue

iUniverse books may be ordered through booksellers or by contacting:

iUniverse
1663 Liberty Drive
Bloomington, IN 47403
www.iuniverse.com
1-800-Authors (1-800-288-4677)

Because of the dynamic nature of the Internet, any Web addresses or links contained in this book may have changed since publication and may no longer be valid. The views expressed in this work are solely those of the author and do not necessarily reflect the views of the publisher, and the publisher hereby disclaims any responsibility for them.

ISBN: 978-1-4401-2874-5 (sc)
ISBN: 978-1-4401-2875-2 (ebk)

Printed in the United States of America

iUniverse rev. date: 6/29/2009

PRELUDE

A little girl played in her room. She was the age of four, she heard her sisters in the living room talking and listening to the records on the record player. Then the music suddenly stopped and one of the oldest sisters, Sue, called and gathered the kids around Lisa's piano and excitedly told them to "Watch the keys." The little four years old wanted to see what was going on but was crowded out by the bigger children. She lightly tugged on Cindy's sleeve and said. "Let me see!" "You don't need to see, ya little brat." Cindy said as she pushed Cloe away from the piano. Cloe made her way around until someone moved and let her in front.

As they all stared at the keys, Sue opened the book to an already marked place and started to chant something the other children could not understand, and stared down at the piano's keys with her blue eyes fixed. Her lips moving to chant the same phrase over and over.

Sue's brow was knitted in concentration and suddenly as if the air got to stiff to breathe, a piano key would lightly plink. Diane, the very oldest, suddenly slammed the piano hood down over the keys. The girls jumped out of their wits. They stared from one sister to the other. Diane told Sue to get out of the house with that book. Cloe had a feeling though that the book never left the house. It could have gone down in the basement where most of the girls slept. And whether they practiced downstairs or not, she knew not. She did know there were figures that darted around the house. She knew she heard voices when no one was home except her or very late at night. She knew she may have even felt someone sit on her bed or lay with her. Only to look and there would be no one. She knew she heard someone walk around or scratching noises.

She knew she wasn't dreaming either.

But she could remember hearing Lisa's guitar playing by itself several times. And how she remembered that when the strings where being played it would wake Cloe up, and she would make her way to the top of the basement stairs and call out for Lisa but no one would answer. The next morning Cloe would ask Lisa if she woke up in the middle of the night and played her guitar. Her answer was always "No." She always caught the girls together whispering about things and sometimes one was scared, she could tell.

So the little house they lived in had one hell of a ghost problem. Sue continued her magic and the girls would do séances and the Ouija boards every chance they got. It was a part of life for that family and the relatives to get together on week ends and play these games.

It wasn't until Cloe got older and started having more friends that she heard from other children and learned that these things were thought of as bad and unholy. Cloe didn't let just anyone know that that was what they did unless someone just begged to find out.

Sometimes Cloe would let them know the secret. Only to have the same friend move away some time later. Then Cloe would be alone again. She always had her imaginary friends though. Imaginary when she was four but she became older they became more tangible. When she had to rid of them, they would become mean and break her most cherished objects in her room.

Then she truly was alone.

PRESENT DAY

As the car sped down the road, Cloe put a CD in the CD player of her Kia. It was a CD her sister burned for her of the old Cher songs from the 1970's. "Dark Lady" was always Cloe's favorite. It seemed like the song was wrote after the life of her older sister Sue. Maybe that's why Sue made that song first on this CD.

As Cher's sultry voice started belting out the song, Cloe's mind went back in time to when she was just a little girl. What a strange mixed up religion her family was. Cloe's dad was part Indian, part German, and was Catholic at a young age but when he quit school in 9th grade and joined the navy, got out on honorable discharge and started a family with Cloe's mother, who was mixed English and German. Cloe's mom's side of the family was full of rumors of witchcraft and her great grandmother was a witch and was evil at that.

Cloe always wondered which genealogy contributed the most to the girl's 'extra senses' to the supernatural. There where 9 children and Cloe was the youngest. All the girls had an understanding of it but the boys didn't show any signs. At least of what Cloe could remember. All her life the family gatherings always included the Ouija board and séances, and visiting psychics. The children of the Smith family always went to church, even though the parents stayed home. It just depended on which bus came by to get them. Mostly it was Baptist, Pentecostal, and then the Methodist bus came also.

And if one child didn't get on the first bus, there was always the other. Sometimes their Aunt Becky took them with her to her Lutheran church.

Cloe could remember that she had a more adult ways of looking at things when she was little. Her friends always told her she acted more adult than she should be and Cloe picked up on things more quickly than most girls her age. Cindy, her sister just before her was the same way but Cindy chose to live life to the fullest and more dangerous, like her other sisters Cheryl and Billie Jo. And the three girls went through their teenage life with drugs, sex, rock and roll. Cloe's dad enrolled Cloe in a martial art class so that she would not take the path the others chose. And over her adolescents she worked hard and became astute in Jujitsu with a touch of Tai Chi. Cloe looked at the clock in the Kia and it read five thirty. She was supposed to be to Sues at six for dinner.

When Cloe talked to Sue on the phone earlier that day, Sue seemed preoccupied with something and when Cloe asked her what was wrong, Sue sighed and said "I'll tell you over dinner." so Cloe agreed to be there around six. Traffic was slowing down for some reason and soon it became apparent that someone was stranded in the road.

As the cars made their way around the stalled car carefully, Cloe was grateful for the distraction. She reminisced way too much, always wondering where her life was going, as if the past would reveal any answers.

As traffic picked back up again Cloe drove two more blocks and turned on her blinker. When the line of cars lessened and an opening came up, Cloe made a left hand turn and went down the street to pull into a driveway. The house was a two story house, and it always reminded Cloe of the houses in New Orleans. It had a big front porch and the color of the house was a dark green.

Sue had apple trees in the front yard and various lawn ornaments scattered respectfully in the right places. Some of which Cloe had bought her from different flea markets and statue places.

Cloe got out of her car and made her way into the front door. Sue's cat came to rub against her leg. The cat was so fat that if a person saw it they would think it was related to Garfield the cat. Except this cat was a long haired gray fluff ball. You could barely see its legs because the tummy dragged the ground. Cloe bent down to pet it and the cat let out an appreciative purr. Cloe stood back up before the blood went all the way into her head, and the smell of spaghetti wafted in the air. She loved spaghetti and her stomach rumbled in agreement.

She made her way through the living room and into the dining room. She walked up to the table and saw the French bread sitting on the table. As she went to sneak a piece off the platter, she heard a voice from the kitchen saying "Put that bread back!" Cloe's shoulders came up and her hand froze in mid air. Sue looked from around the wall that divided the dining room from the kitchen.

"I'm just kidding, you can have one." Sue laughed.

"This smells delicious." Cloe drooled. "How much longer?"

"In just a little bit. Hey, would you call the kids in from the back yard?"

"Sure, where is Greg?" Cloe asked.

"He's at the church doing whatever he does this late in the evening." Sue said softly. As Cloe made her way to the back door she thought about Sue's husband Greg becoming a preacher. *Greg becoming a preacher would really help me out a lot.* Cloe thought. She yelled for the kids to come in and eat and was bomb barded with all of the children running around her and through the door.

"It seems I'm not the only one who's hungry." Cloe said with a huff as a child pushed past her. "Help me get their plates made and then we'll sit down and eat." Sue said over kids talking loudly to each other. Sue's son was telling everyone to wash their hands in an army commander voice.

So as the kids came out of the bathroom one by one. Sue and Cloe handed their plates to them with a pile of spaghetti on it and the kids made their way to the table to get bread and out the back door again to the picnic table. As soon as the children all cleared out the two sisters made their plates and sat down at the table. Sue poured them some wine in two crystal wine glasses. They made small talk about the kids and Greg. Cloe asked, "Where's Megan?" Sue's other daughter. Usually she was home at this time but tonight she was gone.

"Well, that's what I wanted to talk about." Sue declared. "It seems she has found a new group of friends to run with, but I don't know. They seem different…"

"…Different?" Cloe asked in between bites.

"Yes and I don't want to sound over protective, but I think that they are a cult of sorts."

"Oh." Cloe took a sip of wine. "Why do you say that?"

It's not that Cloe thought that Sue was just imagining things. Both sisters have seen their fare share of strange people and strange things. But she needed to hear the details.

"It's the way they look, and act, and Megan acts different now, and there are things in her room that weren't there before, like black candles, ceremony candles, and she's asking for a black robe out of some magazine." Sue shrugged.

"Do you think it's just a phase?" Cloe asked.

"No." Sue shook her head. "And even if it is, it could be dangerous. So I thought I better check but...well, could you do it for me?"

"Yah, sure. I'd be happy to." Cloe exclaimed. "Do you know where they hang out?"

"Mostly at the mall is what Megan tells me, but I don't believe it." Sue mopped up some sauce with her bread. "Besides Lisa and Cheryl both told me they never see her at the mall. And Lisa would know since I think Amanda is with Megan a lot." Amanda being her sister Lisa's daughter, Cloe's other niece.

"Does Lisa think the same thing?" Cloe asked.

"Oh, you know Lisa; ever since she got her psychology degree she doesn't believe in such things anymore. It's kind of like she forgot the whole history of our family." Sue said while rubbing her eyes and yawning.

"Well then it's settled, since they are my family then I have every right to see who they are with." Cloe said with a quick nod and got up to put her plate in the sink.

"Do you want me to wash up here?" Cloe shouted over her shoulder from the kitchen sink.

"Na, I don't know when the kids will be in with their dishes and Greg didn't eat yet." Sue said as she came up from behind and dumped her plate on top of Cloe's.

"Well I hate to eat and run but I'm kind of anxious to see what's up with Megan. Is she out now?" Cloe says as she heads for the door.

"Ya, she's out at the Romp Room with her 'so called friends'." Sue puts up her fingers as to quote in mid air. "I told her to be home at mid night. Hey, I'll walk you out. I need a cigarette." Sue grabs her cigarettes off the table.

They made some more small talk and Sue finished her cigarette. The two sisters hugged and Cloe left with a promise that she would get to the bottom of this. She got into her car and turned the car engine over.

She loved her little car, it was good on gas and all around a good car. Cher came back over the speakers and Cloe swiftly turned it off. *Enough of you*, Cloe thought. She turned on the radio. Nickleback was singing 'Heavens gates won't open up for me' from the song 'Saving me'.

Cloe thought that was more like it. She began to plan ahead about seeking out the Romp Room and what she would do if she actually found out that there was a cult. She has done this work before, and more. Thanks to her own life experiences,

Cloe is sought after from all kinds of people for all kinds of things from cults and missing children to cults and politicians. But one thing Cloe was seeing more of is the seriousness of it all. It used to be kind of like a game to the teenagers, but it has become more ruthless, more surreal. There were the hangings of the three teens down in Dead Mans Hollow with pentagrams carved into their stomachs. The authorities tried to blow it off a as a prank. One detective was hired by the families, but didn't come up with anything. Then there was the cow found headless and tongue less in the middle of the road. Which was again blew off as a hoax.

Cloe's mind went back to a certain time while she made her way through town. Cloe didn't work with any detectives or police, but on her own acted like one. Families called wanting her to find out where their sons or daughters go when they leave the house or just stopped coming home. She got started when she was 19 and after her classmates took her to a graduation party. They drank and danced but Cloe was the designated driver, so she had free soda all night. They went to a sinister place called The Water Cooler. As the night went on, the more Cloe saw. There where group sex and drugs and when the light was just right, some of the people looked wrong. They had a defiant look in their eyes. Cloe could have sworn their eyes glowed. And they steadily watched Cloe walk here and there trying to keep up with her classmates. There were Goth, kids with the biker look, and college kids. It dawned on Cloe what they where doing after watching them a while, which was drinking blood out of someone's arm who seemed to be passed out. Cloe was out of there. She begged her classmates to leave also but they were to far gone from the affects of alcohol. After she stood outside and pondered on what to do, she called another friend Shari, to take her place. Which Shari wanted to go in the first place but wasn't invited. After Shari told everyone she had a blast at this certain hang out before, Cloe was sure she could trust her to come again. She left them and went home.

The next day Cloe called some kids to see if everyone was still in one piece, literally. To her surprise everyone was doing okay. A little hung over but okay. They asked Cloe why she left and when she tried to explain what she thought she saw, they had thought that Cloe had lost her mind. They didn't see anything, they said. But Cloe was going to look into this. By six o'clock that night the news reported a girl found dead on Highway 2 with her wrist slit and most of her blood gone, just gone, disappearing into thin air. Cloe recognized the girl as the one that they were surrounding at The Water Cooler the night before. The news reported that anybody who knew anything about this was to call the local police. Cloe did just that but had only told them that she saw her at The Water Cooler the night before, knowing that they wouldn't believe the rest. Cloe went to a private detective and told him what she saw about the girl. After taking her statement and asking questions, he sat back in his chair and linked his hands behind his head. He looked at the ceiling for awhile and then looked at Cloe. Her eyes were semi wide as she looked back at him as if she was asking *'Well, do you believe me or not?'*

"So, you really believe you saw this?" He asked.

"Yep." Cloe said as she lifted her chin a notch.

"I'll check it out. If she was there someone would have seen her besides you and there still may be traces of blood left." The detective stated. "Thanks for your time."

"Will you call me and let me know that I haven't lost my mind?" Cloe asked.

"Well, I'm not suppose to, but ya, I'll call if I find out anything."

Cloe left with a feeling of self relief. She had done the right thing. But days went into weeks, and weeks went into months. Finally Cloe couldn't stand any more and called the detectives number. The operator came on the other end with the "I'm sorry, you have reached a number that has been disconnected or no longer in serviced." recording. Cloe pulled the receiver away from her ear and looked at it. Her brow was knitted and she whispered "What the..." She dialed the number again, carefully, to make sure she dialed it right, and again the recording was on the other end.

Cloe remembers the sick feeling in her gut as she headed to his office. It was locked and the lights weren't on. She looked in the windows but everything was still in place. No sign of struggles or that he might have left in a hurry. She went to the police station and told them that she needed a number for his residence. The lady cop disappeared behind the door of an office and came out and said he has moved out of state. "I can't give you any information other than that."

"Do you know if another detective took his place at his old office?"

"Ya, I think so." she said with a nod. "I think I heard some of the officers talking about another moving in."

"Thanks a lot." Cloe nodded and turned to leave out the door when she felt eyes on her watching her. She tried to nonchalantly look around and came into eye contact with a man in a suit looking at her. He looked like he was mad with his hands on his hips causing his blazer to be pushed back. Cloe stopped for a second and looked him in the eye before pushing the door open. *What is his problem?* She wondered to herself as she went outside. She wondered if he knew anything about the detective or any of it.

So she stayed away from The Water Cooler from then on. And anytime anybody talked about being there, she got the heebie jeebies. But no one ever said that they saw strange things like she did. And there are only two reasons why Cloe could have thought she saw what she saw. One, was it never happened and her imagination played tricks on her, and two, whoever hangs there is familiar with it and the new comers are drunk so they don t really pay attention. But Cloe started paying more attention to the missing girl reports. She checked out newspapers and read stories on the internet about strange things. Supernatural things, the unexplained. She was pretty sure she could link them together and started interviewing people on her own. I took some lying on who she was of coarse. The more she did it the better she got.

Now it's the Romp Room. Now it's her niece. *Oh great.*

Some months later Cloe had a phone call that pretty much let her know what happened to her detective. She was at home. Her home being an old white church building like the ones you see in Louisiana. The town dried up and there was hardly any one left in the little town. A few houses draped the road on both side and a gas station in the middle. Her little church house was down a dirt road. Sue had brought her to it because it was a steal. And for someone single it was idea. There was some remodeling done to make a bedroom but other than that it was livable inside. The best part that Cloe liked was the kitchen. It was huge with an island, all white and lots of windows. And the second thing Cloe liked was the stained glass windows in the sanctuary. *Her own sanctuary* Cloe thought with a big smile. She was going to love this place. She was away from the big city where her sisters, brothers, and parents lived, but she was just 30 minutes away.

The office she had, had a little library in it and besides the books the pastor had left, Cloe had bought every book she could on every religion, every belief, every cult, fallen angels, good angels, dream dictionaries, charms, spells, healing, herbs, candles, stones, rituals, and even Voodoo and Hoodoo. Anything that may help her in her fight against the unknown. She also had books on finding God, losing yourself and finding God, enlightenment, Saints, Bibles in ever color, and religion. Cloe remembered being in the middle of the Hoodoo book when the phone rang. She tried to get to a place to stop as she slowly got up from the chair. She finished the paragraph and put down the book. Hurriedly she made her way to the phone. "Hello?" she said.

"Cloe?" said the female voice flatly on the line.

"Ya?" she replied

"You went to a detective awhile back for help."

"Yes." she said in a definite tone. Maybe she would hear some news.

"Whatever you saw, whatever you think you saw, forget about it. It's bigger than you and your dumb ass detective. He's gone and if you don't watch it you will be too. Nobody can help you. Keep your mouth shut or else." and the line went dead. Cloe remembered putting the receiver down slowly. Her mind was racing back over the conversation. She replayed it her mind as she stood there with her arms across her chest.

Well, well, well, she thought, so they run him out for checking.

Her mind ran over the reasons of why and how. And then it slowly dawned on her, they had her number and if they know her number, then they will probably find out, if they didn't know already, where she lived. She had to take precautions. Her mind raced to what she needed as she went to her books. There are so many things on protection. Where did she start, thenher mind went to the Hoodoo book and where it stated that Rose brick crushed up would be at most a basic protection for evil or lesser demons. According to the books the church itself was a protection for the bigger bad guys. So she did just that, putting the Rose brick around the house and stable. And to her amazement it worked so far.

Cloe drove through the parking lot of the Romp Room to look for a place to park. She could hear the music's rhythmic thump as she parked. She grabbed her water gun full of holy water and some daggers that were blessed and put them in the back of her pants, just in case. She got out and made her way to the door. There was a man at the entrance collecting an entrance fee from the people who were waiting to get in.

The line moved at a steady pace and soon Cloe was paying the man the three dollars she dug out of her pocket. He asked her if she wanted to buy a membership and she politely declined. She stayed away from these places as much as she could. It was a breeding ground for the wicked and evil. Not everyone who came in here was like that, and as long as you came with a group of people than it would just be a night on the town for most. But if you came alone, you had better be wise to everything.

As she made her way through the crowd she looked across the room at tables and groups of people, the dance floor was in the center of the room, with the strobe light flashing. The DJ was playing a song by Prince called 'Pussy Control' and you could here everyone join in on the main chorus, laughing as they had a good time. There was a female dancer at one end of the dance floor and a male dancer closer to Cloe on the other end. Cloe watched as the man gyrated on top of a table and the women where putting money in his leather pants. She almost had to slap herself to get back on track, and with a shake of her head she pushed of the railing to wonder around some more.

She made her way through mobs of people, her eyes darting here and there when she finally spotted Amanda dancing with a young guy on the dance floor. If there was Amanda, there would be Megan. The two was inseparable. So Cloe decided to hang back and watch the action before she made any kind of move. Usually if you race in and try to reason with younger people, they don't listen to what you have to say, and then do the opposite.

She didn't want to step on any toes…yet. She wanted to make sure if there was any real threat first before she went in with guns blazing.

A waitress came up and asked Cloe if she needed anything. Cloe orders a soda and the waitress walked off. Sometimes she had to stand up and maneuver around to keep her eye on

Amanda. Finally Amanda walked off the dance floor towing the guy by his hand and approached the group sitting at a round table nestled away in a corner. The waitress came back with Cloe's soda and Cloe gave the big boobed waitress a five dollar bill. After taking a drink she moved to a table off to the side where she thought she would have a better view. As soon as she settled in she began to study the group. Some of the kids that were standing in front of the table went back to the dance floor. And she finally saw Megan squeezed in between a bunch of people on the round bench. She noticed an older looking guy at the table that had a tattoo on the side of his neck.

That caused a red flag to go up, but Cloe took her time to process the new found information. Sometimes gangs have a certain tattoo, but sometimes cults do too.

Then Cloe saw a young lady with what looked the same tattoo on the same side, *so there were two* Cloe thought, and probably more. The guy with the tattoo made a gesture like he was trying to shoo away a fly and everyone that was piled on the right side of the table started sliding out off the bench. Then Mr. Tattoo winched his way out of the bunch and after saying something over his shoulder, made his way through the crowd towards the bar. Instantly Cloe took action. She made her way to the bar too. She came up behind Mr. Tattoo and stood next to him to nonchalantly study his design on his neck. It was hard to see at first because he didn't stay still for very long. He would look one way, then the other, and Cloe would try to keep up with his moving without looking like a moron. Finally he was checking himself out in the mirror across the bar and Cloe saw it.

Her eyes widened and her pulse quickened, and she must have sucked in her breath because all of the sudden he was looking at her with his head cocked sideways and his arms folded, rested on the bar. She tried to recover quickly. "Nice tattoo." Cloe said with a nod.

"Thanks." Mr. Tattoo said. One eyebrow went up a notch.

"It looks like the sigil for Botis." she nodded toward him. No sense in beating around the bush.

"Ah, the Botis demon. And how would you know what that looks like?" He said as he straitened up with a grin. He had challenge in his eyes.

"Oh, I uh, am studying cults and religion in college." Cloe replied nervously.

"You look a little old to be in college." He flatly responded, as he studied Cloe's streak of pre-mature gray hair in her bangs.

She looked up at her bangs and shrugged. "Party life."

He laughed. "I guess." and turned to get his drink that just arrived on the bar. He paid the bar tender and turned back to Cloe.

"Well, have fun." he raised his glass up to Cloe.

"I will." Cloe exclaimed with a false grin.

He walked away and strode leisurely towards the table, stopping every now and again to talk to someone. Cloe wanted to leave but decided against it. She had to see the girls tattoo to make a firm decision on what to do next.

If she found out that the tattoo matched then the girls where indeed in over their heads.

Not everyone at the table sported a tattoo like that one but it didn't matter. If the girl matched than it was trouble enough.

She walked to another spot so that she could see the group but just barely. She didn't want to run into Mr. Tattoo again in case he made her. She would just have to wait until the girl went somewhere alone. Those kind of demon wannabes where smart when it came to getting out of trouble. And most have heard of her. But they had help from the demon that was tattooed on their neck.

That's why it was there, because they are loyal to that demon. They worshiped that demon. They gave that demon more strength. There are several demons running several cults here in town. Some demons were more powerful than others. It reminded Cloe of the movie Constantine, when Keanu Reeves stated that there were half breeds that either help or hinder the human race. Except there weren't half breeds. There where good people and bad people, there were people who are saints and very evil people and if a demon could influence the bad or evil people than that's where it started. Cloe checked the group again, the girl still sat there, smiling and laughing at what the others were saying. She thought again about Keanu saying God was like a kid with an ant farm.

She shook her head and thought *boy I hope not.*

Cloe really didn't think so. God was in control on most things but there is always choice for humans. And if a person chooses to be bad then that's what they chose. But she remembered along time ago when she was around five years of age, a preacher told the people on a certain Sunday to 'put on your spiritual armor', and get ready to face the evils in the world. Cloe didn't think anyone really thought he meant literally. It was like he knew what was starting to happen. The way he looked at the people though made Cloe look around to see if only she got the strong vibes from the message. No one seemed to be uneasy like she felt. She felt like the room temperature suddenly went up several notches. But she never forgot the message and after seeing strange things as she had gotten older and around the city more. When she figured out what she was suppose to do, she put on her 'armor'. She ended up facing the evil of this city and banished it when she could.

Finally the girl scooted out of the group and started walking along the other side of the wall. Cloe followed at a distance but kept her in sight. The girl went into the ladies room and Cloe came in about three seconds later. The bathroom was bright with three stalls. The wall opposite the stalls had the sinks and mirrors. Cloe pretended to look at her face and check her hair.

Come on she thought, hoping the girl wasn't going to be very long. A stall door came open and out come the girl. She was busy straightening out her mini skirt and walked up to the sink.

Shit! Cloe thought. *I'm on the wrong side.*

She tried to make the tattoo out in the mirror but that didn't work. She turned off the water and shook the water off her hands and went to the towel dispenser.

The girl turned around and came close to Cloe. *Do something!* Cloe told herself. The girl reached for the paper towel dispenser and Cloe blurted out. "I like your skirt. It's so adorable!"

"Thanks." The girl said and looking down at her skirt. "I thought I looked good in it too." Cloe looked quickly at her neck.

Yep, it was the same one. *Oh boy,* Cloe thought.

The girl raised her head and threw her paper towel away. She walked around Cloe and pulled open the door. She looked one last time at Cloe and Cloe gave her a grin. When the door closed Cloe mimicked the girl, "looked good in it too." she said in a high pitched, whiny voice. She also remembered the movie 'The Devils Advocate' where Al Pachino said, "Vanity, you got to love it." while he was standing up on a balcony. *Ugh, what's with you and movies with Reeves in it, you need a boyfriend.*

She looked at herself in the mirror. *Well that little mystery is solved.* She thought. She looked down into the sink as if it would give her any answers. She was tired but she didn't know if she should go out there and get Megan or just leave and wait to resolve it until in the morning. She dug her cell phone out of her front pocket and looked at the time. It was eleven o'clock. She dialed Sue's number.

"Hello." Sue's tired voice came over the cell phone speaker.

"Hey, it's me, did I wake you?"

"No, I was talking to Greg a little bit. What did you come up with?" Sue asked.

"Well, it's what you thought. And the cult is followers of the Botis demon."

Sue sighed over the telephone. "Do you know anything about that?" she replied.

"Yes, well, somewhat. I don't know how hard it will be to get rid of it, or get the girls away from it. But I can always find that out." Cloe shrugged. "There was a guy with them that I checked out and he had the same tattoo as a girl that I followed around here for awhile. They had the Botis symbol tattooed on their necks. I don't think their alone. I would even put my next paycheck on it that they aren't even the leaders."

"Oh." Sue said slowly.

"So the question is do you want me to go get her? Or do you want to wait until tomorrow until we can speak to her at the house."

"Well, she only has a half hour left. She's usually pretty good about coming home on time. So you can wait until tomorrow if you want." Sue replied

"Okay. But I'm going to go back out I guess and make sure she leaves so call me if she doesn't make it home."

"Okay. Be careful." then Sue hung up the phone. Cloe folded the phone up and stuck it in her pocket. She pulled the door open of the ladies room and went back out. The crowd was thickening and it almost was impossible to make her way through. She got her toe stepped on while trying to get around one group of people. Then she got pushed into another group of people by someone trying to make their way through the mob. *If I make it home in one piece,* she thought, as she blew in strand of bang out of her eye.

She finally got a view of the table where Megan was sitting. Everyone was getting up to leave but it looked like Megan and Amanda already left. She looked around to see if she couldn't find her. No such luck so she made her way through the crowd. Her eyes roved over the peoples faces. She finally made it to the door and carefully looked around before she went out. She came around the corner and heard Amanda squeal. Cloe ducked back and peeked around the corner to find Amanda saying good bye to her boyfriend. It looked like the boyfriend wasn't ready to say good bye yet. He kept grabbing Amanda around the waist and burying his face in her neck. Megan called from somewhere in the parking lot to Amanda and told her to hurry her ass up or else she would leave her. So Amanda kissed her boyfriend one more time and giggling, she ran off.

Cloe waited on the building corner to see if the car left the parking lot. She had a view of the street and if Megan was going home then she would drive right in front of Cloe. A little while more Megan's blue car pulled out from the parking lot and drove in front of her. Cloe sighed and made her way to the car. Hoping she wouldn't run into the bopsy tattoo twins. She usually packs her stun gun or another weapon of her choice. She didn't even think about it tonight. She was sure her little water pistol would be enough.

℘

She unlocked her car door and slid in. The engine came to life when she turned the key in the ignition. She took out her weapons from her back side and laid them on the seat. She put the shifter in reverse and carefully backed up. After putting the stick shift in drive, she made her way through the parking lot. She maneuvered her car onto the street and drove home. Sue didn't call her back yet so Cloe hoped that was a good sign. She was tired anyways. She pulled into her driveway and shut the car off. She run her hands over her face and sat there. Her dog was barking at her to get out, so she opened the car door and was piled upon by her dog. "I'm glad to see you too, Buddy." she said as she scratched his ears. She pushed the dog off her and climbed out. Her horse nickered at her softly and she went over to rub Gigi's nose. She went to the porch and got a coffee can full of horse feed to put in the feeder. As soon as Gigi saw that, he nickered even more and started prancing around. Cloe giggled and dumped the feed. She really loved this horse.

Next was Buddy's turn. She put the coffee can back in the horse feed bag and after closing the container, opened up another container to get dog food. She was meaning to get one of those automatic feeders but she kept on forgetting. As she reached in to grab a can full of dog food, Buddy happily wagged his tail. She dumped it for him and patted his head. He waited for Cloe to walk away and dove in. Cloe went to the door and let herself in.

As soon as she was through the door she dug everything out of her pockets and put them on the foyer table. She took her shoes off and made her way to the couch. She plopped down and let the softness of it swallow her up. She had her eyes closed until she remembered she hadn't checked her messages. Good thing it was a Friday night, she didn't have to work tomorrow. That was unless they called her. She worked for a construction firm that her friend from school had started on his own. She helped with the blue prints and such.

She had an associated degree in the I.T. field. Her friend Chris started the company fresh out of high school. She sat herself up and put her feet on the floor. The phone and answer machine was just on the end table right beside the couch. She reached over and pushed the button. Rose, her other Rose headed friend of 6 years came over the speaker, "Hey, I had a bad dream about you tonight. It's twelve o'clock. Call me when you get in."

Beep.

"Hey, it's Chris, I can't find the blue prints for the bank down town, call me and tell me where it is please, and if you took it home again I'll strangle you. Bye."

Beep.

"You have no more messages."

Cloe reached for the phone. *I wonder what Rose wanted* she thought. She reluctantly dialed the number. She hated to wake anyone up.

"Hey, you." Rose said happily over the phone.

"Hey, Rose. Why are you not sleeping? What's this about a bad dream?" Cloe said back. She loved to talk to Rose. They always had a good time together, made each other laugh. Even when no one else was laughing. Sometimes they even got kicked out of places for being obnoxious. Rose was a practiced Herbal healer, besides a vet tech at a big vacation lodge that sported fish tanks the size of the Titanic and horses to ride. She also made Cloe a lot of her charms and protection amulets and powders.

"Where have you been?" Rose asked worriedly.

"Oh, I have been at the Romp Room for some of the night." Cloe replied as she made her way into the kitchen. "And had dinner with Sue before that." She opened up the frig door and grabbed a soda. She turned around and grabbed a can of Pringles off the counter. Then she made her way back to the couch.

"Why where you at the Romp Room, and without me?" Rose asked sweetly.

"Well it seems as if Megan is running with a cult." Cloe put a chip in her mouth.

"Does she know it?"

"I don't know." Cloe said while chewing. "I'll find out tomorrow."

"What cult group is it, or do you know?" Rose inquired.

"The thing is, is that the two I checked out had the sigil of the demon Botis on their necks. So it wasn't hard to spot. To anybody else it would look like some kind of fancy drawing."

"Oh, isn't that demon a fortune demon?"

"Yes, and you need to make me a protection amulet for this one." Cloe pointed out, and took a drink of her soda.

"You'll have to give me the details on it so I know what to protect you against."

"I'll come over tomorrow if you re not busy, and bring my book."

"Okay. What time?" Rose asked.

"Well first I'm going to Sue's house to talk to Megan and then I can be over after that. I know it takes a while to make an amulet." Cloe stated.

"Okay. I'll do my shopping in the morning then and I'll call you when I get home." Rose replied.

"That's settled. Now tell me about your dream, Rose."

"Oh, that! In my dream we went to a psychic, kind of like the one we saw when we went to that fair on the square? Anyways, she kept on insisting that you were going to die, and we would blow her off and make fun of her and she just kept getting more and more persistent, and you said that she was full of shit and left and when I tried to get up she grabbed my wrist and kept repeating it over and over. I tried to loose my hand but she was strong. And she kept getting closer to my face and I couldn't get up. Then I woke up."

"Wow. That was some dream." Cloe said, and noticed that she was holding her breath.

"Ya, it was pretty powerful. Have you read your cards lately?"

"No, your not suppose to read for yourself, remember? I guess I could ask Sue to."

"Maybe you should." Rose said over a yawn.

"Okay. You sound tired and I know I am, so you ready to get some sleep yet?" Cloe asked gently.

"Ya, thanks for calling. I feel better now."

"You bet. Any time. I'll see you tomorrow, okay?"

"Okay. See ya tomorrow." and Rose hung up.

Cloe put the phone back on the receiver. She thought about putting everything up but decided against it. She stood and stretched and made her way into her bedroom. She pulled off her clothes and put on her pj's and slid herself beneath her covers and didn't even remember falling asleep.

The next morning Cloe awoke to the phone ringing beside her bed. She reached over with her hand and grabbed the receiver and carried it to her ear.

"Hello?" she said sleepily.

"Get up sleepy head." Chris said jokingly.

"What time is it?" Cloe asked.

"Nine thirty, so where's the blue prints for the bank. You didn't take them with you, did you?"

"No. They should be in the drawing room in the last drawer of the drawing desk."

"Why would they be there?" Chris sounded exasperated.

"Because I put them there. I didn't want it ending up with the mall blue print the others where working on."

"Oh, Okay. Good thinking."

"I know." Cloe smiled. "What would you do without me?"

"A lot." Chris said quickly and hung up the phone. He knew he would pay for that remark later. Cloe stretched and got out of bed. She padded into the kitchen and made some coffee. While it was perking she jumped in the shower. She took her time and leisurely let the hot water run over her body. She turned off the water and got out. Dried off and got dressed in jeans and a tee shirt. When she reached the kitchen the coffee was done and she poured her some, doctoring it up with sugar and creamer. She loved coffee. Her sisters drank their coffee black and when they saw what Cloe put in hers; they'd turn their noses up and screw up their face asking "How can you stand that?" and Cloe would always reply with a grin "I like my coffee like I like my men. Sweet and creamy." and they would break out into laughter. Cloe sat at her table and took a sip. Her mind went over last night and she got up to go to her book shelves. She pulled books out on Fallen Angels, Demons and their sigil, and Cults Today. She carried them back to the table and put them down. She went to get the phone out of the living room and went back to the table. Making herself comfortable, she dialed Sue s number.

"Hello?" said Greg's voice.

"Hey Greg, where's Sue."

"Suuuuee." Greg yelled. "Phoooone." pause, "She'll be right with you."

"Thanks." Cloe said. A few seconds went by, "Hello?" Sue said.

"It's me. Did you want me to come over or," Cloe dropped off.

"Come over about noon, that s usually when she gets up and bring some info with you so we can show her with proof." Sue said.

"Will do. See ya." and Cloe hung up the phone.

She took another drink out her cup and went through the books. She found the Sigil of the demon Botis. His sigil looked like a box with one end open. It has two T look a like things and an up side down cross between then two T's, and what actually it was all about. There wasn't very much information. Except that they could take human shape. Her eyes got tired of reading and she finished her coffee. She went to make another cup and went to the living room, which was the part that used to hold the pews. She could imagine the people who used to gather. It was a small church so it couldn't have held very many. Maybe five pews on each side. She could hear them sing hymnals. She loved the stained glass windows and the statue of Jesus was still in the front of the room. She loved it. Everyone tried to talk her out of it that had seen it. There would be no way.

She stopped in front of the statue. *Please be with me again* she prayed *I need your help*. She touched his face and pushed some dust of his shoulders. She needed to wash it really. She stared into his eyes as if he were talking to her and in her head. She imagined herself going for a ride. She downed her second cup while she was walking towards the kitchen. Her cup made a clank as she set it on the counter. Then she walked out the back door and to the stables. Gigi met her with a whinny and she opened the gate. After going to the stall and getting the bridle on Gigi. They took off. She loved riding bare back. Gigi slowly galloped down the pasture towards an island of trees where the underground spring resided. It made a small pool and was canopied with trees.

The water was cold but it was a good swimming hole as well. It had come with the ten acres that came along with the church. She slowed the horse to a walk and they made their way into the trees and to the pond. Cloe slid off the back of her mount and led him to the water. She knelt down and put her hand in it. *Dang that's cold!* she thought. She dropped the reins and walked over to where the water spewed out from the ground. Cupping her hands, she drank up the water that she held. It was so good. After twice of doing this she stood up and wiped her mouth with the back of her hand.

Gigi suddenly spooked and froze, while snorting his head was darting this way and that. Cloe carefully stepped forward the startled animal and cooed to him. "Hey Gigi, what's the matter? Its alright." she said and made another step towards him. His muscles lessened a bit but his ears were still going back and forth. Cloe looked around. Maybe it was a squirrel or fox. Out in the country you never know. It could even be a skunk. Cloe was looking around for something when she noticed that out in the middle of the pond, the water started bubbling and rippling like a wind blew there. It sounded like it also. Cloe couldn't feel it where she stood. "Who's there?" Cloe shouted, feeling a little foolish. The water ripples where still being made, and suddenly a mist of water formed above. She watched in fascination as her hair started rising up on her arm. She didn't know whether she should run or stay. She wasn't necessarily frightened but she felt uneasy at the same time. An image appeared in the midst of the small pool and grew stronger every moment. Finally, she saw a figure of a man standing there looking at her. She couldn't believe it. She had read about it in many of her books but she didn't think it happened to just anybody out in the middle of nowhere.

Not in broad daylight.

Gigi snorted at it and Cloe put up her hand towards the horse. Her head turned sideways but her eyes stayed on the figure. "Whoa baby, its alright." she said softly.

The figure that looked like a man, it was dressed in black and it bled into the air around him. Cloe knew it was a fallen angel but she didn't know which one. She had seen Angels Michael and Gabriel in her dreams and they have guided her, but she has never seen any fallen or otherwise in real life. When they started coming to her in dreams, she did an extensive study on them. It was true that the good angels seemed to like the library, as a movie depicted about them. In the library, they could lead people to the information that they seek. It was nice as it took out the guess work for a lot of people. And if you have an open book they can also make a draft in the air blow to the page you need to read. But she had never heard of where the fallen angels showed up.

Maybe it was like the question about where a bear shits in the woods. Anywhere they want.

Where do good or bad angels show up? Anywhere they want.

Cloe just stared at the figure. The figure just stared back at her as it stayed suspended in mid air. Then it slowly started to smile. Cloe stared back intently. The man made a "tsk,

tsk" sound and shook its head. It must be a fallen angel or demon of doubt. "One of these days," it said with black lips, "You will realize that all of your running around..." it put its hands up and shook them "...and trying to save souls, was for nothing."

"You think so, huh?" Cloe lifted her chin and put her hands on her hips feeling rather big instead of afraid. One thing she learned through out life, is when someone was loosing, they would always try to put a fear in the winner by telling them they where going to lose so they would give up.

As if it read her thoughts it continued "Oh, I know what you're thinking. We are going to lose. But you have no idea. A war has raged for eons over the souls of humans. And you know what's funny. The angels in heaven don't even like you humans because God loves you so much." he rolled his eyes.

"Liar!" Cloe accused, and it was a challenge as well.

"Well of course you wouldn't want to believe it. And what about heaven, it's over rated really." He stated with a shake of his head. "They don't need you." He suddenly started studying his nails. "We are winning on earth. It's very seldom you meet a person who's souls isn't damned. Even your own." he pointed at Cloe. "From the things you did and do and are going to do. God cannot look upon anything but pure innocence. He can't hear you."

"No, He can't hear you. He hears and sees me just fine." Cloe said. "And if you don't leave, I'll make you leave by his words." He jutted out his chin and his eyes squinted. His black lips pierced together. He knew she could. He has seen what she can do. He would never tell her that. "You'll see." he laughed and vanished.

Cloe stared at the spot over the spring for awhile. She couldn't believe it. She knelt to the ground with her legs under her. There must be something big going down. She wandered what. She stood up and brushed her pants off. Gigi was still there, a little calmer now. She strode over to the horse and swung on its back. Gigi wheeled his head around and sniffed at Cloe's shoe. Cloe patted the horse on the neck. "Let's get out of here." she said. She reined the horses head around and made her way back out of the trees. Cloe nudged Gigi's flanks and he took off again to the end of the pasture. She walked the horse along the fence line, looking for any repairs she might need to make. Her mind was racing. Something is going to happen, *what does it have to do with me?* She twirled the thought over and over in her brain. *It must have something to do with last night* she thought. She rode half way up the fence and decided she better get going. She nudged Gigi into a gallop and they arrived at the stable. She made sure the water trough was full of water. She didn't know if Gigi would be comfortable to go back to the spring for a while.

She brushed the horse down and grained him. She hugged the horse's neck one last time before making her way out of the holding pen. She went in and changed her jeans, grabbed her books and keys. She put her money and cell phone in her pocket and went out the door. Buddy whined at her and cocked his head side ways. "Do you wanna go for a ride?" she asked the dog. He gave a bark and a short jump. She went to the passenger door and opened it. Happily wagging his tail the dog jumped in the car. "Spoiled mutt." Cloe said as she pushed the door closed. She went to the other side and started the car. After one minute she was on the road making her way to the big city. Buddy lolled his head out the window on the other side. He loved car rides and Cloe wanted to spend time with him.

She pulled into Sue's driveway in about thirty minutes. She let Buddy out on the other side. She reached into the back seat and got Buddy's leash out. She tied him to one of the trees in the front yard and petted his head. "Stay." she said firmly as she walked away. She went back to the car and got her books out and made her way through the front door and saw Megan and Sue sitting at the dining room table. Megan didn't look all too happy. "How's everyone this morning?" Cloe said in a chipper voice.

"It would be better if it didn't include a lecture." Megan said with her eyes rolling.

"Megan, your mom's right, look." Cloe said and laid her books on the table. She grabbed the one in particular about demons and turned to the page that she had marked. Megan looked at the picture and Cloe explained what the demon was, pointing out the sigil and how it matched the tattoos on the necks of the people she was with last night.

"How do you know who I was with?" Megan stared at Cloe.

"Because I was there last night with my friends and I saw you."

"I think you were spying on me!" Megan said and crossed her arms over her chest.

"If I was spying on you then I would have went over to you and told you to go home." Cloe said and pointed her finger at Megan.

"And don't think I wouldn't have, I'm not afraid of much, and you know it." At one time Megan saw Cloe take on couple of wanna-be bad asses that wouldn't leave then alone at a miniature golf course. With Cloe knowing Jujitsu it didn't take long to put them in their place, but she didn't hurt them bad. They ended up apologizing. "But I can see who you're with, not to be nosy, but to make sure your okay." Cloe said with defiance. "I left you alone though. But now we need to talk about it."

Megan looked at the picture again. She laced her fingers together and thought about it for a second. "So what do I do now? If I just quit hanging around then they'll know something is up. You'll never get Amanda away from them. Her boyfriend hangs out over at their house."

"I'll handle Amanda later. She's to hair brained. It's you I worry about. I don't want you to lose your soul over something you could have avoided. I know that sounds real Holy Roller church go'er, but it s the truth."

"Please." said Sue. "Please, just be careful. I can't be with you every second, but now you have to make some adult choices."

"Okay, mother." Megan said and got up off the chair. "I get the point." she said over her shoulder and went to her room. After hearing the door shut, Cloe looked at Sue. "Do you think she'll listen?"

"I don't know, but at least she knows." Sue got up and headed for the door with a cigarette. Cloe followed her out. They sat down on the porch steps and stared out over the yard. "Sue, I would never let her get hurt. I wouldn't care how many asses I would have to kick."

"I know." Sue said and exhaled smoke. "I just think it's crazy that it's like this in the world. Greg says he has seen some funky stuff even within the church. You never know who to trust anymore."

"Ya, I know. Remember last year when I busted that cult group and they where collecting semen to give to that demon so he could impregnate women." Cloe was snapping her fingers trying to remember. "Ooh what was that, anyways, what I was trying to say is, how messed up was that?"

"I remember. You have sent away a lot of demons. I'm sure you can handle this one."

"Oh hey!" Cloe grabbed Sue leg. "I had a visitor this morning."

"Anyone I know?" Sue said and snuffed her cigarette.

"I hope not. I think it was a fallen angel." Cloe emphasized the word 'think'. As if she came to that conclusion just then.

Sue froze and looked at her. "What makes you think it was a fallen angel?"

"By the way it felt. By the way it looked. It was so damn arrogant."

"But demons are like that."

"But demons are summoned. I didn't summon this one. It just showed up. And it warned me that I couldn't save every soul and yadda, yadda." Cloe stated, she had heard it all before from both the good and evil sides.

"Wow, Really? They just don't show up." Sue got up and went in through the door. Cloe followed her and they made their way to the kitchen. Sue poured her a cup of coffee and Cloe got a glass of ice water. They sat at the dining room table again.

"So what do you make if it?" Sue asked.

"I think something major is about to go down." Cloe said with her head nodding.

"Where did it show up at? Surely not in the church?"

"No. I went riding and I stopped at the spring. It showed up over the water." Cloe went on to describe what happened to Sue.

"Wow. I have a book on fallen angels. I wonder if we could find it. It seems like it needed the water, maybe, to form." and Sue stood up and walked over to the book shelf. Some angels, fallen, and demons were known as elementals, in which they would need the basic elements to form. The basic elements were earth, fire, water and air. After thumbing through some books she pulled out the one she was looking for. She sat back down next to Cloe and pulled her cup over across the table to she could reach it. Together they started reading over the pages.

Megan came out of her room and stood on the other side of the table. "What are you guys doing now, finding out how to send me to church?" she said sarcastically.

"No." Sue looked irritated as she looked up from book. "Cloe may have seen a fallen angel this morning." and she brought her head back down to read something. Megan pulled out a chair and sat down. "Really? Why would it visit you?" she said to Cloe.

"Because they know I can do some damage for one." Cloe smiled a toothy smile. "And I think it has something to do with what we talked about earlier."

Megan sank down on her elbows, she carried a scared look on her face and her eyes were bulging. Sue looked up and asked. "What's wrong?" Megan said slowly "I thought you guys were just trying to scare me because you didn't like the people, but you really think it's more serious than that?" She was looking from Sue to Cloe and back again. Cloe sat back in her chair with hers brow drawn down. "You're weird Megan. Why would we make up such an awful thing like that! Yes, we're serious!"

"It sounds like something Aunt Becky would do to us." Sue said sideways to Cloe, and they both snickered, remembering the past. Aunt Becky was an odd sort of witch in the family. Sue got serious and told Megan. "It will be okay as long as you know what they are about."

"Yah, but what about Amanda? We can't just leave her there." Megan pointed out.

"We're not. I'm going to pay a visit to where ever they hang out."

Cloe stated flatly and turned the page of the book. "How are you going to do that?" Megan asked. "You don't know where that is."

"No, do you?"

"No. I've never been there before. But hey! I could go with Amanda!" Megan's face brightened. Sue and Cloe both groaned and shook their head. "That would be a bad idea." Sue said.

"Come on, we could go there, I could call because I have to check in and Cloe could show up and bitch at me in front of everyone, then I can get out of it because Cloe made me, because you know." she said as she put her hand from Cloe to Sue and back again. "Cause Cloe's a demon hunter and all, and then that will get me and Amanda off the hook and Cloe's in."

Sue sat and looked down at the table for a while. "I suppose it wouldn't hurt." she said and bit her bottom lip. "But you have to be careful."

Megan nodded all too happily. "I will, I promise." She said and crossed her heart.

Sue sighed and said. "Okay." Megan clapped her hands and went back off to her bedroom. Sue and Cloe went back to the book.

"I hope this works." Sue said under her breath.

"I can't believe she came up with that plan." Cloe said under her breath. They both giggled. They had several fallen angels picked out in about an hour and Cloe's cell phone rang. Cloe answered it on the third ring.

"Hello?"

"Hey it's me. I'm home now if you re ready to come on over. I thought we'd BBQ some hamburgers on the grill and whatever." Rose said over the line.

"Sounds' good. I'll be over in a few."

"Okay." and the phone went dead.

കൗ

Cloe folded her phone and put it in her pocket. She told Sue she had to go and gave her sister a hug. Cloe gathered her books off the table and Sue said she would call her later and Cloe went outside and untied Buddy. He climbed in the car. Cloe climbed in the other side and they where at Rose's in fifteen minutes. Cloe got out and gathered her books. Then she opened the door for Buddy and Buddy hopped out of the car. Buddy could run free at Rose's because she had a fenced in yard with other dogs. Cloe opened the gate and Buddy went in first. Rose's dog Puppy came up and jumped into Buddy s face and suddenly they where off running, tumbling, and playing.

Rose came out the front door and watched the dogs play for a bit. They laughed at the dog's obvious game of tag. Then they made their way into Rose's house. Rose had a little house with an open loft where the attic should be. She loved her critters though. There were dogs, cats, and birds. She had horses to, but they stayed at Rose's mom's house. Rose's mom didn't live to far from Cloe but closer to town. Rose and Cloe would go horse back riding together a lot.

"Grab a drink out of the fridge." Rose pointed her spatula towards the fridge and Cloe did what she was told. They both walked out the back door talking about work. Rose had doctored a Draft horse and did a better job than the Vet himself. And she had bragging rights.

She was a fiery Rose head, which stood taller than Cloe by four inches. Cloe complimented her on her job. Rose told her there would be a mangers position open in the stables where she worked. "Are you going for it?" Cloe asked.

"I thought about it." Rose said over chewing a chip. "Unless you want it." Rose was always trying to talk Cloe in working with her.

"Nah. I have enough on my plate the way it is already. And besides Chris would kill me if I quit him." Cloe sat back in the lawn chair. Rose opened the grill lid and salted the burgers. She put the lid back on.

"So tell me about what's going on." Rose said and pulled her chair up to the patio table. Cloe followed pursuit and opened the book up to where The Botis demon chapter started. After reading for a while Rose said. "Well it says here that he starts out a viper. So that's a beginning. And then he takes human form, so maybe if you need to stop him then you need something to keep him as his first form, and then you can kill him." She says like it's that simple. Cloe looked sideways at her and Rose grins and wobbles her head back and forth.

"I know it's not that simple." She says as she exaggerates the word 'that'.

Rose got up and checked the burgers. She flipped them over and put the lid back on. After sitting down again Cloe says. "Guess what I saw this morning?" like it was something nonchalant.

"What did you see this morning?" Rose echoed back.

"A fallen angel." Cloe said and took a drink of her juice box.

Rose's eyes got big in she inhaled loudly. "No way! How do you know that's what it was?" *Why does every one say that?* Cloe thought. She told Rose about the events that transpired that morning. While Rose got up to take the burgers off the grill a voice called from around the corner of the house. It was their other friend Roxanne.

Roxanne was a regular person. No witcheries, no evilness to capture, just a normal person. Roxanne was a bank teller at a local bank.

"Back here!" the other two girls call out. Roxanne smiles and waves, "Hey. I haven't seen you guys for a while so I thought I better come over. Make sure you guys are staying out of trouble." Cloe got up and hugged Roxanne's neck. "What have you been up to?" Cloe says and pulls up another chair for Roxanne to sit on.

"I hope I'm not imposing." Roxanne says after eying the food.

"Of course not." says Rose, "You hungry?"

"Oh you know me, I could always eat." Roxanne giggles and winks at Cloe.

"Well there's enough there." Rose says and opens up the hamburger bun wrapper and unscrews all the lids. She sits down and they all start making there plates.

"So, Roxanne, how's the new boyfriend?" Cloe asks.

"It's going great." Roxanne says and scratches her face. "Notice anything different?"

Cloe looks at her and sees the ring on her ring finger. She opens her mouth to say something but Rose must have seen it too, because all of the sudden she squealed out loud. "Is that an engagement ring?"

Roxanne smiled. "Yes!" she gushed. Cloe and Rose gathered around to look at it. After asking a billion questions about Roxanne and Larry, her fiancé, they all settled down to eat.

"Wow, a full fledged fallen angel. Why do you suppose it was here?" Rose said after a short pause of gushing over the engagement news.

"I'm not sure. I mean, something important is going down I think. But I don't know much more than that."

"Well, I can't make you any amulets against them. They are to powerful for that or anything else."

Roxanne looked back and forth from person to person. "What'd I miss?" she asked.

"Oh, I was tracking some demon cult and a fallen angel comes and visits me to warn me, the usual." Cloe says and bites into her hamburger.

Roxanne's eyebrows come up. "I was wondering if you were still demon hunting."

"Yep." Cloe replied.

Rose tried to lighten the conversation by telling Roxanne about the manager position at her work area. Roxanne asks some questions about what that would involve. Then Roxanne looked at Cloe and said. "Are you guys still working on our new bank?"

"Yah, Chris woke me up this morning and asked me about the blue prints because he couldn't find them." Cloe said in a revengeful tone.

It was getting dark and the bugs started coming in thicker. The girls cleaned up and moved the party inside. They all settled in the living room and Rose brought all sorts of ingredients to the coffee table. Roxanne asks. "What is all this stuff for?" and Rose says a little breathless. "I'm going to make Cloe a protection amulet to wear."

Roxanne moves herself up on the couch "Oooh." she says, and leans forward to watch. Rose was good at making amulets and it didn't take her any time. She followed the ancient recipe, adding this and that.

Then she took wax and sealed the back and dabbed it around the edges. She closed her eyes and said a prayer over it. She set it down on wax paper to set and looked at Cloe. "And that is that." She smiled and brushed her hands together. "When you get ready to use it drop a drop of your blood on it and swirl it around three times. Then it should take effect."

"Thanks a bunch." Cloe took pride in Rose s work as much asRose did. At first when Rose got started they were just goofing around, Cloe and Rose were at a local disco place dancing, when a demon tried to take them both home Cloe showed him the amulet. It starting shaking like he was on the grounds of an earthquake and left running, While Cloe and Rose looked at each other, blinking their wide eyes with their jaws dropped. So when it really worked they took it more serious and began to practice. And the more they practiced the better it got. The time it took to make one got shorter also.

Roxanne cleared her throat and said "Cloe, can I ask you a question without making you mad?"

"Sure."

"Okay. I'm not sure how to put this so I'll just say it. If you are religious, you know, have Christ in your heart. And you do all this witchery stuff. Isn't that like mixing good and evil right there? How does that work? I mean, doesn't God get mad at you for doing the spell thing? Then you go out and banish Demons." Roxanne's voice died off.

"Well, I'll see if I can answer that. I know what you mean. And it is combining the two, kind of. I believe that since God can give knowledge of sacred things, or magical things if that's how you think of it, then I think that Rose helping me is Gods way of helping me. God gave Rose the power to do this and it works. Now it can be reversed. If I were evil and Rose was evil and we just did the same thing as we did now. Then it would work, but it would work because Satan gave us the knowledge, not God. And so that would be evil. But we are fighting for the good, and it works for the good. And If I went to Sue and I said read my cards and she did, and if certain cards came up lets say, and it was a warning, then I think that God helped Sue to give me a warning. And in my dreams, they help me in some of the information and I believe that God is talking to me through my dreams. Even though some religious people wouldn't think so. Good begets good and evil begets evil. I believe that so really you can't mix the two. It is said by some scholars that even Moses had called upon some spirits to help him part the Rose sea. And some scholars believe that Moses used a demon called Abbadon to bring destructive rains to a region. And Solomon had a bunch of spirits help him supposedly, called the 72 spirits of Solomon, but when he started coveting things like local women of the area, and riches, he used the spirits to get them, and more. Then God punished him."

"Wow. I didn't know that. But nobody teaches anything around here but the usual things about salvation and believing and not being bad." Roxanne said. Her head was in her hand.

"At first I used to think about it the same way." Rose said. "But Cloe does a good thing. Sometimes she needs help. And every little bit helps." After a pause Roxanne got up and stretched. "Well I guess I better get going. I told Larry I would be at his house tonight." The other girls got up and hugged Roxanne goodbye. Roxanne told them both to be careful and she disappeared out the door. Cloe turned her head to Rose. "Poor girl, she thinks we're nuts." Rose giggled.

"You wanna watch a movie?"

"Sure, watcha got?" Cloe said and made herself comfortable on the chair.

"I got 'Troy' or 'Mr. and Mrs. Smith.'" Rose held them both up for Cloe to see.

"It seems like someone likes Brad Pitt." Cloe said in a teasing way.

"Can you blame me?" Rose said and raised her eyebrows up and down. Cloe laughed. "Put in the Smiths." She loved to watch Brad or Angelina movies also. She had a collection of both at home. The movie took off and both girls got comfortable. They commented on the movie, the dialog, laughed, Cloe loved the part where Angelina gushed to Brad, "I missed you today." after trying to kill him earlier in the movie. They finished the movie and talked about it some more. It was an excellent movie Cloe thought. She got up and told Rose she was going home. Rose said something about being tired too. Rose walked her out the door.

Cloe called for her dog and they made her way to the car. After waving good bye one last time they went home. Cloe drove in the driveway and parked the car. She got her books and went around letting the dog out. Gigi whinnied at her and they went through the usual ritual of feeding the horse, then feeding the dog. She petted both animals and let herself in. She went to the book shelves and put her books up. She went to the answer machine and checked her messages. There where none. *Tomorrow,* she thought, *I'll work out.* She stretched and made her way to her bed. Once again she was asleep before hear head hit the pillow.

☙

She awoke with the sun streaming in and the birds singing. She looked at the clock. It read nine thirty. She stretched lazily and looked at the ceiling. After awhile she threw back the covers and went into the kitchen to make coffee. She went around and watered some plants in the house that she had neglected. When she was done with that she pulled out her lap top out and checked her e-mail. She would look at the coffee pot every once in a while to see if it was done brewing. She got up and got a cup and put the usually things in it to make it even yummier. She wouldn't drink coffee black. She sat down again at the table and caught up on the news, weather, and everything else the Internet provides. After she had her two cups and finished with reading the news on her laptop, she got up and went to her bedroom. She put on shorts and a tank top. Then she went into the bathroom and put her hair up in a ponytail. After brushing her teeth and washing her face she found her sketchers work out shoes by the front door and put them on. Cloe slowly stretched her muscles. She worked on her neck first and made her way down her body. She couldn't help any one if she pulled a ham string or what ever. After an hour of stretching she went to the punching bag she had hung in the corner of the living room and worked on her usual kicks, jabs and punches. She worked up a sweat, and when it finally was running in her eyes and stinging them, she slowed down and finally stopped.

Cloe went to the chair to get a towel and drink some bottled water. She dabbed her face and took another drink. That's when the phone rang. Cloe walked over and lifted the receiver to her ear.

"Hello?"

"Hey, it's Chris. You coming to work tomorrow?" Like she ever took off that much. "Yah, why wouldn't I?"

"I don't know, just checking I guess since some of the others already called in." Chris said tiredly.

"What's up with that?" Cloe asked.

"I don't know. Some kind of biker rally." Chris said.

"Oh. So, what do you want me to work on?" Cloe sat down on the chair.

"Well, could you run by the lawyers firm on 6th street and see what the bigwigs want to change on the blueprints? Billy was supposed to go but he's one of the ones who called in."

"Yah, I could do that. What time do I need to be there?"

"Nine."

"Who am I looking for?"

"A man named Cory." Chris said.

"Okay." Cloe said and wrote the information down on a pad by the phone. "Is that it?"

"Yep that's it. I'll see you at work after that."

"Okie dokie." Cloe said. "I'll see ya then." and hung up the phone.

Well, so much for a cool down Cloe thought. She walked over to the stereo and put in a meditation CD. She put in something that would sooth her. She went through some Ti Chi moves and then settles on the floor with her legs crossed and closed her eyes. She slowed her breathing down and listened to her heart beat. Her mind wondered over the things that happened over the past few days. She pushed them out, trying to focus. Her Sensei taught her she could see whatever she needed to see. She focused on his words. It starts out like a smoke filled area. Then when the smoke clears then usually there's a vision. She saw blue and white crosses. They were on a corner shelf somewhere. There were five shelves. All were different colors and designs. There were wax crosses, some lit. There where medal ones, plastic ones. She was kneeling down in front of this shelf full of crosses, praying, *was she praying?* Who was with her?

Someone was with her.

She was pulled out of meditation by the sound of Buddy barking.

What was he barking at? She got up and looked out the screen door. She didn't see anything so she went outside and Buddy was standing on the porch with his hair raised. He was barking at nothing. Cloe went to him and knelt beside him and followed his eyes to what he was barking at.

Nothing.

Cloe patted his head and he looked at Cloe as if to say 'Don't you see that?' She told him to settle down, that there was nothing there. But he kept looking out to the road. He would growl and Cloe tried to see if there was maybe a rabbit or something out there. She still didn't see anything. She grabbed him by his collar and made the dog come inside the house with her. *Maybe that will calm him down,* she thought. As soon as he was in the house he went over to the couch and lay down beside it. Cloe followed him and scratched his head. "Good dog." she said.

As he fell asleep Cloe went about her duties of cleaning, dusting, moping and laundry. All of which she hated to do. But she busied herself anyway. It was around three when the phone rang. Cloe stopped folding cloths and answered it.

"Joe's bar and grill." she said with a low gruff voice.

"Yes. I d like to order a pizza and a six pack please." Rose's voice came back.

"Would you like Brad Pitt to bring it?" Cloe asked gruffly.

"Hell yah!" Rose shouted over the phone with a laugh.

Cloe started laughing too. "What do you want." she said after she caught her breath.

"I'm at moms and I was wondering if you want to go riding?"

"Umm." She looked at the unfolded cloths. "Yah, that sounds great!."

"Okay. I'll be there in awhile. I'm already saddled up so it shouldn't take me very long."

"Okay, I'll go get Gigi ready so I should be ready when you get here."

"I'll see ya in a few then."

"K. bye." Cloe hung up.

Cloe knew it would take her at least thirty minutes or more to get to her house. It was quite a distance on horse back. It was usually a good ride for the horses. Rose would come over on horseback by herself, Cloe would join her back to Rose's moms, and then Cloe would ride home alone. One straight shot there and back. A little sunshine and shade along the way. She rolled up the towel that as in her hands and threw it in the basket of clean cloths. She left it on the couch and called for he dog. Buddy always went with when she rode. She went out the back door and went to the stable. Gigi was out to pasture. Cloe whistled and rattled a feed bucket and Gigi came running. She met him with a handful of feed and put a lead rope on him. She brushed his mane out because it had burs in it, then she went to work to saddle him up. She took her time in the process. Making sure everything was snug and tight. She checked his hooves to make sure they were clean of debris. When she put the last foot down she could see Rose in the distance. She thought about going out to meet her, but then thought maybe her horse Spec would like a drink. Gigi began to whinny at the other horse and Rose called out to him. She galloped the horse in and smiled at Cloe. Rose's dog

Puppy came along also, much to Buddy's delight. "You ready?" Rose said down to Cloe.

"You want to see if she needs a drink first?" Cloe nodded towards Spec.

"I guess I better." and she nudged the horse towards the coral. Cloe walked with them to make sure the reins didn't get caught on the side of the water trough. She lifted the bridle over the edge and Spec stuck her nose in it. After about two swallows Spec started playing with the water, splashing Cloe in the process. Cloe let out a shriek because the water was cold.

"Hey!" she shouted.

"Oops, sorry." Rose laughed. "Spec, you naughty girl!"

She backed Spec up out of the water, giggling the whole time. "Well I won't need a bath tonight." Cloe said. She held out her arms and looked down at her wet shirt.

"See? She was just trying to help." Rose chuckled.

Cloe went over to Gigi and mounted. Then they started down the road. The dogs followed with their noses to the ground. Sometimes one would chase the other. The horses got along too. "So, what are you doing over at mom's house?"

Cloe asked. Rose's mom was like a mom to Cloe too. Rose didn't care if Cloe called her mom 'mom'. They were accused of being sisters many times.

"She needed help with the garden and then she wanted to cook out. She asked me about you and I thought I'd ride over and get you to eat with us." Rose said as she looked out over the fields.

"Well, thanks for thinking of me, I was getting hungry." Cloe loved Mary's cooking. She was a retired cook from a restaurant Mary and Wayne, her husband, used to own. The two girls used to go in there all the time and eat. The new owners weren't as good, so they quit going. "Plus dad needs help with the computer again." she said and rolled her eyes. Wayne can do the work, he just likes it better when some else does it for him. Cloe giggled. He was a funny man, very lovable to everyone. Mary was tougher, everybody was scared of Mary. There were always fun things to do at Mary and Wayne's house. They owned forty acres. They had a pool. One of the things that were a favorite is playing witch in the moonlight at night. When you get a lot of people together like the two girls used to do. It was down right hilarious.

As if Rose was reading her mind she asked, "Remember playing witch in the moonlight?" They reminisced about the past as they made their way down the road. Every once in a while they would break out in laughter. They had a lot of memories together. And most of them were quite funny. The conversation was full of 'remember when' as they visited the past. When they got through talking Rose asked Cloe if she wanted to race. Cloe didn't wait for a reply; she kicked her horse into high gear and took off. Rose shouted out at her but Cloe knew that Rose would have done the same to her. As they raced down the road, each girl was laughing and yelling at their horses to keep up the pace. They ran into Mary's lawn and slowed down to a stop. After taking the saddles off they walked the horses around so they had a proper cool off. They let them go in a holding coral and made their way to the porch where Mary and Wayne were sitting.

Mary shooed them away from the food and told them to get washed up first. They went into the bathroom and washed up. Cloe told Rose about her meditating and about the blue and white crosses. Rose told her that either color was linked to inner intuition. White to some scholars could mean death, as the same with crosses. Rose went on to tell Cloe that five was the human and the five senses, which all together, or without any, would lead to the sixth. Cloe thought that that was a good assessment. She made a mental note to herself to remember that and write it down later. They all sat down after making their plates at a covered picnic table and had a conversation about the girls work with their meal. After about four hours of visiting and looking at the garden. Cloe told everyone that she must get home before it gets too dark and everyone hugged her and said goodbye. She called Gigi back up to the gate and Rose helped her put the tack back on her horse. While they were busy putting everything back on Rose asked, "Are you sure you're going to be okay?"

Cloe looked over the horses back at Rose. "Why do you ask that?"

I don't know." Rose said with a shrug but wouldn't bring her eyes to look at Cloe. "With everything going on and then this vision, it's got me worried, that's all."

Cloe knew Rose worried about her, but she has never really come right out and said it before.

"It'll be okay Rose." Cloe came around the horse to study Rose.

"I know. I m just being silly I guess."

"No. I know what you re thinking because I think the same sometimes. One of these days I am in for a world of hurt, my luck will run out. But then I think that if I had any belief at all in God then I know he will protect me because that's what he does. And not to mention I had some pretty powerful angels on my side." Rose knew of the dreams Cloe had where Archangels Michael or Gabriel had talked to and guided her. Rose nodded and handed Cloe the reins. Cloe took them and mounted the horse. She looked down at Rose. "You going to be okay?"

"Yeah. It's true what you say. I should have faith." Rose smiled.

"Okay, then. I'm going to go. We got to work tomorrow ya know."

Cloe nudged her horse. Rose waved bye one last time before Cloe set down the road. Cloe waved bye over her shoulder and took off at a gallop. She arrived home after a peaceful ride. She had to make sure Buddy followed her home. Sometimes Cloe thought he'd rather stay with Puppy. She thought about what Rose said about her dream. She knew she had to be careful. Something felt like it was going to happen. She was being warned. She thought about the other figure in her meditation dream. *Who could that have been?* She felt like it was a man but she could be wrong. After putting everything away in the barn and brushing Gigi down. She fed them all and went into the house. She looked at her messages. None. She went into the kitchen and got a soda out of the fridge. Then she sat down and finished the laundry she had left earlier. After putting everything away she showered and got ready for bed. She said her prayers that night for help, guidance and protection. She climbed in and shut off the light. After staring at the ceiling for awhile wondering about her meeting tomorrow she dozed off.

જ

The alarm went off at seven thirty. She always put the alarm on radio because it put her in a bad mood to hear the constant repeating beeps of the clock. After listening to the news and weather she reached over and shut it off. She laid there for awhile before she pushed the covers back and climbed out of bed.

Then there was the usual ritual of walking to the kitchen and making coffee. She picked out her cloths carefully. She wanted to look professional today since she had a meeting. She picked a cream colored pant with blazer suit. After getting dressed and picking out brown shoes, she went back into the kitchen and drank her two cups. She went to the closet and got out her briefcase that had a calculator and bidding guide lines in it for new businesses. While she drank her coffee she sat at the table she looked at the e-mails and the news on her laptop. She looked up the clock, it was eight fifteen. She put every thing away and after grabbing her keys, money, and cell she went out the door. Cloe started down the highway in her car. She hated being late to anything, so she always gave herself enough time to get where she was going. Her cell phone rang.

"Yah." She said when she saw it was Chris.

"Are you on your way?"

"Yes, boss." Cloe said sarcastically.

"Okay, okay, don't get your panties in a wad." Chris said. "Now you know what to do, right?"

Cloe sighed. "Make him happy but don't give him the impossible. Bid the right hours and charge accordingly."

Chris has had some men that worked for him go in and underbid a job which ended up costing Chris. It was hard to find a good bidder.

"You got it. You'll do well." Chris said as if he reassured himself.

"I try." Cloe said through her teeth.

"Okay. Hey, thanks for doing this for me."

Cloe softened. It was a good thing they were good friends since kindergarten. "No problem. I'll catch you later." And they hung up. Cloe turned on the radio and drove some more. Finally she made it to her destination on 6th street. It was an old firm but it was huge. It had at least ten floors. It took up most of a city block. The owner wanted to remodel some of the offices, starting with his own. She parked the car and got out her briefcase. She straitened up her clothes from sitting. Cloe walked through the front lobby to the secretary that was sitting at a round desk. The lady was helping someone so Cloe looked around. Everyone here was very professional. They were very dressed up. Cloe looked down at her own clothes. She felt under dressed somehow. *Oh well,* she shrugged and looked around some more. There were some very peculiar paintings along the walls of the waiting room they have for the ones who want to wait to see the lawyers. Cloe looked at her watch. She had time. She moved from the desk and stood and looked at the paintings. They were paintings of angels and angelical scenes.

But then she ran across a painting of Lilith. *That's very odd,* she thought.

Then she noticed the ceiling.

It looked like a small cathedral ceiling. It was the renaissance picture of heaven and hell. She was deep in thought as she studied the colors and images. As she was looking at it, a manly soft voice said from behind her. "You must be Cloe." She jumped and whirled around.

There in front of her stood the most gorgeous man she ever laid eyes on.

And he was a tall, built man. He wore a tailored suit but his muscles were very prominent through the fabric. He was gorgeous. He had dark hair and light blue eyes. His dark eyelashes really made his eyes shine. He had a straight nose and prominent cheek bones. Cloe shook herself inwardly; *keep your eyes open* she told herself. She extended her hand to shake his.

"Yes, I'm Cloe. Are you Cory?"

"I'd feel like a fool if I wasn't. Sorry I scared you." he said with big white teeth. They shook hands.

"That's okay. I was just admiring your art work." *And you.* Cloe pointed up over her head.

"It's beautiful, isn't it?" He walked to the middle of the room and looked up. "It makes me wish I could be there." He said softly.

Cloe's hair began to rise on the back of her neck. *What a strange thing to say,* She thought.

He turned around as if he quickly pulled himself out of a trance and stared at Cloe. Cloe looked nervously around the room. He began to walk up to her and said, "So are we ready to get started?" Cloe wanted to leave really, but she nodded and followed him as he walked past her.

They made their way down the hall towards the elevator. Along the walls were more paintings. She'll have to come back one of these days and look. She had business to do now. They stopped at the elevator doors and he pushed a button. The doors slid open and they walked in the tiny box. He pushed a button again and the doors shut. Her stomach did a little flip as the elevator started moving. He turned toward her and asked, "Have you been with the company long?"

"A little over three years." Cloe said.

"What did you do before that?"

"I was in college. This is my first job." Cloe nodded.

He put his hands on the railing on either side if him. "What did you go to college for?"

"Information Tech." Cloe answered.

"That's a good field." he stated.

The elevator stopped and the doors slid open. They walked down another hall and there was a secretary at the end. "Hold my calls Linda."

"Yes sir." Linda said.

They made their way into his office. It was a vast room with everything a boss could need. It had a wet bar and a big screen TV. A couch and chairs scattered along the wall opposite the TV. The desk was by the windows, on the other side. He moved around his desk and sat down. Cloe followed him and sat in a chair in front of his desk. He brushed some papers aside and pulled out a quote from the company she worked for. "At first I wanted the room to look like this." He slid the blue print to her. She picked it up and looked at it. "But now I've changed my mind. I want it like this."

Cloe mimicked him in her head. It must be nice to 'want and get'.

Cloe picked up the second blue print and compared the two. It had an added gym area and a hide a way bed in the wall. She scratched her forehead hoping he didn't see her blush. She could just imagine what that was for! *I'm going to kill Chris,* she thought. "Do you have the quote for the first print?" she asked Cory, hoping that he didn't hear the squeak come out. He slid that to her. Cloe noticed he hadn't taken his eyes from her. She studied the old quote and looked at the new blueprint again. Putting them down she asked. "Is this all that was quoted?"

He sat back in his chair. "I told Chris that if it turns out then I would want other offices done as well, but I gave him this one project first."

Cloe nodded and said she understood. You don't want to be stuck with someone who can't do the job by a contract. It was a smart move. Cory got up and went to the wet bar. "Would you like something to drink?" Cloe turned around in her chair and asked, "Do you have water?" Her mouth was dry for some reason. He opened up the little frig and pulled out a bottled water. As he handed it to her he asked, "Have you lived here long?" *That's a weird question,* she thought. "Yes, all my life." She turned the top off the water and took a drink. He was at the bar making himself a drink. When he was done he came around the desk and sat back down.

"What's your last name?" Cory asked.

"Smith." Cloe answered, but wouldn't look at him.

"Smith." he said, as if it was something he should know. Cloe's eyebrow went up and she looked at him. She was getting peeved. He noticed and sat forward in his chair. "It's just that I wondered how I could have not seen you all these years. You are quite interesting." Cloe's other eyebrow went up and she cocked her head sideways a notch.

Was this a pick up line? "How so?" she countered back.

"Well, I can tell by looking at you that you are very lean and muscular." She looked down at her leg that was crossed over the other one, *did he have x-ray vision?* He went on. "Do you work out?"

"Yes." She wasn't delving out any more information than that.

"And you seem intelligent, mysterious too." he smiled.

"Thanks." Cloe said and smiled back.

"I haven't met anyone like you for along time." He leaned forward more as if to hone the point into her mind how much he was really interested in her.

Cloe just looked at him. As if he could sense her irritation, he sat back and gave her one last serious look and cleared his throat. "Okay, back to business." He said as he relaxed back in his chair. "Please forgive me. It's just that when I see something beautiful that I want, I usually get it." He went on to say something else but Cloe put her finger up in the air so he stopped what he was about to say.

"I don't mean to be rude. But I'm not interested." She stopped at that.

He smiled. "How would you know? I haven't had any complaints yet, but okay. I give up. So now, what do you need to make this new quote happen?"

She got up and looked around the room, still extremely uncomfortable, but thankful to be up and moving. She didn't know how much longer she could have sat there with him staring at her. "I'll need to walk around and measure and calculate this." she said over her shoulder.

He got up and walked past her. "Okay. I'm going to step out for awhile then since you don't need me."

She looked at him and said, "That'll be fine."

He went out the door with one last look. After the door closed Cloe let out a long breath. There was something else about him. He acted strange but she didn't want to ponder on it here. Sometimes she had to do her job first. If he was something evil and he didn't start any trouble with her then she would leave him alone, for a while anyway. She wondered that if he was who she suspected, a deadskin. *Did he knew who she was?* She got out her briefcase and went to work.

She wrote on a paper pad everything she would need and on a separate piece wrote down the prices. She walked around the room and wrote some more. It wasn't to far off the original blue print. After about an hour she was finishing up. She opened her brief case and put everything away. She straitened up and looked at the painting over the couch. She was focusing on the painting. It was one she had never seen before. She looked at the colors of swirling pastel. All of a sudden her ears heard a piercing sound. At first she thought maybe a bug was buzzing in her ear, but it got louder and louder in both ears. It was so loud she thought her ear drums would bust. She looked around, there was nothing there. Suddenly she felt little bites upon her skin. She doubled over and was trying to push off whatever was biting her but there was nothing there.She was trying to look around for something that was causing this, but she was alone. She didn't know if she was screaming out loud or if the noise that was in her ears was making that high pitched sound. She fell to the floor and balled up. *Say a prayer,* she tried to control her breathing, *calm down and think,* she started to recite the Lords Prayer, *calm down*, she continued on praying, *it's going to end soon,* she put her hands over her ears. By the time she got done with the prayer, which seemed like an eternity, everything had diminished. She lay on the floor breathing heavily.

She knew she had just been attacked demoniacally.

She had been through it before. It was never the same though. She sat up and rubbed her ears. *I've got to get out of here!* She picked herself up off the floor and grabbed her briefcase. She quickly put the quote on Cory's desk. She ran to the door and went out it. After she closed the door behind her she looked around the hallway and noticed the secretary looked at her and smiled. It was amazing bright here compared to his office. Cloe smoothed out the front of her shirt and tried not to look hassled as she made her way past Linda's desk. Linda tried to stop her but she wasn't stopping. She made her way to the elevator briskly and just before the door shut Cory came out of another office and was looking at her, smiling that white smile. She made her way out of the firm at a fast pace. She didn't want to seem scared. Most was looking at her quizzically. Some was just looking at her with a smirk on their face like they had known what happened. When she reached her car she got in and locked the doors. What she didn't know was that Cory watched her from his office windows. She pulled out of the parking lot and made her way to work. She drove into a gas station a good distance away and after putting the car in park she put her head on her steering wheel. Her thoughts were racing. She knew something was different about that place. She knew it. A preacher once said Satan has his hand in everything about money, because everybody wanted it. There was money and politics, money and education, money and law, money and love. Not all humans were like that though. Not everyone relied deeply on money. She was wrong about Cory, she should have known by those eyes. They were white. That's how you can tell the Fallen apart. And a deadskin at that, which is a term she used to describe that a fallen can take over a dead body and make it their own. They're walking deadskins. Demons can do it to but it takes them a lot more effort. And you can tell because either they have some mark, like demons and their followers. Or their eyes are void of color which would be a fallen angel. What they wear can make you think there's color. But if you got close enough to look, there wasn't any. She got out and pumped some gas. No wonder he said he wished he could be there she realized when he was looking at the painting. She shook her head and looked down at her shoes.

She was sure Chris was getting a phone call right about now. *Great.*

The nozzle clicked off and she went to pay for gas and something to eat and drink. She got a sausage biscuit and a cappuccino. Maybe food would settle her nerves. She rubbed her ears. She got back in the car and drove to work. She carried in her goodies and made her way through the door. The building was a warehouse so it was all open inside. That was all except for the bathrooms and Chris's office. It used to be an old furniture warehouse but the company went belly up. Cloe made her way to her desk and dropped everything. Chris was at the drafting desk with some other guys and when he saw her he made his way for her.

Here we go, she thought, as she saw him coming towards her. He'll want to know why she was so rude to leave like that. Chris came up to the desk. "Hey, I'm proud of you. You did a damn good job. You sure you don't wanna be the quote person?" He sat on the corner of her desk.

Cloe's eyebrows went up. "Did he call you?"

"Yes. And Cory recommends that you do all the quoting from now on if we do well on this one."

"I don't think so." *So he didn't say anything.*

"Why not? The way he gushed over you, he obviously likes you. We could use that to our advantage."

Cloe sat down at looked at Chris in disbelief. She shook her head and sighed. "I can t believe you said that."

"Hey, it's business." He giggled and pushed her shoulder. "There wasn't anything wrong with him, was there?"

If only you knew, she thought. Chris knew some things about her demon hunting but didn't believe in it, he thought it was about teenagers or just sick people in general playing a joke on society.

"I don't ever want to go back there." Cloe said and took a bite of her food. It was cold so she trashed it.

"But he said he wanted you to do the quotes!" Chris protested.

"I don't care. I'm not the quote person. Billy is. HE can do the quotes."

"He said you left without saying so." Chris stated.

Ah, here it is.

"I did. I was finished and I couldn't find him so I put the quote on his desk and left. He found it, didn't he?"

"Yah, I guess." Chris said indecisively.

"Okay, then." she said wanting to end the conversation.

"Can I see what you quoted him, please?" Chris asked.

"Sure." She pulled the papers out of her briefcase. He went over the papers and the new blueprint. Nodding his head he got off the desk and patted Cloe on the back. He headed over to the drafting table and went to work on it. Chris took his work seriously. That's why he was in high demand.

Cloe went to work as well and stayed busy putting in account numbers and blue prints for various other jobs. It was two o'clock when her cell phone rang. It was her mother. Cloe talked to her for about fifteen minutes. Her mom just wanted to say hi and was in the neighborhood. She wanted to know if Cloe wanted to go out to eat. "Sure." She said, and her mom said she be there in five minutes and hung up. Cloe stopped her work and got up to go to the door. She told Chris she was having lunch with her mom. Chris said okay and waved her off. That's what she liked about working at Chris's Construction. He was very lenient with his employees as long as they didn't screw around. He was very watchful though so if an employee tried to be lazy, and get paid for it, he would end up with his ass given to him by Chris. She waited outside the building and saw her mom's car make its way towards her. She opened the passenger side and got in. Her mom squeezed her hand and drove off. "I believe I owe you dinner, where would you like to go." She asked.

"Oh, it doesn't matter, mom. Where ever you want."

"How about Chinese?"

"Sounds good." Cloe said. No matter if she was hungry or not, she would never pass up Chinese. Her mom chose a place close by. She didn't get out much. And her car was a very beat up one. Half the time she couldn't rely on it but it was all she could afford. She was out of work, so she stayed home a lot. The girls would make sure she had food in the house often. They went in and waited to be seated. The waitress finally seated them and asked what they wanted to drink. Cloe ordered a soda and her mom got tea. They told the waitress they would eat at the buffet and the waitress waved them to it and went off to get their drinks.

After they filled their plates with food they sat down to eat. The waitress had already put their drinks on the table. Cloe took a bite and she closed her eyes. She hoped they had Chinese food in heaven. *This is so good* she told herself. Her mom watched her and asked. "It's really good food here, isn't it?"

"Yes. I love this place." Cloe answered.

"So how have you been, dear." her mom asked.

Cloe thought about earlier today. She could tell her mom anything. Shirley had seen her own grandmother practice witchcraft so she knew what it was like. Her grandmother was mean to her own kids though. And Shirley told a story that once when her mom, along with her sisters and brothers, came home from school one evening, that they found Shirley's grandmother, their own mother, hanging from a rafter. The girls all dropped to their knees crying and hid their eyes. The boys were crying too, but being older, they made their way to get their mother down. Before the boys could reach her though, she opened up her eyes and started laughing. To her it was a joke. Cloe told her mom about what had gone on that morning. Her mom listened attentively. Cloe finally finished the story and took a deep breath. She didn't have to be strong in front of her mother. Her mother knew. She patted Cloe's hand. "You go through so much, why don't you get out of it?" Cloe shook her head. "Because I have a gift mom, I should use it for something good. You know this, you have it too, but you never used it."

Shirley knew she spoke the truth. She didn't have the guts to do what this daughter does, even though she has dealt with demons before. She pretended it never happened. She was proud of her daughter, but scared for her also. She had seen movies and read books where a demon can tear apart a human. She hoped secretly it wasn't like that in real life. Shirley had never asked. Cloe changed the subject and asked about her dad and Shirley filled her in on what they did in their spare time. They thought about traveling to another state. Cloe said that sounded like a good idea. "You know your dad. One day he wants to do something and the next he can't because of something or the other." Shirley said over her plate.

"Do you want me to talk to him?" The kids could always talk him into anything.

"I don't know. I'm not sure I want to go."

"Come on mom, sometimes getting away is a good thing." Cloe persisted.

"Only if you want to. It would be kind of nice to see the ocean." Shirley shrugged.

"I'll talk to him. Why don't you have a potluck dinner for all of us and I'll bring it up then. That way I'll have back up." Cloe smiled. She knew her siblings would chime in if they knew their mother wanted to go off on a vacation. They seldom went anywhere. All the kids would chip in on funds to help them out.

"That's sounds good, I'll put on ham and sweet potatoes." she said brightly. "Well then, set a date and call everyone."

Cloe said happily. "And don't forget to tell them to bring something."

"I won't. You're such a smart girl." Shirley said. It brought Cloe to remember earlier that morning. She had heard the same thing from Cory.

"Are you alright?" her mom asked. She noticed Cloe having a glazed stare.

"Yah. I was just thinking about this morning. Mom, there is something else. There is something going to happen, big, I think. I don't know what." and went on to tell her mom about the incident at the spring in her pasture. Her mom's eyes got big. "Has that happened to you before?"

"No. That's why I think it's big. Usually it's just demons. Now there's fallen angels' coming into play. I don't know if they've always been around and are showing up for something, or they are just now getting out in public for the first time from another place."

"Hmmm, I don't know either." Shirley studied the ice in her glass. "You know some religions think that the fallen angels where locked someplace in heaven, I think, and are waiting to be turned loose."

Cloe nodded, she had read that somewhere. Her mother went on. "And some religious scholars think that some are already here.

"Either way." Cloe stated and held up two fingers. "I have possibly seen two already, it's just that one disappeared into thin air."

"That is very strange. Is that all the action you've seen?" Shirley thought maybe there was more. "No. There's a cult Megan started hanging with. Sue caught that in time luckily, but I've got to get in their hangout and try to get Amanda out as well."

"Oh, gosh! How did they get caught up in that?"

"I don't know. I didn't get that detail. Sue was just scared that the group of people she started hanging out with was a cult and it turns out, after checking, that they were."

"Well it's a good thing Sue caught it then. So what is it?"

"The cult? It's for the demon named Botis. He is a truth seer, but can lie, be a trickster. He looks like snake but can take human form. I hope to banish him before he takes form."

"Can he be real dangerous?" Shirley knew some demons cannot possess other beings, some can.

"Not as much as some, but his specific goal is a seer into the future. And can tell where hidden treasures are."

Cloe liked that kind best of all. She had rather done without any of it, but if she had to take her pick, it would be one like this. The ones that can possess are rather hard to capture. They keep jumping around from one person to the next. They got done eating and made their way to pay. "Be careful, okay?" her mom said to her. "I will mom, I promise." Cloe knew it was probably painful for her mother to know things about her and not worry. Nobody wants to lose a daughter. Cloe stepped up quickly and laid the money on the counter. She didn't want her mom to pay. She paid enough though out life. Her mom protested but Cloe told the cashier to take her money in a very warning tone of voice. The cashier took Cloe's money carefully while eyeing her. Her mom sighed and put her money back in her purse. They walked out to the car and got in. Her mom started laughing and Cloe asked "What was so funny."

"Did you see the look on the poor little girls face?" she was talking about the cashier and after thinking about it, Cloe started laughing to. "I bet she thinks I'm a total bitch." Cloe said after they had a good laugh. Her mom giggled again and said thanks for dinner. She drove Cloe back to work and they hugged each other quickly before Cloe got out. After she shut the car door she turned around and said through the window, "Don't forget to call everyone now, for that potluck dinner." Cloe said, leaning over.

"I won't. I love you." Shirley said.

"I love you too, mom. Drive carefully." and Cloe stood up to wave her off.

Cloe went back to work until six. Then she got up to go home. Most of the workers went home around five. Cloe wanted to finish up. She hated leaving work undone. After putting everything in the computer she looked for Chris.

"I'm going home." She said as she leaned on his doorway.

"Okay, then. You really did a good job today. How's your mother?"

"She's doing well. She wants to go on vacation." Cloe smiled.

"Can they afford that?"

That was another thing they had in common. They both came from poor families. They both lived two blocked from each other in a poor neighborhood. Both he and Cloe's parents still lived there. So Chris knew how hard it was for Cloe's parents.

"We'll make sure they can." Cloe said.

"Let me know if I can help." Chris said. He has helped her family out many times.

"I will. Thanks. I better get home."

"Yah, me too, Samantha will be mad if I miss dinner." Samantha was his girlfriend. It was hard for Chris to have a girlfriend for very long. He was very committed to his work and the long hours. Some women didn't like it when a man didn't make an effort to show up some of the time. They walked out together and made their way to their cars. Chris drove one way and Cloe went the other.

❧

Cloe went home and after doing chores she relaxed on the couch. She turned on the TV. Then she turned it off. She sat there with her head in her hand thinking of the day. How strange that it would happen in broad daylight.

She's never been attacked in daylight hours.

I should have known she thought.

The phone rang. It was Sue. "Megan wants to talk to you." she said.

"Okay, put her on."

"Hey, Aunt Cloe. I just wanted to tell you that there is a party that I am invited to Saturday night with Amanda. I think it's at that guy's house with the tattoo. So if you're ready then we'll do this thing Saturday night."

"Okay, sounds good. How do you know it's at that guy's house?"

"Cause I told Amanda I had to know where it was for mom's sake or I couldn't go. Amanda said it was at the guy's house with the tattoo on his neck. I played stupid and she asked me if I remember going to the Romp Room with a bunch a people and she described him to a tee. So that's how I know."

"Wow, Megan, you're getting pretty good at this." Cloe said amazed.

"Thanks!" Megan gushed. "You want to talk to mom now?"

"Ya, I'll get in touch with you on Saturday okay?"

"Okay." Megan said then she was yelling for Sue.

"Hello."

"Hey, are you still okay with this?" Cloe asked.

"Ya, it'll be okay, I think. Your biggest problem will be Amanda."

"I'm not sure what to tell her except if she wants to see him then she needs to get him away from that group." Cloe said while rubbing her forehead with her fingers. "But since she is over eighteen I don't think I can do anything."

Amanda was older than Megan by a year and a half. But they were close for cousins. Cloe knew that Megan was worried about Amanda now, so all she could do was try for Megan's sake.

"So how'd your day go?" Sue asked.

"I had lunch with mom today. She wants to have a potluck dinner sometime." Cloe said.

"What day is it?"

"I told her to call everyone with a day and time so she'll call when she's ready."

"Okay, that sounds pretty good." Sue exclaimed.

Cloe didn't tell her about the vacation thing, she'll wait until everyone is there at mom's house then she'll spring it on them. It's pretty sneaky but it works. Cloe told Sue about her meeting that morning with Cory. Sue was nervous for Cloe. "Had they ever attacked in the daylight before?" Sue asked astonished.

"No, not at me they haven't. What concerns me is it was a public place. But I think the whole bunch at the firm is souled out." That was a term Cloe liked to use for describing someone being evil or selling their soul.

"Really?" Sue asked.

"Yes. It was the way they looked at me when I was leaving, as if they knew what happened and it made them glad."

"Creepy." Sue said in a wobbly voice and Cloe thought she might have shivered.

Cloe told her about Cory and how he looked at the picture and said he wished he could be there. If Cloe was right and he was a fallen angel. Then that would make sense for him to wish to be back there again. A fallen angel's worse regret is being away from the creator. They want to go back but can't. It's anybody worse regret really. After talking to Sue about it, it made Cloe feel a little better. And they talked some more before Sue hung up to get everyone ready for bed. Cloe wasn't ready for bed yet so she went to her personable library and pulled out her bible to read it. She studied with a man on TV who she thought was a pretty good preacher. She had his bible tapes ordered through the mail. She had some catching up to do. After an hour of reading in the book of Isaiah she turned off the TV and went to bed.

Her night was full of dreams and she didn't sleep well at all. The alarm was soon going off and it was time to go back to work. After the usual routine of coffee and reading the news on the Internet, she took off to work. She liked being at work because it took her mind off of everything else. She helped Chris and the others at the big drafting table. They had lunch together at a local restaurant. Then came back to do some more work. The phone rang over the speakers and Chris went to answer it in his office. He came from around the door and hollered at Cloe. When she looked up he held the phone receiver for her to see. She had a phone call. When she got to the phone she asked Chris who it was and Chris shrugged and left the office. Cloe watched him walk away for a second and put the receiver to her ear.

"Hello?"

"Don't hang up." The man's voice said.

"Tell me who this is or I will." Cloe insisted.

"It's Cory." Cloe eyes went wide and she froze.

"I just wanted to apologize for the other day." Cory hurriedly said.

"Why." Cloe said. Maybe she would get him admit to what went on that day.

"I didn't mean for you to leave without saying good bye."

"Why would you care?"

He sighed. "I couldn't stop thinking of you."

"I bet." she said. Chris studied her through the office glass windows and Cloe shot him a dirty look. Chris smiled. In his innocence of trying to set her up, he had no idea what was really going on.

"No. Really. Why did you leave so suddenly? You looked like you saw a ghost."

"Don't pretend like you don't know what's going on." Cloe said through clenched teeth and squeezed the receiver.

"I really don't." Cory said as he pretended innocence.

"Are we done here?"

"Why are you so hateful? Don't you know a good Christian is supposed to love everyone?" Cory purred over the phone as he put emphasis on the word Christian.

"Cory, you are asking for it." Cloe said slowly and hung up.

She sat there for a second and then she put her shoulders back she went out of the office. She went over to the work table and joined the others working on the blueprint of a bank. It had to get started on building it tomorrow but they were almost done. A representative from the bank had come in and was helping make decisions. Chris looked up at her when everyone else was busy talking amongst their selves. He moved his eyebrows up and down and asked who it was on the phone. Cloe stopped what she was doing and stared at him with her lips pierced together.

"You know who that was, don't you!" She said with her hands on her hips.

"Yah, he called me at home last night and was asking questions about you, like if you were single, and what you liked to do." Chris said and drew a line on paper.

"You didn't tell him, did you?"

"What is wrong with him? He's rich and smart and good looking." By the time Chris got that sentence out everyone was listening to him say something about Chris thinking a guy was good looking. Some eyebrows went up and snickering went around the table. Chris looked at everyone. "What? I can think a man's good looking, I'm comfortable with my masculinity." he said with his hands wide apart as if he was challenging someone to say something. He shrugged his shoulders as if he was putting on a coat before he went back to work.

"Chris, I don't want a boyfriend right now, besides, we don't really know this man, do we?" Cloe said as she was studying the drawing. "For all we know he could be an ax murderer."

"Oh, please!" Chris said and shook his head. He rested his hands upon the table.

"Fine, have it your way. If I know anything about him 'cause I'm a guy, he won't give up that easy."

"That's what I'm afraid of." Cloe kept the rest of her thoughts to herself. She looked at Chris and Chris just shook his head at her. She smiled at him.

He really was an adorable person. She couldn't stay mad at him long. They finished up and went home for the evening. Before Cloe went home she went shopping for food and feed for the animals. While she was at the store she ran into several old acquaintances from school. It took longer than she thought to get everything done. By the time she was on her way home, it was around eight at night. She was driving home when her cell phone rang. She looked at the number on the screen, just in case Chris gave her number out. It was Rose.

"Hey, you. What are you doing?"

"I'm on my home from shopping." Cloe said.

"Oh. I wish I knew you were going, you could have come and got me. I just went myself."

"Sorry, I would have picked you up if I'd known."

"That's okay. So how is your week going?" Cloe told her about the whole Cory business and Rose was shocked. She asked the same questions Sue did and Cloe answered them the best she could. Rose couldn't stand it anymore and said she was on her way to Cloe's house. She was going to spend the night because she had something to tell her that she found out but didn't want to discuss it on the phone. Cloe asked her if she ate yet and Rose said no. Cloe told her that she'd cook up some frozen pizza's and to come on over. It wasn't unusual for them to spend the night at each other's house. Cloe hung up and went home to cook pizza. Rose showed up about thirty minutes after Cloe got home and of course Puppy was with her. She turned Puppy loose and the dogs took off. The two girls fed the animals and went in the house. Cloe stuck a pizza in the oven and they say down at the kitchen table. The chairs were almost like big office chairs so it was comfortable to sit in them for long periods. Rose was excited about something and Cloe asked her what was going on.

"I went to the herbal store and there was that lady in there that I always talk too. We got to talking and she said she had heard of you. Well, not really of you per say, but that there was a demon killer is what she called you. The word is on the street but nobody really knows what to expect."

"That's good." Cloe replied. "It ruins the element of surprise." Rose nodded but she went on. "So anyways, this girl was telling me of a hoodoo couple that live here in the city and she told me how to get there, and said that I could buy some of the stuff there and that owner would give some pointers but that this couple could really help you out."

Cloe's eyebrows went together. "How can they help me?"

"I don't know, the lady really didn't say." Rose shrugged. "She just said that they could help us. Well I know how they could help me but I don't know about you."

Cloe got up to switch pizzas out of the oven. Her mind went to an old Cajun couple that used to live in town. The old man went to jail for laundering money but she didn't hear of anything more. They were practiced Hoodoo also, and Cloe had went to see he old lady for advise on some demons when she first really put in the hours on demon hunting. As she could remember they were called Papa Whitney and Madam Agnes. Madam Agnes was a like a gypsy lady, very peculiar. Cloe had forgotten about the odd couple. Cloe put the pizza on the table and got some plates down. They served up the pizza and Cloe asked Rose. "She didn't give you any names?"

"No, just an address. I asked if she knew the names but she said she had never been there herself yet. But she thought I looked trustworthy of the information, since they don't let just anybody in to see them. All that's passed around is this address. And it's given only to a person that you absolutely trust."

Cloe took the paper and looked at it. It was somewhere downtown. There was a lot of really big houses downtown. Most of them turned into businesses like realtor's or plumbers or doctors offices. "Are you going to check it out?" Cloe asked.

Rose finished chewing and shrugged. "Do you think I could?"

"I don't know. Do you want pointers from a hoodoo witch?"

"They are pretty crafty." Rose pointed out.

"They can be pretty dangerous in the black arts." Cloe countered back.

"Yes I know, but I'm not a black witch, so I wouldn't even go there. You yourself use Rose brick dust to surround your property. That's a form of Hoodoo." Cloe nodded. "But if she could let some good secrets out, we'll be the wiser. Maybe I'll even ask for her to read my cards." Rose giggled. Cloe could read cards but didn't want to for her best friend. It's hard to read for someone who she cared about. They finished with the pizza and cleaned up. Cloe told her about the old Cajun couple she used to know and wondered if that was the same couple. After they got done they went to the living room and settled in. It was going to be a late night but either one didn't mind. They loved to stay up talking. Rose then asked about Cory.

"What about him?" Cloe countered back.

"What's he like. Are you certain he's a fallen angel?" Rose fluffed up a pillow for her head.

"He's got to be, but no, I'm not certain. He could be a very powerful demon."

"And he likes you? Boy, are you in big trouble! You know what that means, right?"

"Do you mean that he'll try to win me over to their side." when she said it, it sounded like something out of 'Star Wars' and could hear a voice say "Luke, come to the dark side." But that was the only way she could put it. Cloe told Rose about the Star Wars thing and they laughed. They sobered up after about fifteen minutes of making fun of what she said. "No, really," Rose said and wiped at her eyes, "He won't leave you alone until you have to put the hurt on him."

"Ya I know. And if he's a fallen then that is going to be real hard." she drug out the last two words.

"I feel sorry for you. Does Chris know?"

"No. He wouldn't believe me if I told him. He would think I'd lost it." Cloe said.

"I guess you could always try to turn him." Rose said softly. Cloe thought about that. "That would take a lot of hard work." Cory would have to want it, but man, if he was a fallen, what would heaven do? Rejoice? Send him back? Cloe thought about the other angels in heaven actually getting a family member back. Rose broke her train of thought. "How come you just didn't tell him to leave you alone?"

"Well, there is an old saying that goes something like this." Cloe pointed a finger in the air. "Keep you friends close, but your enemies closer." After a short pause Rose said, "You sound like a fortune cookie." and they went off on a laughter trip again, making fun of what she said and adding to it, trying to talk like the Chinese dialect. They once again got serious and Rose asked "What the hell does that mean anyway?" about what Cloe quoted earlier before.

"It means always pay attention to your enemies, that way when they turn on you, then you already know what damage they can do. Then it's no surprise."

"Oh." Rose said and got quiet. "That's actually pretty smart." Then she turned toward Cloe with her eyes pulled back by her fore fingers and said. "Your one sthmart cookie."

in a Chinese voice again and Cloe threw her pillow at her. They laughed some more over what she said.

It was midnight and they decided to go to bed. They brushed their teeth and Cloe got an extra pair of pj's for Rose. They slept in the same bed because it was king size, and Rose was scared of the dark. They didn't have to worry about the alarm because they pretty much got up at the same time. They got under the covers and talked some more, laughed some more, and dozed off to sleep. The next morning the two girls got up and got ready for work. Rose had packed her clothes for work so she could get dressed at Cloe's without going home. Only Cloe had coffee but they shared the laptop. Then they took off to work, promising to call each other shortly. The rest of the week was pretty much the same and soon Saturday came around. That evening on Saturday Cloe went to Sue's to get ready for the big rescue she was going to fake with Megan. They talked it over and made a plan. Cloe was going to barge in unannounced and go after Megan and in the process of that send her home.

Hopefully this all took place in front of Mr. Tattoo.

They got it all settled and Megan left to pick up Amanda and go to the party. Cloe followed from a distance. Cloe did her hair and makeup so that if you did know her, you wouldn't recognize her at all with the make up on. She got the protection amulet ready that Rose gave her also. After Megan picked up Amanda, they started to drive out of town. Cloe still followed at a distance, hoping she wouldn't loose them. After a while they turned down a country road that was graveled and drove for twenty minutes more and came upon an estate.

The gates were open and cars where everywhere. When Cloe saw all the cars and people she had an idea it will be easier than she thought. She waited in her car for another ten minutes so that she wouldn't run into Megan and Amanda. She was thinking that she would snoop around first before she became a party crasher. She got out of the car and made her way to the front door. The house had double doors and they were both open. People were pouring in and out. It was quite a party. She went in through the doors. It was a beautiful place. It looked like the old colonial houses with the grand staircase up one side of the hallway leading up to a balcony. There where people everywhere. The hallway led all the way to the back where another set of double doors stood wide open. People where going in and out of that also. There where rooms off the hallway on both sides. One was a sitting room, one was a billiard room. There was a big chrome filled kitchen and one room was a library. *Ah, the library*, Cloe thought. That was a good place to look. She sauntered her way from shelf to shelf. The library looked like hers, almost. It had some of the same books but a lot of different ones, darker ones. Some where about rituals and rising the dead. Some were store bought, and some were homemade. That was the ones she looked for. After looking around she took an old black covered homemade book off the shelf. She looked around again and opened the pages to where every marker was. Quickly scanning the titles, she saw some of interest. She found a peace of paper and quickly opened it. It had something about a Catholic church on it. It was dated yesterday. She stuck that in her pocket. Then after looking around she put the book back. She quickly looked over the desk. Some calendar dates were circled. She thumbed all the way to the end of the year. Halloween seemed to be a big date.

She made her way through the room and was just about to go out the door when she spotted Cory.

She ducked behind a grand father clock in the hallway. She peeked around the edge of it to see him talking to some other rather handsome men. They all looked like they just took off their business jackets and loosened up their ties. Cory had women draped on each arm. As if he could sense she was looking him he suddenly started looking around and studying faces.

She ducked back behind the clock. *Oh shit, oh shit, oh shit,* she thought.

A bead a sweat started to form on her forehead. *What am I going to do now?*

Problem number one, Mr. Tattoo.

Problem number two, Cory.

She didn't need any more problems.

If he sees her he'll relentlessly bug her. If she doesn't do what he wants she may have another attack to deal with. She took a breath and scratched her head, *oh well*. She had to get Megan out of this. She'd deal with Cory later. She made sure to get past Cory with out him noticing. The people he kept company seemed to capture his attention quite well.

Maybe this was his house she thought.

She looked around from room to room and didn't find anyone she was looking for. She was at the back door and made her way out. The yard was great big and was packed with people. The music was hard core. Cloe walked across the spacious patio. There were all kinds of walk of life here, as Cloe run into two women petting each other and kissing. She averted her eyes to the ground and she made her way past them. She went out into the yard. Cloe made her way towards the bon fire. That's when she saw Mr. Tattoo. He had quite a crowd around him. Deciding that she didn't want to take on all of them, she waited for the perfect moment to confront him. It ended up taking longer than she thought, but finally he broke free to wonder around. He had a girl on his arm but that didn't matter to Cloe. She followed him for awhile and he made his way to a group that Megan was standing with. This was now where she came in. She walked up to Megan and put on a big scene, of course Megan was protesting. Amanda came up and looked at Cloe like it was the first time she ever saw her. Cloe then turned on Amanda and told them both to leave this place, and that they didn't belong here.

That's when Mr. Tattoo stepped up. *About time.*

Cloe whirled around on him. "You got a problem?"

"Ya, I do. Who are you to tell these ladies what to do?"

"Keep your nose out of this."

"What's wrong with being here, you're here." he said. Cloe thought for sure he was gonna give her the Z snap action.

"Well, I'm here for you." Cloe all but whispered as she stepped closer to him.

He smiled. "For me, uh huh, what do you want with me?" and looked down his nose at her like he was some stud.

"Your library books are due, I'm here to collect." Cloe was like that, being a smart ass. He laughed. Cloe grabbed him by a wrist and spun him around in front of her with the same arm up behind his back. She started twisting his wrist. She pulled him up tight as he struggled and whispered in his ear. "I know your demon, I'm a demon hunter. I think you get the rest of the story." and pushed him away. He looked at her with such hatred. He rubbed his wrist and came at her again. She rolled backwards on her back and stuck her foot in his gut, tossing him over her and onto the ground above her head. She quickly got up and so did he. By then they had a crowd gathered around. She looked at Megan and told her to leave. Megan's was about to and Amanda stopped her. Cloe sighed. She looked back at Mr. Tattoo, and he was coming at her again. He connected a punch to her jaw and it snapped her head around. She staggered backwards and wiped her mouth. She looked at him and smiled. It startled him and he came at her again. This time she side stepped him and jumping up, brought her knee up to his chin. Then she slapped her hands over his ears with everything she had. He grabbed his ears and she punched his throat. He went down on his knees and she finished it with a kick to his face. As he lay on the ground trying to breath she turned towards Amanda and said breathlessly, "Get out of here now Amanda, or you'll be next." through clenched teeth. Megan started to walk off and Amanda looked from Cloe to Megan. Finally she ran after

Megan. She was trying to grab Megan's arm and demanded to know what's was going on. Megan finally had enough and told Amanda to get her ass in the car, she would explain it on the way home. By that time Mr. Tattoo was getting to his feet. Before he could charge again there was voice from behind her boom out "Stop!" and he immediately froze.

∾

Cloe turned around to find Cory and his peoples standing behind her.

"What is going on here?" Cory asked with a commanding voice. It sounded like he was disappointed in Mr. Tattoo. About that time tattoo pointed at Cloe and said "She started it!"

Cory looked at Cloe.

Cloe was willing him silently *don't notice me, don't notice me.* It was too late. It took Cory a second but he did.

At first it was as if he doubted himself, and then he stepped out of the women's arms and asked, "Cloe?"

Shit!

"Yes?" Cloe stepped out from between Cory and tattoo. She didn't want to be sucker punched because she was looking at Cory. She doubted if Cory would have stopped it. He probably would have been more like 'oops, sorry.'

"What are you doing here?" Cory asked.

"Taking care of business." Cloe answered back.

"What business would that be, beating up little boys?" He looked at tattoo in a manner that said he wasn't giving him a compliment.

"No, I don't want my nieces here and he thought I couldn't tell them to go home. I proved him wrong."

"Why can't they be here?" He asked like there was nothing wrong with that.

"Because they don't need to be here." Cloe said impatiently. Cory just stared at her. Cloe's eyes squinted down. She was getting peeved. As if he decided against further arguments he looked at tattoo. The boy went to him and whispered something in his ear while looking over his shoulder. Cory looked at tattoo, and then looked at Cloe. Tattoo must have been pleased because he grinned at Cloe one last time before leaving. He took most of the crowd with him. Cory said something to his peoples and they dispersed also. Then he came toward Cloe to stand in front of her. He put his hands in his pockets but his jaw was clenching.

Cloe watched his jaw bulge in and out.

He looked over her head at the people who was still around. As he made eye contact with them, they slowly moved away. He looked down at her. She looked up at him.

They were on opposites sides of the fence.

They always would be.

There would be no playing nice. They both knew it. As Sue always said about fighting evil, it was a chess game. He seemed hesitant as to what to do with her. Finally he said, "I'll walk you out."

"No need. I came in by myself. I can make my way out."

He looked at her with his head cocked sideways. As if he wished they didn't have to be enemies. He had a big eyed deer look as he studied her. She crossed her arms over her chest. *Too bad, big boy* she thought. He seemed to read her mind and straightened up.

Suddenly he had his hand on the back of her neck and was beside her, effortlessly making her walk. He had a death grip on her neck and Cloe walked beside him, not willing to show the pain that was coursing through her. He had the other hand behind his back. She was almost on her tippy toes.

To anybody else it looked as if it was a fatherly gesture as they walked toward the back door. They walked at a slow pace. Only Cloe and Cory knew what was going on. When someone said hello to him he would politely smile and wave. Once in a while she would try to break his hold but to no avail. She had no choice but to pretend with him. Every time she moved he squeezed harder and she didn't want her neck broke. It felt like it was awfully close to the snapping point. He whispered in her ear. "Is this what you like? Pain? I can bring you plenty, you have no idea." He nodded with a smile at a guest that waved at him.

"You're a dumb ass if you think I have no idea." Cloe said with a false smile.

"You are in over your head little girl." He politely said.

"Ha!" was all she said. He gave her a quick shake as if to warn her, which just made her madder. "You're playing a game you're going to lose and you know it." she spat.

"I'm not losing anything. Did it ever occur to you that some of us like our life as it is?"

"Did it ever occur to you that I don t give a shit?" Cloe countered.

She just wasn't giving in.

"Such a potty mouth." he said through clenched teeth and run her into the door jam. It was very quick so no one really noticed. If they did, they weren't tangling with a big guy like Cory. She quickly rubbed her head where there was a searing pain. She looked at him as if to say you're going to pay for that. He rolled his eyes. They slowly walked down the hall. He was still waving friendly at everyone. He whispered in her ear again. "Do you know that I wouldn't even have to touch you?" He pointed at a bunch of his peoples that were with him earlier. "Those girls would tear you apart, if they thought for one minute you were a threat."

"Well, they don't have to worry about that, they can have you!" She replied and smiled sweetly as she looked at them. They all had the same colorless eyes with hardly any pupils.

A bunch of deadskins no doubt

Cory shook her again. She winced inwardly. They made it to the door and Cory still didn't turn her loose. Instead they went through the door and down the walkway, taking his time.

He finally stopped and let go of her with a shove. She whirled around to face him and, rubbing her neck, said "You sure have a funny way of showing a gal a good time." She should have kept her mouth shut because he was suddenly towering over her and whispered.

"Oh, I could show you a good time," as he nuzzled her hair. Cloe was back peddling.

"That's okay." She said out loud to make people look. "I don't like you Cory!" She said again loudly stepping away from him. He took two large steps and reached her. She was about to get all wild on him when he reached up and pulled her amulet that Rose had made her, off her neck. Her head jerked downward as he did. He stood there looking at it. She was thinking *oh crap!* He slowly stared down at her and smiled. He threw the amulet at her feet. "It doesn't work on me." he said as a matter of fact.

"It wasn't for you." She said as she picked it up.

"It was for Allan?"

"Who's that?" Cloe asked.

"The one you beat up." Cory stated.

"So, dumb ass has a name." Cloe nodded in acknowledgment.

Cory laughed. "So are you the demon hunter we've all heard about?" emphasizing the word 'are'.

"Yep." Cloe said and put her amulet in her pocket. Cory rubbed his chin. He was thinking. He dropped his hand and looked at her. "I should have known there is a reason why I want you and hate you all at the same time. This is new to me." As if it were a game and he couldn't wait to play.

"Well, don't worry your big head about it. We'll just go with the hate part." Cloe said and turned around to leave. She had better get out of here before her alligator mouth overruns her hummingbird ass.

"Oh, I'll see you again, I'm sure of it." Cory said with a wave.

಄

Cloe made her way to her car. She unlocked the doors and got in. She got out of there as fast as she could. She shook her head at herself. She could have gotten seriously hurt. For some reason though, she knew that Cory wasn't letting that happen. They could have easily killed her and nobody would have ever known. She thought about that. Cory must have plans for her. That was alright. She had her own plans. Cloe dug her phone out and called Sue. Sue announced that Megan showed up with Amanda and that they were discussing the events of that night. Sue asked Cloe if she was okay. Cloe told Sue that she got a little ruffed up but was nothing she couldn't handle. She didn't go into details. Sue told her their mom called and dinner was tomorrow at mom's house. Her mom tried to get a hold of her but Cloe shut off her phone. Cloe told Sue she would call mom in the morning to see what to bring and after talking awhile more about the party, they hung up. Cloe got home and did her chores. She went into the house and drew a bath. She put some powder in it that Rose had given her to draw out soreness from over worked muscles. She would need it for her neck. As she soaked she thought about the night. She shouldn't have been surprised to see Cory there really. She should have kicked his ass, and went down swinging. Then she changed her mind, what good was she to anybody dead? She thought about what a smart ass she was at times. She giggled. She did come back with some pretty good ones. She was always a smart ass when it came to confronting any type of people. It made them mad and then they made mistakes. It was a lot of people's weakness to be made a fool of. One she capitalized on. The promise of Cory saying it wasn't the end rung in her ears. She grimaced. She'd have to really watch him next time. He was surprisingly fast for a big guy. He wouldn't need any help from anyone to fight. The fallen have extra ordinary strength like the regular angels do. She had better start doing more exercising that's for sure. She needed to go jogging.

She got out of the tub and after wrapping a towel around her, made her way to her room. She pulled out the paper she swiped earlier from the library. It had Sibylline Oracles scribbled on it under the words Catholic Church. She would have to check that out. Tomorrow she could ask Greg when they were at mom's house having dinner. She got on her pj's and tried to sleep. Her mind kept going over the night. She kept giggling to herself at her boldness. Nobody else would have thought she was very funny. Not even Rose. Rose would have clobbered her in the first place for getting herself in such a predicament. She giggled again. If Rose was there, there really would have been a fight. One mouth was bad enough but when two bold mouths were running, there was hell to pay.

On her part, usually.

She drifted off to sleep with Cory's last words hanging in her dreams.

The next morning she got up around nine thirty. She went to the kitchen and drank coffee and called her mother. Her mom said to be there at two and bring rolls and paper plates. She said she would be there and hung up. Today was the day to exercise. She began with a warm up, and then did her Jujitsu, then her cool down. As she meditated she pushed all thoughts aside and let her mind wonder into peacefulness. She suddenly saw the Cajun couple, saw Madam Agnes sitting at her round table with her crystal ball. She smiled at Cloe as if to say welcome back. Cloe's eyes slowly lifted open. She got up and stretched. She knew she would have to go see who actually lived at the address that Rose had. She remembered it and wrote it down. She started doing laundry before she went to her mothers and almost had it done by the time she left. She had to stop by the store to get buns and paper plates, so she left a little early. She went to the store and was making her way around the store. She was walking at a brisk pace when she rounded the corner. She almost ran into a lady but she had side stepped her. As she was steadying herself she grabbed the woman's arm so that she too didn't fall. She looked at the lady and was going to apologize when she saw her eyes. It was the same eyes from last night and Cloe remembered that this was one of the people standing with Cory last night. There is no mistaking the women. They are drop dead gorgeous. They have all the right parts, and all the right curves. They say all the right things to seduce. They are sent to make men weak, and to bring jealousy to women. The lady looked at Cloe and smiled. Cloe knew she recognized her from last night. She had a look in her eyes though. They said she would like to hurt Cloe very badly. Cloe wasn't scared. The females weren't as strong as the males. The lady jerked her arm back out of Cloe's grasp. Cloe just stood there, waiting. The lady moved past Cloe in a slow snaky kind of way. She made her way down the isle. Cloe wondered how maybe there could be no gender in heaven with angels, or was there? So many people believe so many things. If there wasn't any gender than if they get booted from heaven then suddenly they are one or the other? Cloe went about her business and picked up her food and plates. As she was checking out she could feel eyes on her. She looked around and saw the lady standing in front of an end cap of food but looking at her. She slowly gave a sweet smile to Cloe and blew her a kiss. Cloe flipped her off. The lady lost her smile and strode off.

Cloe went to her mom's house. Everybody was there. The place smelled like delicious food. Everyone was scattered around the tiny duplex home. It wasn't very big because it was just her mom and dad living there. They all talked and smiled. It was good to be with family. Cloe made her plate after some siblings made their way through. There was a picnic table outside and some chairs sitting in the lawn. Everyone made their way outside to eat. Cloe brought up the vacation deal and much to dads disagreement and mom's meek ways, they settled on a trip. Cindy was in charge of collecting money for the next few weeks. The parents felt bad but the family insisted that they go. One of Cloe's brothers even offered up his travel trailer for them to take. Mom was delighted and dad gave everyone a round of hugs.

When she had some alone time she cornered Greg, Sue's husband. "Can I ask you something?" she said to Greg.

"Yah, what's on your mind?" Cloe liked Greg. He was cool for a preacher.

"I found this at a house. It was in a ritual book. What is it?"

Greg read the piece of paper. "I don't know." he said. "You want me to find out?"

"Could ya?" Cloe asked after taking a drink of her soda.

"Yes, I'll ask around. I can let you know by late tonight." Greg said.

"Okay. That sounds great."

Greg nodded his head and stuck the note in his pocket of his shirt. He would go to church after the dinner and get ready for the sermon. The rest of the day went by with a few games of horse shoes and laughter. Soon it was time for every one to go. Everyone hugged everyone and made their way out. Shirley hugged Cloe and said "Thank you." in her ear. She told her mom not to mention it and Cindy was telling everyone don't forget about the money as they left. Cindy told Cloe that she'd be by later that week if she didn't catch her at work. Cloe's dad walked her out to her car. Cloe was the last of the kids and spoiled rotten by her dad. She was bomb barded with questions about how she was doing and was she still working. She loved her dad but he was bit overbearing sometimes. He just wanted what's best for her. He always did. He didn't agree with what she did though. He always argued if she wanted to take on the bad guys then maybe she should be a cop. He always wanted her to join the armed forces. She got done talking to him and hugged him. He told her to be careful and she promised. She gave one more hug to her mom and she went home. She read some more out her bible and rode Gigi down the road and back. She didn't feel like dealing with any more surprises. She knew next week would be full of them. As she returned back home it was getting dark. She brushed her horse down. Then she fed all the animals and turned in for the night. While she watched the news the phone rang.

"Hello?"

"It's me, Greg. I have some information for you. I have sent it to your e-mail though because it's a lot to read. The name you found on the piece of paper is a book that was written by women seers' way back before Christ was even born."

"Wow, that's interesting. Okay I'll go check. Thanks Greg."

"You're welcome. Let me know if you need any more help."

"Oh, you know I will." she laughed and they hung up.

She went to the kitchen to get her laptop. She sat on the couch and pulled her laptop on her lap. Opening her e-mail she found what Greg had sent her. Supposedly the books where written by females who could read the future and where heavily guarded. They were feared because they shaped a religious outlook. It had different doctrines and teachings. Some chapters were wrote by Jews and some were wrote by Christians. Some where wrote by both. She finished up and was told where to find the book at a book store so she could read more about it. She checked other messages as well before she closed the laptop. She sat there for a second and then she turned off the TV. She wondered what this had to do with the cult, the fallen and Halloween. As she got ready for bed she thought about what she read in her e-mail. She knew that women didn't play an important roll way back when, and this book would prove differently. She went to bed early. She had a busy day tomorrow.

At sometime during the night, she had a bad dream. As she tossed and turned she dreamed she was being tortured. They were stabbing her with daggers. She was tied up. She couldn't get loose. She awoke and sat up and stared out at nothing, breathing hard. She wiped her hair out of her face. Was there a shadow by her bed? She adjusted her eyes. Her door stood open. She thought she had closed it. She got up and went to the door. A breeze was coming from somewhere; she could fill it on her legs. She walked out into the living room. Something moved and it caught her eye. She moved her head to focus on it, and then it was gone. Her front door was open. She screwed up enough nerve and charged out the door. She ran off her porch and landed with a roll on the ground. She froze at a crouch. Her eyes roved at the front of her house. She looked at the car, at the road. She stood up and looked all around. She didn't see anything. Where was Buddy? "Buddy!" she called out loud. "Buuuudyyyyy!.." she called out with her hands cupping her mouth. She heard a yelp from the barn. Buddy! She ran towards the barn and went in it. She looked around, but didn't see the dog. "Buddy?" She said and heard a wine. It was coming from the cabinets that she kept the tools and tack in. The cabinet was eight feet tall, and built into the wall. She slowly opened the door, afraid of what she would see. At first nothing, then Buddy came out from the bottom cubby and slowly made his way to her. He was whining as he came towards her. She knelt down and looked him over. He didn't have any marks but his hair was scuffled. He moved like he felt real sore. "How'd you get in there?" she asked and looked into his eyes. He whined again and Cloe patted his head. "I guess you'll have to start coming in the house, huh?" He moved so she could close the door. They made their way into the house slowly. Buddy was beginning to limp. Cloe picked him up and carried him up the stairs after he tried himself and fell off. She put him down and he made his way in the house. She followed him in and closed the door behind her. She locked it this time. She checked it to make sure it was latched by pulling on it. She went to the couch and petted Buddy, who had climbed on the couch to lie down. Whatever got him did a number on him. He wasn't cut up but he was awful sore and tired.

Like someone was kicking him and he couldn't get away.

She wondered about the Rose brick dust she had laid down. *Didn't it protect him?* Maybe he went off the property. He was still closed in the cabinet. *How did he get there?* Cloe went back to bed. She lay there thinking of Buddy. *He couldn't get away,* like in her dream, she couldn't get away either. The more she thought about it the more she got mad, and after tossing the incident around in her head, she fell asleep.

Her alarm clock went off and she got up. She walked to the living room and checked on Buddy. He was sleeping on the couch still, his breathing was labored. Poor thing, it even hurt to breath. She went to the kitchen. She would leave him in for today. She made coffee then poured some water in a mixing bowl and set it by the couch. He'd find it later. She sat down to her morning coffee and after that went to work. She came into work and there were gobs of donuts and coffee on the reception table. She wondered what the big deal was. Chris and everyone were gathered around the table. She worked her way over to them and Chris called everyone's attention to him. As soon as everyone quieted down he began his speech. "We'll have visitors today. They are from the Birchtree Firm where we are redoing an office for them; some of you know what I am taking about. I know it's just one office but they are bringing by more prospects from all over town, even out of town. It is famiy and friends of our clients and they are very wealthy. They are looking for someone to build everything from offices to homes. I want these guy's business very much. So you know what you have to do, right?"

Every one mumbled in agreement, and Chris said to finalize the speech. "Be on your best behavior." and shot Cloe a glance. "And be nice. Help them with every question. If I can't because I'm busy then I'm relying on you to fill in the gaps." His eyes looked at everyone as if he wanted to make sure everyone was on the same page. "Okay, let's get to work." he said with a clap of his hands.

Cloe went back to her desk and put her hands over her eyes.

Great!

She sucked in a breath and held it. Maybe she'll pass out and get to go home.

Maybe she should have called in sick.

Maybe she still could.

She was running that possibly over in her mind when she felt someone looking at her. She let out her breath and uncovered her eyes. Chris was leaning on her desk looking at her.

"It can't be that bad." he said.

"How did this come about?" Cloe said in a whiney tone.

"He called me again and we set it up over drinks on Sunday."

"Are you becoming friends with him?"

"He's a pretty decent guy, Clo, and very powerful. Don't you see? This is great for business."

"I know, but I'm telling you Chris, and I'm being straight up with you." She pulled at his tie to bring him closer to her. "He's very dangerous, like the mob or something, I can feel it!" She had to use some sort of analogy, she couldn't tell him the truth but she could make it just as bad.

"You're just being delusional." Chris said and pulled his tie from her hand. "Now come on."

"Can I go home?" Cloe begged.

"No!" He said and straightened up. He smoothed his tie back down.

"Please, I really have a sick dog and he needs me!"

"No!" he said over his shoulder as he walked away.

Any body else would have left if they really didn't want to be here. She didn't know if she really wanted to go, but she didn't want to stay either. She couldn't leave Chris in a bind either. He wanted to look good and he always included Cloe. So she took a deep breath and decided to stay. She could check out the competition. She shook her head. She went to work and tried not to fret about it. It was nine o'clock and they showed up. All of the sudden the room started filling up with navy and gray suits. Chris welcomed them with a handshake.

Cloe watched Chris and he looked nervous, even though he tried not to appear to be. They laughed over something Chris had said. Chris was a smaller guy in height but he was stocky. He was swallowed up standing next to these guys. You could tell there was some regular wealthy men in the bunch so not all of them where fallen or demon. Humans carried themselves different. The fallen have an air about them that's screams majestic arrogance. Her eyes caught white ones as Cory looked at her. Next to his Navy blue suit his eyes seemed light blue. They just stared at each other. He was smiling and Cloe's nostrils flared. She put her head back down and went to work. Or at least, look like she was. She had a feeling she wasn't getting nothing done today.

She might even ask him about her dog.

They made their way to the drawing table where a buildings life began. Chris was brilliant when it came to building plans and molding it out of nothing. He had a great imagination. Their heads were bent as they all looked at floor plans and blueprints. The desk lights lit up there faces. One little group would be looking at one print, and another group was looking at something else Chris was showing them. Cloe studied some of them and there was one that held a more chiseled look about him, they all could have passed for models, but this one, well Cloe hated to say it, but he looked like portraits of Jesus. He had golden brown hair that was semi long and wavy and a straight nose. He was not as stocky but he was just as tall. He seemed to be the boss of all of them. Cloe looked at his eyes, yep, a fallen. She looked back down again as some of them were scanning over the workers. She didn't want to be caught staring. She was sure Cory filled them in. That's why they were here, to check out the competition. And to gets their moneys worth.

They went on to Chris's office. They surrounded his desk. They were laughing again. Chris was showing them quotes she was sure. She got up to go to the bathroom. She needed a breather. She did her business and washed her hands. The she let the water run over them while she stood there. She didn't want to be here. Maybe it wouldn't be so bad. She shut off the water and dried her hands.

She went back to her desk and piddled. Someone had called her name and she jumped. She turned around and Jessica was motioning to her to come to her desk.

Cloe rolled her chair over and Jessica grabbed her arm excitedly. "Are they gorgeous or what!" she pronounced every work slowly.

"Whatever." Cloe said and snickered, Jessica was a little older then her and a single mom.

"You don't think so? Ashley and I do." She turned towards Ashley. Cloe followed her gaze and looked at Ashley. Ashley wiped her forehead as if she was fainting then smiled and gave the thumbs up. The girls giggled.

"Do you see any rings?" Jessica said as she peered around her shoulder to look them. One of the guys was looking back and Jessica quickly turned her head around towards Cloe again. Cloe just stared.

"I think their single." Cloe said. "But they'll break your heart!" she said in a warning tone. She hated to have this conversation because really, no one ever listened to her. And second no one knew what she did on her time, so even though she knew about them, she could never really make anyone understand.

"Who cares! Could you imagine being with a guy like that for one night? I bet he could teach me a thing or two." Cloe didn't know what it was, but whenever someone talked about sex with a demon or otherwise, they could always sense it. It was like as if the person talking gave off this big arrow that pointed at them and it read SEX in big bold letters. She had seen it a million times. Maybe it was because someone was talking about them in general, but it really caught their attention. Cloe was looking at them as Jess was saying what she said, and sure enough heads was going up and looking at each other and looking out the windows. She didn't even think they were listening to Chris anymore, they were distracted. Cloe just watched with a grin on her face, she couldn't help it. They were getting uneasy. Like a pack of wild dogs who could smell a female in heat. The boss looked up all of the sudden and looking at his people, he followed their gaze outside. Cloe told Jess to look busy and they pretended to look at accounting numbers. Out of the corner of her eye she saw the blinds go down in the office windows. *Well, hallelujah!* Seeing that, Ashley scooted her chair over and the women gushed over the men. Cloe shook her head and went back to her desk. Rob came up to her desk with his chair and asked. "So, what's going on?"

"I don't know. What do ya mean?"

"You think we'll get their business?"

"Yep."

"How can you be so sure?" He asked

"Because Chris is the best, you know that." Cloe said.

"Well yah, I know. That will be great." he said eagerly.

"Why's that?"

"Because then he'll hire more people and I can get some friends on. I heard if that happens though he'll need another quote person, you going to do it?"

"No way!" She answered.

"How did you come to know how to do quotes in the first place?"

"I did it before he put Billy on the job." Even as they spoke Billy was gone making bids on new customers to quote.

The bank building started going up today as well. Chris had his own crew doing the building and construction work. The men and some women on the building crew made more than half the company. The other's where office workers like her.

"I did it when Chris was a small business. When he grew I was gone all day running around town. I didn't like it so he hired Billy to take it over."

"Boy, I sure would like to do it." Rob said as he looked down at his shoes, swiveling his chair back and forth.

"Why don't you tell Chris to train you?"

"Do you think he would?"

"You could try. I don't know what Chris would do but I imagine if you had someone to take your spot then I wouldn't see why not."

"That would be so cool." Rob said. The office doors came open and the men all filed out. Rob quickly squeezed Cloe's arm, Cloe got the hint and they pretended like they were going over what Rob had in his hand. Rob said. "Thanks for your help Cloe." out loud and scooted back to his desk. Secretly Cloe was saying don't leave but she let him go.

Cloe looked down at her desk, counting the steps as they made their way over to her desk. They were meeting and greeting every one. Chris led the way and there they stood as Chris beamed. "And this is Cloe. She has been with me since I first started this company. We go way back though. We were actually friends since kindergarten." He secretly put his hand under Cloe's arm and pinched her to make her stand up. Cloe jumped off her seat and went to shake everyone's hand. *Oh I'll charm them alright!* She thought.

"This is the one I was telling you about." Cory said with a smile. "She is very good with… her job." He looked hard at Cloe as if he were saying I dare you to say something. They all looked at her and she felt like she was under a microscope.

"I didn't do anything but charge you more money." she said sweetly and they all laughed.

"This is my boss, Lance." Cory said as he emphasized the word boss, but only Cloe heard it. Lance put out his hand again and Cloe grabbed it. There was something different about Lance, even though he definitely was a fallen.

"Its nice to meet you, Cory can't stop talking about you." He said in a more quiet but deadly voice. Cory didn't look embarrassed either when Lance said that. He just stood there staring.

"That's funny, I thought all you guys ever talked about was sports." That got a laugh out of everyone. Lance wasn't done. "He says you are a very smart young lady. I can see why now. You're very comical too."

"Well, I try." Cloe said and they snickered.

"Well if there is anything that we can do for you please let us know. I'm sure we can find a place for you at our law firm." Lance said.

"I'm very happy where I'm at, but thank you." *The gall of this man,* she thought.

"Well if you would like to make more money then I'm sure you might be interested?"

"No thanks." Cloe said with a shake of her head.

"Maybe you're not as smart as I thought." Cory said, sarcastically.

Oh, no, he di'nt!

"Touch my dog again and I'll show you smart." Cloe said in return. "Or did you think I was not smart enough to figure out that any time I get attacked in any way, shape, or form, that you're behind it."

Cory hands moved but Lance kind of got in the way, intentionally, but quietly, as not to draw attention. Lance and Cory exchanged looks and then Lance looked at Cloe and said "Nice to meet you."

"Like wise." Cloe said snidely.

The fallen walked away from her and went on to meet other workers. The girls oohed and aahed over them. And then they were leaving to go see a job sight. The warehouse seemed big again when they left. They took Chris with them. Chris asked her if she wanted to go when he could sneak away. She said no. She thought that wouldn't be a smart move. One little accident and Cloe would be gone. They could make it happen.

❧

So Cloe finished out the rest of her day. After she clocked out she called Rose. There was no answer. She went home to check on her dog. He was getting around. When she came through the door he was on the floor. He slowly stood up and padded over to her. She reached down to pet him and He wagged his tail.

"You're doing better, aren't you?" she said baby talk. 'You wanna go for a ride?" she asked and his tail wagged again. So she fed the horse and took off. She took Buddy with her. She got the address off the table that Rose had. She made her way back in town and went down the city's main streets. She read the street signs until she found the block she needed. The house was in the middle of the block so that meant she had to take the alley and park in back. She found a parking spot and left Buddy in the car with the windows cracked. She made her way towards what looked like a dark brown two story stucco house. The door was opened and she stopped and called out "Hello?" She was startled when a cat ran out between her feet. She went through the door and made her way down a dark corridor. She put her hands along the wall to keep from tripping over anything she couldn't see. She came to a living room and looked around. There was jazz music playing softly and Papa Whitney was sound a sleep in a Lazy Boy recliner. She went over to him and watched him sleep. So it was them after all. He looked good for just getting out of jail. She touched his shoulder and he woke up, looking at her. She waved to him and he sat up rubbing his eyes.

He was trying to focus on her and welcome her at the same time. When he finished rubbing his eyes and put on his glasses and he looked at her. "I'll be." he said and got up. "Madam told me yous a comin, but I din't belief her. Let me look at cha chil." he said and turned her around. "Why, you hasn't changed much no siree." He said with a laugh.

"You haven't changed either Papa." she smiled. "Where's Madam at?"

"Where's my hat? I never wore a hat, chil." He said and touched his head.

Cloe laughed and cleared her throat. "WHERE'S MADAM AT?" she said slowly and loudly.

"Oh, she's down ata store getting me's some Red beans and rice. She's told me not to fall asleep so don't you be-a telling her. She's says someone specials was a comin. Have a seat dear, no sense in standin da'. Tell me watcha been doin wit ya self."

"I have got myself in a predicament." She said loudly.

"Whacha mean gir?"

She explained to Papa that she is heavily hunting demons and banishes them. He shook his head and asked. "Watcha doin a thing like dat fo? Yo got a death wis or sometin? I never thought ya git far wit that."

"It's my duty Papa." She said.

Madam walked in on them talking. She looked at Cloe and exclaimed "Isa knew you be comin. Didn't I tells ya Papa? I says we's havin a special visita today. How ya doin girl?" She went to the kitchen and they followed her. Papa helped put the groceries up and Madam gave her a hug. She had a special connection with these people. Madam Agnes had always told how the cow ate the cabbage. If she was in trouble then Madam would say "you's in danger girl!" just like that. Most people sugar coat it. And when she screwed up Madam would say "Gitcha head otta yo ass, girl." Cloe loved it.

Madam put on some tea and they sat at the table. Papa went back to the living room to watch the news. Madam took at look at her and got up to grab her mojo bag full of bones, twigs and rocks. Somehow she could read into someone's future. As if that wasn't good enough when she shook them on a mat, she shuffled a deck of playing cards and laid six down on the table.

She studied them and Cloe knew to be quiet. She took a sip of her tea Madam got her. After a while she looked up and Cloe and said "Who'd ya piss off dis time?" Cloe opened her mouth to answer but closed it when she looked back down at the cards again. She looked up a second time and said "I sees ya in hot wata gir. But I sees ya haf help wicha biznis. I donts sees an endin. I sees a maja scrap comin atcha. It's as the devil him sef watchin ya. Sometin about a great writin." she said and let her voice trail off. "It aso says sometin about a man not changing hiss ways." She looked at Cloe, "Yo got che sef a man?"

"No. No man. A bunch of fallen angels though." Cloe said cheerfully.

"Whatcha doin wit dem?"

"I'm pissing them off according to you." Cloe laughed and scooted around in her seat. After Madam looked at her like she was insane, she explained what was going on. Madam nodded her head and listened intensively. She closed her eyes and listened. She was concentrating on Cloe's words. "Ya haf divine help chil. Ya fightin on da right side." and she patted Cloe's hand. Cloe knew that that was the end to the discussion so she changed the subject and asked how long had they been back. Madam Agnes told her about her moving to be closer to Papa when he was in jail. She said it was good to be back. They filled in all the missing parts. Cloe looked at the clock and said it was time to get home. She gave hugs all around and told them she'd be back. They waved her off when she drove away.

She made her way down the street and called Rose again. Rose answered the phone. Cloe said it was her turn to stay the night and Rose was excited. She said "Hurry up." and hung up. Cloe drove into her drive way twenty minutes later and parked the car. She let Buddy out. Buddy wagged his tail and walked into the yard. Cloe closed the gate behind her. Puppy was jumping all over Buddy and he didn't return the excitement. He kind of was like 'Please don't hurt me tonight.' as he walked away slowly.

Rose asked as she put her thumb in his direction. "What's wrong with him? Cloe told her the story. Rose asked if anybody else got hurt and she said no. Gigi wasn't up there at the time but he was eating in the corral that morning. Then Cloe told her about meeting the rest of them at work. She also told her what she said about touching her dog again. They giggled at that, then suddenly Rose slapped her behind her head. "Are you crazy? You are really going to bring it down on you."

"I know, but I get so mad!" and went on to tell her about the paper she found, the book it involves and visiting Madam Agnes and Papa Whitney.

"So it was them. What did she say?"

"She said it looked as if the devil himself was watching me."

They went to the kitchen and got ice cream and cake that Mary had dropped off for Rose. They were both homemade. It was delicious. They went back to the living room and made themselves comfortable. As they talked and ate Cloe told Rose about the book and what it was about, that the original was held in a Catholic Church. They tried to make a connection between everything but didn't get anywhere. They guessed that there maybe a connection between the demons and the fallen, but where would the book comes in was a mystery, and Halloween? It seemed that nobody cared about Halloween except if you had kids. The book was written by women priestesses. Why would the fallen want a book written by women. Why would demons? Maybe it had something to do with a birth? They didn't know.

Cloe told her that Madam Agnes said she would have divine help. They talked about that. That could mean anything. She already had divine help. Rose asked about Lance. "Do you think he's a higher rank then Cory?" Rose knew angels had ranks in hell like they did in heaven. The lower the level, the higher the rank. It was confusing sometimes.

"Cory said it was his boss, and I think he meant it. You ought to have seen him. He was just awesome. Like royalty walking in. He looked like if a human mixed with a lion. His hair was the color of the mane on a lion. He was very prideful. He was very quiet, but if you looked at him he was very stern. He didn't get excited at all. Cory wanted to hit me I think and all Lance does was softly touch him and he backed down."

"I can't believe Cory wanted to hit you."

"Come on, Cory always wants to throttle me. I was disrespectful to his boss, it's his job. If someone disrespected you, I'd wanna punch them."

"I never thought of it like that." Rose said and stared at the ceiling. She felt the same way. "But still, he must be very confused. Or maybe he's just entertained by you."

"Something. I think it's like how girls are attracted to bad boys? They want them because they're free to do what they want and they act tough, but in the end they're a bunch of losers." Cloe stated.

"Are you saying you're a loser?" and Rose broke into the song called Loser by Beck. They laughed and were singing the chorus together.

Who needed alcohol with these two girls around.

When they finished they settled down again. *Never a dull moment* Cloe thought.

"I understand what you're saying though." Rose said. "But were you describing your feelings for him, or his feelings for you." Cloe thought about that for a second before answering.

"Now I'm not saying I'm totally blind. They are good looking that's for sure. But they were angels once, so it's totally explainable. And it's a challenge, maybe that's why I'm such a smart ass. I like to push buttons. But I think." and Cloe paused for the right words, "That he thinks he can get me to change my ways, and I know that I can try to change him, but in the end I know it won't work. So that keeps me grounded. I don't think he sees it the same way. They have always won the smaller battles. And to them I am probably a bug. I know they have probably heard about me, but they haven't seen me in action, yet." Cory was sure pushing for some.

They cleaned up and got ready for bed. Cloe was glad that the day was over with. She wanted to relax before doing it again tomorrow. They talked and laughed. It was the usual. And talking about the good old days, they fell asleep. They woke up the next morning and got ready for work. Rose didn't have a coffee pot because she didn't drink coffee so Cloe visited for awhile and left early to stop at a convenient store and get a cappuccino. She brought gas, breakfast and a cap. Then she took off to work.

She walked in and made her way to her desk. Chris had everyone around the drawing table again. That meant it was speech time. Cloe brought her coffee with her. Chris got everyone settled down when everyone showed up. He raised his hands and the noise died down. "I just wanted to thank you all for yesterday. You did a wonderful job and they really liked us!" A bunch of hoots went out and Chris waved his hands to settle them down. "We will get more business from them in the future!" More hoots and hollers from the workers. "And lunch is on me today, pizza will be here at eleven and you can work after words if you want but you got the rest of the day off if you want also!" The last announcement made everyone hoot and holler even more. Chris had to shout the last half of the sentence because they were so loud that the clamor was almost deafening. Cloe winced at the small pain in her ears. Chris yelled. "That's it." And everyone scattered. Cloe almost made it to her desk when someone grabbed her elbow. She turned around and Chris was behind her holding her. Another co worker had his attention at the moment so Cloe stood there and waited until they finished talking. Chris finished and turned towards her. "Can you come into my office?"

"Let me get my breakfast and I'll be right there." He let her go with a nod and went to his office. Cloe walked to her desk and picked up her breakfast. She turned around to make her way through the desks. Everyone was in high spirits, and there was visiting everywhere. Today they could get by with it. Today Chris was on cloud nine.

She went through the door and closed it behind her. The noise disappeared with the close of the door. She walked to a chair that sat in front of his desk and sat down. Chris was going over quotes and put them aside when she sat down.

He looked at her and smiled. Cloe smiled back. He looked really good. He looked really tired too. His blondish hair was kept messy with a mouse style but he didn't sport a suit today, just a tee shirt and jeans. He looked relaxed compared to yesterday when he wore a suit. He looked stuffy.

"Are you happy?" Cloe asked.

"I'm ecstatic." he said with a grin.

"You look good today; you must have slept good last night."

"Like a baby." Chris's mind is always on his work that he can't sleep at night.

"So, what's on your mind?"

Chris looked at her while slowly rocking back and forth in his office chair and Cloe got an uneasy feeling. She hoped he wasn't trying to play match maker again. He looked at her some more as if trying to find the right words. He knew he was in big trouble. "I don't know how to tell you this, so I'm just going to say this. I'm going to need your help." Cloe groaned and put her head in her hands. Anytime Chris says he needs her help that usually means he's volunteered her for something she didn't want to do. He also knew that Cloe didn't have the heart to say no. She tried to help him the best she could.

"What is it this time?" Cloe raised her head up.

"Well, they want me to come to dinner at their house."

"So? Go."

"So, you're invited also." Chris said forwardly.

"I'm invited, that doesn't mean I have to show up." Cloe shot back.

"I told them you'd be there." Chris winced.

"Chris!" Cloe shouted.

"Well? They told me to bring you. They loved your work..." He trailed off.

"Loved my work?! I only did one quote for them. It doesn't have anything to do with my work!"

"Please!" Chris sounded disparate. "I need you to be there so that I make them happy. It seems that they want you around. Just one last time, please?"

Cloe sat there and thought about it. It would be like going into the lions den. Nothing light tempting fate. Cloe sighed. "Okay, but this is it Chris, I mean it!" She looked him in the eye. "I don't like them. Any of them!"

"Okay. I got it. I don't understand why, any girl would give their arm to be with these guys." He said as he held up his hands in defeat.

"I can't help that, I'm not one of them."

Chris sighed and shook his head. "Dinner is this weekend. I can pick you up?"

"No, that's okay. I'll drive myself. That way when I'm ready to leave I can. But I'll follow you to where ever we're going."

"Okay." Chris gave her the details about date and time.

Cloe walked back to her desk and visited the co workers. Then it was Pizza for lunch and then everybody took off. Cloe took off also. She was going to search for the Sibylline Oracles.

First she went to the public library. All the copies were gone. So she went to the Catholic Church. The deacon met her and she asked to use the library that they have. They have helped her before also, and she was welcomed in their church. They knew that she was a demon hunter, but they did not think that she did it with the help of God. She was just a lowly human, nothing more. Cloe found the library and helped herself. After searching across the shelves she found the book. She opened it up and began reading. It was written like the bible; it had the creation of earth, of man, the angels, the sins, the saints, everything. It was not a book about Jesus and his teachings. But it was a book about God and his love, or his wrath, which ever man provoked. And it was about the end times, when the devil would return. The end times were pretty parallel to the bible. Cloe copied as much as she could, that held interest to her. Father Scovley walked in and when he saw her, he came to where she was sitting. He sat down beside her and she quit was she was doing to squeeze his hand. He was younger then the other priests. He lifted up the book cover to read it and put it down. He had a concerned look on his face. "What are you doing with this book?"

"I'm trying to find out what it's about." Cloe answered.

"It's rubbish." He countered

"Well, there some fallen angels and demons who don't think so."

"How would you know?" He asked.

Cloe proceeded to tell him of what was going on. He listened and when she was done he said "We knew of some activity going on, we just didn't think it would happen here."

"Where did you think it was going to happen?" Cloe countered back.

"In China."

"Why China?" Cloe asked.

"It doesn't matter. How certain are you of this?"

"Well I know what demons and the fallen look like. And I know that the title of this book was written on a piece of paper within the pages of a rituals book. It was dated two weeks ago. This means they already have a copy by now. As a matter of fact the public library was out of their copies."

"So it appears that whatever is going to happen will happen soon."

"It appears that way to me." Cloe didn't say anything about the date on Halloween. To them it doesn't matter, it's just a pagan holiday. And it may be nothing anyways but a big celebration or sacrifice. Either way she'll remember the date for future references.

"I will tell the others. I don't know if they'll help you. I don't know if they'll do anything. It's the way it is."

"I know Father, and that's okay. I'll get to the bottom of this." And she squeezed his hand one more time before he left.

She finished up and put the book away. She stuck her notes in her pocket and made her way out of the library. As she walked down the hall she passed by a woman. At first the woman held her head down, but at the time that Cloe was passing evenly with her, the woman looked up. She had blacked out eyes. At first it didn't register to Cloe because she was thinking about the book. But then it dawned on her and she whirled around. She saw the woman turn the corner and was smiling at her before she disappeared. Cloe froze for a split second and then took off after her. She rounded the corner but no body was there. It was another hallway. Cloe jogged down the hall looking in the rooms as she passed. *Where is she*, she thought. She finally ran into the deacon that had led her to the library.

"Did you see a girl in here, brown long hair, kind of tall?"

"No, I saw no one come this way."

"Thanks." and she went on some more. She came to the end where there was an exit door. She opened the door and looked around. Nothing. She came back through the hall way at a jog again. Still nothing. *Maybe she went to the library like I did.* She made her way to the library but there was no one there. She left the library and went to the sanctuary. She walked through the pews, looking around. Then she saw her. The woman was up in the balcony. Cloe ran to the stairs and ran up them taking two at a time. She came to where the woman was sitting with her head bowed, her hoody covering her head. Cloe slowly walked in front of her and said. "What are you doing here? This isn't exactly a place where you like to be, is it?"

"It doesn't matter. I'm here for one reason. I won't be here long."

Cloe realized that this was the demon Druj. She had seen her before and had several one on one confrontation with her. Suddenly Druj jumped over two pews and landed a kick at Cloe's chest. It had just landed when Cloe grabbed her foot and twisting it violently, making Druj twist two times in the air before landing on the floor. Druj was on her feet in no time and Cloe shook off the blow and took her stance. Druj came at Cloe with fist flying and then tried to punch Cloe's face. Cloe swung her fist away and came in with a blow of her own. Druj blocked that and carried her knee into Cloe's ribs. Cloe dropped from the blow after it landed on all fours and kicked out Druj's knee. Druj fell to the ground and Cloe landed on top of her. Cloe reared back to put her fist in Druj's face but Druj brought her legs up and hooked them around Cloe's neck and dragged her backwards. Cloe fell on her back and continued the flip to land on her feet. Druj was coming at her again with her foot leading. Cloe fell back down on the floor and kicked up into Druj's ass, catapulting her forward and bringing Cloe around on her feet again. Cloe turned around and went in to attack first. She punched Druj in the gut and when Druj bent down from the blow Cloe round housed her in the head, sending her flying into a pew. It split her head open and a trickle of blood was running down her face. Druj became enraged then and charged Cloe, wrapping her arms around Cloe's waist and carried her to the edge of the balcony. Cloe had a feeling of falling backwards and started grabbing in mid air. She grabbed a hold of Druj's shirt and was looking down at the floor that was a story down. Her legs tightened on the ledge and she looked up at Druj. Druj was smiling and looked down at her. Then lightening quick, she took off her hoody. Cloe fell backwards with a scream and Druj brought Cloe's legs over the balcony ledge to finish Cloe off.

Cloe started falling and looked around. As she fell she grabbed onto a cloth flyer that draped the banister. By one hand she hung on as one side came loose and it slammed her into a statue of Mary on the ground floor. She fell over the statue and landed on the ground floor. She moaned and lifted herself up her elbows. She looked up and didn't see anyone looking at her. She lay back down and caught her breath. Everything hurt from hitting the statue. She slowly got up and went to the pew and sat down. She was waiting for Druj to come and finish her off but she didn't see any more of her. She sat there for along time. They must be really worried about me she thought. She looked up at the statue of Jesus holding the world in his hand. She put her hands together and said a prayer. She made the cross sign over herself and got up to leave. She was slow and she limped so it took her awhile to get to her car. She should have gone to the hospital, but she didn't.

She went to Rose's instead.

Even though Rose was a vet tech, she made a pretty good doctor as well. She drove into her driveway in a matter of minutes and honked her horn. Rose came out and looked at Cloe's car. Cloe waved her over and Rose saw the look on Cloe's face and came quickly to the car. Rose swung open the car door and while trying to get the whole story helped Cloe into the house. Cloe sat on a chair with her arms up while Rose taped her ribs. Then they taped her knee and Rose made her some tea to help with pain. She helped her into the living room and sat her down on the couch. Every movement was torture to Cloe. She was thankful she didn't hit a statue of a Saint with a sword. That would not have been good. Cloe pulled the notes out of her pockets and gave them to Rose to read. Rose looked them over and asked Cloe "Why would they want this information?"

"I don't know." wheezed Cloe.

"This is getting pretty serious."

"Yah, want to know what funny part is?" Cloe asked

"I didn't know getting your ass kicked was funny."

"But see, the flyer that I grabbed said 'fly through the mist of heaven'"

Cloe started laughing but it hurt to laugh. Rose tried to keep from smiling but when Cloe grabbed her side she mocked Cloe and pointed at her and laughed. They sat there for awhile and talked. Cloe could feel the soreness settle in and she was stiff. She needed to go home to her animals and thought about Buddy. He was still here. "So how's Buddy doing?"

"He's fine. He's getting around better. I think Puppy ran it out of him." That made them laugh.

"Maybe I need to go out and stay with Puppy." They laughed some more.

"Are you going to stay here again tonight?"

"Yah, I wonder how Gigi is doing?"

"I'll call dad and tell him to go check."

"Do you'll think he'll mind?"

"Nope." and Rose got on the phone. Cloe heard only one end of the conversation. From what she could hear it seemed as if Wayne asked Rose why. Rose told him that Cloe was at her house with the flu and didn't make it home. He said he would and after a few uh-huh's, Rose hung up. "Dad told me to tell you that he hopes you get better."

"Thanks, I'll try."

Rose didn't tell her dad the truth because then they would worry about her and there was no need. Cloe stayed on the couch the whole night. Rose let Buddy come in and see Cloe. Cloe petted him for a bit and then he went back outside. They watched some TV and Wayne called back to say that Gigi was fine and that he fed him some feed and left him sound. It was eleven when Rose decided to go to bed. Cloe said a prayer and went to sleep on the couch.

☙

The next morning Rose was standing over Cloe gently shaking her. She was asking her if she wanted to go to work. Cloe woke up enough to use the phone to call in. She left a message on Chris's cell phone telling him that something came up and that she wouldn't be in. She gave the phone back to Rose, in return took the three pills that Rose handed her for pain. She drank them down and went back to sleep. She didn't even remember Rose leaving. It was noon and her cell phone was ringing. She looked at the number. It was Cindy her sister. She flipped the top and said "Hello?"

"Hey, I came by your work and Chris said you called in. Where are you?"

"I'm at Rose's house."

"What are you doing there?"

"Resting."

"Are you sick?"

"No, I got my ass kicked last night."

"By who?"

"No one that you know." Cloe said. Cindy was a scrapper, and she loved to fight. If Cloe couldn't get the regulars, Cindy would. She wasn't afraid of much. A lot of people knew Cindy and didn't want to tangle with her.

"I'm coming over, don't move!" Cindy said and hung up. *Don't worry!* Cloe thought and fell back asleep. She didn't know how much time passed by before Cindy knocked and came through the door. Cloe opened her eyes from the knock and tried to sit up. It was a slow process. Cindy came in and sat down.

"Gees, I guess you really did get your ass kicked, are you all bandaged up? Who did that for ya?"

"Rose." Cloe said while trying not to breath. It hurt to breath.

"What the hell happened?"

"I got into a fight with some one at the Catholic church. They threw me off the balcony." No sense in telling her any more than that.

"Who'd ya piss off this time?" Cindy asked incredulously.

"The wrong group of people I guess." Cloe weezed.

"At the church? What were you doing at that church?"

"Researching something."

"Oh, this has to do with that demon chasing stuff your into, doesn't it. I told you not to do that, you're barking up the wrong tree. I can't help you. Now if it was normal stuff I'd be more than happy too, but I just can't get involved with this." Cindy said with a quick shake of her head.

"Cindy, it's alright. I don't want you to get involved, believe me, you don't want to."

Cindy stared at her. "It's that bad?"

"It didn't start out that bad, but it's gotten there fast."

"What are you going to do? You'll end up dead one of these days. I don't mean to sound bossy but you need to stop while you're ahead."

"It's too late for that." Cloe said slowly.

"Why? Just hold up a white flag or whatever and tell them you're not involved anymore."

"I can't Cindy. This is a do or die thing. I've already got in the middle."

"I can't believe you don't have more sense than that!" Cindy said frustrated.

"I have sense, this is big. I've got to finish it." Cloe argued back.

"I guess I don't understand. There are demons and evil everywhere. They'll be other days. Right now you need to back down."

"It's more than that, Cindy." She didn't want to say it but it had to be said. "It includes fallen angels."

Cindy got up and started pacing. "You're messing with fallen angels? I didn't know there where any here." She paced some more. "I guess if a devil can roam the earth though, I don't see why they can't. How did that happen? You can't win against them. They are supposed to be real strong. Did a Fallen angel throw you off the balcony?"

"That would the work of a demon." Cloe said as she watched her sister pace back and forth.

"God, Cloe, I wish I could help. No, maybe I don't. How are you going to kill a fallen angel? That would be virtually impossible."

"Thanks for your vote of confidence." Cloe said flatly.

"Well, really, did you think about that part?"

"No Cindy. I didn't think that there was going to be a 'that part'."

"How did they get involved?"

"I beat up a family member."

"What do you mean a family member? I didn't know they could have family members!"

"I didn't either, until I beat up one."

"Well can't you say 'hey I'm sorry. I didn't know'?"

"Well...there's more. There's also one that likes me, I guess you could say."

Cindy sat down and slapped her forehead. "How did that happen?"

"That wasn't my fault. I was doing business for Chris and he happened to be at a firm that I had to do a quote on."

"What? They have businesses? Oh my God!" She got up to pace again. "What is this world coming to? It really is the end of days." she said sadly.

"Now Cindy, It isn't the very end. It was said for a very long time that some fallen were sent to earth and the rest were captured in heaven. I'm just now finding the ones on earth I guess."

"How many are there?"

"I don't know."

"I can't believe it!" She chewed on her bottom lip. "I'm just going to pretend I didn't hear a thing. This is hard to deal with. It breaks my heart. Why would God let them come here? Never mind, I don't wanna know. End of discussion. I came here because I wanted to collect the money for mom's trip."

"Oh, ya. Hang on." And she called her bank. She was put through to a loan officer she knows and knows Cindy also. Cloe told her to take out three hundred dollars out of her account and Cindy would be by to pick it up. That was settled and Cloe hung up. "Okay, all settled." Cloe said and leaned up against the arm of the couch.

"Can I get you anything?"

"Ya, would you hand me more aspirins?"

"Okay." Cindy went to the kitchen to get her a soda out of the fridge. She handed Cloe the pills and soda and sat back down. "Have you eaten at all today?"

"No."

"I'm going to go get you something, you want a burger?"

"That sounds good."

"Okay, I'll be right back." She left out the door. Cloe lay back down and relaxed. She wondered how long it will take for her to get better. Cloe was thinking about Cindy and how much she looked like their dad pacing back and forth. She dozed off and woke to Cindy standing over her saying "Cloe, here's your burger." Cloe sat up and took her food out of Cindy's hand. Cindy sat back down to eat her food also. They ate their food in silence. When they were done Cindy said that she better get around and finish getting the money. Cloe thanked her for the food and Cindy walked to the door telling her it was no problem. Before she left she turned and said "Cloe, I don't agree with what you do. But I'm glad there's someone out there fighting for us. I wish it wasn't you, but as they say 'God has a plan for us all' and so I'll remember you in my prayers every day. I love you and you be careful."

"I love you too and I will Cindy, I know I don't look like I'm being careful. But I'll be careful."

"Okay then, stay in touch."

"I will."

Cindy left and Cloe went back to sleep. She woke up and was trying to go to the bathroom when Rose walked in. Rose asked her if she needed help and Cloe declined telling her that she needed to move around on her own. A little R and R helped her a lot. She wasn't one hundred percent but she was better than last night. She made it to the bathroom and came out a few minutes later. She sat back down on the couch gingerly.

"Cindy came by to see me." Cloe said

"She did? How is she?"

"Freaked." Cloe said

"I suppose. It's hard for some to grasp."

"Exactly. That's how she acted. It was hard to see her so upset."

"How did she know you were here?" Cloe went to tell her about her going by work and told her about the conversation. Cloe finished and told Rose she should probably go home tonight. Rose didn't want her to leave but knew she had to. Rose said that she should stay for supper at least one more time before she went. And Cloe agreed. Rose made sandwiches and brought a bag of chips and they played cards while they ate. After dinner Cloe got her dog and they got into the car with Rose's help. Cloe thanked Rose for all her help and Rose carefully hugged her and closed the car door after Cloe say down behind the wheel. She drove home and Gigi came cantering to the fence. She got out and petted her horse. She checked it over to make sure it was okay while she was gone. Then she fed him and Buddy before going in the house. She sat down again to rest her muscles. She was really straining them to move around. She took it easy for awhile. She checked her messages. There wasn't any. She wanted to do something but she was to sore so she read her bible along with her tapes for awhile. That made her tired so she went on to bed.

The next morning she went to work and she walked stiffly but not to bad. She made her way to her desk and every one told her they were glad that she felt better. She said thanks and sat down. She had a pile of quotes and account number to put in the computer. It took her pretty much all day to do the task. Not because there was a bunch to do but because she couldn't move that fast. She asked were Chris was and Ashley said he was out at a job sight. It was four when she clocked out, telling everyone she wasn't quite up to par yet and needed to rest. She wasn't exactly lying. She went home and lay on the couch again, resting her straining muscles. She clicked on the TV and watched it until it was time for bed. Rose and Cindy both called her to check on her. She assured them she was doing better. She fed the animals and made her way into her bedroom. She was just about to shut off the light when her phone rang. She thought it was Chris calling to make sure she would be at work tomorrow.

"Hello?"

"I'm sorry you're not feeling well." Cory's voice came over the line.

"Why do you say that when you know it's a lie?"

"It's not a lie, besides, it's a polite thing to say."

"Since when are you worried about being polite." It wasn't a question Cloe was asking.

"I'm just making sure you're not trying to get out of dinner Saturday night."

"Oh, don't worry. I'll be there so you can kick me while I'm down."

He laughed. "I won't kick you, but I think Lance may."

"And that's funny?"

"You deserve it, with your smart mouth." Cory dropped off.

"What is it that you want Cory? If you hate me so much than why do you call me and bug me at work. You can't have your cake and eat it too."

"Says who? I don't know. I really don't. Lance says it's because you are close to God and it's just a reminder of a place I can't be. He says to kill you or leave you alone. I don't want to do either, but I guess it will come down one or the other, won't it?"

"Yah, one or the other." *I'm betting on the first for you* she thought.

"Why can't you just join us? Why can't you make my God your God? You can have anything you want. I'd give it to you."

As if that was a good sales pitch.

"I love my God; you're supposed to love my God, that's why you were made. You follow the wrong God now. You're damned Cory. Unless you ask for repentance. Why don't you come back home?"

"You think your slick don't you?" he was getting hateful.

"You think about it." She said and hung up. Then she turned the ringer off. That should shut him up for awhile. For once she said something that surprised him. For once she got the upper hand. She lay in bed and ran the conversation over in her head. What was she suppose to do. She wished someone would help her. Did God really want her to kill one of his creations? Would it damn her soul? Was she supposed to turn the other cheek or was she supposed to send them to heaven where they can be judged again? Maybe God would let her know soon. Time was running out.

The next morning she went to work and was dreading the day ending. That would mean Saturday would be here and the dinner party also. She busied herself at her desk. Chris came to her and said "Are you ready for tomorrow night?"

"I guess. Is it casual or what?"

"It's casual. I'll meet you here with Sam okay? About six?"

"Sam is going?"

"Of course, she said she wouldn't miss this for the world."

"Oh, okay. Yes six will be fine."

"Okay, don't forget!"

"I won't." she said irritated.

She went back to work and Rose called her and wanted to know if she wanted to meet for lunch. Cloe agreed and they met at a Mexican restaurant for lunch. As soon as Rose saw her from the table she said "I see your getting around better?"

"I feel better. Tonight I think I'll take off my bandages and take a shower."

"Wow, I'm glad to here it. You had better be on your toes tomorrow night. Since they know your hurt, they might try to go for the sore spots."

"I thought about that too." The waitress came up to take their order and went to get their drinks as they waited for the food. Cloe told Rose about the call last night from Cory.

"Cloe, Cloe, Cloe, pissing him off again. When you going to learn?"

"I didn't do it on purpose. I just told the truth."

"Well I'd be surprised if they both don't go after you." The waitress brought them there drinks and Rose filled Cloe about her day at work. Rose has some very funny kids that work for her and she always has a funny story to tell about them and the customers. Cloe listened and chuckled. The drinks came and soon the food followed. They ate their meal and talked about normal things. Cloe didn't want to be reminded for awhile of her life. She asked questions about the horses that Rose worked with. The grand lodge that she worked for had their very own horses for trail rides, and wagon rides as well. The horses there were some of the best and very beautiful. Cloe liked to go visit Rose on her job and see the horses. Rose told Cloe that she was thinking about going to Madam Agnes's house today for some supplies. Cloe reassured her that she would like Madam.

They left the restaurant and went back to work. The day didn't take long to end and then it was time to go home. Chris told Cloe not to forget about Saturday night. She told him she wouldn't and left. On her way to the car her cell rang. It was Cindy checking up on her again. Cindy told her that mom and dad were leaving tomorrow so everybody was meeting at their house to see them off. Cloe said she'd be there. She drove home and took off her bandages, she was still sore but it was gradually lessening. She made her self stretch. She gingerly did some twists. She wanted to work out with Jujitsu, but felt that would make her ribs worse, so instead she opted for lifting weights. She had a Bow Flex system in the other corner of her living room. She went over and sat down. She took a deep breath and cleared her mind. She focused on her breathing. She also focused on her pain. It was kind of good in a way to bring pain while moving around. That way you can focus on it and still motivate yourself. She would be ready for anything tomorrow, she promised herself. It was time to fight back. If she could. She wasn't going to worry about what the people thought. She was just going to start going wild on them. She worked out for three hours. She worked her arms and legs. She left her mid torso alone for now. She had a bar that sat across the bathroom door for her. She would strap herself into it and while hanging upside down, would do her sit ups. She was going to wait for that. Overall she felt good.

She hopped into the shower and let the hot water run over her sore muscles. She hadn't been this sore since she had chased a demon named Amy. While fighting Amy he had pushed down a flight of stairs at the local park. She got away. Cloe got to recuperate for a few days. Big demons are hard to capture. Whatever body they posses, they abuse it. The bigger demons don't care because they can always jump into another body. Cloe tries not to hurt them to bad so that she can excavate the demon out. The only thing is you have to draw a square and begin the Litany of the Saints which makes the stronger ones come out of the body. Then you finish the prayer and trap them in the square. That's hard to do while they're kicking your ass. The weaker ones are easier to manage. All you have to do is lay your hand on the body that they possess and say the Lords Prayer. They leave in a matter of seconds. They don't have quite the power to fight skillfully. Although some have surprised Cloe a time or two.

Cloe got out of the shower and dried off. After getting into her pj's she read some more of her bible and went to bed. As she laid there she told herself that tomorrow she would work out some more. That was after she saw her parents off on their trip. She fell asleep with her mind wondering what tomorrow would bring. She woke up early, round seven. After her morning coffee and reading the news she headed to her parents house. Every one was just showing up. The kids helped the parents pack and load the travel trailer. The kids gave more money for the parents to buy whatever and after a round of hugs for everyone, they were waved off. After they left the siblings stood in the front yard and talked. Cindy and Sue were asking Cloe's questions. It seems Cindy had told Sue that she had concerns for Cloe.

"How are you feeling?" Sue asked and looked sideways at Cindy. "I'm fine, see?" And Cloe did a turn around for them to see.

"How come you didn't tell anyone you were hurt?" Sue said.

"Because you guys would just worry, like you already are."

Cloe would rather face a room full of demons than her sisters when they were upset with her.

Here it goes.

"You wouldn't have said anything if Cindy didn't find you like that."

"As I said before…" Cloe countered.

"What's in it for you?" Cheryl asked.

"What do you mean?" Cloe said back to her.

"Why are you risking yourself? You don't have to do this to get into heaven, there are other ways, ya know. Like going to church and just being a good person. Normal things like that."

"It's too late now. Why are you guys busting my balls over this?"

"Because it's getting dangerous." Lisa said. "We don't want to go to your funeral."

"So don't go to her funeral." Her brother Ivor said in a smart ass way. Lisa hit him in the arm as he was behind her motioning to Cloe jokingly while pointing to himself that he'd come to her funeral.

"If ya ask me sis," Ivor said while rubbing his arm. "You're doing a great job." and when the sisters started to protest, he held up his hand and talked above them. "She's doing what she's supposed to do. It's her calling. Think of it like Joan of Arc. The man upstairs has her back, I'm telling you." and they all were pointing and shouting at each other. Cloe let them vent for awhile, then she put her fingers to her lips and gave out a shrilling whistle. Everybody shut up and looked at her. Then they separated out of the circle that they where in and stood looking at her and each other.

"In a way Ivor's right. Out of all the people that could have run into these things it was me. I think I have to take care of it. I'll get hurt every now and then, it's true. It would be no different if I were a bull rider or a cop. There are chances you take. I like what I do, and I'm good at it. Yes the fallen are new to me. But, I'll learn something about them to my advantage, I always do."

"So we can't talk you out of this?" Lisa said.

"No, I got to do this. Listen! Something big is about to happen! It needs to be stopped. I don't know how I know this, but I feel it in my being. In the end you'll see that I was right. If you're so worried about me then say a prayer for me and that will help surely."

They all were looking somewhere else. Some were looking at the ground and some were looking to the right or left. Cindy shrugged and said,"Alright, I thought that if all your family would ask you to quit then maybe you'd consider it. But I guess not."

"Not everyone is asking her to quit." said Mike, her other brother.

"You support her to?" Cheryl asked.

"Yep." They went to argue some more but Sue told them that she was going home. Pretty soon they were all hugging and leaving. Some had agreed to meet at a local restaurant for food. Cloe was the last to leave. She waved bye to them as they drove off. Then she got in her car and drove home. When she got home she began to work out again. She concentrated on Jujitsu in her mind. If you can't do it then the next best thing was visualizing your moves if someone was going to attack you. Then she hit the Bow Flex until she couldn't pull another handle, then she soaked in the tub again. She got ready, taking her sweet time. She wore tan dress pants and a button up white shirt with a tapered waist and collar. She put on a diamond cross necklace that caught the light beautifully.

It had a white gold angel charm with it also. It was the most expensive jewelry she owned.

It was five when she left her house. She was supposed to meet Chris at work and drive out to the house, where ever that was. She waited for his car in the parking lot. Finally he drove up and waving at her turned around and made his back the way he came. She followed him to the rich part of town. The houses were huge and very modern. They had wooden privacy fences around the back yards, and heated driveways for when the winters come. They parked along the side of a long driveway. Cars were parked on one side only. Cloe and Sam said their hello's to Cloe and talked about work while they made their way up the drive. They came to the house and went upon the wrap around porch. As they came to the door, Chris rang the door bell. He was stating to the girls that he didn't build this house. He went to say that if he did build it he would have done this different or that. Cloe and Sam smiled at either as Chris rambled on. The door came open and a butler was standing there ushering them in. There were a lot of important people here. There where presidents and CEO's. There were politicians and models. Cloe wasn't surprised. Sam was though. She marveled at the string of people here. To her delight Chris introduced her to them. Cloe stood back. Most were normal, a few were fallen or demons. Cloe didn't need any introduction, they knew who she was.

Cloe's gaze went around the house. She'd have to check out the office or library here too, if she could get by with it. She imagined there would be eyes on her at all times. Chris and Sam slowly made their way through the people, Cloe tagged along behind. Cory came up from behind them and grabbed Cloe's arm and squeezed hard as he said "You made it." Cloe secretly brought her heel down on his pinky toe. His eyes got wide but it looked like it was because of something Chris had said. They laughed and Cory took his hand off Cloe's arm.

He shot her a look, and Cloe returned a sweet smile. Cory told them to follow him. It was a good thing she decided on small heels. They made their way to a crowd standing in a living room by a fire place. Lance was there along with some others. They shook Chris's hand and kissed Sam's hand, telling her how beautiful she was. They nodded to Cloe. Cloe just looked at them. It was a good thing Chris and Sam were engrossed in a conversation, or they would have thought Cloe was rude. Lance came up to Cloe and asked her to join him as he went to the bar.

Chris was absolutely beaming.

Cory looked confused.

Cloe really didn't know what to expect. She nodded and took his arm as they made their way to the wet bar. He had a server for the night. Cloe looked back at Cory one last time. He didn't look pleased. They got to the bar and Lance ordered a whiskey. Cloe got water. He waited until the bartender busied himself and then he looked at her.

"We are old souls Cloe, you and I. Must we fight? When I look at you I see a world I haven't been to in along time. You don't see it though do you." he sighed and continued "This war will go on as it always has. My job is a lot easier than yours I think. Are you sure you won't reconsider the offer Cory made?"

"What offer would that be?" Cloe played stupid and leaned upon the bar with one elbow.

"Please, don't do that. Don't make me beg. You would be the greatest partnership we could ever wish to hope for. Your strong, don't get me wrong. But you're not strong enough. Give it up." He whispered the last, drawing out each word.

"I think you're missing the point." Cloe said with a smile.

"What would that be?"

"How about that I have Michael and Gabriel on my side?"

"Oh...that." he sounded tired. He looked down at his hands as he rubbed them together. "How are they? I miss them sometimes. If they're on your side, then why are they not here? They should be here. I would have invited them ya know. Maybe they don't like me." He said more to the air than Cloe. "Oh well, no sense in crying over spilled milk. I don't think they are with you, I think you're pulling my leg." He said with a smile and play slugged Cloe's arm. It still about knocked her into someone else standing behind her.

"They don't have to be present to be here. You know that." Cloe said and rubbed her arm while looking around to see if anybody noticed.

"Yes, all to well. When it comes to your death, I won't be part of it. But I won't stop it either. I could, mind you, if you said those magic words I would just love to hear."

"There's no way you'll hear those words from me." Cloe said proudly.

"Well, then!" and he slapped her on her back, about knocking her to the ground. "You're on your own. Cory has his orders. Oh by the way, I don't know when he'll carry them out. He still thinks there's hope for you yet. I guess when he gets tired of you than you'll be the first to know." He grabbed his drink and went to leave her standing when she grabbed his arm. He looked down at her like he just saw her for the first time.

"I want to know one thing." Cloe looked up at him.

"What's that?"

"You said that you play no part in this then if the tables were turned and I kill him, does the same rule apply then?" He laughed a hardy laugh. Everyone looked at them as if they had never heard him laugh like that. He sobered up and nodded his head and put his hand on her shoulder.

"You really are comical, just like Cory said. But okay I'll make you a deal, if you get the upper hand, there will be no interference from me. A fair fight." he said and made it a toast.

Cloe raised her bottled water and hit his rim. "A fair fight." she said and they drank on it. Somehow Cloe believed him even though he made his way through the crowd laughing as he disappeared.

Cloe waited a while to calm her nerves. She stayed at the bar and took another drink. She looked around and saw Druj heavily leaning on a male model. She was all sex appeal as she whispered in his ear and traced his jaw with a slim manicured finger. As if she sensed Cloe looking, she made eye contact with her. Druj eyes widened a fraction and then became slits. Cloe made the choking act for her to see then started laughing, shaking her head. Druj took her man by the arm and walked off. They'll meet again Cloe was sure of it. She'll have to start carrying a smudge stick around all the time. Since that's how it was going down. Cloe made her way towards Chris. He would wonder about her if she didn't show up. She came up to the group and came up beside Chris. They were standing with some normals so Cloe touched his arm. He turned around and his face lit up.

"I saw you walk off with Lance. What was that all about?"

"Oh we just talked about Cory. He thinks like you do."

"See? I'm not the only one who thinks you'll be a perfect match."

He went on to say some more but Cloe's mind went some where else. A perfect match, so all I need to do is figure how to get to me and turn it around. We are the same, just different. Chris was asking her a question and Cloe shook her head. "Huh?"

"Are you evening listening to me?"

"Sorry, repeat what you said." Cloe stammered.

"I said Sam has to go to the rest room, will you take her?"

"Oh yah, sure." and the girls made their way to find the bathroom. They found it down the hall and to the right. Sam went first, and then Cloe went. Sam asked Cloe on the way back. "Chris says that one of the guys here likes you."

"Na, Chris is just trying to play match maker."

"Oh I don't think so. I've seen the way he looks at you. I've never seen such…." and she looked for the right words with out sounding foolish.

"…Such what?"

"I don't know, this sounds stupid but…it's like a real hunger shows in his eyes." She looked side ways at Cloe.

"Are you sure? I think its pure jealousness." Cloe said as she looked ahead of her at the people.

"Why do you think that? He obviously has everything. They all do." Sam pointed out.

"Because I have a chance and he doesn't." Cloe said over her shoulder at Sam. Sam looked confused and Cloe shrugged. "It's a long story." Cloe said and Sam just said "oh." They made their way back to the group and Chris was playing pool with a couple of norms. Sam stayed with him and Cloe went off to snoop. She saw the same paintings here as at the firm. There was a new one of Lilith with a snake. Cloe was studying it and looked in the back ground. There was a sign painted into a wall behind Lilith. Cloe tilted her head to read it. It was scribbled so it looked like a part of the wooden building at first. It read Sibylline Oracles. At first Cloe blinked a couple of times to make sure that's what she saw. But it was there. It wasn't there to someone who didn't know what to look for. Cloe pondered on that. She'd have to make notes and piece them together later. She stepped back and was studying it some more to see if there was something else she missed. She felt a presence behind her. With out looking she said out loud. "What was she like?

"She was bold and demanding. Nothing pleased her. Everything was second class. Lucifer himself didn't like her. She was like him, but more so. She didn't like what any one did, but she was too lazy to do it for herself. Sloth was her closest friend." To anybody else that last remark would have been confusing. But Cloe knew that there were demons called after the seven deadly sins.

"Wow, I didn't think she was that bad. I guess you don't miss her then?"

"No, but I will see her again soon enough." Cory said. Cloe thought about that last comment. But she didn't say anything. *So was she coming here, and the book had to do with it?* She thought to herself. She stared at the painting some more. Lilith had dark flowing hair. She looked spoiled. Cory put his hand on her back and that startled Cloe. She looked at him and he said "There's another painting I want you to see." He gently guided her towards a painting by the hallway. It was a painting of a war for souls. Michael was in it, so was Lucifer. It was deep and dark, with a lot of black and red color. Heaven even looked sad. "This is my favorite painting of all, who's going to win? Anyone would wonder. It makes me want to jump in and start fighting."

"It doesn't for me, it makes me sad." Cloe said softly.

"Sad?" Cory asked in astonishment.

"Yes, sad. It was a war that could have been avoided. It should have been. The only one who had to suffer was Lucifer. You and the others didn't have to believe his lie."

"He didn't lie, Clo. God made man above us. If you were an angel, and was made to live in the glory of heaven and be blessed to look upon God, how would you feel if a human was put above you?"

She looked at him, she understood somehow, but somehow she didn't. "I would feel like God had a purpose, and he did. He gave us choice, yes, but that isn't such a good thing Cory. You didn't have choice but you didn't need it! You were already where we humans struggle all of our life to get to! You had it made! Do you know how many humans love and worship angels? Do you know how many baby girls pretend that they're angels? You were everything to us, our protectors, and our messengers to God. I don't really know why you wouldn't want that except that somehow there in your heart jealously started and it took off from there. But yes Cory, Lucifer took a single truth about humans and blown it up so that it put that jealousy there. And you took the bait."

Cory just looked at her.

His eyes stared into hers as if to see some truth to her words.

She stared back. She was not backing down.

She almost saw something in his expression that gave her hope, but then he shook his head, as if to be pulled back to reality and stared at her like she had just slapped him.

"Oh, you're good. You're damn good. I can't believe you. You thought you had me, didn't you?" and let out a laugh. Cloe inwardly sighed. She didn't have what it takes to make him listen. He went on to mock her. "Humans love and worship you." he said as he wildly shook his head and his hands danced around. "You are wrong about that. God wouldn't allow that to happen." he said close to her face with anger in his face. "We might have been everything to you lowly humans, but we were nothing to him." and he pointed upward. "Lucifer just wanted us to have what we deserved. We are better than you humans, we deserved to be treated better. Did he not flood the earth when we wanted to love human women? Then we loved them and were punished for it. Where's justice in that?"

"The justice in that was that your kind gave away Godly secrets and God told them he didn't want them to procreate and they did. And it wasn't all about your race either. They had false gods then also."

"And it's justifiable to flood the whole world and kill all humans?" Cory asked.

"If that's what he chose, he made us." Cloe said with a shrug.

"Unbelievable!" He said with disdain.

"Sorry, I'm not one to ask God why. We humans have a saying that God has a plan for us all."

"Well, I'm here to tell ya. He doesn't as much as you humans think he does. His plan is for you to love him and each other. The rest is up to you."

"What would you know?" Cloe asked quickly.

Cory made a hissing sound and came at her. Then he remembered where he was at and stopped short. He looked over her head as if to focus on something else for awhile, gritting his teeth together before returning to look at her.

"You sure can piss me off." He said slowly through clenched teeth.

"You started it." Cloe countered.

"Okay, I'll start something else if you like." he purred in her ear. She scooted away from him and shook her head. "You know better."

"Do I? I think we'd make a pretty good team. If we got together, you make me want to run away with you so bad. I'd either convince you or kill you. But together we'd be stronger than Lance." Cory eyes went to where the old fallen stood with other norms and demons.

"Does Lance know you talk like this?"

"No, and he doesn't have to either." He warned her.

"Cory. You know its no use. I'm not interested."

"Let me show you." Cloe could tell he was raring to go and it was making her uncomfortable. She needed to put distance between them. He started whispering fast what he could do for her, how she would feel. She pushed him away and made her way for Chris. She was shaking and stood with Chris for awhile. When Chris seen her he included her in on conversations of work. Cloe gladly got involved.

After a while Cloe wanted to go home. She told Chris she was leaving and they said they're good byes. She was just about to the door and Cory was there again. He followed her out.

"Are you leaving?"

"Please Cory, leave me alone. I've had enough of you." He moved to the side and let her pass. He must have felt sorry for her. Either that or he felt the same way about her. Their conversation was pretty intense. Cory wasn't used to anybody talking to him like that. He must have gotten mad at himself because he called out in a loud voice. "You can run but you can't hide!" to threaten her.

❧

She kept going until she reached her car. She got in her car and went home. She was glad to be there and for the night to be over with. She fed her pets and sat down to write on a pad. She wrote down in one column fallen, in the next demon Botis, the next Oracles book and Lilith, and next Halloween. They've got to be connected Cloe thought and worked through all the different ways. She went to bed and thought some more. Maybe they wanted to bring Lilith to earth with that book on Halloween. She'd have to go see the Catholic Father Scovley to see what he thought of the matter. She made plans for that tomorrow after she worked out. She would call him in the morning. She fell asleep and dreamt all night.

The next morning she had coffee and read the news. She called Father Scovley and told him she needed to see him and he told her to be at the church at two. Then she worked out in Jujitsu for along time. She had a lot of things on her mind, a lot of things to work through. She knew in her heart the truth, but Cory's words made her think. He was there so he would know. It's strange that she can see different sides to the same situation. She wondered why on a lot of things. She knew she shouldn't have. She couldn't help it. Cloe thought everyone probably tried to figure the way things are at one time or another. Unless your simple and didn't care. Some people were like that. God's God, Satan's Satan. People are good or bad and going to one place or the other when they die. It was that simple. She wished it was. She got tired and finally did her cool down. She didn't want to meditate. She didn't want to think, she didn't want to know. So she skipped it. She went out and rode Gigi instead. She went to the spring. It was quiet. She prayed and cried. She knew she would need help. After she got her emotions spent she mounted her horse and made the usual rounds of checking the fence for repairs. There wasn't any to do so she went back home.

She went in the bathroom and washed her face. She put on some makeup to hide the puffiness. She did some laundry until it was time to go. She drove to the church and parked on the side of the building. She went in through a side door and found Father Scovley's office. He was sitting in his chair reading when she knocked on the door. He looked up and said. "Come in."

"Hello Father."

"Hello Cloe. How are you today?"

She lied. "I'm doing great, how 'bout yourself?"

"I'm wonderful. Every day is a good day if you wake up."

Cloe liked that saying, it was just what she needed to hear. She perked up a bit. "I was at Lance West's house last night, are you familiar with him?"

"Yes, a little. He's very rich and has donated money to us, but he doesn't come to this church. Why do you ask?"

"Because he had a painting in his hallway of Lilith, and in the background it has the Sibylline Oracles inscribed in a wall of a wooded building." Cloe said and sat back, relaxing in the seat to be more comfortable.

That sparked his interest and he sat up closer to her. "Can you draw it?"

"Well I'm no artist but it goes something like this." and Cloe sketched out the painting with a pencil. She didn't bother with the little things, she put in what he needed to see.

"I have never seen this painting. How do you know its Lilith?"

"I have seen paintings of her before Father; I know what she looks like."

"Why would it be hanging in Mr. West's house?"

"Well I hate to tell you this but he's a fallen too." Her voice dropped off.

"How do you know this?" He asked as he leaned on the desk with his elbows.

"He told me."

Father Scovley rubbed his face with his hands. If it were anybody else sitting here, they would think this young girl sitting in front of him was nuts.

He looked at her. He knew she was serious. He knew she was special, even if no one else believed it. He wasn't sure how she knew all this information, but she did know a lot.

Sometimes more than any of his brotherhood.

He entwined his fingers together and put the fist to his lips. "I must speak with the others about this."

"So you have no clue as to why the painting is this way?"

"All I can tell you is, and this is just from my speculation, that maybe Lilith helped to write the Sibylline Oracles. They were written by women prophets. That is, if you want to call them that. It would make some sense."

"And if they were found in a ritual for raising the dead book, then maybe they'll try to bring her here?"

He still had his fist held to his lips. "I don't know. I don't know what she would have to offer to anyone, let alone demons and fallen angels. She wasn't anything really."

"Oh. Could she help them? Does she do anything special?"

"Special?" Father Scovley's eye brows went up.

"Ya, you know. Make the plagues come, bring fire down, special."

"I don't know. We really don't know anything about her. I'm afraid you're on your own." He said but the look on his face told Cloe he wished he could help out more.

"Okay. Thanks for seeing me today." Cloe said and stood to leave.

"Thank you for coming in. You are very resourceful, even though we don't get involved much. I will say a prayer for you." He truly meant what he said. He did care about her, even though he did not understand her ways.

"I'd like that, thanks."

Cloe left the office and was going to go out the door when she thought she heard someone whisper her name. She turned around to find no one in the hallway. She turned back around towards the door. Then she decided to follow the whisper. She didn't really know if she heard it or not, but she was going to find out.

She made her way down the hall. When she got to the end she could go down another hallway or go into the sanctuary. She was about to go down the hallway when a noise came from the other direction. She turned around and went to the sanctuary.

It was so big. They could easily fit five hundred people in it. The stained glass windows took up more than half of the church wall that were easily 10 stories high on either side. They were of all the saints. Cloe made her way down the middle of the pews. There was a man sitting by himself in the front row. Cloe looked at his back for awhile. That must be where the noise came from she thought. She looked around to see if she could see anything else. After she was satisfied that she was hearing things she turned to leave. No sense in bothering the man with his thoughts.

"You are not bothering me, Cloe, I am here for you." the man said. Cloe froze.

Not again she thought.

She didn't want to fight today.

The man turned around and looked at her. No, this was no demon Cloe told herself. Who was this man? She moved into the front and came close to him and sat down. He looked harmless but almost like a thin jolly Santa. He had a twinkle to his eye and a grin on his face. He looked at her and her back at him. He had sky blue eyes.

"Do I know you?" she asked him.

"Yes." He said matter of fact.

"Okay?" Cloe said in more of a question.

"I am here to help you."

"How do you know I need help?"

"Because I've heard your prayers."

Cloe took a moment to digest this. She was wondering how he heard them. He sat there and let her have a minute. He liked to be here. He liked this church. Yes, she could take all the time she needed, he thought. Cloe was looking at the stage where the sermons were held. And then as if she had an answer she turned to him and asked "Are you Michael?"

"Yes."

"But, I thought you were a strong muscular type angel."

"We can be any type we chose."

"Oh...It's nice to see you. I usually talk to you in my dreams."

Cloe didn't know how to treat him.

She wanted to jump up and down like a little kid at Christmas but she didn't.

"I will always be with you. But for now I have something for you to use in your fight against the ex-watchers."

"So I will have to face them." Cloe said more to herself than him.

"Just one, for now. You know which one I'm talking about."

"Why just him."

"Because the others will know not to interfere. You've made a deal with Mastema. He will stick to his word."

"Mastema?" Cloe asked thinking what in the world is he talking about?

"Oh. The one you call Lance." He nodded.

"That's Lance's real name? What is his roll?" Cloe knew that hell had ranks of angels, demons and devils, kind of like heaven did.

"He is the leader of the offspring of the fallen angels who mated with human beings."

"So he's just a babysitter so to speak."

"So to speak." Michael said.

Cloe sat there and absorbed it all. No wonder Lance made that deal with Cloe. He wasn't a prince or an ambassador, he was just leading the way to fame and fortune. No wonder he was so rich and powerful. He had to be in order to put every fallen in play somewhere. Then she thought about Cory.

"What's Cory's real name?"

"Vetis." Michael said.

"And that is…."

"Vetis is a demon who was born from a fallen who mated with a demon, not a human. He specializes in tempting and corrupting the holy, or even the ones who believe the most. He's not truly a fallen because he is a descendant, but he is stronger than most demons also, so he has fallen traits but is a demon. He has the best of both worlds."

"That would make sense." Cloe said.

She didn't know if she herself was holy, but she knew she believed and he did a good job tempting her, and making her feel like she was going to fail.

"Yes." Michael said.

Cloe looked down at her shoes. It felt strange to be sitting here talking to one of Gods chief angels. She didn't want it to end. He must have sensed her hesitation because he said. "Don't worry, I will be here when you need help."

"But I don't want to kill him." Cloe said and slumped backwards. Banishing demons is one thing, the body still lives. Killing a body is another thing. One that Cloe has had a hard time doing.

"You will have to I'm afraid. It will not be punishable by God, for you are doing his will. It is time Vetis comes home."

"Are you sure?"

Michael looked at her as if to say 'are you kidding me?' Cloe shrugged and said sorry under her breath. Michael stood up and motioned Cloe to get up too. Cloe did and Michael went on to explain.

"When you get the chance. And that is up to you dear one. I will give you the power to make the Deaths Dagger appear in your hand. You will not see it until you are in the correct position. So now, put your fist in a ball and put it over where my heart should be. Pretend like you've just stabbed me."

Cloe just stared at him. Then she looked around. This time it was her turn to look like 'are you kidding me'. She looked at Michael and Michael got impatient with her, and said "Do as I say." in a demanding tone that boomed through the sanctuary that Cloe quickly did as he said. She did not want to be on his bad side. Michael went on to instruct her, keeping her hand where it was with his own hand.

"Now when you do this, you have to say their name, their true name. Now say Michael."

"Michael." Cloe said awkwardly

To her surprise, there appeared a dagger handle in her hand. She looked at in amazement then she followed the handle up into Michael's body. The blade was buried deep into his chest. Cloe eyes got big and her jaw dropped. She sucked in a breath and pulled it out the dagger in a quick swipe. When she had it all the way out, it was gone again. She looked up at Michael and he looked at her with wide eyes. His mouth was working but no words were coming out and he grabbed at his heart. Cloe went for him and started to apologize profusely.

"Just kidding." he said as he straightened up and brushed something imaginary off his arm. Cloe just stared at him. "Hey, we need a good laugh too, you know."

Cloe sank down on the pew scarcely breathing. She could here him chuckle and say something along the lines of "Wait till I get back to tell everyone that story…." as she put her head down between her knees.

That was not funny.

"So that's how you use the dagger, got it?" he asked her.

"Got it." she said. After she caught her breath she brought her head up and asked "What about the…." but she was alone.

She looked around and nobody was there. She took a deep breath. She said a prayer of thanks. Then she went to the door and got into the car. On her way down the street she realized that she wasn't sore anymore. She touched her ribs roughly. They were good. She said thanks heavenward once again and went home.

Before she got home she decided to stop by a Chinese restaurant and take home carry out for supper. She filled her container up that they gave her and paid for it.

Then she started for home again. When she got there she went in and put it on the table. Then she came back out and fed her dog and her horse. She then decided that she wasn't hungry anymore so she put it in the microwave. She worked out some more on the bow flex. It made her feel better that Michael had seen her in the church. It made everything clear. She still was uneasy about having to deal with Cory. But she knew in the end, and he did to, that it will come down it. She wasn't ready to die yet. She might not have a choice.

She needed to find out what the Botis cult was up to. That ritual book was in Lance's nephew's house. So there must be a connection. Botis was a demon of hidden treasures. Maybe Botis knows why the Sibylline Oracles is in the picture. There's one way to find out. She hadn't run into him yet. Maybe the ritual book was to bring Botis in through a ritual. Then Botis would tell about Lilith. Cloe decided to concentrate on the cult for now. She'll figure out the fallen later. She took a shower and warmed up her Chinese food. She had a plan. The more she thought about her, the more she realized that she was sidetracked with Cory and everything else. She groaned out loud. So much time has passed that she had to get back on track. She wondered if Cory did that on purpose.

Cloe watched some TV before going to bed. She watched the news and weather. The food in her belly was making her sleepy. She finally went to bed, thinking of how clever they were to get her attention while the cult worked behind the scenes. She went to sleep thinking of her meeting with Michael.

The next morning she woke up with a great perspective on things. She was smiling to herself as she made her coffee. She read the Internet on her laptop and got ready for work. She looked at Buddy and was feeling around for hurt spots but Buddy seemed to be doing as well as she was. She patted his head and got into her car.

The work week went by smoothly. No run-ins or calls from Cory. She was almost surprised but mostly grateful. She wondered if he somehow knew that she had met with Michael. They worked on a different plane of existence, was it possible to know what the others are doing? That would make it hard for her if he knew that could call on the Deaths Dagger when she needed it. Then he wouldn't trust her. Did he trust her now?

After work Cloe went to Sue's to see Megan and to see if Amanda still went to that house because of her boyfriend. Megan let her know that she still did. Cloe asked her if they bug her or anything. Megan said she hadn't heard any more from them. Amanda still asked her to go but Megan says no every time. Cloe told her she was glad. She left after visiting and went home. Her mom called her to let her know they were at Mount Rushmore. She told Cloe funny stories of her dad. He was Foghorn Leghorn, Sylvester the cat, and Daffy Duck all rolled into one. Even when he was annoying he was quite hilarious. Maybe that was where Cloe got her comical side from.

Her mother also said that Chris had put in a thousand dollars in their account. She went to withdraw and checked the balance to her checkbook. The teller told her the number the bank had showed. Shirley said she had a thousand less which prompted the bank to investigate. After researching the extra funds they told Shirley a deposit was made by Chris. Shirley told Cloe to tell Chris thank you. Cloe promised she would before hanging up. Her mom had to call the others.

The next day Cloe made her way to Chris's office. He was at his desk and studying a quote that Billy had drew up. She sat down and he looked at her.

"You look tired." Cloe said.

"So do you." Chris countered back.

"I'm not too bad. I have a lot on my mind, what about you?"

"It's all this business rolling in and only Billy doing the quotes. I'm trying to help him but then I'm getting backed up also. You wanna help?"

"I'll tell you what, I'll do the quotes here but I am not going out running around town. I thought you were going to hire someone to do quotes?"

"I was but no one seems interested."

"Robbie is."

Chris raised his eyebrow and thumbed toward the door. "Robbie Anderson?"

"Yep."

"Do you think he can do it?"

"I'll teach him as I catch you up."

"You'd do that for me?"

"Yep." Cloe said, feeling generous. Actually she would do a lot for Chris. He was like a brother to her. "Think of it as a way of me saying thank you for putting money in moms account."

"Oh, you found out about that. I ran into Cindy in the store the other day and she told me that they had left. I told you that I would help out but you never mentioned anything, so I figured you were mad at me for trying to set you up."

"I wasn't mad, just a little irritated. I know you mean well. I'm just not interested right now."

"So we good?" Chris said in a funny tone.

"We good." Cloe said, mimicking him.

"Okay then. Send Rob in here and let's get this boat rockin' so I can do what I need to do, and here, take these with ya, will ya?" He handed her a pile of quotes that he gathered from going to Lance's dinner last Saturday. She left his office and went to get Rob. As soon as she told Rob Chris needed to see him he had a worried look on his face. Cloe reminded him of their conversation about quoting and he smiled and hurried in.

Cloe sat at her desk and went through the quotes. She saw almost half was from Lance and his bunch. There were some where from some of the politicians in the city, some from rich people that she had only heard about. Plus some others that were getting old from along time ago. Rob came up to her and asked if he could pull his desk up to hers so he could begin learning. He didn't want to wait until tomorrow. Cloe laughed and told him to go ahead. The rest of the week the two went over the quotes and one by one Rob learned what to do. Billy would have to show him the running around town part.

Friday came and Megan called Cloe to tell her there was a party that night at the same place she had been before when she beat up Allan, Lances nephew. Cloe thanked her for the information and made plans to be there. She'd have to figure out how to get in. After work she went home and worked out. She figured tonight she wouldn't screw around. She'd find out what's going on. After she took a shower she got out leather pants with a skimpy shirt and high heel boots. She went for a light Goth look in her make up so that they wouldn't recognize her right away. She hoped none of the fallen would be there. She didn't want to tempt Cory more by having these tight cloths on.

It was eight that night when she made her way to the party. She walked in and nobody looked at her except for some guys. She expected that. She needed to find out some information but she was sure Allan wouldn't tell her if she cornered him. He would probably call his uncle in, *that little punk* she thought to herself.

She made her way through the crowd and found Allen and the girl. This time they were all over each other with a crowd watching. It reminded her of a movie she watched about Rio. She scanned for a groupie and when they were done and the crowd split up, she found her mark. He was a younger kid with black hair and brown eyes. The kid followed Allan everywhere and when Allan sat, he sat. When Allan moved he went with. Allan would introduce him to a bunch of girls and he would laugh at something Allan had said. He was probably talking bad about them, without them knowing it. *What a bastard* Cloe thought.

Cloe followed them around. Every once in a while some guy would try to make an advance on her. She would put them on another girl and walk off. Finally the guy made his way somewhere and Cloe followed. He went to a back room and stopped at a group of people who were using nose candy on a glass table. After getting his fix and high fiving a few men he went on to the bathroom.

Perfect, Cloe thought. No audience.

She waited until he opened the door to step out when he was done, and Cloe pushed him back in. She heard him cuss and protest until he saw her. Then he was Mister Macho. He looked her up and down and Cloe let him. She leaned against the sink and smiled seductively. He was nodding his head and came towards her. He ran a hand up her side and around her neck but she held him off.

"I don't make it with anyone who's not a member."

"I am a member." He said as sexy as he could.

"I don't see any marks." Cloe countered lazily.

"Its right here." he said and showed her the inside of his wrist.

"Why is that there? When did they start doing that?" she asked as she traced it softly.

"It's because of a demon hunting bitch, they say she's real psycho."

"Really? It's a she?" Cloe asked and nibbled at his fingers.

"That's what they say." He said and watched her nibble. She hoped he washed his hands when he was done pissing.

"So tell me something than if your involved, what's the big plan?"

"What do you mean?" he said and she traced his jaw. *Keep him talking* she thought.

"I mean are they bringing in Botis or have they already done it?"

"No. They will begin the ritual next Friday." He said as he looked at her cleavage

"Can I come with you?" She purred.

"If you want." he giggled and sniffed at her neck.

"What are they going to do with Lilith?"

"She's going to help Botis and some other bad dudes." He answered in almost a slur as she put her fingers through his hair.

"Do what?"

"Why are you asking so many questions?" he sobered and went to back up. Cloe let him. She came forward and said "Oh I just wanted to be sure so I wouldn't miss it."

"How do you know so much anyways, are you a member?" he asked.

She showed him her wrist "No, just a lucky guess." She said with a smile. His eyes searched her wrist and then her face. It must have dawned on him because all of the sudden his eyes got wide and he started stammering "You." She didn't waist time; she put one leg behind his and tripped him backwards. He fell on the ground and she was instantly sitting on top of him.

"So now that we know who I am, and I know who you are, why don't you tell me what you know?" she said over his head.

"Screw you bitch!" He spat.

"Now, now, is that any way to talk to a lady?"

"I ain't telling you shit."

"You had to make it hard on yourself." Cloe said and grabbed his bottom lip and squeezed. He let out a yelp and starting cursing her. "Now be a good boy and tell me how is Botis and Lilith suppose to help the fallen."

"I don't know." he said as best as he could with his lip in her fingers.

"I don't believe you." Very swiftly Cloe punched him in the nose. He screamed in agony and started bleeding.

"What is going to happen?" she jerked him up by his bottom lip again.

"Please!" he begged. "I really don't know. They are calling in Botis. Botis is suppose to know how to call in Lilith, and Lilith is suppose to help those dudes, but I don't know with what, hardly anybody does." he said and spit blood to the side. Cloe looked at him for a second. He was telling the truth. She could see he was scared in his eyes. She got off of him and said "Now that wasn't so bad, was it?" He got up and went to get a towel and then said "You won't make it out of here! I'll get twenty of them after you and…." Cloe punched him out and then caught him before he hit the floor. She put in him in the bathtub and closed the shower door. Then she shut off the light and went out, closing the door behind her.

☙

She made her way out of the house and got into her car and left. She'll pay for that she was sure. But for now she got out without a scratch. She went home and called in Buddy. They slept in the living room.

The next morning she awoke with a start and went outside to check on Gigi. He was out grazing in the pasture. She whistled loudly and he brought his head up instantly. She made kissing noises at him and he chewed his food while he looked at her then he put his head down to eat some more. She went back in to make coffee. After coffee she did dishes and dusted around. She concentrated on her Jesus statue and washed the dust off him, and then she washed her windows. The stained glass really shone when you took the grime build up off. It was gorgeous to look at.

She was in the back yard washing her bucket out when she heard Gigi start to snort and neigh. He put his tail up and started prancing to the barn. Cloe shut off the water and went to go see what he was excited about. In the distance Rose was trotting down the road on Spec and Puppy happily trotting beside her.

Cloe waved and smiled, Rose waved back. If the two of them could have lived in the western days, they'd be tickled pink. Cloe went over to pet Gigi but he wasn't very interested in her. Buddy ran up the road to meet them. They came in the yard and Cloe asked "What are you dong here?"

"I want to swim." Rose said and shook her bathing suit at Cloe.

"Lets go swimming."

"Sounds like a good idea; I just got done dusting and washing windows."

They put Spec in with Gigi much to his delight and they ran off racing. Rose laughed. "I guess we won't be riding to the spring." They went in and changed their cloths. Rose had a two piece, Cloe had a one piece. They donned flip flops and went out the back door. They went through the little wooden gate and made their way through the pasture. The sun beat down on them as they walked.

"That water is sure going to feel good." Cloe said.

"I know." Rose said and stuck her tongue out in a pant.

They felt like kids again and talked about everything from family to work. They made their way to the trees and came upon the spring. Cloe took her flip flops off and touched her toes in. "That's cold!" she said and stepped back.

"Let me see." and Rose followed Cloe's motion. "But I bet it will feel good."

They made their way around to a rock that had the deep side. They had fun jumping off the ledge. "I know, we'll go in together." Rose said.

"Uh-huh, you'll stand there and let me jump." Cloe said while shaking her head.

"Okay I'll tell you what; we'll hold hands this time. That way you can drag me in if I don't go."

"Okay." Cloe said and grabbed Rose's hand. They counted to three, while they did that Rose went to plug her nose. When they got the end Cloe jumped and Rose let go of her hand. The last thing Cloe heard was Rose laughing. The last thing Rose heard was Cloe cussing. She made a splash as she went under, and then came back up laughing. "I knew you'd do something!" she sputtered as she came up.

"Is it cold?"

"No, actually it's pretty nice." Cloe lied, hoping Rose didn't see her give a little shiver.

"Here I come." she said. With a plug of her nose she jumped in. When she came up and screamed "You lied, it is to cold!" Rose hated to be cold.

"I had to get even with you some way." she said. They splashed each other and swam around. They went to the bottom and came up again. They played old games they used to play when they were in school. They spent the whole day there at the spring. When they got tired they laid out in the sun. Rose told Cloe she went to see Madam Agnes.

"Really, what did you get?" Cloe asked.

"Oh some herbs at a cheaper cost then the store had them for. She showed me a book that had some new herbal remedies that I never heard of. I'm going to try them on you. When I told her I was your friend, she took out a bag and threw some sticks and stones and shells out on a mat. What is that all about? Then she told me that my worries are for a good reason, but it will be alright in the end. She's hard to understand because of her Cajun accent."

"Ya, but she means well. So what are your worries?"

"You, my parents, my job, a bunch of stuff really."

"Well see, you don't need to worry, everything will work out fine."

"What about you?" Rose asked

"Oh I got help from a certain someone the other day." Cloe said and went on to explain how Michael showed up in the church to help her. As she told the story of Deaths Dagger they made their way back to the house. They were getting hungry. She told Rose of their real names, and how he scared her at the end. Rose laughed at that. "So they do have a sense of humor. I've always wondered."

"It scared the crap out of me. But after I caught my breath I went to ask him about the book, he was gone. I didn't get any answers there but I did from some one else. I went to the party at that house I told you about? Anyways, there was a kid there who I tricked into spilling that the cult will bring Botis, and Botis will bring Lilith, and Lilith is suppose to help the fallen with something, but he didn't know what."

"How did you make it out with out him squealing?"

"I had to knock him out actually, and then I hid him in the tub." Cloe went on to explain about the whole situation with the kid. Rose shook her head and told Cloe she was crazy. Cloe told her about the 'psycho part' and they laughed.

They made tuna sandwiches and had chips out on the front porch. They brought a pitcher of cool aid to drink. Cloe asked Rose "So what do you think I should do?"

"About…"

"…About the ritual thing. It starts this Friday."

"Well you can't just waltz in there; they'll kill you for sure."

"I know, but I need to get in somehow."

"Well even if you get in, then what, you got a plan?"

"No, that's what I'm hoping you'll help me figure out."

"Okay, well, let's see. Botis is a demon that can look like a snake, and turn human?"

"Yes." Cloe said between chews.

"So how will they raise him?" The girls pondered on that for awhile. *How would they do that?* Cloe thought. She didn't know what the ritual book would say. She didn't own any raising the dead books. She didn't think she needed them. She wondered if her other books would give an insight. She told Rose she'd be right back and went to her library. All she had was a cults book. She took that back to the table and her and Rose went through it. They found a spot and Cloe skimmed the page at a faster rate than Rose.

She pointed to a passage and said "Rose, listen to this. It says most cults try to raise their leader in their true form and would need the actual form before them to manifest the spirit." Cloe looked at Rose and said "That means they would need an actual snake before them. Then It says 'after days of constant ritual the spirit will take form. If it is a person that is forming, the person(s) would need an adept magician to manifest the form fully." Cloe put the book down and Rose said "Well they have that, they'll have demons and the fallen."

"Okay then, you can make a charm to keep the snake a snake?"

"How you gonna make the snake wear it?"

They were back at square one. It was getting dark so Rose decided to spend the night. She was too interested to leave now. They needed to come up with something tonight. They moved into the house after doing the chores. Each girl was thinking about what to do. They sat on opposite ends of the couch and thought.

"Okay. We're agreed that we got to be there to do whatever right?"

"Right." Rose said.

"Okay then lets say we're actually there, what do you think we may see?"

"A bunch of people chanting around a snake." Rose answered.

"Okay, then, is the snake on a table, on the floor?"

"I bet it would be on the floor." Rose nodded.

"Ya, I think so too. But it would have to be caged wouldn't it?, or it would slither away and then they would be trying to get the snake back the rest of the night." They laughed about that, that would be too funny. Everyone hunting for a snake. Rose said "Okay, but couldn't someone hold it?"

"I wouldn't think so, then the holder might take away from the ritual being performed."

"Okay, so we have a snake on a floor in a cage, don't forget it would have to be in a circle of conjugation for the ritual to work."

"Okay." Cloe said and they visualized it.

"I still don't see how we can be there to keep this from happening."

"Could we say a spell against them?" Rose asked.

"I don't think it would work, there would be a lot of them against us. We need to keep it from happening."

"We could steal the snake?"

"They'd just get another one, I thought about that to, except I thought about killing it."

"Cloe!"

"No, after they had actually brought the spirit into it then I thought about it."

"Oh." Rose said.

"We need something around the snake that they wouldn't find to keep it from happening."

"Then they would eventually find that, then it would be like Fort Knox to get in again." Rose said with a sigh.

"Okay then, we'll just have to steal it."

"I knew you'd say that." Rose said and let her head drop down on the arm of the couch.

"Well, Rose, if we prevent it on any level, they'll figure it out. They can always get a new snake and start over. So we need to let it happen, then we need to get the snake. We could always donate it to the zoo or something, after we put a charm on it so it won't change back or forward."

"Okay then, how do you propose we do that?"

"We could…" Cloe stopped and looked at the ceiling.

"Exactly."

"So we need a diversion." Cloe said.

"And time. It wouldn't take them much to figure out the snake is gone, then it wouldn't take them long to start looking for us."

"Okay then, it needs to be during the night. We can be more sneakier at night."

"But most fallen will be there at night, we need it to be during the day, when most of them act like people and work."

They both said together "We could switch snakes!"

They both got excited. They started jumping around and dancing doing a little 'oh, ya' routine. Then it hit them that they would have to actually pull this off. They knew they'd have to be lightening fast. So they made a plan. Rose would go in Friday night and take pictures. Then they buy one that looked like it and do the ol' switcharoo. It would take them both when that happened, Cloe would be the diversion and

Rose would have to do the switching. Cloe went on to draw the house's floor plans to Rose so she would know where to go in case she was found out. They'd didn't think that would happen. No body has ever saw Rose before. She was a secret helper. Then they high fived each other and got ready for bed. It was past midnight. The next morning they decided to go to church with Rose's dad. He went to a church just outside the city. They rode in and caught him and Mary at the table having coffee. They put the horses up and went into the house to tell him. He was surprised, and delighted. They climbed into the Ford and went to the church. Cloe and Rose prayed hard for God to help them with their plan. They went back home and had lunch, eating greenery out of the garden. It was so good to Cloe. She loved Mary's cooking. They visited for awhile and Cloe made her way back with Gigi and Buddy.

When she got home she worked out some more on both the bow flex and Jujitsu. When she got tired she did a cool down. She meditated to some music. She passed her day leisurely until she got ready for bed. The next morning she went to work whistling and got started on the quotes with Robbie. He was catching on quite well. He had this week with Cloe then he was on the road with Billy. They were almost to lunch when Chris motioned to her that she had a phone call in his office. When she got there she looked at him, and he nodded and said "It's Cory, but I didn't have anything to do with this."

"Hello." she said after she took the receiver from Chris's hand.

"So you're talking to me?"

"What do you want?"

"You know what I want."

"Besides that." Cloe said shortly.

"I want to see you again."

"Poor baby. I know you have other women to occupy your time."

"Sounds like you're jealous."

"You wish."

"Come on, see me."

"Only if you'll play nice."

"I promise."

After a pause "Okay then, how about supper Friday night."

"I was hoping before then."

"I'm hanging up now." Cloe said and put the receiver away from her ear.

"Okay! Friday night. I'll pick you up."

"Not so fast, I'll meet you."

He reluctantly agreed and they picked a spot in town. A fancy place that he knew of. She'd have to dress up. But at least she knew were he'd be when Friday rolled around and Rose was at the house taking pictures.

But was she crazy?

Why was she going out with him?

Cory would be the only one she'd worry about catching her. He's very smart and very quick.

Was that the real reason?

The rest of the week went by in a blur. Cloe stayed to herself pretty much. She seriously wondered about her sanity. A few phone calls from her sisters and one from her mother kept her from missing anyone. Friday came around and after she got home the phone rang. It was Rose.

"I'm nervous."

"It'll be okay, just get some pics and get out of there. Don't rush though, or you'll look obvious. And don't forget your cell phone." Not only just in case she needed it but it was taking the pictures.

"You don't have to worry about Cory either I've agreed to have dinner with him tonight so that he won't be there with you." Rose breathed out over the phone "Okay, I can do this." Cloe reassured her and then hung up to get ready for her date.

She was nervous also, but she repeated Rose's words "I can do this."

She got into her car and made her way across town. She decided to wear a one piece sleeveless dress that was more fitting than frilly. She wore her hair down with big loop earrings. All her jewelry was silver. She parked her car and went in. There was a man standing at a podium and asked her if she was expecting someone. She explained she was having dinner with a man name Cory, and was interrupted by him saying "Ah yes, he's expecting you. Right this way."

She followed him into the restaurant which was big in itself. There where crystal and brass things every where. She finally saw him sitting at a table for two. He looked gigantic at the little table. He saw her and smiled. She inwardly groaned. Why did he have to be so damn good looking? The man pulled out the chair for her and she sat down. He left and she turned towards him and asked "Been waiting long?"

"No, as a matter of fact I just got here."

"Good, I hate to wait."

"Me to." he said and smiled at her.

It had been a while since she had seen him smile. It reminded her of the first day they met. He looked relaxed. She would bet a hundred dollar bill he thought he would make progress with her tonight. He'd kill her if he really knew why she was here. The waiter came up to give them menus. Cory ordered a bottle of wine for them both. When the man walked away again Cloe started to protest about the wine.

"Would you just relax? I gave you my word. No fighting tonight."

"You had better mean this, Cory." She warned.

"I got what I want; I'm not screwing this up. I promise." He crossed his heart.

They went on to look at the menus and when the man came, Cloe ordered a steak with baked potato, and he ordered the same. The waiter took their menus and poured them a glass of wine. The he was gone again. Cory lifted his glass of wine and said "To us."

"Us?" Cloe asked. He sounded so normal.

"Yes, to us."

"Why do you say that?"

"Because you know what we are. We're enemies, but yet here we are having dinner. That's funny, isn't it?"

"Oh, yes I guess that kind of is funny." And they drank their wine at the same time.

"So, I'm curious, why did you decide to have dinner with me?"

"I don't know. I guess when you're not being mean, I like to listen to you talk. I bet you have a gob of stories."

"Yes, you could say that." He said and there was a gleam in his eye "Can I ask you a question?"

"Sure." Cloe said carefully.

"If I were a normal guy, would you be interested?"

"But your not." Cloe said.

"I know but if I was just a human, would you be?"

"Yes, probably." Cloe said sadly.

"Oh." he said and looked down. It almost looked like he was sad, but then he looked up at her and said "So you do like me."

"I thought you said you'd behave?" Cloe asked getting uncomfortable.

"I am, I'm just making an observation."

"Well don't read more into this than what it is."

"What is it then?"

"Curiosity on both parts." she said.

"That's all it is to you, you're curious?"

"Yes, I'm curious about a lot of things."

"Like." Cory raised an eyebrow.

"Like why do you persist on getting me into your bed."

Cory laughed "You are good at figuring things out. I want you because I've never knew any one like you my whole life." That was saying a lot. Cory had been around along time. How can anybody not be like her. She wasn't that different. He had a lot of women, she would put her life on that. She decided to ask him.

"How is it that you've been alive along time, and you've never met anybody like me?"

"I've never met someone who didn't give into their hearts desire or fight what their body wanted. You wear your heart on your sleeve but yet you don't give in. You are truly noble for that."

"And how do you know what my heart desires?"

"I see it in your eyes Cloe, you can't fight the way we feel about each other. Well, you are, and I don't want to." He shrugged and took a sip of wine.

"It's the way it has to be." Cloe said with a shrug.

Cory was about to say something but the waiter showed up with the food. He leaned back and watched her. She didn't want to look in his eyes so she looked around the restaurant. When the waiter left she slowly looked at her plate. She practically jumped out of her seat when he said "Enjoy." She started eating and then she had an idea. She asked Cory "Have you seen Cain around?"

Cory stopped cutting his steak and looked at her. He tilted his head back and let out a laugh. She was looking around to see if anybody thought he was insane. No one seemed to care. He stopped laughing and he looked at her. She drew her eyebrows together as if to ask why he was laughing. He must have knew why she looked at him so queer because he said "I have never been asked that question."

"Really?" a lot of people never realized that in the bible, when it told the story of Cain and Able, that God punished Cain to the earth forever.

"Why would you think of that?"

"I don't know, I guess cause I always wondered where he went; now I have someone I can ask." Cloe said and took a bite.

"You are an amazement." he said in awe.

"So, where is he?"

Cory entertained her as he told her that Cain lived in New Orleans. It was a place that someone like that could live and not be bothered. He had a little bungalow in the swamps. He was doing miserably. He wanted to go home and couldn't. It was real torture on him. They tried to visit him as much as they could. They've offered him a decent place to live but he wouldn't leave the swamps. He hadn't changed a bit Cory said.

"Wow." Cloe said "That's cool."

"I guess." Cory said with a shake of his head at Cloe.

"So now its your turn."

"What do you mean?"

"Tell me how Michael and Gabriel are doing."

Cloe froze. Did he know about the visit? "How would I know?"

"Come on, I know they help you out, or you wouldn't be so successful. Don't you see them in dreams or whatever?" Cory wiggled his fingers in midair.

"Oh, yes, I see them in dreams, except I've only see Gabriel's face usually. And she's doing fine, just as beautiful as ever I imagine. But I never see Michael, I just hear his voice." She hoped she was believable.

Cory snorted "Michael! That's his favorite thing to do, the voice command thing. He thinks he's so big and powerful." he snorted again.

"Don't you want to be with them at all Cory?" He looked at her side ways, as if he debated whether he could tell her or not. He sighed "Yes, some of them I do. Gabriel's voice could calm even Lucifer himself at times when he lost his temper.

She is beautiful. And a few others…" He let his voice drop off as he looked down at his plate.

"I've even met Metatron!" Cloe blurted out. That got his attention. Cloe was just trying to have a conversation. Cory had his head titled down but he looked up at her from under his eyelashes. His face almost went crimson. It didn't seem to please him at all when she said that. Cloe looked around nervously. "Did I say something wrong?"

"When did this happen?"

"Oh, way before I met you." Cloe said carefully.

"Why would he help you? He's just a record keeper."

"Because he shows me sigil shapes of what I need to know about what demon."

Cory straightened up. He played with his wine glass but stared at Cloe. "You must truly be privileged if Metatron helps you."

"Why do you say that?" Cloe was almost giddy at the sight of Cory being so angry. Maybe she had one up on him.

"Because Metatron is a very by the books angel, he has no fun at all with anything. I personally thought he was quite a bore. But he's one of Gods closest angels. He is anything God needs him to be."

"I know. That's why I think it's great!" Cloe said and took a bite of her food.

"And I am starting to understand a lot more too." Cory said as he studied his wine.

"Like what?" Cloe asked. Why was he so angry?

"I really underestimated you. Now I know it's more serious as to why we can't be together. But yet, it tortures me to think I can't have you. Do you know what I would do if I saw someone else touch you the way I want to?"

Cloe throat was tightening up. This was getting out of hand again. So if she thought of having a boyfriend while he was around. Was he saying would kill them in a heart beat. She was glad it would soon be over with. Her phone rang and she was glad to answer it. She put a finger in the air at Cory and he calmed down while she was on the phone. It was Rose and she said she was done, everything worked out and she was looking at the pictures right now, they were good. Cloe just said "Really?", so that she didn't have to say more. Rose hung up after she told Cloe all was okay. Cloe hung up to.

"So, was that a friend?"

"No it was my mother, she's sight seeing and they are having a wonderful time. She thinks she has to call me every time she sees something big."

"Oh, how lovely." he said coldly.

"Are we done here? You seem distracted."

"Yes, it's getting late." He said and looked at his watch.

"Okay then. I'll get out of your hair."

"Thanks for having dinner with me. We won't be doing this again." Cory stressed the word 'won't'.

"I'm glad you came to your senses." she meant it, and got up to leave.

Cory looked at her coldly. He waved her on like he was bored with her and she got out while the getting was good. She went to her car and took off. She was glad another night of hell was over. She did however enjoy the story about Cain. She had always wondered where he went.

She got to Rose's house and they went over the pictures. Within a week they would have to find a snake that looked just like the one in the picture. Rose told Cloe about her night and Cloe told Rose about hers. "You what? I guess I didn't quite hear you on the phone." she said when Cloe said she had dinner with Cory.

"I had to; I was worried about him being around and you getting caught."

"Uh-huh." said Rose as if she didn't believe her.

"No, really, Rose. He's super smart and he'd have spotted you with your red hair and all. Then he'd be bugging you to sleep with him, believe me, he's a tough one to turn down."

"You really like him, don't you."

"I'd really like him if he was just normal, but no, he's not worth my soul to have."

"Would that be the punishment for sleeping with a fallen?"

"Yes."

"Oh, I didn't know that. Okay, I'll quit bugging you about him."

"That's okay, I think he is adorable. And he told me a story about Cain." Cloe went on to explain who Cain was and how Cory had visited him. Rose said when she was done "I feel sorry for you."

"Whys that?"

"Because you meet someone you like and you can't have him. That must hurt."

"It does."

"Can you change him?"

"No, if he would turn to the good again, it wouldn't matter. Fallen Angels or demons can't be with humans. So if he wants human women, he'd be better off staying whatever he is."

"Oh."

"So the best he could hope for is to change me, but after tonight. I'm not sure if he wants that so much."

"How come?"

"Because I told him that Metatron helps me out to and that really pissed him off. I think he hates Metatron."

"I wonder why?"

"He didn't say really, he just said he was a bore." Cloe said with a shrug.

They laughed at that and made fun of Cory for awhile, quoting how everything was 'such a bore'. Then they went over when they would steal the snake. It would have to be on a week day, they agreed. So they decided to give it a week and then talk about it for the following week. Cloe went home and got ready for bed. As she lay there she wondered why she kept him so close. She knew she couldn't change him. She knew he was dangerous. They knew how to say the right words and tempt people. That's what they were all about. Cloe thought maybe she just missed having a guy interested in her. Not that guy's aren't, but she would never have a boyfriend in the line of work that she does. That would be like putting a target on their back and saying to the enemy "Come get 'em!"

She rolled over on her side and sighed. Maybe she should date all of her friends and sisters exes. Nobody would ever miss those bastards. She giggled to her self and shook her head. Soon she fell asleep.

๛

For the weekend she decided to go rock climbing with her sister Cheryl and they stayed in a motel two hundred miles away. Cheryl's boyfriend was an avid rock climber and they invited Cloe to stay with them. Cloe needed to get away so she went. She had went rock climbing before at the malls when they would have a weekend special and put up a simulated rock climb. Marty and Cloe would usually race to the top. Sometimes she'd win, sometimes she wouldn't. There was no racing this time. This was a real mountain. They needed to take their time and be careful.

When they reached the top they stood on the edge overlooking the land and catching their breath, the sight was beautiful. The land looked greener from all the tree tops. When they got done 'oohing' and 'aawing' over everything, they repelled back down. Cloe didn't know which was more fun, going up or coming down.

They unhooked their harnesses when their feet touched the ground and rolled up cables and put everything in the back of the truck. Cloe didn't want to ride back to camp though and told Cheryl to take off with out her. She wanted to hike the trail back instead. After Marty asked "Are you sure?"

a couple times, they waved at her and drove off down the dirt road. Marty was saying something about needing some alone time anyway. Cheryl slugged him in the arm. Cloe smiled and shook her head at the two.

When they were out of sight Cloe looked for the sign that marked where the beginning of the trail started and took off down it. Every once in a while she would come across a sign that said how far she hiked or what special bird or animal was seen most times in that particular area. She looked around at the sky scraper trees surrounding the trail. They where spaced out enough where you could see far into the woods. Cloe walked at a steady pace and let her mind wonder. She didn't want to think about what she left back home, but her mind went there anyways. She made her self think about other things and finally the thought of owning something like this resort back home kept her mind occupied. She thought about what it could mean for the children or young adults to have a place like this to go to.

As her mind went over plans and dreams she didn't realize the force that was developing behind her until she felt her hair stand up on the back of her neck. She froze and her mind came back to the woods. She looked around with squinted eyes and studied the trees.

Surely not here she thought to herself.

She heard rustling behind her and with her eyes leading her body, she slowly turned around.

She noticed a small breeze blowing some leaves around in a circle, but she didn't feel anything herself. She sighed and turned around fully to watch the leaves swirl and grow. The taller it got with leaves and limbs the more it took shape. Finally at 9 feet it formed into a humanly shape and Cloe ducked at the last minute as a tree limb was swung at her head. Cloe said loudly "But I'm on vacation!" at it and took off running down the trail. Every once in a while her foot was grabbed to trip her up and make her slide on her belly to a stop. She got up to sprint off again. She zigzagged down the path to avoid the things grasp or tree limbs being thrown at her.

When she heard something above her head she would try to look up while running to find that the form would be going from limb to limb to drop tree limbs on her head. She would duck and jump. She would stop just in time to avoid a limb dropping on her head only to take off again. She didn't know how long this trail lasted but she hoped she was close to the camp. Her lungs were on fire. Finally she came across a sign that said 'camp just ahead' and gave it all she had to run into the clearing.

She ran out on green grass but there was loud sounds behind her as limbs were being broke because the thing was hurrying also, trying to get to her. Then she was out in the clearing and the cabins where surrounding her. There were people out everywhere, playing games or picnicking and just walking around visiting. When Cloe came into the clearing the people stopped what they were doing and looked at her. She made her self slow down to a stop and while bending over and grabbing her ribs, looked back behind her at the edge of the forest. All that came through was a small breeze that carried some leaves as the form disappeared into thin air. One of the resort workers came running to her and was asking her a bunch of questions. Cloe was listening but her breathing made it unable to answer his questions of what was going on.

All she could do was breath.

He took it upon himself to figure that an animal was chasing her as the crowd grew around her. She nodded at his inquisitions and thought he provided a good cover to what really happened. Finally she straightened up to wince at the pain in her mid torso. She walked off with a limp toward her cabin as everyone was inspecting the tree lines as if a rabid animal was going to run out at them. The resort worker took that opportunity to remind the visitors how important it was to stay in groups when ever they ventured off.

She made it into the door of the cabin to find Cheryl and Marty at the table having wine with some fresh food. Cheryl took one look at Cloe and put her fork down and got up to come over to Cloe. "What happened?" she said as she looked at Cloe's cut up body. Cloe looked at her knowingly and said for Marty's sake "I fell." Cheryl looked at Cloe as if to say 'here?'. Cloe nodded. Marty came to where they were standing and looked Cloe up and down "Did you fall off something?" and Cloe just agreed as she walked into her room. She knew Cheryl would handle it.

She grabbed her towel and a change of cloths and went to the bathroom to take a shower. As she gingerly undressed she looked at herself in the full length mirror. *Damn!* she shook her head at herself. She took a deep breath and turned the water on and set it to the temperature she wanted before she climbed in. She knew it was going to sting on her fresh scrapes and it took all she had to keep from screaming out as the hot water hit the open cuts.

She got out and dried off. She put ointment on her wounds and after bandaging them up, got dressed. She put on a long summer dress with short puffy sleeves. She put flip flops on her feet. Dinner was tonight with everyone at the resort. It was a special occasion to welcome the guests. She went out to find Cheryl and after everyone was ready they made their way to the big log building in the center of the resort where every one originally checked in or out.

There were a lot of new faces and everyone was so friendly. Some of the people asked her if she was doing better after that episode from earlier that day. Cloe nodded and smiled but didn't offer any explanation. She figured it was better not to. For dinner they had several round tables that had the guests names to seat them. When Cloe found her seat she sat down. Then Cloe had to tell every one what she did for a living. It was like that around the table. Everyone was introducing themselves and telling a little bit about themselves. It was an enjoyable time. The night ended and Sunday came and they packed up and went home.

❧

Cloe drove home and busied herself around her house. She worked out and meditated. She saw her and Cory. They were at a stand off. Then suddenly he was choking her. She was fighting for her breath. She came out of her meditative trance trying to catch her breath. She got up and went to see Madam Agnes. She drove her car through the alley and parked in the back. She made her way through the door and went into the living room. Madam was sitting there watching Oprah. Cloe said "Hi." as aloud as she could and Madam looked up from the TV. She got to her feet and said "Watcha doin chil?" Cloe told her the plan on stealing the snake and asked if Madam could help in any way. Madam said she could and she cooked up an invisibility spell for Rose. She would need it, but she had to use in the five minutes she needed, then it was no good. Cloe waited for Madam Agnes to charge the powder. Madam went into her ritual and dance. When she was done she handed the little pouch to Cloe. "Takes care ovit chil, it will protec' her when she needz it."

"I will Madam, thanks for your help."

"Noda problem chi, now I gots ta as ya sometin."

"Anything."

"I think I seen yer fella at da store de udda day."

"I don't have a fellow, Madam."

"I knows ya don't chil, butcha gotta watch this in, becuz I seen the look in hiz eye, and he wants ta be wit yo real bad like, I seen it az plain az day, when I sees him, I haz a vision of yins togetha. I gots an eerie feelin. He'll make ya mad in the mind, and he'll take your soul."

"Yes, I know Madam Agnes. I'm watching him. He's part fallen angel, part demon."

"Maybe dats why he was watchin me too. Like he knew wat waz in my mind."

"I'll be careful. I promise."

They hugged each other and Madam looked sad as she left. She went to Walmart and shopped around for personal items. She looked at cloths and went to the music and movie sections. She picked out some new releases that she could watch when she got back home. She paid the cashier and left. Then she swung by a fast food joint and got her some food for her movies. When she got home she fed her animals, checked her messages, and plopped herself down on the sofa after she put in a movie. She watched Fifty First Dates with Adam Sandler and Drew Barrymore. It was hilarious. Then she watched Click with Adam in it to. When she was done with that it was time for bed.

The next morning after coffee she went to work. Chris was in a sour mood. "What's the matter?" Cloe asked.

"I don't know. All the sudden Cory is backing out of the deal with me about the rest of the firm. I don't know what we did to piss him off but he's pissed. He looked at her suddenly and said "You didn't do anything stupid did you?"

"What's that suppose to mean? And no, I just had dinner with him, thank you very much."

"Then I don't know what's the matter!?"

"Let me go talk to him." Cloe said as she bit her lip. She hated to see Chris upset.

"What good would that do?"

"I don't know, maybe it will do something, maybe it won't. I don't think you'll have anything to worry about with the rest of them though, if that's what you're worried about."

"That's what I'm worried about!" Chris said as he slammed down the quotes on his desk.

"I'll go see what's up. I might even kill him!" Cloe said over her shoulder as she left Chris's office.

She knew he wouldn't take the killing part seriously, even though she was.

She got into her car and drove the 6th street. She parked her car and made her way into the firm. She didn't bother with the lady at the desk, she knew her way up. She couldn't tell if the lady was protesting or not though. The elevator doors closed shut. Cloe pushed a button to go to the top floor. With a ding she was going up.

What was she doing?

She was asking for it.

It's for Chris she told herself.

She didn't know what she'd say to him but she had to make him change his mind. The doors came open and Cloe walked with determination towards Cory's office doors. With Linda trying to stop her she walked past her and flung the doors open to his office. The doors banged against the wall and she walked in. Cory was on the phone and by his expression; he was surprised to see her. He stared at her while he talked to who ever was on the other end. He finally said his good bye and hung up. "What are you doing here?"

"Why are you treating Chris like this, he didn't do anything to you!"

"Why are you so protective of him?" Cory shot back.

"Because he has been my friend for years, ever sense we were five, he's like a brother to me."

"Well maybe I don't like his work."

"That's not it and you know it! You're taking it out on him that I won't give in to you."

"So what if I am. Are you here to say he's worth you changing your mind?"

"Do you really want me to change my mind because you made me, or would you want me willingly?" Cloe said and folded her arms over her chest.

The words just came out of her mouth.

If she was smart she would just tell Chris there would be other prospects.

She didn't know what she was doing or what she meant by the words she spoke. Cory seemed to think this over. He stared at Cloe and he slid his eyes down her body. She rolled her eyes at him and shook her head and he grinned. He picked up the phone and dialed Chris's number. He apologized for his behavior and said that everything was back on schedule. After telling Chris that he thought he found a mistake in the blueprint, but it was a misunderstanding on his part. He promised that it would never happen again while he looked at Cloe as if to say 'there' and then he hung up the phone.

"There, now what do I get for that?" Cory asked as he sat back in his chair.

Cloe heard his promise and was taken back. She didn't know why but she was very grateful.

She would die for Chris.

"This!" Cloe said and walked over to him and kissed him on his lips.

If he could have fallen over he would have.

He should have grabbed her and kept her there but he wasn't thinking straight.

"Now isn't that better? You can draw more flies with honey, not vinegar." she said to him and she walked out. Cory let her; he was still trying to figure out what just happened. She went back to work and Chris hugged her as soon as he saw her. He patted her on the back. He said he didn't know how she did it, but she did it. Cloe wasn't telling him what she did, she didn't want him to get his hopes up. She sat down at her desk and put her face in her palms.

What am I doing! she thought.

The rest of the week came and went. Cory called her on Saturday. He wanted to know if she wanted to go horse back riding. She said yes and promised to meet him at the local riding stables. He offered to use Lance's ranch horses but Cloe wanted some place public. She had to be there at one. She didn't know what she was doing, always going out with him. She knew she had to kill him one day. Cloe guessed that was why she did it. One day one of them would not be here. Maybe Madam was right, he was getting inside her head. Would it make her chicken out when it came time? She didn't want to delve in the possibility.

She arrived at one and he was there in jeans and a tee shirt. She thought she would write a country song about something that goes along the lines of when a fallen angel wore blue jeans and a tee shirt. He was fine to look at. Cloe swallowed real hard and walked up to him. He had already paid, so there was nothing left to do but pick out a horse and ride. He picked a strong black gelding. She picked a Paint. They went off on a well beaten trail. They did not talk much as the horses made their way down the trail. Cloe looked around and enjoyed the scenery. Cory was watching her. Finally he cleared his throat and asked "Are you enjoying yourself?"

"Yes, I love horses."

"You do? Do you ride much?

"All the time, you?"

"I have no use for a horse, really. Along time ago Chris told me you might like this."

"Yes I do. The other day I went rock climbing, have you ever done that?"

He looked at her. "Why would you want to do that?"

"It's great exercise. It's hard to do sometimes." She looked at him sideways. *He wouldn't have much trouble* she thought.

"You humans do the funniest stuff for entertainment." he said with a shake of his head.

"And what do you do for entertainment?"

"Gamble, we love to gamble. And…other things." He said coolly.

Cloe didn't want to know what the 'other things' were, she had a pretty good idea, after all, she quoted a hide-a-bed for his office. They rode some more and some people passed by them coming in off the trial ride. A woman looked at Cory with bedroom eyes. He waved at her with a smile on his face. Cloe rolled her eyes. Cory saw her and laughed. She shook her head at him.

"What's the matter with that? She was just showing her appreciation for a good looking man." he quipped.

"Is that all we are to you fallen or demons?" the question slipped out before she had thought about what she had just asked.

"Yes, pretty much. You can't give us any thing but. We have our own money. This means we have our own…everything. And with money we can have a lot of women. We don't need someone to think for us or give us any help. We are stronger than humans, and smarter."

"Gee, thanks." she said.

"Well, you and a few others are an exception to the rule, I'm not the only fallen or the demon who has thought of you, but the others know not to mess with you, Lance's orders."

"Why?" Cloe asked, surprised.

"I don't know. I think Lance has a side purpose, but I don't know what it is. Lance is the boss though. Lance thinks highly of you as a human. That says a lot."

"I don't know why, after all, I beat up his nephew." Cloe snorted.

"Allan is a hair brained idiot. Lance really doesn't need him for anything. If you fight with a fallen or demon, which I know you have done in the past, it has nothing to do with this group of fallen that you have currently got involved with. The demons just hate you basically."

It made Cloe think then over Allen's purpose in anything, except there's strength in numbers as far as the ritual goes. They rode some more and Cory asked her "Why did you kiss me?" Cloe laughed at the question. Cory got red in the face; he wasn't used to being laughed at. Cloe thought *good, now you*

know how it feels and said "I don't know. I guess I wanted to."
She looked ahead of her at the scenery.

"Really?"

"Yes, I wouldn't have done it if I didn't mean it." She all
but whispered at the end of her answer.

"But I thought you said…" Cloe didn't let him finish. She
put up her hand to hush his words.

"I did say it, and I meant it, and you know it. There will
come a day when we'll have to be who we are. I guess it's up to
us when we decide on when. But I cannot have sex with you
Cory. I can't lose my soul for something that is short term and
useless. Even, and I use the term loosely, even if I did sleep
with you, I'd hate you for it and still would try to kill you in
the end, so, its better if we just skip that part. You wouldn't
make me happy anyways. I want one man and I want one man
to want only me."

"Why do most women insist on that?" Cory asked.

"Do you know how many diseases are spread because of
infidelity?"

"We don't have to worry about that I guess." He said with
a shrug.

"Well, we do." Cloe said flatly. "And there are other reasons
that would take me all day, so I really don't want to talk about
it anymore."

"So, the kiss, it was just to get your way?" Cory said
incredulously.

"Did you not get your way too?"

"But I want more!"

"You can't have more!"

Cory sighed and looked at the saddle horn. He was
thinking and Cloe wondered what about. Cloe looked at him
and he said "You know, I never met anyone who made me
wish I was something rather than what I am now. But I know
I could never have just you, I'm not made that way."

"I know, its not your fault. There are a lot of things that are out of our hands Cory, whether you like to believe that or not." They made their circle and came in off the trail ride. Two ladies took the horses from them and Cloe thanked them and told them they had lovely horses. They just nodded at her but they smiled big at Cory. Cory winked at one while handing the reins over. Cloe watched over her shoulder as they made their way to the parking lot. The girls were giggling and watching Cory walk away. Cory didn't seem to care. After awhile he stopped in front of Cloe but she walked forward and around him so she could stop a few feet away from him. "I guess I'll be seeing ya around." Cory said softly. He stared at her.

"I'm sure of it." Cloe said with a nod.

"Do you ever tell yourself your crazy for being here?" He asked.

"All the time." she said.

With that he turned and got into his truck. Cloe watched him drive away and waved. When he was out of sight Cloe put her arms up to her head and screamed.

Then she jumped up and down and kicked at a rock. *Why couldn't it be different?* she thought. *God, I hope you've made a human that looks like him and I find him* she thought as she looked up above her into the sky. *That would be nice, right Cloe!* Cloe got in her car and drove away.

She got home and fell on the sofa and put a pillow on her tummy. When's the last time she had a boyfriend anyways? She really didn't have time for one.

Maybe that was what her problem was.

Maybe she needed male company.

She knew of plenty of men that would take her out. No strings attached. She went to her bedroom dresser and found a little address book. She began to look up some numbers. There was Rob from work, he's kind of a dork though, and she didn't need any drama at work. So any males from work were out of the question. She paged through the pages. There was James. She had met James at a grocery store. He asked her out and they went once. He said at the end of the date that he would like to do it again and for her to call him. Then she never did call him again. She tried to remember why. Oh well. She dialed his number.

"Hello?" the voice said.

"Is James there?" Cloe asked nervously

"Speaking."

"James, this is Cloe. Remember me? We met at the store you worked at some time ago and went on a date."

"Ya, I remember you, whacha been up to?"

"You know how you said we could go out again sometime? Well, I was wondering if we could tonight."

"Hell ya. I had plans but I'll cancel them. You wanna meet somewhere?" he said happily.

"Wherever you want."

"How about Cowboys, that all right with you?"

"Yep, thanks. See you around eight?" Cloe asked

"Okay, see ya then, sexy." he said and hung up.

Sexy?

Now she remembered why she never called him back. All he wanted to do was go out to bars and taverns.

And play pool.

And call her sexy.

She was bored the last time. Oh well, maybe she'll get lucky and be done with him.

You're no better than Cory she thought.

Oh well, she didn't do this all the time.

She wasted time around the house and eight o'clock came. She dressed in a mini skirt and tank top. She put on ankle boots and went to find Cowboys. It was on 27th street and it was packed. She didn't know how she'd find him in here but she'd try. He was waiting by the door for her and when he saw her he grabbed her and yelled "Wow, you look great." over the music.

"Thanks." She said and followed him to the table.

"You want something to drink?"

"Ya." and she ordered a mixed drink.

They drank and got caught up with each other. A song came one over the speakers and he grabbed her hand "Lets dance!" he yelled. She followed him to the dance floor and they danced. She was having fun. If she had her head in the game she would have checked the place out first. That was the furthest thing from her mind.

So she didn't see Cory off to one side with a bunch of other deadskins. Cory was worked up over what happened that day that he had to get relief. He planned to get it somewhere tonight.

But he saw her, instantly.

He saw her dancing with a young man. He felt enraged, and went to get up and go to her.

But then he smiled.

If she would have seen him, then she would have remembered that the fallen or powerful demons can project themselves into another human body. Cory smiled; he couldn't pass up an opportunity like this. It would put him in a slow mode when he returned; it took great strength to pull this off. The fallen can't do it all the time or their body would age quicker.

She'd be worth it he thought.

"James, I have to be honest with you, I kind hoped we could have some, um, alone time?" Cloe said in his ear while they danced. Suddenly James was pushed into her by another person who wildly dancing next to them.

Or so she thought

He hung on her shoulder for a minute. She pulled back to check his reaction.

He took on an eerie appearance to her, like he couldn't breathe.

She took his arm and shook it gently.

"James, are you alright?" The way he stared at her, she had a feeling she'd saw that look before, somewhere else. Then he shook his head and asked "Did you say something? Let's get out of here." If Cloe was paying attention she would have seen that James wasn't the same.

James was in Cory's body, sitting at a table.

The others at Cory's table would know that Cory had projected himself, and that Cory left them a new victim, who couldn't do much but sit there. The demons liked it when the fallen let them have their fun.

James looked at Cloe and said "Where would you like to go?"

Cloe blushed and said "How 'bout my place?" James smiled and said "You drive."

It was James body, which that was it. Cory had complete control now, even down to feeling her hold his hand. She led him to her car and he got in the passenger side. She got behind the wheel and went to start the car. He grabbed her all the sudden and kissed her deeply. He didn't want to stop. Cloe was pulling away.

"Um, you wanna wait till we get to the house?" she said with a giggle.

"Do I have to?" He asked.

"We are in public." she replied.

"So?" He said with a low tone.

"You'll have to wait." She giggled.

He smiled and nodded. As she drove James would play with her hair or trace her jaw line.

She drove out and James looked out the window. He was remembering every inch of the way. She drove for a half an hour. James kept sliding his hand under her mini skirt.

She didn't remember him being so bold, or handsy.

Oh well she thought, she didn't mind tonight.

Tonight she was going to forget everyone and everything. She parked her car, Gigi was out to pasture but Buddy started growling. Cloe bent down to scratch his ears "It's alright boy." James just stared at the dog. Cloe fed him and the horse quickly. Buddy wouldn't move from his spot and his hair stood straight up.

"I've never seen him act like that, I'm sorry."

"That's okay. He's probably just being protective." James said looking down at the dog.

Cloe brought him into her house. And like the vampires myths, now Cory can come in when ever he wanted. The rose brick dust that his sight caught like a glowing line around her house didn't work anymore either, because he didn't mean to hurt her, just the opposite. Cloe didn't notice a thing, except that he was unusually quiet. Cloe turned to ask him if he wanted anything and James grabbed her and kissed her all over until she was breathless; His hands were everywhere as he took off her clothes. When she was fully undressed he held her back and looked at her. She had to focus on his face. The way he looked at her was as if he was imprinting her to memory.

"You alright?" Cloe asked.

"You are so breath taking." he said softly.

She looked around the room nervously. She tried to move in but he stayed her. He was quite strong for as little as he was. She started feeling uncomfortable. He sensed it and brought her to him. They kissed again and she undressed him. Her mouth going places and he groaned. His hands went in her hair and his head fell backwards. He had done this with so many times with so many girls. But it will never be like this. He brought her head up after awhile and pulled her to him.

He dropped her on the couch and he entered her. He thought he was going to go mad. How many times had he wished to be doing this very thing? Cloe gasped. She didn't know he was this good, or she would have suggested it along time ago. They made love all night long. They were gentle with each other at times, rough the next. She did every position she could think of, and he even knew more. He was strong, she was amazed. They were finally spent and it was five in the morning. She took him by his hand and pulled him into the bedroom after she asked him if he wanted to leave. He refused and they went to her bed.

They kissed tenderly, and Cloe thought she could get used to this. As she lay in his arms she fell asleep. When he felt her breathing, James let his mind wonder and found Cory's body sitting at a house with a demon woman doing him.

He smiled to himself.

He really enjoyed this. He didn't want it to end, but he couldn't stay in this body forever. When he certain that she was in a deep sleep, he crept out of the bed slowly. He looked at her for as long as he could. She lay there naked. He kissed her lips one more time and left the room. He crept passed Buddy but didn't wake him and made his way home.

∽

The next morning Cloe didn't wake up until one in the afternoon. She opened one eye then the other. Her brain was remembering and she brought her head up to look for James. She looked around the house for him but he was no where to be found. Maybe he had a friend come and get him she thought. She didn't worry about it though. She laughed and skipped around the house and had a world of weight lifted off her shoulders. There's nothing some good sex couldn't cure. She worked out and did her cool down when the phone rang. It was Rose.

"Where have you been all night and day?"

"Oh I've been out. And I got me some, and I'm feeling groovy" Cloe said and giggled.

"Really? Who was it?" Cloe went on to tell Rose about last night and how amazing it was. She gushed about James and how amazing he was. Rose said "You lucky dog." Rose was dating too, but she was like Cloe, it was hard to find someone decent.

"I just called to ask you about tomorrow." Rose finally said.

"What's tomorrow?" Cloe went blank.

"Wow, he really did screw your brains out!" said Rose, laughing.

"Oooohh," said Cloe as she remembered and started laughing too. "The snake thing."

"Yah, the snake thing. Are you sure you'll be able to do this?"

"Yes, and by the way I have some powder for you from Madam Agnes." Cloe went on to explain about how to use it and the warning Madam gave. The news made Rose feel better. "Okay. So are we on for tomorrow?"

"Ya, I'll swing by for lunch and we'll do this."

"Okay, we can do this."

"We can do this, Rose." Cloe said.

They hung up. Rose would do whatever she needed to calm herself and Cloe did the same. It was a big thing to pull this off. *God, please let us do this* she prayed silently. There was a knock at the door and Cloe went to go answer it. There was a lady standing at the door holding flowers. Cloe pushed open the screen.

"Can I help you?"

"Yes I'm looking for Cloe."

"That's me." Cloe said.

"Well then, these are for you my dear." The lady smiled.

Cloe took the big bouquet of flowers. There were all kinds from white roses to tiger lilies and some wild and exotic flowers were included. The lady drove off leaving Cloe to look at the flowers. She found the card and it said 'for last night, I'll never forget it.' It wasn't signed. Cloe smiled happily and went in the kitchen to find a vase. She didn't have one so she used a decorative drinking glass. She smelled at them again. Then she set them on the table.

She wondered if she should call James to thank him but decided against it. She wasn't looking for a boyfriend anyways. He would know she appreciated the flowers. She was on cloud nine the rest of the day. She brushed Gigi down after she went for a ride and hummed to herself. She even gave Buddy a bath. The phone rang and she answered it. On the other end was Roxanne and she sounded breathless. "Cloe?" she asked.

"Yes, it's me." Cloe answered.

"Are you busy?" Roxanne said in an awkward way.

"No, why? Are you okay?"

"Well I was kind of needing your help."

"Ya, sure. What's the matter?"

"Well, my sister had her friends over last night at her house and they played with the Quija board. She called me and said they are actually locked in the house and weird things are happening. I wouldn't have believed her if she didn't sound so frightened. Can you come with me over there and see what's going on?"

"I'll be right over." Cloe said and hung up to quickly grab her things and got into her car. As she drove she had to remember where Roxanne lived. She made it in thirty minutes and Roxanne was outside waiting on her. Cloe pulled up to the curb and Roxanne opened the door and climbed in. Cloe pulled away as she was shutting the door.

"Why didn't they call you last night?" Cloe said.

"I don't know, I couldn't make anything out because she was so hysterical and screaming over the phone."

"That doesn't sound good." Cloe shook her head. They made it to her sisters' house in an hour. Roxanne's sister lived on the outskirts of town. It was a small two story white house but Cloe could tell immediately when she stepped out that there was something very wrong there. The air was still and nothing moved. The house looked sad. There was no noise coming from the inside either. All the windows were blacked out but not by human hand. Roxanne looked at Cloe and said "Well?"

"Ya, there is definitely something wrong here, you wanna come or stay behind? I understand either way." Cloe said over hear shoulder. Roxanne looked around nervously and then shrugged. "I guess I'll come with you." and started walking with Cloe up to the porch. It was as if whatever was in the house knew Cloe because it groaned all the sudden and the porch jerked once and creaked. Roxanne froze and her hands came out as if she was falling. Cloe looked back at Roxanne and after checking her and they made eye contact, Cloe once again started walking to the front door. She tried the knob and it wouldn't turn. She looked around and Roxanne said "Should I call the girls and let them know we're here?"

"No not yet. They'll just get more hysterical and then I couldn't hear anything. Whatever is in there is now focused on me; the girls will be alright for a moment." Roxanne nodded and Cloe stepped back to look at the windows, She was frantically going over everything she knew about spirits and entrapment or breaking an entrapment. She needed a mix of cayenne pepper and sea salt with sulfur. Cloe went back to her car and opened up the trunk to find the mix in a duffle bag. She brought out a clear bottle that had the mix inside it and after shaking it while seeing how much was in there; she hoped she had enough as she closed the trunk to make her way back to the door. She began pouring it in her hand and sprinkling it at the front door and window on the porch as she chanted...

"The presence that stands upon the stairs,
The unseen hands that move the chairs,
The lights that play across the wall,
The stains that stay, the plates that fall,
The mist, the chill, the wandering scents,
This spell must remove them hence."

As Cloe worked around the door and windows the house groaned more and the windows started vibrating, Roxanne started backing down the porch stairs and the girls inside started screaming out. Cloe hoped it was for fear and not pain. After the shaking stopped it almost seemed as if the air had suddenly got lighter and the sun began to shine down. Cloe heard a bird chirp somewhere in the distance as she went to try to the door again. It came open and Cloe went in with Roxanne not far from her but with less confidence. Roxanne called to her sister and suddenly there was scampering from somewhere above them as the girls made their way to the stairs. The girls all but knocked each other down trying to get down the stairs and out the door, rushing by Cloe. Roxanne's sister grabbed Roxanne's arm and begged her to leave with them. Cloe told Roxanne to go ahead and calm them down and get the story while she looked around. Roxanne put her arm around her sobbing sister and they walked out while Cloe put her hands in her pockets of her pants and went into the living room to look around.

The Ouija sat on the floor with the candles around it. The candles burnt all the way down and wax was every where. There was a notebook beside it and Cloe picked it up. It had the questions that the girls asked and the answers the Ouija gave. At first, like always, it was just a bunch of garble but then the answers started making sense. They were real simple answers and the more they played the more the answers became sentences, and the sentences became meaner and more threatening. Cloe looked for a name because people always asked for one and how they died.

She noticed Eomiahe was spelled and she nodded in acknowledgement.

To the girls it probably looked like more garble.

They had a serious spirit on their hands.

Cloe looked around the room as everything was a mess, as if someone was looking for a hidden object. Sometimes Cloe would find blood splatter here or there and her thoughts went to the girls. The crucifix on the wall hung upside down and Cloe went to it and with it cupped in her hand, said a prayer over it, then put it back on the wall upright.

There was a scurrying noise and Cloe saw something from the corner of her eye move. She looked back to the board and the planchette was beginning to move by itself. Cloe looked around and then went to it to see what was going on. She knew that it could move by itself if the spirit was still in the room to move it. Cloe didn't waste time "Who are you?" she asked it. The planchette spelled out Y O U A R E G O I N G T O D I E. Cloe just shook her head. "Ya someday I will... well, dipshit, enjoy your time here because when the priest comes to bless this house then you, are, going, to, die." and after giving her evil laugh like on the movies, turned around and went out the door.

Cloe walked down the stairs and looked at the group of girls that were standing beside her car with Roxanne. They looked scared and tired, some of them had makeup smeared around their eyes from crying. Cloe walked up to them and said "What happened?" All the sudden the girls started talking at once and Cloe put up her hand and said. "One at a time, please." and Roxanne's sister began to speak and told Cloe that it was all okay at first and they even stopped playing because they were getting tired. But when the lights went off then things started happening like objects flying through the room or noises or a figure of a man appearing in the bed with some of them. They all were nodding their head as Roxanne's sister talked. She went to explain that some of them got cut out of no where and one got pushed down the stairs also. "Why didn't you call last night?" Roxanne asked.

"Because every time we went to use the phone we were hit with something!" said one of the girls and another one went on to add, "So we all just huddled in the closet until this morning."

"Well is everyone okay or does anyone need to go to the ER?" Cloe asked. After everyone mumbled no then Cloe said "Get in your cars and go home, everything will be alright for now and if you notice anything weird going on with you or your surroundings again, call me and let me know right away." She stressed the last part sternly. The girls nodded and got into their cars to drive off. Roxanne's sister waved everyone off after hugging them. Cloe turned to her and said "You need to stay somewhere for a while until a priest comes out here to bless your house. It's not safe in there until then."

Sheila shivered and looked at the house and then asked,"Can I get any clothes out of there?" Cloe nodded and said "Ya, I'll go with you." They made their way back to the house. Sheila bulked at door and Cloe put her hand on Sheila's back. "Its alright, they'll attack me before they attack you again." and Sheila continued on and they went to her bedroom so she could pack quickly. Sheila asked when would the preacher come out and Cloe answered she did not know but she would let Roxanne know something soon. They went back outside and Sheila locked up her house. They got into Cloe's car and drove away. Sheila's tension was leaving her as more miles were put between them and the house. Cloe took them to Roxanne's house and told Roxanne she would call her later and drove back home.

She went in her door and saw her flowers and felt better. She got on the phone and called Father Scovley. He answered and Cloe told him about the house and what went on there and asked him if he would bless it. He agreed and got directions and Cloe told him the owner would bring the key to him sometime tomorrow. He was fine with that and they ended the conversation and Cloe called Roxanne.

"Hey, it's me, Cloe."

"Hey." Roxanne said

"How's your sister?" Cloe asked.

"She took a shower and fell asleep here on the couch. Did you find out anything?"

"Yes, go by the Catholic Church tomorrow and ask for Father Scovley, he'll need a key to the house so he can bless it. Also he wants to know if your sister wanted to be cleansed and blessed also, so be prepared."

"Oh, okay. I bet she'll go for that after what happened last night. I think she learned a lesson."

"Well that's good. Make sure she keeps an eye out for her friends for any weird stuff so we can nip it in the bud right away. I can't stress that enough."

"Okay. I will, and thanks Cloe, for everything. I don't know how you do it so calmly."

"Ah." Cloe shrugged, embarrassed. "I've seen worse."

They said there good byes and Cloe hung up. She smelled her flowers and sat on the couch and remembered her night with James and smiled. She got up and leisurely made some supper and turned on the TV to watch for a little bit.

That night she went to bed early and was excited, happy and nervous all at the same time. She had butterflies in her tummy. She thought *I bet this is what it feels like to get married.* She shook her head at herself. *Give me a break* she sighed and went to sleep cuddling the pillow where James laid his head. She could still faintly smell him.

The next morning she went to work and kept looking at the clock nervously. Rob was out with Billy learning that end of the job and she caught Chris up so she was back to her old job. She busied herself as much as she could and finally it was time to do what they had planned. She picked Rose up at work and Rose said to stop by the car to get the snake. It was in a mesh bag. It was big. Rose had to by a big back pack so she could get into the house with it. She bought it at a pet store out of town. It was the only store that had one the same size and color.

"You owe me some money also, that thing was expensive!" Rose said.

"Okay. When did you buy it?"

"Saturday morning, it stayed at dads in the barn. I had my brother feed it, Yuck!" she said and shivered. "It eats mice whole."

"Eww.." Cloe squinched up her nose.

They made their way and to the house and parked down the road. They wanted to have a clean getaway. Cloe hid in the bushes as Rose nonchalantly walked in with another group. They didn't seem to mind and she was in. Cloe told her not to forget she had the powder. They had two way radios and Rose would tell Cloe when she needed the diversion. Rose made her way through the people and everyone mostly wanted to see the snake. It slept to gather energy, but it was transformed. You could tell because it wasn't in a cage anymore, it was just lying in the circle. It was a good thing they just fed this snake, as it lay sleeping also. Rose hoped it would stay asleep as she switched them. She would have to be real careful. When she got as close as she could, she whispered to Cloe through the two way "Now!"

Cloe was outside and she took a baseball bat to some of the lawn ornaments and went all bizzerk. She started hollering and screaming that she wanted justice and that she will avenge her God to these people. Sense all the big shots were gone to work; there wasn't really one there who could take on Cloe. When Rose had enough people gone outside to see what Cloe was screaming about, she took the powder that Madam Agnes gave her and threw it in the air. As it floated down she stepped into it and waited a moment. Then she was lightening quick. She gingerly took out the snake as to not disturb it and laid it down, she cautiously grabbed the other and put it back in her bag, She zipped it up and walked away.

Rose looked around and was amazed that no body seemed to care or notice as she was walking out the back door. They went about their business as she made her escape. She radioed Cloe she was out and heading to the car. She would be in the car in a jiffy and go after Cloe. Cloe was getting ready to take on two guys, who was really no match for her. They had to try to subdue her though or they'd pay for letting her get away. She ran around the lawn though trying to stay away from them. She called them names and they went after her, only for her to dodge their moves and watch them fall to the ground. Every one else just watched and laughed from the front porch area.

Rose drove up and went through the circle drive and Cloe got in, yelling for everyone to repent and search for God. Then they drove away and headed out of town again. Cloe and Rose went to the capitol where you can adopt or give away pets to a certain save the animals foundation. When they got at a safe distance, they traded sides and Cloe drove. She was the fastest driver and Rose worked her magic. She did a spell on crossing the demon and painted some fancy emblems on the snake so that it couldn't transform back to a spirit until the snake itself died. That would buy them some time.

They went into the building and filled out all of the papers. They told the lady that her boyfriend was trying to kill the snake and that was why it was here. So if anybody should call asking about it then to keep it a secret. The lady wrote all of this down on the snake's papers and said she totally understood. Before they left they went to see it in its new cage. They didn't have a snake like this, so they were going to keep it for display for the kids to enjoy. It was much larger than it should be, so they were more interested in it for study, they told Cloe and Rose. The girls smiled at each other. Then they saw that on the cage was a name plate in gold that read 'Mr. Slithers'. The snake was awake now, and was going around the cage putting his nose in the corners. It couldn't talk like before when it was at the house, because Rose put a crossing spell on it. All it could do was stick out its forked tongue. Cloe and

Rose smiled at it through the glass and said "Good bye Mr. Slithers."

⌒

They made their way home. They were nervous as heck. They hoped that nobody noticed the snake being different. They would realize it when it snaked off the circle. By then it would be too late. And they wouldn't be able to conjure Botis because he was trapped in the other snake. Even if they were found out, they still had the upper advantage. Rose wasn't in any real danger; it was Cloe that they would blame.

Cloe's heart skipped a beat when she realized that Cory would come after her, no doubt, and he would be down right enraged. Oh well, it had to be that way. They made their way back to work and Cloe dropped Rose off, telling her she would call her later and Cloe went back to work. Nobody showed up and nobody called. She imagined the snake was still in the circle then. Which it was, just sleeping in a curled up ball. Cloe thanked the Lord for letting her pull this off and went home. When she got there her mom and sister called. She talked to one while looking at her flowers. She hung up on one. Then the phone rang again and she talked to the other. Then she made some supper and looked at her flowers some more. Then did her usual chores and went to bed.

The rest of the week went by and Cloe heard nothing. On Friday morning she walked in and Chris had everybody around the drawing table again. Cloe made her way over and Chris had his hands up and everyone shut up to listen.

"We have visitors again this morning, and it's the same group that has the law firm on 6th street, they are doing a check up so it shouldn't be anything big, but still you know what's expected of you, right?" and everyone nodded their heads and murmured yes.

"Okay then. Lets get to work." and everyone went back to their desks. Cloe knew though, that they had found out the truth. They were on their way over to see Cloe. She took a big breath and exhaled through her lips. She didn't think they would do anything here, but one never knows. Her stomach was in knots. It didn't take them long to show up. There wasn't very many of them. There were mostly fallen and few humans. Cory and Lance were leading the group in. It didn't take long for Cory's eyes to find her. She could feel it but she didn't dare look up. She pretended to be busy. She finally looked at him and could tell by his set jaw that something was up. Lance almost had the same look. They greeted Chris with false kindness. He didn't catch it. They made their way to the drawing desk and looked at blue prints. After they checked on their business, they made their way around the room, without Chris. He was busy changing something on a drawing.

They made their way to Cloe's desk and Cloe looked up at them. "To what do I owe this pleasure?"

Cory leaned on her desk "Oh, I think you know." He said through clenched teeth.

Cloe looked innocently back and forth from Cory to everyone else in his group. "Know what?"

Cory smiled "You want to play that way, huh?"

"I don't know what you're talking about Cory."

"Where were you Monday?" Cory leaned in.

"I was here." Cloe pointed down at her desk with one finger.

"You expect me to believe that?"

"You can ask everybody here, I was here." It's a good thing nobody really paid any attention to her. They knew she came in, and they knew she went home. Cory straightened up and crossed his arms over his chest. Cloe said "suit yourself." under her breath and called Ashley's name out.

Ashley, of course, came right over.

Cloe looked at Ashley and asked "Ash, was I here Monday for work?" Ashley looked confused but looked at the ceiling as if to think about it. Her face lit up "Yes, I remember you walked in behind me and someone was teasing you 'cause you had a smile on your face, and they said you got laid cause you had a hickey on your neck and…"

"That's enough Ashley, thanks!" Cloe interrupted suddenly, and stood up to turn Ashley around and gently shove her away. She had forgotten about the hickey. Cory caught every word and reaching out, made Cloe turn her head sideways. He touched it with his thumb lightly before Cloe jerked away and cleared her throat. "Are you happy?"

Cory's gaze was on her, but he really wasn't quite there, he was remembering.

Cloe looked at him and drew her eyebrows together. She'd never seen this look on his face before, like he had just completely forgotten where he was, and his focus slowly shifted back to her and he really looked at her this time. He sighed and said "I don't know how you did it, but I know you did."

"Did what, what happened?" Cloe said impatiently.

Lance came forward then, he was mad but it showed very little. Cloe stared into his eyes and she could see the red in them. Cloe's eyebrows drew up as if she said aloud "Humph, look at that." and Lance didn't say anything. He grabbed Cory's arm and they left. Cloe knew that Lance would tell Cory it was time to deal with her, and Cory had to listen because Lance was the boss. She got lucky today, she should have been an actress.

She finished the day and she went home. She had a thought they may steal her horse or dog for a trade. She called Rose and told her about the meeting, and that she feared for her own animals in case they would come and steal them, making Cloe trade a snake for her loved animals. Rose agreed and with her mom and dads permission, she came with a truck and trailer and brought Gigi to her parent's house to board him and Buddy went home with Rose.

She went to Rose's later to spend the night. She was bothered by Cory's reaction. The way he touched her neck, it was strange. Why would he want to touch another man's mark? Unless he wished it was his. She knew he was probably furious with her right now. She didn't want to stay alone. She called Sue from her cell phone to see how she was doing. They visited for awhile and Sue invited her over for the day. They were going out on their boat for the whole day. Cloe said that sounded good and agreed to be there around nine in the morning. Then they hung up. Rose and Cloe went out to eat at a local taco place. She was grateful to be someplace public. She knew it wouldn't last forever. It kept her mind off of how much trouble she was in. They went home and watched movies. It was a love story and Cloe's mind went to the night she had with James.

The next morning she went for a boat ride with her sister after stopping by and checking on Gigi. She was enjoying watching her sister and her husband ski and soon it was her turn. She hooked up her skis on the dock and motioned for Greg to take off. She landed on the water with a tug and took off. She loved to ski. As she darted back and forth effortlessly she looked around at other boaters on the lake. Some other boaters waved to her. As she skied she noticed that a wave runner was coming towards her on her right. She wasn't alarmed at first until it seemed that the wave runner wasn't going to stop. Then it drove right for her and at the last minute she maneuvered to avoid a collision with the wave runner. She was looking at the driver to see if maybe they were drunk. That was a common thing on the lake. As she darted back and forth she kept looking at the person on the wave runner. After it missed her the first time it turned around with a splash of water and took after her again. Finally Cloe saw the face. It was a demon! Cloe yelled at Sue because they were talking and really not paying attention. Cloe screamed at Sue and after the third time Sue looked back at her. Cloe was yelling at them to drive faster. Sue was looking at Cloe quizzically and then saw Cloe avoid another collision with the wave runner. Sue finally understood and told Greg to move it. Cloe kept her eye on the wave runner and had to do a lot of maneuvering to avoid it. Any chance she took she made a wave into a ramp and jumped up and over the wave runner as it aimed for her over and over again. Sue and Greg was watching her but also moved quickly around the other boats in the water. Cloe saw Sue motioning at her and pointed for the beach. Sue told Greg to go toward the beach. Sue didn't know what Cloe had planed but she trusted her. Greg gunned it for the beach and at the last minute turned the boat around. Cloe let go of the ropes and headed straight for the sand. She slid across the sand for a moment before falling into the ground. She took off her skis and stood up waiting for the wave runner to either follow or turn around. She knew she had a better chance on something solid. She could be beaten more easily in the water. As she stopped at the edge of the water she saw the wave runner slow down and after watching her for a second, turn around and take off.

She stayed at the edge of the beach and watched for Sue and Greg to come around. They didn't show up and Cloe started getting worried. After watching the water for a few more moments she saw them heading toward her. She waved at them and they waved back. They pulled up some distant away from the beach were people were swimming. Cloe trotted over to them and after wading through waist high water, climbed in the boat.

"Did you see the wave runner?" Cloe asked.

"Yea, Greg chased it for awhile to make sure it went the other way before turning around to get you."

"Oh. That's what took you. I was a little worried that it was after you guys." Cloe said and put her skis up.

"We wanted to make sure it wasn't coming back" Sue said. They talked about it some more while they made their way back to the boat trailer. They loaded up the boat and went home. After she got to Sue's she helped with making supper.

She expected Chris to call her saying that Cory or Lance had pulled the plug at work. He never did. That night after having supper with Sue, and made her way home. While she sat there she knew that the cult was probably trying to figure out how to bring Botis back. They didn't have the snake but there was more than one way to skin a cat. She knew it had to do with the book. She looked at her notes again. She lit some candles and sat down to meditate. She needed answers. She quieted her mind until she couldn't hear or see anything but black. She let her mind drift. She saw angels, she saw them happy and friendly. She looked around, she saw a black cloud. The cloud became angels in the air. There was fire falling from the sky. The angels on the ground were taking a stand. She saw one yell "Guard the Informatory" at her. She looked around. There were angels in a hollowed out circle in the clouds. They were just standing there. Why were they not moving? It was as if they couldn't. Are they prisoners? She looked back at the angel who commanded her and suddenly a big mouth of a dragon opened up, and all she saw was flames engulfing her face. She came out of the trance with a start, and stared down at the floor. What was that all about? she asked herself.

She prayed to God to help her understand the dream. She got up and went to the kitchen. She got out her pen and paper and started writing down what she saw. She looked at her flowers and smiled. She cleared her mind and focused again on the paper. She got several books out and didn't find anything to help her, she went to get the book called 'The Passages of Jubilee', she thumbed through it and found a passage that says the fallen Watchers may be bound in the third heaven, but such books are not studied by any church, many scholars thought they were rubbish.

She went back to her paper and kept the passage fresh in her mind. If the fallen Watchers were in prison in heaven, then is that what she saw? Did she see others trying to free them? Why would they do that? Who would want to free them?

Well, she thought maybe Lucifer for one. But why? If Lucifer is freed then the end is near. She rubbed her eyes. She saw a war in heaven, but it wasn't the old war, it couldn't have been, why would God show her an old war? Then Sue's words hung in the air. She had always said history repeats itself, in as much as the bible as everything else. And it was suppose to be like the days of Noah in the end. Which were the days of giants caused by the fallen mating with humans?

So there was a war coming. And it had to do with Lilith? How did she play into this? There were so many angles and questions that it gave Cloe a headache. She stopped looking at the paper and got up to take some aspirin. She couldn't forget the angels voice command her to guard the informatory. Who was that angel? She had never seen him before. A wise preacher told her that if she didn't understand something, to put it on the shelf. If she was meant to get it she would. But no sense in pushing the answers, God would let her know in time. So she did just that and went to bed.

She woke up and thought about her strange dreams that she had. She dreamt of James but he would turn into a snake and try to kill her, but Cory would rescue her. She was up early so she decided to go to church with Rose's dad again. She checked on Gigi and rode with Wayne to church. When they got back she had lunch with them and Rose showed up. When they had a minute alone, Rose asked if she had heard from anyone yet. She said no but told Rose she felt like they were missing something. When Rose asked what, Cloe couldn't answer. Rose didn't like to see her like this and asked if she heard from James. Cloe smiled and said no. It was a nice change of subject. Cloe went home after her and Rose rode the horses around the farm. She sat on the couch and thought about her vision some more. She wished Michael would come see her. But she knew she would figure it out. She hoped she did it in time. The phone rang and she answered it.

"What are you doing?" It was Cory's voice.

"You know what I wish?"

That put him off guard "What's that?"

"I wish you'd tell me what it is that I'm supposed to do."

"With what?"

"With you."

Cory paused "I think you know the answer to that." he said.

"I know the final answer, I don't know what's suppose to happen between here and then. And you know what?" Cloe asked

"What?" Cory answered.

"You do, but I know you won't tell me."

Cory laughed "What makes you so sure I know?"

"Because you keep me distracted, because we keep playing this game. You either want me to turn and be yours, or you're trying to figure out how much I know that you know."

"Did I ever tell you that you are smart?"

"Yep."

"I can't help but to want you. Would you like to go out?"

"Nope, I think we don't need to go out anymore."

"I see, I'm sorry you feel this way. Is it because you have a boyfriend?"

"I don't have a boyfriend."

"Oh, okay then, do you want a boyfriend?"

"Cory?"

"Yes."

"You remember when we first met?"

"How could I forget."

"Why did you attack me in your office?"

He sighed. He didn't answer for along time, she said his name to make sure he was still there "I'm here. I guess I did it because I was told to look out for you, everyone is made aware of you. I was told that that you were the enemy. I knew you were a demon hunter before I met you. I wanted to hate you, but when I seen how strong you were, it got me scared. So I attacked you."

It was Cloe's turn to sit there and think.

"So now what?" Cory said impatiently

"I don't know. Cory?"

"Yes."

"I'm hanging up now." She placed the receiver slowly and quietly on the phone base. She went to bed feeling sad. It sucked that they were so wrong for each other, yet Cloe had an attraction to him. She knew the day would come and she knew she was going to win.

But she didn't look forward to the fight.

The next day was Monday and it was back to work. Cloe worked at putting in quotes and customer numbers and soon it was lunch. She left and went to a local sandwich and soup diner. She was sitting there eating and across the room she saw James at a table with some other people. She smiled to herself and got up to see him. As she walked up to his table and he was laughing with some guy friends. When he saw her he suddenly looked scared, which slowed Cloe down. She slowly came up to the table and asked James "Can I talk to you?" He acted like he didn't want to but he politely got up and walked away from her.

"How are you?" she asked.

"Fine, I guess." he said quickly and acted like he was in a hurry. He moved around slightly and wouldn't look her in the eye.

"I had fun the other night." she whispered. To her surprise he looked at her like she just slapped him. He stammered and mumbled and Cloe was confused. "What?" she asked "What's wrong with you?"

He looked around and said "I don't remember anything of that night."

Cloe shook her head as if to say 'what?!' "What do you mean, you don't remember?"

"I don't know how to explain this." he said nervously and his brow started to sweat "What I remember is being somewhere I haven't been to before, with some girl I don't know. And it was weird. I had no control of anything but I could see out my eyes. Other than that, it was like I was a...a...puppet...or something."

"Are you kidding me? If you didn't like what happened the other night, just say so!"

"Cloe, I'm telling you the truth. I watched you walk out with me, but it wasn't me. I was somewhere else, in some else's body." he said as he grabbed her arms to make her understand. He thought he was going crazy. Cloe searched his face, he was serious. She didn't know what to say. She said in a whisper "Okay. I believe you. It's alright. Let go of me now."

James took his hands off of her and ran his fingers through his hair. "I don't ever want to see you again." he said and shaking his head, he walked off.

Cloe went back to her seat and stared at her food. She threw it away and drove to work, but she didn't remember doing so. She went to her desk and sat there. Everyone was asking if she was alright, she had a frightful look on her face. Chris asked her if she felt okay. Cloe just nodded to everyone and stared down at her paper with her head in her hand. She replayed the night in her mind started asking herself who was she with then? She went over the night again in her mind, she could swore she heard James whisper "I love you." in the dark. But James swears it wasn't him. He said he saw her walk away with him. How is that possible? She sat up suddenly, so someone was at Cowboys and saw her with him! And what, whoever, jumped bodies and became him? She put her hands to her eyes, *oh my god*, *who was it?* No wonder he didn't act like himself and then it hit her like a ton of bricks.

He looked at her and she had seen that look before, she had seen that look on Cory!!

But how, when? Was he there?

He must have been. *That son of a bitch!*

He got his way after all.

Cloe wanted to jump up and down and scream. She went outside and walked around in the parking lot. She slugged the wall every now and again. *How could she have been so stupid!*

She leaned against the wall and slid down it.

She didn't know, she said towards heaven, she didn't know. *How could this happen?* How could he get his way?

She totally blamed herself, she led him to it. She tried to make him see the ways of the heart, instead she led him on. No wonder he touched the hickey on her neck tenderly, he put it there, he was remembering. He almost looked love stricken. *Give me a break, he can't know love, he's a demon!* she told herself.

She straightened up, well there's no turning back. This was a lesson well learned, but yet, she had feelings for him. She did, even though she didn't want to. But that's what he was good at, seducing women. She shrugged to herself. It was over now, and deep down in her heart, she guessed she had something to remember him by.

Now she was going to kill him.

Then she thought it's a good thing I'm protected. Her mind went to if she had a child, what would that be like? It would be a nightmare. She went to work and everyone stayed clear of her. She had a different look to her and it wasn't very friendly. It was time to stop this madness. She decided it was time to act. She would do something about it. She wished she could ask him. She knew he wouldn't tell her. All of the sudden she had an idea. She was going to see Lance. She told Chris she was going home and didn't wait for a reply. She got into her car and drove to Lance's house. She parked in the round driveway and went to the door. When she rang the doorbell, the butler opened shortly after and said "Ah, the master has been expecting you." Cloe staggered before she went forward. *How could Lance be expecting me?* she thought. She didn't even know she would be here. She was ushered toward the library, where in a big chair Lance sat, smoking a cigar. Suddenly Cloe didn't feel so brave, suddenly she felt like a fool coming here. What would Lance tell her anyways?

He motioned her in and said "Have a seat."

She did what she was told. As she settled in, he offered her a smoke. "No thanks." Cloe said.

He closed the box and said "Ya, it's a bad habit. What about a drink?"

"Water." Cloe told the butler. He disappeared through the double doors.

"So what brings you here."

"I have a question."

"I think you have more than one."

"Well, I do, but we'll start with one." Cloe said. She wanted to be sure she could trust him. As if he read her thoughts he said "You can trust me. I'm not here for any one purpose. I'm here because God put me here to oversee the fallen here on earth. I'm neither black nor white, I just am. But you know that don't

you? I have imagined you have learned our true names by now?"

"Yes." Cloe said. She didn't feel compelled to lie.

"Call me Lance though, it wouldn't do you any justice to call me by my name."

"Why?"

"Because you would see the horror of the fallen."

"I don't understand." Cloe said, confused.

He sighed "Say my name then if you must, and see for yourself why we chose to use your names instead of ours."

Cloe's eyebrows went up and she said slowly "Mastema."

She didn't see any thing at first, then the air started shifting around Lance, as his cloths disappeared, his charcoaled body became apparent, his face was grotesque, and his wings were burned nearly close to his body. All they were was burnt stubs, with black feathers melted together. Cloe smelled the smell of burnt flesh and it was pungent enough to almost make her vomit. Smoke bellowed out from his body. She shut her eyes and held her breath. He must have sensed her discomfort because after a few moments Cloe heard him say "You can look now."

"I'm so sorry." she said after she took some breaths. She opened one eye slightly and he was a man again.

"Why are you sorry, that's a funny thing to say to a angel who's damned."

"Because I am. I'm sure you were once a beautiful angel."

"I don't know really, I've been this way for so long, I don't remember."

"Is Vetis that way?"

Lance looked at her sternly "No, Vetis was not thrown out, Vetis is just one of the demons of temptation. He is an offspring of one of the fallen."

"But he's not a true fallen." Cloe said as a matter of fact.

"No, but what difference does it make? If your great grandmother was of German heritage, then are you not somewhat German yourself?"

"Yes." Cloe saw his point.

"And if you loved him, you would still damn your soul to hell."

"Yes I know, but that's not why I'm here."

"I know. You're here because you want me to tell you what we are going to do with the book the Sibylline Oracles."

"If you could." Cloe nodded.

"You are a brave soul, do you know that? I could kill you right here and now if I wish."

"I know."

"But you still feel compelled to ask me?"

"Yes. I don't believe you want me dead or you would have done it along time ago."

"You are wise, so you have seen visions?"

How did he know so much? "Yes, of a war in heaven."

"Yes. A war that I do not wish to happen. If this war was to take place, then all the fallen are loosed from heaven. With all the fallen loosed from heaven, they plan on staying to free Satan. It will be the end. I, my dear, am not ready for the end. I'm sure most humans agree. There are fallen and heavenly angels working together to see that this won't happen. But with the help of demons and all the evil on the earth, there is no way to stop the fallen who are trying to free their brothers. That's where you come in. You have already hid Botis, which was very clever I might add, but that was just the beginning. They will find a new way to call on Lilith, and try to talk her into helping them."

"What does Lilith know?"

"A lot, but she keeps her secrets to herself. She does not give out information willingly without some sort of sacrifice. And right now, you are the sacrifice. If they catch you."

"I have to deal with Lilith also?"

"I don't know, that's up to God."

"But I have to deal with Vetis."

"Yes, and you know how already. Michael and I have talked about this. It's either you or him, but it has to be. Vetis is a very damaging demon, without him some of the others will flee. It is your job to take care of this with no help. He has no help either. We have agreed to that. It's just a matter of when."

"Great." Cloe said with a sigh.

"Oh my dear, don't worry. It's easy to have feelings for those you want to help. You can't help Vetis though. He is what he is. But he can try to make you lose your way, that's what he does best. It's up to you about how your going to handle him." After awhile the butler brought in the water. Cloe took a long drink and put the cap back on. She stared at the painting on the wall.

"So will Vetis help in bringing Lilith?"

"Yes, that's why we're hoping you'll deal with this before its gets that far."

"So there is a time frame, sort of."

"If you want to call it that. Vetis will do his bidding when he gets tired of trying to win you over, then he'll punish you and because you didn't slacken. In his rage, he will help to bring Lilith back."

"So I have been prolonging it with my being nice to him."

"Yes, only God knows why you do it though, the more you wait the more you risk losing yourself and losing your nerve to kill him."

"Ya, I know, I can see it happening already."

"You mustn't lose sight of what you were called to do."

"I know." She sighed. "Why didn't you just tell me at the party instead of being mean to me?"

"Because I am being watched and I didn't want to give them more to suspect. They want to overthrow me as well. Vetis is trying to see to that also. He is not one to be reckoned with, but you'll know what to do when the time comes." He got up and said "Now, if you'll excuse me. I've got work to do. I suggest you quit wasting time.", and he walked out and left her there to sit and think.

Cloe left and went home. She knew what she had to do. She had to do it soon. She'd call Cory tomorrow and set up a date with him this week end.

God help me she thought.

When she got home she worked out and knew she had to get in a frame of mind. She went to bed with a new outlook towards the whole thing. The next day she called Cory at the firm, he wasn't in so she left a message for him to contact her. It was time to go home from work when he called. Cloe answered her cell phone while she was walking out the door. "Hello?"

"Cloe? It's Cory, they said you called?"

"Yes, I wanted to discuss something with you."

"Over the phone?"

"You might want to hear what I have to say."

"Okay." he drawled out.

"I ran into a friend of mine the other night, do you know who that was?"

"No clue." Cory said hesitantly.

"It was the man who gave me this hickey, except you know what he told me?"

Cory didn't say anything; he knew where this was going. Cloe stood outside her car pacing "He told me he didn't remember anything, can you believe that?"

"Uh.."

"Well, of course I was pissed, 'cause I thought maybe I wasn't that good."

"Oh, I'm sure you would good." Cory said in a low tone.

"Well, now, see? How would you know that?"

"I can use my imagination." he said quickly.

"Oh, no, you can use it because you were there, weren't you?"

"Cloe, I can explain." Cory began but was cut off.

"You can't explain anything, how could you do that to me?" Cloe asked.

"It wasn't that hard actually." Cory kind of snickered.

"And did I hear you whisper you loved me?" Cloe asked incredulously.

"Maybe, would it make a difference?" Cory sounded hopeful.

"How can you 'love'?"

"Well, I can't."

"So why would you say that?"

"I don't know!" Cory sounded as confused as Cloe did.

"Well now you got your way, didn't you?"

"And you hate me, don't you." he said sadly.

"Actually." she hoped she could pull this off, she crossed her fingers for luck. "I was wanting to get together Saturday night." Cloe heard him suck in his breath, he was nervously breathing on the phone. He said shakily "Are you sure?"

"Yes Cory I'm sure. We know we have feelings for each other, and now I'm in over my head. Now that I've had you, I just want more. We're already together, so will you see me?"

It was if he had melted. He had thought he had won. In his mind he was going to be king. He could see her by his side. "Come to Lance's house. We'll throw a dinner party there. I want to tell everyone I know. Is that alright?"

"Sure, whatever you want." she purred.

"Cloe, you will not regret this, I'll make you the happiest, and you'll have everything you want and more. You'll be my most cherished mate, I promise. You have made me so happy!"

"Okay then, I'll be there Saturday night okay?"

"Oh, Okay darling, I'll see you Saturday, Are you sure I can't see you before then?"

"Now Cory, don't rush me, this is big for me and I have to deal with it in my own way."

"I'm sorry. It's just that I can't wait, but I will darling, I'll wait for you."

"Okay then Cory, I'll see you Saturday night." He hung up the phone and Cloe went home to make plans.

Most cherished mate! she thought, how pathetic.

She would have to go through the whole ritual to get him alone. Whatever she had to do, she would do it. He will pay for what he did. Did he really believe her?

She was amazed at how simple that was. Maybe it was a trick. She would have to be careful. Everyday of the week he sent her flowers expressing his undying devotion to her. Everyday she took her flowers home and put them in a vase. They made the little church smell wonderful. The more it got closer to the day the more nervous she was. She went to a formal shop and picked out a renaissance dress for the occasion. She was dressing up. After all it was kind of like a marriage, *until death do us part.* she thought.

೧

Saturday came and she dressed up in her beautiful dress of deep reds and purples and blues. She put her hair up in a bun. She was reminded of Juliet of Romeo and Juliet. *This is what she must have looked like*, Cloe thought, as she looked in a full length mirror. She didn't tell anyone she was doing this. She didn't want to frighten anyone. They'd think she was crazy. All she needed was God. Michael said she had that.

She drove out to Lance's house and parked way down the street and made her way up the drive. Cloe saw that that there were people who looked like they were looking for someone and when the saw her, they were coming at her and ushering her to hurry. When she walked through Lances door, with everyone ushering her in, she stopped short as she saw Cory. *You can do this*, she told herself. He was talking to a bunch of fallen and demons when they all stopped talking and stared. Cory turned around and his jaw dropped open. It was almost as if he didn't believe it quite yet. But he did now. She was dressed so beautifully to him, he couldn't have asked for anything more. He walked over to her and she kissed him passionately, at least she didn't have to fake that part. Everyone cheered and he picked her up and twirled her around. They laughed and went to say hello to everyone.

She was still treated coldly, and when Cory saw this he apologized for them and told Cloe they'd get used to it. They made their way to Lance. Cloe hoped secretly that he knew what she up to. He went to the couple and shook Lances hand and said to her "So you've come around to our way of thinking."

There was a gleam in his eye and Cloe knew he knew. She bowed and said "Master." Everyone hooped and hollered.

The night went on with drunkenness and orgies. Cloe tried disparately to not notice. Most of them kept their distance, the wanna be's came around to congratulate Cory in his conquer. He told them stories of fighting for her and finally making her fall for him. They kissed a lot, which Cloe didn't mind. Cory was a good kisser that he would have taken her in front of everybody, if she would have let him. She finally told him that she'd like to be alone and he readily bid everyone good night and took her upstairs. There was a ritual bed that they took new comers too, to make them fully evil by sexual rituals. Usually more than two went up to that room. She could feel the evilness of the room weigh down on her. There was hardly any light in this room. She could have sworn she saw shadows move out of the corner of her eye. She tried not to falter. When they got by the bed Cory kissed her hungrily but she stopped him after a moment. She cleared her throat "Cory, please, can we have it like the first night? Where you were patient with me and undressed me slowly, but this time, I want to undress you first."

He looked at her and laughed a happy laugh, If it were anybody else, she would say he truly looked in love, it was so storybook to her. She wished it were real.

But this was Cory.

And it wasn't.

He agreed and slowly she undressed him, every piece if clothing she took off, she kissed his skin. She got his pants off and stood there looking at him. *You can do* this she reminded herself. Her heart was beating fast. She went to his arms and said softly "Did you ever think if we were to make a baby?" At first it was like he didn't catch what she said, but then he looked down at her tummy and he asked "Did? ..."and she laughed "No, not this time, but would that be a good thing? After all I was how I was, and you are who you are."

He rubbed her tummy and thought about it. "You are so smart; did I ever tell you how smart you were?"

She slowly traced his chest and he shivered "Yes you've told me that many times."

She brought her hand over his heart and made a fist and whispered "Vetis..." He looked at her as if he didn't hear her right and then he realized that she had said his true name.

He felt a pain like he had never felt before in his chest and he looked into her eyes, and saw tears.

He went to raise his hand to wipe them away but Cloe pulled back and he felt cold and sticky.

His hand made it to his chest and he felt something protrude out. He looked down and saw Deaths Dagger sticking out of his own chest.

He looked up and Cloe and had a look of horror, as he fell to the ground. His white eyes turned black as did his lips and nails. She fell to the ground and looked at him.

She suddenly felt another presence in the room and looked around. There on the balcony of the room stood another angel, and in his arms he had the soul of Vetis. The angel was white like the glow of the moon, even the eyes shone like white diamonds. Vetis's eyes were cat yellow, and his withered body looked like old dried up leather. The yellow eyes glared at her, and then suddenly he fought to get to her, hissing at her. Cloe jumped back and then they disappeared. He would be in that informatory that he worked so hard on planning to break.

She had to get out of here.

She knew that Lance knew it was done. He would see to it that she would escape. After that she was on her own. Some demons would fear her and the fallen would hate her now.

She got up and pulled the dagger out of the body that used to be Cory's. She whispered "I'm truly am sorry, I wish it could have been different." The dagger disappeared as she whispered to him. She took off her dress, it had blood on it. Earlier when she got dressed for this she had put on shorts and a tee shirt under the dress. She stepped out the window and made her way down the trellis on the side of the house. There would be a lot of people still partying so she made her way to the pasture along the road and stayed in the dark. She walked in the dark all the way to her car. They wouldn't disturb them for along time. By then she'd be long gone. She looked back one last time and saw a shadow in a top window. The figure waved at her. She waved back and made her way to her car.

She drove to Sue's house and of coarse Sue was up. Cloe walked in and Sue said "What happened?"

She looked at Sue and said "What?"

"You've got blood smeared on your face."

"Oh." she went into the bathroom and Sue followed her. She told Sue what had happened, how she planned it and how she had help. She washed her face and Sue rubbed her back. She told Sue about how Cory had tricked her and switched bodies with James. How she ended up with James but not really. How it had to happen this way, and about the war in heaven. After she dried her face they sat down at the kitchen table. Cloe told her the whole story and Greg made her a cup of coffee. Greg didn't really know how Lilith could help with anything either unless she had some special knowledge. Cloe told them about Michael and that Lance said that some where trying to stop this war from going on, because then that meant that Satan was loose. And everybody knew what that meant. "So now you have to face Lilith?"

"I don't know." Cloe said with a shrug.

They visited for a little while, and Cloe went home. When she got there she missed her animals. She sat on the porch wishing she could pet Buddy. To her it seemed like a dream. No matter what the deed she needed to do, she hated to lie to someone. It was a bad thing to play into a roll that you've pretended to be someone's friend, to destroy them. It was better to just do it quickly and get it over with. She had never really gotten to know the victims. But she did her job. It was too easy she told herself. She couldn't believe that Cory fell for it. But she guessed he did, because he's gone. Did he not once question her motives? Maybe in all the weirdness he was really, really wanting to win her over. Maybe he did think he caught the biggest catch of all. She went to her couch and lay there. With Cory out of the way, she'd focus on the cult and the ritual book. And Lilith. She needed to research her. She needed to see the painting in Lance's house again. She would call him and ask to borrow it. After all, he wanted to help, didn't he?

She thought about the war in heaven. She had a feeling that it could still take place, and then Vetis would be loosed, and she imagined he would have a vendetta against her. She really needed to stop this now. She might have won the first time, but she didn't think it would happen again. After she fell asleep she had a dream of Michael. He was in an old abandoned building. She walked in climbing over the rubble. She walked up to him and said "I did it!"

""Yes, you did good. A bit theatrical, but it got the job done."

"But it's not enough." Cloe realized.

"No, it just stayed them for awhile, but the fallen won't give up that easy."

"Can I stop it?"

"You could with help, but it will be worse than before."

"Where do I get help? From you?"

"No, not now, someone you know, he can help. He has the answers."

"Do you have a name?"

Michael slowly disappeared. She screamed for him to come back. Then she realized he wasn't leaving, she was. Somewhere there was a sound, a bell ringing? Where was it coming from? She came to and opened her eyes. She realized the phone was ringing beside her. Some people had bad timing. She reached over and answered the phone. It was Rose checking up on her. She was going thrift store shopping and wanted Cloe to go with. Cloe opened her eyes and the sun streamed in through the window. She looked at the clock, it read eight. She told Rose she'd be right over after a shower. After showering and making herself a cup of coffee to go and she was out the door.

She drove to Rose's house and after petting Buddy and running around the yard with him, she got into Rose's jeep and they drove off. Rose's was excited to go shopping, especially thrift stores. They had a lot of trinkets she liked to buy. Cloe looked for art and books. They made their way all over town, looking at this and that. Rose bought gobs of stuff. Cloe didn't see anything yet that caught her eye. It was lunch time when they settled on a pasta place that had outside dining. They both ordered Chicken Parmesan and a margarita.

"Rose, you remember James?"

"How could I forget." said Rose rolling her eyes.

"Well, it was really Cory that was in James body."

Rose froze while taking a bite of a bread stick, then she set it down and said "Come again?" Cloe explained what happened and went on say that there was no more Cory. Rose swallowed and said "So what about Lilith?"

"I don't know. Michael said something about how 'he' would know how to help me."

"But you don't know who the 'he' is?"

"No."

"Could it be Greg?" Cloe shrugged, and took a drink of her margarita. The food came and they took their time and enjoyed it. It was really good. They didn't talk anymore about what happened for the rest of the day. They just enjoyed spending money. Cloe finally found a picture that interested her. And for five dollars she now owned it.

They made way back to Rose's house, and Cloe put her picture in her trunk. She went into Rose's house and sat down to look at the neat little things that Rose bought. She loved bottles of all shapes and sizes, and she put her potions and lotions in them. Rose and Cloe cleaned them and put them on a shelf, where the different colors and shapes made it look festive. They sat back down on the couch and talked about what Cloe needed to do. She told Rose she wished she knew. She knew that she had to focus on Lilith. Rose suggested they go to the local library, and Cloe thought that was a good idea.

They hopped in the car and went to the library. It was a huge building that was well lit with skylights and had balconies five stories high. There were stair cases everywhere and a lot tables and chairs on the main floor. And some on other floors also. Cloe loved the library. To her it was a bigger version of her house all lit up with the outside light and very peaceful.

They searched on the book shelves that held religion and other books. They could have used the computer to find it, but it was more fun to search and see other titles that may interest them. Cloe knew of another way. She looked around the balconies and mentally called out to the angels there to help her. She knew they heard her and all she had to do is look for signs. Cloe felt a breeze on her left cheek so she walked left until she felt an invisible tub and her right hand and turned right. A book would magically poke out on a shelf and it caught Cloe's eye. They looked together and found all kinds of things on Lilith. They took all the books down and went to a table and spread out the books to passages that thought might be helpful. They read that Lilith was a myth, even though she is mentioned in every language and nationality. There are supposedly two Liliths. A Great Lilith who was Satan's grandmother, and there was little Lilith. Some scholars believe that she is quoted in the bible once in Isaiah. And some scholars point out that she is mentioned in Hebrew manuscripts. Some books says she has a body but no feet and hands. Some books say she has fire for feet and hands. The books do say that she was supposedly Adams first wife, but when Adam tried to be celibate for God she got mad and mated with demons, and had demon children. When she was ordered to go back to

Adam she said no and God killed her babies. She in return was angered and she takes her anger out on human women and takes or kills their babies. After Rose and Cloe made notes they put the books in the bin to be returned and went home. When they got comfortable on the couch they went over their notes and Rose asked Cloe "Do you think, if this were true, that Lilith could be Cory's mother?"

"I think it's possible. But if she's a myth, how are they going to bring back a myth. Lance didn't say she was, neither did Michael."

"Why wouldn't religions want you to know about her?"

"Because then it wouldn't be Adam and Eve anymore. Could you see all the years of teaching us that, and then having to change it? The bible even says Adam and Eve. Maybe God does not want to us know her because she has no purpose. If she was real, then all she did was created evil." Then Cloe remembered looking at the painting of her in Lance's office. "You know what? Even Cory said that she was 'to good for anyone fallen' and he didn't like her. She could still be a fallen angel even if she wasn't Adams first wife. I've never asked that question."

"Did you read that part where some scholars think that Adam was lonely and God created Lilith first?"

"Ya, I read that. It would be hard to fathom that she came first. But who's to say she didn't. Maybe God is like us, and doesn't mention the mistakes that came out of trying to do what's right for mankind. A serious study will say that God created evil as a checkpoint for himself and lets evil upon the earth to tempt us. In the bible it mentions Satan, Devil, and Lucifer. It mentions that Lucifer took one third of the angels. But it doesn't give any names. So you know there's evil, and you know there's fallen, but that's it. It's hard to think that these three with the help of other fallen, are the ones who are responsible for all the evil of the world. But that it is the Bible, Gods word, which it can't mention every little thing, that it gives outlines only, of how one should live and believe, because it's the Holy Bible. And Jesus is mentioned as a role model and savior. Because he was God incarnated. But that doesn't mean that evil doesn't have names, and different sexes and different duties. It would be like God telling me to make cake. And I made a cake but I wanted a different cake, so I added a filling and different toppings and layers, and now I have different cake. God made an angel, but the angel went evil because it followed Lucifer, say it was an angel of virtue, now it's an angel of no virtues. Well no virtues could lead to no caring, no listening, no loving, etc, etc. So now the no virtues angle names these, as selfishness, there's an evil, doubting, there's and evil, hate, there's an evil. So it goes on and on, because there are different angels for different things, but when they followed Lucifer they became the opposite. But these evils become something of a spirit and so who ever created them named them and charged them with this job to bring to humanity. Now God probably has replaced his angel with a new angel of virtues and so on and so forth, that way we have them, but now we have the others, does that make sense, Rose?"

Rose just looked at her in amazement. "You are really something else. You got all of that out of Adam being lonely?"

Cloe paused for a second then remembered that Rose had asked her about Adam and she starting laughing, Rose joined her and they laughed and made fun of Cloe and the cake thing. Rose's voice boomed "MAKE ME CAKE!!" and they were falling off the couch from laughing so hard. When they got done, they were holding their ribs and Rose said through breaths "Speaking of cake, I have some that mom brought over, you want some?"

"Ya sure, I am hungry for some cake." She giggled some more.

"You nitwit." Rose said over her shoulder and Cloe followed her to the kitchen.

For the next hour Rose would mention something about cake, and Cloe almost had it going out her nose from laughing so hard. That's what they liked about each other the best, no matter how serious the situation, they would find a way to laugh. It was a well needed break. When they got done eating they went back to their notes. Rose said seriously "By the way, you did make a good point and it is a good theory."

"Thanks." Cloe said, trying not to start laughing again.

"And I understand what you're saying, but that still doesn't tell us if Lilith is coming and if she is, then which one."

"I know. I think she is coming because the fallen along with the demons will bring her, they still want to free their brethren."

"And who the 'he' is that is supposed to help you." Rose joined in.

"I guess I could call Lance later, I was going to anyways and ask to see the painting on his wall of Lilith."

"The one Cory talked to you about?"

"Yes."

"Do you think it's the 'he'?"

"I don't know, I thought of Greg, but I wouldn't put Greg in such a predicament because he has a family. I thought about the Catholic Fathers that I talk too, but they don't want to get involved much either. I really don't have anyone else."

"I wish I could help." Rose said with a sigh.

"Thanks. It'll come to me."

They finished up and ended up no where closer to the answers than when they started. Cloe told Rose she needed to get going and Rose walked her out. Cloe petted Buddy one more time before she left. He whined to go with her but she told him "Not yet." Then before she went home she stopped by and seen Gigi also. He didn't care where he was at as long as he had grass to eat. She laughed and let him go after standing out in the pasture petting him. She went home and went to the table to check her e-mail. She would have to work tomorrow. It would be strange not having Cory bug her anymore. She didn't understand her hang up over him. He was a fallen/demon. She did her job. She shouldn't be standing here thinking about him. She busied herself until it was time for bed, she'd call Lance from work tomorrow. She wondered if he would help her. She fell asleep thinking about Lilith and the painting.

The next day she was at lunch and called Lance. His butler answered and she said she was with Chris's construction with some questions on a bid, in case anybody was there watching him, like he said they often do.

"Hello." his distinct voice came over the line.

"It's Cloe, can you talk?"

"Yes, go ahead."

"Can you send me your painting of Lilith or can I come and see it?"

"I can sent it if you promise to take care of it, its the only one there is."

"I promise." Cloe said

"I'll send it to your work."

"That will work."

"Anything else?" As if he knew.

"I was told by Michael that some man was supposed to help me, would that someone be you?"

"I don't think so dear."

"Oh." said Cloe with a sigh.

"I helped all I can. The rest is up to you. Don't forget, watch your back. They are hounding for you. It will get dangerous if you don't get the help you need."

"Is there any messages from...?"

"No, if Vetis somehow gets a message through, it will come right to you. Surely you don't think it will be a good one, do you?"

"I thought maybe he would be the 'one' to help."

Lance laughed over the phone. "He would hate you to the depths of hell, there will be no help from him. By the way, look out for his replacement at the firm. Good day dear." and then dial tone was in her ear. Cloe hung up the phone. She didn't think about the replacement. Oh great, she thought, *well, he better stay away from me, or I'll kill him right off the bat.* She bit her bottom lip as she stared at her computer screen. Who could it be to help her? She didn't know very many men that would. Chris came in and made his way to her. He sat on her desk and said "Did you know Cory moved to another country to do business?"

"No, I didn't know that." She almost laughed at his words. If Rose was here, they would have.

"Well I was told this morning by his secretary, and she informed me that his replacement was another partner of the firm. His name is Benjamin."

"Oh, have you met him yet?"

"No, I haven't."

"Well I'm not." Cloe said with a tone to her voice.

"I can't talk you into it?" Chris asked innocently.

"No, you're on your own, buddy. Not after what happened the last time."

"Okay, I'll take care of it." Chris said.

"I thought you would see it my way."

"He should be here tomorrow." Chris started walking away from her desk.

"You already knew that? You're such a smart ass sometimes." He dodged the pencil coming at his head. He told her he'd fire her for that, she told him to go ahead. The end came and Cloe drove by the Lances house on her way home. She needed a plan for stopping Lilith. She didn't know if she should stop it all together or if she would have to defeat Lilith. How would she stop a whole mob? She imagined that was where they have it. It was bigger than Allen's house by far. Not only that but they brought Botis there and lost him. She imagined that screwed up his chance for any more rituals. He proved to be incompetent.

ברים

She went home and thought about it. October was just a month away. She didn't have much time. She wondered if Madam Agnes could help her. Maybe Madam knows a man that would help. She wondered. She worked out and meditated. She wondered of the man she saw pray by her in one of her meditating dreams. Was that her helper? The rest of the week came and went. Cloe spent her time with Rose, or her own family. Her mom and dad came home from the trip and showed everyone what they got for them from their travels.

Cloe was at the park a week later with Sue and her kids when she saw Druj talking to a man. She was trying to seduce him no doubt. Cloe walked up behind her and said calmly in her ear. "Trying to pick up another one, Druj? If you had as many things poked out of you, as you had in ya, you'd look like a porcupine?"

Druj whirled around, eyes flashing. "Are you trying to compete with me, Cloe?"

The man didn't know what to think, so he sat there and watched. Cloe was plain compared to Druj, who was blond haired and big blue eyes among big other parts of her female anatomy.

"I don't have to compete dear, I don't sleep with just anyone."

"No, you kill them first." Druj said with a shrug. That was enough for the man, he got up and left without looking back. Druj and Cloe watched his back as he walked away. "Now look what you've done." she purred "You've scared him away."

"You scared him away, I didn't do a thing."

"What do you want, I'm sure you don't want to go down right here?" and she waved her hand even with the ground. "You don't want to be embarrassed."

"It would be you that's embarrassed. The only thing that saved you last time was throwing me off the balcony. There's no balcony here."

"Next time you won't be so lucky!" Druj said quickly.

"Don't count on it." Cloe countered. "But no, I don't want to fight. I just wanted to save that poor creature from you." Cloe said as she went to walk past Druj and back to where she came from in the park. Druj gave a hissing sound "He would not suffer the same fate as our beloved Vetis. You will pay dearly for that one."

Cloe walked away with a wave and a smile. She knew Druj wouldn't fight here. Cloe's family was close by and could help her if Cloe shouted out to them. Then Cloe could banish her. She was planning on it any way. When she made her way to Sue, Sue asked "Who was that?"

"That was Druj, a demoness."

"The one that pushed you off the balcony?"

"Yep."

"She can hang out at the park?" Sue asked incredulously

"Where else would you pick up homeless people to possess them."

"In the daylight?" Sue pointed out.

Cloe giggled. "There not vampires."

"But...my kids play here. Some days yours will to."

"I know. I'm trying the best I can."

Sue sighed "I know."

They went home and Cloe ate supper with Sue and her family. Greg talked about the bible and God. Cloe didn't mind, she liked to hear Greg's theories. And if she didn't agree, Greg didn't get mad because someone had to think his way. If Cloe didn't leave or someone get tired and go to bed, they would talk all night. Cloe went home thinking of what Druj had said. Her warning was well meant and Cloe knew it. There where probably legions waiting to get a hold of her. She didn't know why they didn't except she was protected in this house.

She fell asleep and had dreams of Druj fighting her and throwing her in a den of ravaged wolves.

When she went to work Monday, Chris was already there with a strange man. They were at the drawing desk looking the firm quotes. Cloe guessed that he must be Benjamin. She went to her desk and sat down, just to get up again when Chris called her over to the drawing desk. She went over and stood by Chris, he introduced her to Benjamin. They didn't shake hands, neither one gave their hand for a handshake, they just nodded at each other. Chris told Benjamin what Cloe's role was at the company.

"I've been told a lot about you." Ben nodded. He had a tone in his voice that Chris didn't catch.

"Really, I hope you didn't hear bad things." Cloe said with amusement. Ben just shrugged and gave her a 'go to hell' look. Chris looked from one to the other. He cleared his throat and said "Anyhow…" and went on about the work he were doing for the firm. Cloe stood there and listened to Chris. She wasn't excused yet so she had no choice. Chris walked to the office with them in tow and pulled some stuff up on the computer. He was telling Ben about the work he did for Lance. Ben said "Yes I saw you there at the party."

"You were there?" Chris asked.

"Yes I am there for all the parties, I never miss 'em." He said, and as he drew out the 'all' he looked at Cloe.

"Can I please be excused now, I have a lot of work to do." Cloe said and got up as if she was electrocuted out of her chair.

"Sure, I'll get with you later." Chris said.

"Nice to meet you, I'm sure I'll see you around." Ben said with a wave.

Cloe nodded and went to her desk. So he knows to, great. *Well, what did she expect* she told herself? He was watching her as he left some time later. Cloe watched him walk out the door. She had a feeling that he wasn't going to make the same mistake as Cory and try to get to know her first. Cloe left work at five and went home. She was headed down the highway when she saw a stranded car on the side of the road. It looked like an old man was bending over the hood, and Cloe stopped. She couldn't leave an elder stranded; she wasn't taught that way from her parents. She made a u turn and then drove around the car and made a u turn again to pull up behind the stranded person. Maybe it was something simple like a jump to the battery. She shut off her car and got out. She went up to the figure bent over and asked "You need some help?" She just ducked in time as a tire iron came down for her head. It landed on her shoulder instead. She reacted by falling to the ground and rolling away, but this time the tire iron kept coming down where she had just been. She held on to her shoulder as much as she could until she jumped up on both feet and stopped the tire iron from cracking her face open between her hands. She had the iron in one hand and she punched the figure with the other hand. The old mans hat fell off to reveal a demon without human skin on. She had seen one without a human body before. They were like old dried up raisins with hands, feet and a head. But they were strong and fast. He went to punch her back and she put the iron in the way making his fist land on it. The iron went to the ground. She kicked him backwards and he landed out away from her, only to come at her again. She dodged a few swings before he jumped up and connected an elbow to the top of her head. She heard the thump inside her ears and shook her head. She tried to clear the stars from her eyes as she dodged his advances. She got tired of fighting him off and ran on top of her car. He followed but only made it to the hood before Cloe kicked up and put two feet into his face and made him flip backwards unto the ground. That bought her some time to pull it together. He picked himself up and looked at her through yellow eyes. It reminded Cloe of Cory. The eyes seemed to look at her and around her as if to contemplate his next move. Cloe had an idea. She got back on her feet and ran over the car top and put the car between them. It only lasted a moment as the demon jumped on the roof of the car. It squatted there and hissed at her. Cloe put her hand in her pocket and pushed the button to activate the alarm sound, which in turn made the demon jumped backwards, and fell off the roof and put its hand over its ears. Cloe activated the trunk and it popped open. She grabbed the flare and shut the trunk lightening quick. When the horn stopped honking the demon straightened up, and jumped back on the roof, except Cloe wasn't there, she ducked down and waited for it to leave the ground before sneaking to the front of the car as he looked for her in the back. By the time he realized she was in front, she was ready for him. He came back over the roof of her car at a leap for her, she waited, then ducked and he landed on the engine of his car. She took his head and slammed it down on the fuel injector. She took a fuel line and poured gasoline over his face and shoulders that she had loosened when he was looking for her. He swung wildly as the gas went in his eyes. When he was a little ways away from the car she lit the flare and threw it at him. He screamed and flailed around as he burned. One might think that gas fire and fire from hell is the same thing, but it isn't. A gas fire is a gas fire, and if demon is on fire from gases, then their going to burn to a crisp.

The fire followed the gas trail from the demon to the stranded car though and Cloe saw it.

Oh shit!

She ran towards the other side of the road and hit the deck, putting her arms over her head. There was an explosion and after the racket died down Cloe got up and looked at the damage. Her car was very close but not hurt.

Cloe ran and got into her car. She started it and threw it in reverse as fast as she could. When she thought she was a safe distance, she looked one last time before turning around and driving away. She didn't want to be there when the cops came around. Someone would come by eventually and investigate.

Cloe got home and went into her house. She locked the door and went to the bathroom. After she pulled off her shirt she saw the bruise from the tire iron on her shoulder. It was red and swollen. She was lucky it didn't crack her collar bone or hit her head. She got a rag and walked into the kitchen and got ice to put on it. She felt the top of her head and there was a lump. *Great*! she thought. She was going to go to work stiff, *again.*

She went to the bathtub and ran a hot bath, She put some more of Rose's potion in her water for sore muscles. She sat on the toilet lid waiting for the water to fill the bathtub. When it was full enough she undressed and climbed in. She soaked for a long time, even putting her whole body under water. Her head needed a good soaking too.

She went to bed with a pain in her shoulder and it was hard to get comfortable so she had trouble sleeping. She needed to be prepared better, because this was just the beginning.

The next week nothing eventful happened. She went to Rose's Friday night because they were going out with some co-workers from Rose's work. They wanted to go dining and dancing. Rose knew Cloe would protest but she begged and pleaded. Cloe finally agreed to go out with Derek and Fred. Cloe ended up with Fred. Rose had told Derek she'd go out with him but neither wanted to go alone.

They picked up the girls at Rose's house and took them to a Mexican restaurant. They ordered their food and a drink. Then Fred filled in Cloe on what he did at work, which was accounting. Derek and Fred interchanged stories and had Cloe and Rose laughing. They were pretty funny together and they didn't even have to try. When they got done they went dancing at a local honky tonk. Rose loved to two step and partner dance, and even line dance. Cloe like to fast dance but Rose said she had two left feet for that. So Cloe two stepped with the best of them.

They were dancing a type of square dance and had to change partners for a while. Then Cloe got a new partner. Her smile died instantly when she looked into the eyes.

It was another demon.

He smiled at her in an evil way and squeezed her hand hard, and they danced together until it was time to leave him to go to the next partner. She tried to act like she was having a good time but she kept her eye out for him. They made it all the way to their original partner before the song ended and everyone clapped before they went to sit down or dance the next slow country song. Cloe and Rose made their way to the table. Cloe asked Rose if she would accompany her to the ladies room, and they excused their selves.

When they got into the ladies room Cloe said. "Rose, there is a demon out on the dance floor!" Rose started pacing and began talking to her self as if she was trying to figure out what to do, then suddenly she snapped her fingers and quickly pulled her lipstick out of her bag. "Turn around!" she told Cloe and lifted up Cloe's shirt. "What the..." Cloe said and Rose quickly stilled her and drew a protection star on Cloe's back with some figures around it. After she inspected her art work, was satisfied then drew the image on the mirror. She gave the lipstick to Cloe and said "Now draw on my back and make it look like yours." Cloe did the same to her and drew the figures that Rose showed her how. They were protected, but their dates weren't, and there was no way to protect them.

They went out and went back to the table. Derek and Fred were sitting at another table visiting other people and when they saw the girls coming, they excused themselves and walked with the girls back to the table. They sat down and talked some more before getting up to dance a two step. Derek and Rose went one way and Fred and Cloe went the other, talking as they danced. As they made their way around the floor at a fast pace a man came and cut in and Fred went off with another female before Cloe could stop them. It was the demon with Cloe and he made a toothy smile and showed all his pointed teeth. When Cloe saw that she released him to another girl and stole her partner. But the demon kept jumping bodies, so when she thought she got away, she would end up dancing with the demon again. Finally she seen Rose and danced her way to her, but the demon jumped into Derek instead. Rose didn't know it and the demon whisked her off away from Cloe, Cloe dropped her partner and tried to get to her, only to be run into time and time again trying to get to her. By the time Cloe made her way to Rose, Rose had figured it out by the way it talked to her. She was trying to get away when Cloe cut in and danced off with Rose, leaving the demon standing there looking around. Cloe asked Rose if she was okay and they got off the dance floor.

They looked for Derek and Fred and the men were looking for them. They made their way across the dance floor separately and asked what happened. Fred said "I started dancing with you and all the sudden I'm dancing with God knows who, and then I end up by my self." Derek chimed in that it was the same for him. Cloe and Rose played dumb and said it happened to them too. They didn't know what happened. They made there way back to the table talking about how it was a strange thing to happen.

Cloe and Rose looked at each.

ↄ

They sat down for awhile and enjoyed their drinks. Cloe sipped at hers but didn't want to seem like she wasn't drinking any. Fred and Derek were putting theirs away at a good rate. Rose was just taking swallows here and there. Rose wished she could put a star on their back but they would never go for it.

Fred wanted to go out on the dance floor and line dance. Derek asked if they were coming, Cloe and Rose said they'd sit this one out but to go have fun. The guys left and Rose told Cloe "I'm glad we're protected but I wish there was some to protect them."

"Ya I was just thinking the same thing."

"Is there a way?"

"Unless you took their hand and drew it on them"

"That's it! I'll draw it on them in pen. It'll be crazy to them but oh well."

Cloe and Rose watched the two guys saddle up to some girls as they lined danced. They weren't exactly Cloe's or Rose's type but they were pretty fun. Cloe also spotted the demon. He was sitting at a table by himself, watching Cloe. When the dance was over the guys came back and Cloe said that it looked like they were having fun. That's when Rose chimed in "Fun, you know what fun is? Drawing on people's hands, that's fun. Can I draw on your hand Derek?" like a mad lady.

He looked at Fred with questioning eyes "Uh, ya, sure." Rose grabbed his hand and drew the same sign that was on the girls back. When she was done she looked at it and said "there, that's better."

"What is it?" Fred asked.

"A star with some shapes in it, and squiggly lines around it" Derek said.

"It's your turn Fred." Cloe said with a grin.

"Why is it my turn?" Fred asked.

"Because it's fun." Rose said with wide eyes and a laugh.

This time it was Fred's turn to look at Derek as he slowly gave his hand to Rose. When she was done Fred looked at it and asked "Where's yours?" to the girls. Cloe sucked in a breath and said "We already have ours."

"Where?" Derek asked

"On our backs." Rose answered.

"Really, is it a tattoo?" Fred asked

"Not really." Cloe said.

"Can we see them?" Derek asked excitedly.

"No!" the girls said together.

Derek backed up in his chair "Why can't we see them?"

"Because." said Cloe "Uh...we don't want to pull our shirts up out here, that'll be embarrassing."

"We can go somewhere else and you could show us." Fred said in a sultry tone.

Not in this lifetime, putz. Cloe thought.

Cloe looked side ways at him and turned back to her drink. A song came on and Cloe said quickly "Ready to dance some more?

The guys chimed in "Yes." together and the four made their way to the dance floor. They hit the dance floor but they didn't have to worry about the demon in these two men, they just to worry about someone cutting in. Which happened to Rose. She suddenly realized she was dancing with the demon when she called out Cloe's name when they were close, the demon wouldn't let her go. Cloe looked around and saw them dancing. She told Fred "I gotta go get this." and pointed at Rose. Fred's eyes followed and he watched Cloe walk over and stomp the demon's foot. The demon let go of Rose, which to anybody else, looked like a regular human. Cloe stood there and Rose stood beside her. Rose's said "Leave us alone you bastard!" and the demon went to lunge but looked around. Cloe looked around also and they had a audience. So Cloe used it to her advantage "Leave us alone." She said loudly "We don't want to dance with you, we have our partners." She said it like she was remembering a script and said it slowly. Everyone looked at him and the bouncer came up and ask if there was a problem, Cloe said "No problems, we're just setting him straight."

Everyone started to dance again and the four went on dancing. They didn't have anymore problems for a while, until the demon jumped into the bouncer. Cloe was dancing with

Fred when all of the sudden there where big hands on her shoulder. When they came down on her shoulder, it hit the place where the tire iron had bruised her shoulder and Cloe's winced in Fred's arms. Fred couldn't

say anything, it happened to quick. Cloe went sailing backwards and slid on the ground after a thump and traveled five feet on the floor. People scattered everywhere. Cloe got up and said "That's it!" Cloe dusted off her butt and pulled down on her shirt. Cloe was peeved. She hollered at Rose when the demon laughed and came at her again saying "There's nothing you can do this time, I work here." and laughed again. Cloe jumped over the dance floor railing and the demon came behind her. Cloe could see Fred telling Rose something and pointing and when Rose found where Fred was pointing, she was chasing after the demon.

The demon was smart though, as he wasn't the only bouncer. He called on his radio for backup. The other bouncer went to Rose was trying to retain her from moving. Rose got mad and so did Fred and Derek, Fred trying to tell the other bouncer they didn't do anything. While they where in heated discussion Cloe was maneuvering around chairs and tables to buy her some time. The demon got tired of the cat and mouse game and charged her. Cloe jumped on a table to get away. She didn't want to hurt the bouncers' body. It was the demon inside she needed to make leave. He was swinging at her legs with his hands and Cloe was jumping from table to table. She spilled drinks on people and said "Sorry!" as she passed by them. She finally fell though when a pissed off lady came up and grabbed her leg, tripping her while yelling at her for spilling her drink. Cloe fell to the floor and started crawling between the peoples legs. She was suddenly under the bar but she was trapped, she went to turn around but it was to late, the demon had her by the foot and was dragging her out on her belly. Cloe was trying to grab anything to stop herself, but there was nothing to grab.

She stopped for a second and was going to turn around, but he was coming at her and she hurried and tried to scramble away. He grabbed her by her back and picked her up, slamming her down on a table. She moaned and got up slowly. He put his arms together and came down on her back. She splattered to the ground. She rolled away from his foot coming down on her face and got up quickly and took off running. She ran into Rose and the guys. When the demon came through Rose jumped on its back. He was whirling around trying to get Rose off. Rose was used to a rough ride, she broke many horses in her lifetime. She held on and squeezed his throat to drop him. Cloe turned around and was keeping in front of him saying "Who's your mama!" and dancing around like a prized fighter. "Hang on Rose!" Cloe yelled to Rose as Rose hung on with all her might. The demon slammed Rose up against the pole in the middle of the dance floor. Cloe saw the look of pain on Rose's face, but it just infuriated her more and she squeezed even harder. Cloe looked around for something to draw a box with. She grabbed peanuts off the bar and made a human size square. She yelled at Rose to hang on again and made symbols around it with pool cue chalk. After she did that she ran and got the demon with Rose still on his back. He was slowly blacking out, Cloe had to get him in the square. She took his hand and led him to it, zigzagging the whole time. He finally dropped in it and passed out. Rose quickly got off his back and out of the square. The square kept the demon from jumping into another body. The demon came out of the body looking like a dried up raisin with yellow eyes and teeth gnashing. Everyone saw that and screams went everywhere. People were falling over themselves trying to get away from it. Fred and Derek just watched in amazement. Cloe started chanting the Litany of the Saints and made a sign of the cross over her and walked around the square doing the same thing. Rose joined her as she chanted and the demon was jumping as if something invisible was shocking him and he screamed out in terror. After about five minutes the demon started to smoke and caught fire, only to be ashes on the ground in the end.

The people that stayed and watched were amazed, if a pin was to drop on the ground some one would here it, it was that quiet. Cloe and Rose gave themselves a high five and the crowd started hooting and hollering for the girls. Fred and Derek were freaking out. Cloe asked them if they were alright, as they stared at the ashes smoldering on the floor. Fred looked at Cloe and asked a little hysterically "What is that thing?" Cloe scratched her head and looked at Rose.

"We don't know." Rose said.

"How did you know how to kill it?" Derek said.

"We don't know." Rose said again in monotone.

"Is that why you put this on our hand, is this some sort of witchcraft stuff?" Fred said and his voice was getting a higher pitch as he finished the sentence.

"We don't know." Cloe said and shrugged at Rose. Rose shot her a dirty look. Derek huffed "Well, I don't know what you girls are into, but I don't want anything to do with it. Come one, I'll take you home." After discussing who was going to pay the bill for damages with the owner, who insisted it was Cloe's fault, but everyone saw the bouncer trying to beat up Cloe so she got out of it. They all made their way to the car. Derek and Fred didn't say much on the way home. Cloe could tell Rose wasn't happy about the way the events went down. They both looked out the window on the way home. It was painfully quiet. When they pulled in Rose's driveway Derek never turned around but thanked them for going out with them. Rose mumbled something and got out and Cloe stayed behind until Rose got to her gate and told the guys "If you mention this and Rose gets her feeling hurt in any way at work, I'll find you and do the same to you as I did that thing at the dance hall, got it?" and didn't give them time to answer before she shut the door. That was all she needed was Rose to lose her job over rumors. Cloe sat on the porch after petting

Buddy with Rose. Rose was staring out into nowhere. "You all right?" Cloe asked.

"Ya, my back hurts though." she sighed. She moved her shoulder around in a circle.

"Besides that." Cloe stated.

"Ya, I really liked Derek too, but oh well, he already made known how he felt about the witch thing." she quoted in mid air.

"I'm sorry about that."

"It's not your fault." Rose told Cloe.

"Well it kind of is. There wouldn't have been any demons if I didn't tag along."

"I know, and it's funny because I've always wanted to be there when that happened, but now that it happened, I almost wished I wasn't there. But maybe I wish I was there if it was just me and you. But then it wouldn't matter, it would be bound to happen, so I don't know what to think but I do know one thing. I feel sorry for you. That really hurt when he slammed me into the pole."

"Lets go see if you got a bruise." Cloe said and they went into the house. Rose took off her shirt and she had a purple and blue line going down her spine between her shoulder blades. Cloe got a cream that Rose made for bruises and smeared some on. She told Rose she really needed to soak in the bathtub with some sore muscle potion in her water. Rose said she would do it tomorrow. She didn't feel like sitting in a tub tonight. She went to her cabinet and pulled some Tequila Rose and two glasses full of ice. Cloe and Rose carried on with their own party until early morning having fun.

❧

The next day the girls finally stirred. It was a rainy Saturday and the girls went to the local gas station down the road to get some cappuccinos. Rose was in the mood for one. They went back to the house and Cloe told Rose about the demon

218

that attacked her on the highway, showing Rose her bruised shoulder. Rose said "I thought I heard about that, didn't the car blow up? Dad said it was talk of the church that the cops found a car burning on the highway and a pile of ashes that they thought was a dog. The cops were investigating whose car it was."

"It was probably stolen." Cloe said over her cup.

"Ya, you're probably right. Now you'll have to pay close attention from now on, the attacks are getting closer together."

"Ya, I know."

"You know what we need to do, don't you." Rose asked

"What's that?"

"We need to tattoo these protection symbols on us somewhere."

"I knew you were going to say that one of these days." Cloe groaned. She hated needles.

"Well, it's true, and there's nothing like a rainy day to get a tattoo. Come on, lets go." Rose all but dragged Cloe to her jeep. They spent most of the day at a tattoo parlor putting the symbol for protection on them. Rose chose across her lower back and had a bigger circle than Cloe's, which put hers on her ankle. After words they went shopping for cloths at local thrift stores, Rose loved thrift stores. When they got done they went to Rose's parent's house to check on the horses. They stayed until midnight riding and watching movies with Rose's mom and dad. Cloe agreed to spend another night with Rose and the next day she went home. When she got home she did Jujitsu and Tie Chi for five hours, and then did her household cleaning. She waited until it got dark to meditate. She lit some aroma therapy candles and played some meditation music then sat in her comfortable spot on a bean bag chair and closed her eyes. She drifted off and pushed everything aside. She drifted some more. She was in a hallway, it looked like a corridor to a dungeon, and it had the torches along the way. She followed the path down to a room. In the room there were two figures standing there talking. One was a higher rank than the other. They were disputing something. Cloe couldn't make it out. She leaned against the wall as flat as she could to hear. "We must stop her from seeing him. He has the answer to help her."

Who's her? Cloe thought.

"How can we do that? She is strong."

"Find a way." The higher ranked one said "Or we will all be destroyed. The brethren on the other side will help her anyways, even if he don't."

The lessor one argued back "I don't care. You know what she did to Vetis, she'll do that to us all if she gets to him, we must stop it" Cloe focused, *they're talking about me...see who?.. I wonder what they're talking about...I better get out of here before they find me...*Cloe brought her self out of meditation and stared at the floor.

What seemed like seconds actually lasted an hour. She got up and went to get something to eat. Her mind went to what they were saying about her. She didn't know who they were. They talked about Vetis, so Cloe knew somewhere on another level they had known what she did. And what she can do. But she didn't know who she was suppose to see and they did, how is that fair? She knew one thing, they would try to stop her at all costs. That's why they were coming at her on a regular base. That wasn't good. Cloe went to her cellar and turned on the light. She had guns of all kinds, holy water bottles, big cross daggers and various other knives. She went to her favorite gun though, it was built by a friend of hers as a potato launcher, but they modified it and instead of shooting potato's, it shot little ball clusters, what Cloe calls demon busters. They are made from mixing holy water and dirt from the ground where Christ was crucified in Jerusalem. They harden into mud balls quite well, and when that lands on a demon head, it can be quite a killer. Otherwise it disintegrates where it touches. It's hard to get off because it sticks to them. Along with her flame thrower, she's quite a little terminator.

She needed to get a hold of Jax, who was the one that made her the demon busters by trial and error. Jax is another demon hunter down in Florida. She found him on the Internet one day by chance on a forum. Everybody gave him a hard time and said he was full of shit when it came to demon hunting. Cloe believed him and they started talking. He showed her a lot of tricks. She was almost out of busters and she knew she would need more. She carried every item she needed up into her house, then she went to sit on the couch. She had a thought, was Jax the one to help her? Maybe that's it, she got excited as she dialed his number.

"Hello?" came a man's voice, he had a little British accent.

"Jax? It's Cloe from the south."

"Hey, I've haven't heard from you in a while, how's the demon chasing getting along?"

"Horrible. Hey Jax, I am dealing with fallen angels, have you see any fallen?"

"Not that I'm aware of, love. I didn't know they would come into play."

"Well they're here and I've pissed some off, so their sending more demons after me. I've overheard a conversation about how someone is suppose to help me, and I'm trying to figure that out. They're going to bring in Lilith, so I'm going to try to stop them. Do you think maybe it's you?"

"Well...lets see, No, I don't think it's me, I've been doing this for along time. But I haven't dealt with any fallen. You say they are bringing in Lilith? Her I have dealt with. She started the vampire existence. You must not let her survive. I'm the one who killed her the last time. It wasn't easy either. You may be way out of your field I'm afraid. How did you get yourself in such a fix?"

"It's a long story. What I really need are some busters. You still got any?"

"Yep, I just got a case in from Zova not to long ago. It's a good thing I ordered extra. But they won't be effective against the fallen."

"I know, I have a weapon for them from Michael."

"Michael? Michael who?"

"St. Michael, Archangel Michael."

"You've got to be kidding me! He came down from the heavens personally to help you? I've never heard of such a thing! But I never seen any fallen either so...you lucky dog, you. Well, if he's in you must be doing alright for yourself. Either that or you need all the help you can get! Say I've got to run. I'll send them pronto, and I'll keep my ears open from the demons down here in case their up to something. I'll get in on the action myself maybe, don't know, well love, I'll beg off now. Be safe, and remember what I said about Lilith."

"I will, and thanks." Cloe hung up the phone. She went outside and dug her target out of the barn. She target practiced for awhile. When she was happy with her aim, she shot a few more rounds then went to the flame thrower. That was pretty easy, just point and shoot. When she started a target on fire she smiled.

It was getting dark so Cloe brought back everything in the house. She cleaned it and shined it up and she had a thought so she called Rose. Rose answered in the third ring.

"Hello?" she said breathlessly.

"Rose, are you alright?"

"Um...ya." She giggled and muffled the phone. Cloe's eyebrow shot up. "Can I call you back?"

Cloe laughed "Don't forget." and she hung up. Well, it seemed someone was being entertained tonight she thought. She knew Rose deserved a great guy and maybe this was it. Cloe went on cleaning her equipment and stocked the vest that holds the holy water and busters full. By the time she got done with that and cleaned up herself and the room, Rose called back. Cloe answered the phone and Rose gushed over the other end "Sorry 'bout earlier. I was detained for a while."

Cloe laughed "I guessed, with who?"

"His name is Dewayne. You haven't met him yet."

"And how do you know this Dewayne?"

"From work." Rose said and giggled.

"Well, I'm glad you had fun."

"Thanks, I needed that. So, what did you call about?" Rose asked

"Can you not make a protection collar for my dog. And something for my horse?"

"Yes for the dog. Beer for your horse." Rose said and they started laughing.

"No really, I don't know…I'll have to look it up. Why, you missing your animals?"

"Like crazy, I feel like my children have left home." they both laughed.

"I'll look it up and call you tomorrow on it, okay?" Rose answered.

"Please don't forget."

"I won't. I'll see ya tomorrow."

"Bye." Cloe looked at the clock. It read nine o'clock. She went to bed to get ready for the next week. She was sure it would be full of surprises. The next morning Cloe loaded her things in the car to make sure she always had them. She had holy water in a bottle that looked like a drinking water bottle but was designed for holy water. She would leave it on her desk at work. She also had two throwing stars tucked down by her socks strapped to her ankles. They had points that were harmful to a demon because they were blessed with gold dust by Saint Bernard of Clairvaux, a Cistercian Monk. Presents bestowed upon her from Jax.

Nothing happened at work and Rose called at the end of the day to tell her that she can put protection symbols on animals and that it should work against demons but not the fallen, if they chose to hurt them. So Rose was going to work on Buddy's collar, that would be easy, but the horse was a different matter. Cloe said she'd be over to get her dog then if Rose didn't care to do it tonight. Rose said "That'll be fine with me, come on over." On her way to Rose's from work Cloe was going through a green light when all of sudden a figure came up from behind her in her own back seat and grabbed her around the throat. Cloe looked into her review mirror and saw yellow eyes staring back at her. Cloe was trying to fight off the demon and drive at the same time. The demon's short stubby like fingers were ripping into her skin. She started swerving in and out of traffic. She was punching him in the head but it didn't effect him any. Cloe reached into her sock after dodging a car and grabbed her throwing star out of her sock strap. She took it and jabbed it into the demons arm. He fell back wards in the back seat and Cloe grasped for breath. She pulled the car over just in time as a big truck turned in front of her. The demon came again and Cloe reached down and pulled the other dagger out. She stabbed his good arm with it and he wailed in the back seat as his arms started to melt away. Cloe got out and popped open her trunk. She got out her flame thrower. She hung it on her shoulder by the shoulder strap and opened the car's back door. She reached in to get him but he kicked her in the gut, sending her two steps back. She cursed and got even madder and reached in again. The demon again kicked at her but Cloe grabbed the foot and drug it out. It landed with a thud and Cloe drug it another ten feet before she let it go. It got up and hissed at Cloe "You will payyy for thisss". Cloe said "Oh yah, well this is for getting into my car with your stinking ass." Cloe blasted it. It caught fire and Cloe watched it burn. She reached for her throat and felt some blood on it. She knew the cops were called. There were cars back up and some were driving by slowly. A man was asking her if she was alright and she nodded. The cops showed up and asked what was wrong. They took a statement from Cloe that there was an animal in the back seat and Cloe destroyed it. The cops looked at each other with raised eyebrows as Cloe told the made up story. They asked her if she always carried around a flame thrower, even it if was a small one. Cloe told the cops you never know when you'll need to build a fire. That comment really made the cops look hard at each other. One cop got a message to bring her in for questioning. Against her wishes they cuffed her and took her to the precinct.

When she got there they put her in a holding room for questioning. A man walked in with a suit but showed her his gun in a side holster and looked at Cloe. Cloe looked and it and brought her eyes up to look at him.

She couldn't believe it.

A demon was a cop.

Some demons can look closely like humans, only their eyes are different. *Now how is that fair?* She thought. The demon sat down and asked Cloe "You don't remember me, do you?"

Cloe huffed and said "Should I?"

"You were in here along time ago looking for a detective." Cloe went back in time in her mind and remembered a cop watching her walk out the door after talking to the lady cop at the front desk. "You!" she said.

"I haven't seen you in a long time, now you're going around town killing my kind. Can't you keep your business more quiet than that? You're starting to make me look bad."

Cloe couldn't believe her ears. "Well, can't you tell your kind." she said the last two words sarcastically "To leave me alone? It isn't my fault they attack me in broad daylight."

"Well, they must have a reason to, or else they wouldn't."

Cloe looked at him and shook her head "Do you even know what's going on?"

"No, as a matter of fact I don't and I don't care. My job is to make sure there's enough crime in this city to keep my precinct happy. I don't care about you and your problems. I've got enough of my own."

"But how could you not know, you're a demon?"

He mimicked her through screwed up lips and face. Then he sobered and said "I'm not here for the end of mankind, or the fallen, I am here to cause crime so Justice can prevail."

The way he said Justice, it wasn't just a saying. Justice was a good angel for humans and it was a check and balance system that he was talking about. Cloe didn't know that certain demons didn't pay attention to others. She nodded her head slowly and said "Oh."

"So you see, your really pushing the issues here sweetheart." he said and sat back in his chair.

"Well, honey pie, if the demons didn't attack then I wouldn't be making your life hard but if they want to play then they gotta pay. So, why don't you set me free and I'll be out of your hair."

He sighed and walked her out. He didn't have more to say to her. He would be glad when she was dead. They gave Cloe back all her belongings. They tried to keep the flame thrower but after Cloe said she has a bigger one at home. The captain demon gave it back to her. She grabbed it and her other stuff and went out the door with the demon captain telling her she ought to really get her throat looked at with a laugh. She went on to Rose's house and when Rose saw her, she went to get her medicine as Cloe told her about the demon captain on the force. They talked about the demon in the back of the car as Rose put ointment on a gauze bandage and taped it to Cloe throat. Then she wrapped her throat and it looked like Cloe had on a priest collar. Rose said it was fitting. Cloe asked to see the dog collar and Rose called in Buddy. His collar was donned with symbols of protection and Rose guaranteed it would protect him at all times unless, and they said it together, the fallen went after him. "I know, I know." said Cloe and

Rose said "Now as for Gigi, I thought we could permanently paint him or something."

"Won't that hurt him?" Cloe asked.

"No, they make body paint for horses for shows when you want to dress them up. But it does wear off eventually, so you'll have to Redo it every once in awhile." Rose pointed out.

"Okay, I can handle that."

"This week end we'll do it and you can take him home."

"Sounds good. Well I guess I'll take Buddy home now."

"Take care of that wound on your neck."

"I will." Cloe said and she and Buddy went home. Buddy would lick her every once in a while she was driving. She said "I missed you too." and pet his head. Cloe took him to a fast food hamburger joint that he loved. She bought him two cheeseburgers and one for herself. When they got home she let him out and he happily went over the grounds sniffing and wagging his tail.

Cloe opened both car doors to let it air out. A demon that doesn't possess a human body smells like burnt flesh and her car smelled like it now. She grabbed her daggers and wiped them off. She went in the house to put the daggers on the counter to clean and got out her cleaning supplies for carpet and upholstery cleaning. She got out a shop vac also. When she was done she was sweating but her car smelled better. She had a spray bottle of New Car Smell and sprayed that heavy. She had a thought and remembered the protection symbols that Rose had drew on them and took a magic marker and drew them on all the doors, small but visible.

Cloe was satisfied and went in and took a shower. When she was done she went back down in her cellar and got some more daggers out that were the size if her palm. She came back out and put them in various places in her car, just to make sure. She also had a kid toy squirt gun that made a pretty good pistol for holy water, and she could leave it in the car without the cops pulling her over.

Cloe went back in and put some more ointment on her throat and covered it. She called in Buddy who came in at a trot. She closed the door and went to bed. She was sound asleep when Buddy was in the living room and started barking towards a window. The next morning she got up and made coffee and looked for Buddy. He was sleeping under the window in the living room and the window was opened. She froze. She didn't remember leaving that window open. She called for Buddy and he got up and strode happily to her. She petted his head and said

"Good Boy, did someone try to come in the window?" He jumped up and she went to the window to examine it. It didn't have any tool marks. She looked out it and shrugged. She shut the window.

She got a cup of coffee and walked out to the outside of the window. She put her cup on the window sill and stooped down. She examined the ground and there was bent down grass where someone was standing. Cloe stood up and grabbed her cup of coffee, she took a drink and wondered. A human was here but got the window open with the help of something else. She drank up her cup and put it on the porch as she made her way to the cellar again. If humans got involved she didn't want to have to kill them but she had just for thing for them. She had a bean bag gun that shot out little bean bags at a terrible force. Just like in the movie Walking Tall with the Rock, it took a man his size down in a hurry.

Cloe grabbed the gun and some bean bags and took them in the house. She would have to look at it later after work to make sure it was still on target. She went out to the porch and got her cup. She had another thought of putting blue sticky powder underneath all the windows, that way she could track her peeper. She went to work after checking all around and in her car. She told Buddy to be good and she went down the road. She got to work and everyone crowded her to ask her about her throat. Someone said they knew of someone that heard on the scanner that it was her involved in a car incident on the road and was taken in for questioning. She answered that she didn't know what it was in her car, some big rabid animal and they took her in for questioning because she killed it by a flame thrower. They didn't ask anymore questions. They couldn't get over the part where a big animal attacked her in her car, in the city. They were walking away and some were saying they were going to start checking their back seats more often. Chris came out and handed her some more paper work and asked if she was alright. She said she was and asked how Rob was getting along learning the new job. Chris said he was really good at it and patted Cloe's back before walking off.

The work day came and went and Cloe made it back home without any mishaps. She got home and went to her walk in closet and got out the blue powder bottle that sticks to whatever walks through it. Jax said he used it to see if demons or people would come up by his Florida home. Demons without human bodies have raccoon like feet. He could see the difference because in sand it was hard to tell. He sent Cloe two big bottles and Cloe never had a use for them until now.

She went around all her doors and windows and dumped some. In the dark it would be hard to see. It was almost black. She would find whoever thought they would sneak in her window at night. Even if she didn't catch them she was sure to run into them somewhere along the line, especially if they run with demons. Not all humans had to be possessed to run with demons. They just are wannabes like Allan and that other girl with the tattoo. They will do biddings for a demon like kill someone or steal something valuable, and was promised fame and fortune in return.

When she got done she put the bottle up and sat down to bible study for an hour. Then she went out and fed Buddy before she made herself supper. When she was done eating she went outside with her beanie bag gun and shot it a few times to make sure it was still on target, when she was satisfied with it she went in with Buddy. She watched TV before she went to bed. At one o'clock in the morning her phone rang. At first she didn't hear it but she slowly answered it.

"Hello?" There was static and crackling on the phone, Cloe opened her eyes and sat up, touching her lamp to turn it on. She sat there listening before she said "Hello." again. She listened through all the static and heard a voice in the distance, it blended in with the crackling but it slowly said "You-will... pay for what... you did-to... me!" Cloe listened and it sounded like a demon scream before she quickly hung up. She stared at the phone for a moment before she unplugged the phone. Jax taught her that spirits can come through transmissions over phone, TV and radio. He told her to watch the movie called White Noise to see what he was talking about. After she watched that she hated to hear static over the radio and TV and would quickly shut it off. She researched it for later use because a medium who was possessed by a spirit by using the RSVP. The family called her and she extracted the spirit who was a singer for a big show in Vegas. The medium attracted it because she was using the radio to get her messages. She laid back down but didn't shut off the light. She thought she was retarded. Nothing big scared her.

But that static noise made her hair stand on end.

She hated it.

After she watched The Ring, she wished she'd never watched that movie either. She hated it. That's why she hardly ever turned on the television or radio anymore. She was happy listening to her Cd's or watching movies. One time she had a radio that kept jumping off the Cd player and onto the radio, which was a usually a blank station. She got tired of that and threw it in the dumpster at work. She knew who's voice that was over the phone. She didn't want to acknowledge it but it was Vetis. He had found a way to get a message to her. And if he could get messages to her, then he could get them to his helpers also. He probably spent more effort on the latter. So he was pissed at her. Oh well. What did she expect?

She dozed off lightly with the light on and woke up to the alarm. She got up and checked on Buddy and let him out. She did her morning thing and went to work. Checking her car again before she got in. She went to work and had a busy day. Chris had to go out of town and left Cloe in charge. Cloe had to put in quotes and go over quotes of Billy and Rob, which had more than doubled now that more business came in and their were two people on the outside.

☙

At six she clocked out and went home. She checked her windows and found nothing. She worked out for a while before jumping in the shower. She read some more of her bible. She got on the Internet and did some research and then she went to bed. She slept on the couch and Buddy laid on the floor beside her. She set her beanie gun and some holy water balloons beside her also. She dozed off.

At two in the morning Buddy started growling and it woke Cloe up. She sat up on the couch and petted Buddy's head. She didn't dare make a sound. She wanted to catch them in her house. She saw a figure out the side window and she grabbed her beanie when she saw the figure stop. It looked like it turned around and said something to the air. Her window locks slid open by themselves and she watched them as if invisible hands turned them and pushed open the window. Buddy growled again and Cloe petted his head. The figure stopped talking and turned to the window. The figure slowly levitated as if there was a small escalator outside her window. Then like in the movies it slowly slid through her window. When it was about half way through it looked up to find Cloe on the couch looking at him. Cloe smiled and 'humphed' and the human man got big eyes before Cloe shot it in the face with a beanie. The man started yelling at something to get him out, his nose bleeding all over him as he backed out of the window at zero speed. Cloe grabbed her water balloons and put her beanie gun on her shoulder and her and Buddy went out the front door. By the time she reached the corner of the house, she could hear a whirring noise as the figure got whisked off by something down the road. For all Cloe knew it could have been a big bird, it sure sounded like it she thought. She called after it "And don't come back, or I'll kick your ass!"

She went into the house and laid back down on the couch, huffing. Buddy came in with her. She'd have to check the window in the morning to see if there are any prints. She thought about if they ambushed her through all the windows. It might come to that. She had to have a plan. She waited and listened and dozed off only to hear the alarm clock go off. She got up and after she made some coffee she went to the window outside. She bent down and saw tracks by boots from a rather heavy male by the way he sunk in the blue powder. So now she could track the intruder, if she got lucky enough to find blue powder on someone's shoes, hopefully before they tried again. She went in and drank some coffee and dressed to the hilt for an attack before going to work. She would have to be heavily armed until this whole thing blew over.

She caught Chris up on his work and helped some others out that would have normally went to Chris. She had a busy day. Rose walked in and took her out for dinner. She gushed about Dewayne. Cloe asked "So is this a boyfriend?"

"I don't know yet. They never last more than a few weeks. I'll let you know later." She giggled. They were fine with her until they found out she practiced spells and other witcheries. Then they all but ran out. Cloe's phone rang and it was her mother. Cloe talked her into going to lunch with Rose and her and they picked her up on the way to a restaurant that Rose was dieing to try.

The pulled into a crowded parking lot and Rose told the others about how everyone at work ranted and raved about this place. When they walked in they waiting to be seated and ran into Derek and Fred with two other girls. The men were cowing at them like they got caught doing something wrong and Cloe and Rose giggled and waved. Cloe even blew a kiss and they laughed as the guys quickly acted like they never saw them.

They got seated and ordered with out any problems from the people that worked there or other wise. They enjoyed their meals and talked and listened to Shirley tell the girls about Shirley's vacation with Cloe's dad. She had some funny stories and Cloe and Rose laughed a lot. Rose paid for all of it and then they went back to work.

When Cloe was dropped back off she told Rose she would call her and walked into the front lobby. She stopped short as she saw Lance standing there with her painting and Cloe greeted him with a hand shake. She led him into Chris's office and invited him to sit down. He looked at the chair as if it was blessed but he sat down anyways. Cloe sat in Chris's chair. "How are you Lance."

"I am fine. I thought I would bring you this painting personally. And see how you where fairing."

"I'm getting my ass beat by demons every time I turn around. Don't suppose you could put a stop to it can you?"

"I'm afraid not since it isn't my doing. But even if I could I wouldn't dare seem that I was sticking up for you."

"Fair enough. I suppose you wouldn't tell me who it is I'm suppose to see for help that has everybody's panties in a wad then?" Lance laughed as if she amused him but annoyed him at the same time. He just looked at her, white eyes met hazel ones. The smile faded from his face.

"Well." said Cloe "I thought I'd ask."

"Yes, well, I wanted to tell you that a ritual will start in three weeks to bring back Lilith."

"Already? They must have found another way."

"Yes, they have."

"I'll work on it."

"Then I must get back. I'll see you around I imagine."

"Bye Lance, thanks." He left with swift grace as he had always had. He didn't nod or say anything to anybody as they said hello to him or watched him pass. He disappeared into his Limo and drove off. Cloe went out of the office and brought the painting with her. She took the cover off of it and set it up by her desk so that she could study it. Everybody commented on it asking her a bunch of questions. She didn't get to concentrate on it much. She put the cover back over it and decided to take it home where she could look at it more. She stayed until five and went home. She took the painting with her and when she got home she took off the cover and stood it up against a wall. She studied where the book title was scribbled in the wood. She could hear Cory's voice talk about her. She wasn't a myth. She was real. How could one stop her? Cloe got her notes back out and studied them. Pulling books off the shelves of any that would give something about her. She read about crossing and banishing spirits. She didn't think that Lilith would qualify as any of those.

She thought some more while looking at the painting. Who ever she was to see was suppose to have the answer she bet. She just wished she knew who it was. Cloe kept remembering something about a man. She didn't know who it was. She decided she needed to see Madam Agnes. Maybe she could help her. Cloe thought about meditating but went to the bow flex and worked out instead. She would need all the strength she could muster if she had to take on Lilith. She worked out until she couldn't possibly pull another time and she went to take a shower. She forgot all about jogging until now. It was too dangerous.

When Cloe got done she went to study the painting. She remembered Jax telling her that some teachers teach students in an art class that sometimes painters that painted in the 300's on up painted angelic paintings but they always painted both angels and demons in a picture. But the thing was, Jax had told Cloe, is that you have to look for hidden pictures of the demons in other areas.

So Cloe thought maybe I'm just not seeing what I need to see. She tried shifting her eye sight to focus on others things in the painting. She didn't find anything. Then she tried to look at each object individually straight up, sideways, and upside down, still nothing. She got out a magnifying glass and sat in front of the painting. First she checked Lilith, her cloths, her hair, and found nothing. Then she checked the building that the book title was scribbled on, nothing. She got up and rested her eyes. She went to the fridge to get out a soda, popped the top and got a drink and went back to the painting. She checked the tree, nothing, the leaves, still nothing. She looked at the snake hanging out of the tree. Lilith was lovingly holding its head in her hand as she lay the other hand on her stomach. Cloe dropped her magnifying glass and looked at the painting and took a drink of pop.

After a sigh she went back to work looking at everything she thought would be something. After awhile she got a crick in her back and neck and got up to pace in front of the painting. Where did Jax say it would be, or did he even say? She wondered. She thought about calling him but dismissed the idea. She thought he had said. Cloe thought and thought. Then it hit her, it was usually around the whole picture by the frame. Cloe set the picture up higher so that she wouldn't have to sit on the floor any more to see it.

She got out a kitchen chair and set the painting on it. She set to work looking carefully around the picture. She looked for another half hour and still found nothing. She got another kitchen chair out and sat in front of the picture. She sat back and studied it. She needed to relax, she told herself, she was trying to hard. She closed her eyes and kept them closed. She slowed her breathing down.

She opened up her eyes and didn't look at the painting, she just went to work. She forgot that it was a painting because it blocked her thoughts. She was scanning the bottom of it when she saw it. It was a tiny demon with horns looking up and pointing. Cloe sat back and put down the looking glass. She couldn't see it with the naked eye. It was tiny, maybe a half of an inch big, and it was in the blacks and dark browns.

She looked at it again through the glass, she decided she needed a stronger magnifying glass so she went back to her kitchen drawer and got a bigger one. When she sat back down again and looked the glass made him bigger.

"Ah, that's more like it." she said. She looked around where he may be pointing at and saw another demon holding a book and reading it, he was looking forward. She followed his gaze and there in front of him was a group of short winged angels and a figure laying in a upside star. One had his mouth open and he looked to be yelling and was looking up. She followed his gaze and brought her glass up slowly. There above where angels looking down at him with their big wings spread and their hands out. One was looking up and Cloe followed. Above them was Michael, you can always tell Michael, he has a sword with him, but in the other hand he had a symbol shining that looked like a Christmas tree with wings. Cloe looked above him and saw the eye of God, the all seeing eye. There was nothing above him so Cloe went down again and looked at Michael. She put her glass down and got a pen and paper. She sat down and was just about to copy it when she heard Buddy bark wildly. She looked over her shoulder and felt that feeling around her. It was a feeling of the air not moving and it carried a charge that made her scalp tingle. It was her own built in warning system and she quickly put the painting down and backwards so it faces the wall then she dropped to the floor, and crawled to the couch.

She armed herself and got her remote to shut off the light. She crawled to the back door and opened it and whistled real loud. She was on her knees and Buddy came running through the door. She kicked it shut and scooted up to the

wall and Buddy was beside her. She petted the dogs head and whispered for him to be quiet. She waited to hear a noise. She didn't hear anything at first, but then she heard a window slide open.

She stayed where she was at. Due to the island in the middle of the kitchen she could surprise them if they came through the walkway on the other side. She heard footsteps and hoped they didn't see the painting, or they would know Lance was helping her. The footsteps walked around the living room and Cloe had to keep Buddy still. He let out a low growl but the stranger heard it. Cloe's heart beat went up and Cloe tried to steady herself. The foot steps came into the doorway of the kitchen and Cloe let Buddy go. He was a good distraction as he went for the leg of the intruder. About the time the intruder was going to cut Buddy with his sling blade Cloe shot him in the head with her beanie. The blade fell out of his hand and he fell to the floor. Cloe was on top of the island and launched off of it and flew through the air to drop a holy water balloon on him as she landed on the floor above his head. She spun around and had her beanie gun on him again. The water didn't affect him so he wasn't possessed by, or wasn't a demon. Cloe went over and called Buddy off. She tied his hands up and waited for him to come too.

He finally quit seeing stars and shook himself into reality. She had him leaned up against the wall and the light over the island was on. She sat on her island with her gun pointed towards him. Whoever brought him left with a big whirling noise. Cloe looked up at the ceiling as the noise of beating wings faded. She wasn't leaving her prisoner this time. He didn't have any old blue powder on his boots, just fresh, so he hadn't been her before.

He looked at Cloe and was going to go for her when he realized his hands where tied. She cocked her head to one side and humphed with a smile. "So what are you doing here?" she asked nicely.

"What do you think?"

"You came here to kill me?"

"Gee, aren't you a genius." He said and found a short dagger suddenly inches from his head, singing as it vibrated in the wall.

"I don't believe we have to be nasty here, it was just a question." Cloe said calmly. He looked at her with wide eyes. "Answer this question, how did you get here?"

"I flew." he said with a wicked smile.

"Some how I believe you, even though your being a smart ass again. So answer this question, what flew you here?" She said as she spun her fore finger around in a circle at him.

"You wouldn't believe if I told you." he said.

"What's your name?" He looked at her like she had lost it.

"Please don't make me repeat myself." she said as she picked up another dagger and started cleaning her fingernails.

"Nick, my name is Nick, what's it to ya?"

"Well, Nick, don't make assumptions about what I will or won't believe. Now, answer the question, and this is twice I've had to repeat myself. The third times the charm. What. flew. you. here?" she said the last four words slowly as if he couldn't understand.

"A. big. demon. with. wings." he said slowly back to her, mimicking her, as he sat up.

"That's better, you can talk slowly if you want to, I kind of like it." He rolled his eyes.

"Okay, who told you to come here?"

"I don't know."

"Now Nick, we're friends, I know your name, you know mine, your even in my house, alive." she said the last word with eye contact and loudly "so I feel like we know each other well enough that you can tell me anything."

"Why would I do that?" He found out why as she took an apple and hit him in his groin area with it. She was a damn good aim. As he groaned and called her names she let him. He finally caught his breath and looked at her.

"So know you know why." she calmly said with a smile.

"You are so dead." he said through clenched teeth.

"So I've been told, and you are too if you don't answer."

"I really don't know, I was hired over the phone. No names are mentioned. They wire you the money into your account when the jobs done."

"How did they find you?"

"Word on the street, they hire people like me to do their dirty work for them in exchange for money. No questions asked. You never hear from them again."

"What's the bounty on my head?" Cloe asked.

"Ten thousand dollars."

Cloe jumped off the counter and Nick flinched "Ten thousand dollars! No wonder you maniacs are coming for me. That's a lot of money. Hell, I may even turn myself in for that!" Cloe paced in front of him ranting about the money and what she could use it for. Nick looked at her again like she was crazy. Cloe settled down and picked Nick up. Nick was bigger than her but she managed. He was surprised at her strength, she looked littler than that. She made him walk out her front door and Buddy was with her. She let his rope loose as she told Buddy to watch him. He growled but kept his distance. As soon as she untied him she kicked him off her porch and had her beanie gun on him before he could pick himself up off the ground.

He stood there rubbing his wrist and looked at her. He just stood there and Cloe shook her head, and said in her best country slang "Well, I reckon you know where towns at. I'm not giving you a ride so you best get walking." He looked at her for a moment as if trying to figure her out and took off walking away. Cloe watched him go down the road in the street lights until there where no lights left and he disappeared into the darkness.

She went back in the house and closed the door and locked it. She went to the window and closed it too. She went to the painting and put it back on the chair. She put her gun beside her as she sat down. Buddy laid behind her. She picked up her pen and paper and went to draw the symbol that Michael was holding. It must have been something important. She got her looking glass and went back down the figures.

Where she had see the first demon looking up she went past him and there were other short winged angels in a circle, bound by fire it looked like. Cloe thought maybe that was the fallen bound in hell, but some scholars believe hell was a place in heaven across a great abyss. She dropped her glass back down and went to take a drink of her pop. Something told her not to drink it so she threw it away and got another one. She went to the fridge and decided to grab a juice box instead. She went back to the painting and looked at it. She looked at the clock. It was almost midnight.

She finished up her juice and cuddled up on the couch. She put the cover back on the painting. There's been no way she wanted to look at that thing and wake up to it. She was thinking of the little figures as she dozed off.

The next morning she took the painting to work and had a postal carrier take it back to Lance. She would have returned it herself but there was no way. She knew he wanted it back as quick as possible. She doubted if he wanted to pick it up.

Chris called and was checking to see how things were going. Cloe reassured him that everything was on schedule. He said he would be back tomorrow. He thanked Cloe before he hung up. Cloe told everyone that Chris would be back tomorrow. Most workers groaned but there were a few yippy's out of the bunch. Cloe was to lenient on them compared to Chris.

Cloe clocked out five and started to go home but remembered she wanted to go see Madam Agnes. She turned down Pine Street and made her way downtown. As she got two blocks from the house a swarm of black birds attacked her car.

She didn't see them coming at first until she noticed a swarm of black behind her in her review mirror. She cussed and went to roll up her window. One bird got in half way and Cloe was beating on its head. It had Rose eyes and was trying to peck her and cawed in her face. As she was trying to get that one out more was trying to come in. They were pecking her hand as she tried to push them out and some were trying to peck her face. She was swerving all over the road again. People were just staring at her in disbelieve.

She rolled up the window as much as she could. Some blood began oozing down her window from the birds that were trapped. She made her way for the alley and skidded to a stop. The birds were still flapping and hitting her windows, sometimes rocking the little car. She laid on her horn for help. It seemed like forever as she sat there looking at the birds swarm her car. She herd a ping against her roof, then another one and some more followed as birds were falling off her car. She looked through her window at the building. She saw Jamar with a BB gun and he was shooting off the birds. He was Jamaican and he lived next door to Madam and Papa. When Cloe saw an opening she went for it.

She opened the car door and went to run into the door. Jamar was yelling at her to go but she didn't quite make it. All the sudden the building was moving. Cloe froze in horror as bugs of all sizes, shapes and breeds came at her from the building. Cloe ran towards the car but it was covered too. She looked around and ran for another car. She jumped on the hood and up on the roof. She looked around for another place to go, which took her to a privacy fence. She scaled that until she saw the fire escape. She leaped into the air and just caught the bottom bar and hoisted herself up and climbed it as fast as she could towards Jamar.

Jamar had traded his BB gun in for a can of bug spray and a lighter. He was yelling at her to move her sorry ass. She shimmied up the latter and jumped through his window before he slammed it down. The bugs found another way in through little cracks and crevices and began filling Jamar's apartment. He told her to run to Madam's door and he followed blasting anything that moved. She went out to the hall and made her way to Madams door, beating on it frantically. Madam opened the door and Cloe fell through along with Jamar against her back.

Madam looked at Cloe and Jamar on the floor. They were breathless and Cloe's hand was bleeding. Papa helped them up and Madam told Cloe that she was trying to get a hold of her but the same things happened to her. They had been trapped there for some time now. Madam had strange dreams about Cloe and had wanted to warn her but she couldn't. Cloe said as Papa bandaged her hand. "Madam, I was told several times that there is a man to help me with something. I don't know who the man is or what he is supposed to help me with. I thought maybe you could tell me, and now I know I'm on the right track." she said as she caught her breath. Madam looked at her and said "You brings thiz to all of us. I pity you. I know of a fella who could of helped yo along time ago, but thiz fella don't do bizniss anymore, other than that, I can't help yo."

"But Madam, I fought my way here for your help." Cloe pleaded.

"I sorry chil. I can't help yo wit thiz. It'z outa my handz. You are only getting yoursef in more hot wata!"

"Madam, please, I need to find this guy who can help me. We are all in danger, not just me. I gotta find away to stop Lilith from doing whatever she's going to do. It's the end to us humans, let me go to him myself, I'll try to talk him into helping me. Just tell me where he is." Cloe begged Madam.

She didn't understand why Madam wouldn't help her until she saw her looking at Papa sideways.

Cloe looked at Papa as if he would tell her where to find him. She said "Papa Whitney, do you know where to find him? I disparately need his help."

Cloe said softly. Papa seemed to disappear somewhere inside himself. Madam was holding her breath. Finally Papa spoke and said "It is me that yunz seek."

Madam went to stop him but Papa held up his hand "Mama, you don't need ta worry yourself. Its time someone elze knew now. We always said we wou share it wit someone who waz worthy, well, if she ain't worthy I don't know who iz. See" he looked at Cloe "I used to be a voodoo docta. When I wou chaze away demonz sometime dey had a counta part dat waz stronga than I waz. I hads to find a way to defeat the one who waz stronga than da demon so dat da demon hads ta let go of the body. A man came up ta me one day az I was prayin in the ol catholic church down da road. He showed me dat if ya hold your fingaz like dis." and he showed Cloe a symbol with his palms facing her and his hands intertwined with the first two fingers criss crossing and the second fingers touching the tips and the thumbs touching, the rest was just spanned out as far as they could go "Dat you cou call the authority spirit to ya and can fight it or give it a sacrifice. I couldn't fight it zo I gave it a sacrifice…" his voice breaking off and his eyes closed. "I gave it peoples I didn't like. It waz wrong of me I know. But back den I thought I waz doing justice. I used dat symbol only three times before I quit being a voodoo doctor."

"Do you know who that was that showed you the symbol?" Cloe said.

"No, I never seen him agin. And at de church he just seem to disappear."

"Papa, that was St. Michael who showed it to you." Papa looked at her and his face lifted out of his scowl. He looked at Madam and said "Do you hear dat mama? Cloe says it was

Michael." and Madam smiled at him. "And you know what Papa? You were suppose to help me. I've been told time and time again to see a man who knew the answer. It was you all along."

"Yez, yes. It waz me. I'm so glad to let it go. I'm free now." Papa and Madam hugged and Madam wiped Papa's tears away. Cloe practiced the symbol on her hand and asked "Is that all I do?"

"No." said Papa. "No, you have ta command dem to come. You have to say 'Three times I call ya holy name' and whoever it iz you want, say da name and continue and say 'make dem come, humiliatin and repentin', to me by da most holy of holy' and dey should appear before you. But dey are mad when they gets there, so be ready."

"I will." Jamar cleared his throat and everyone looked at him. "Well, that's all good but how do you expect to get out of here?"

Cloe looked out the window and saw every creature in the city ready to attack. Madam took Cloe by the arm and said "Come on, I'll show ya anotha secret. Jamar, get in my car and drive it to 7th block. She'll meet ya dar." Jamar and Cloe looked at Madam and she stomped her foot at Jamar and said "Wahz you waitin fer, get haulin." and she took Cloe downstairs into a basement where they do laundry. Madam looked around and pushed on the wall.

It opened to reveal a tunnel.

❧

"Its a tunnel dat was here before even I waz born. But itz a good tunnel. There used to be a jail here and thiz waz a tunnel the Indjuns used to escape. Keep on it and it will take ya all the way to 7th block. Jamar shou be there with de car. If you don't minz driving my car, dat is. That's the only way your gonna get around without being zeen until ya ready to be zeen. Do ya trus me with ya car? I should haf asked you dat huh?"

"Its alright, we'll switch for awhile. When ever you're ready to switch back just come to my work. I can't complain. You've done enough for me. Thanks for everything."

"Itz okay, here I put da words on paper so's you don't fo'get." and Madam shoved it in Cloe's hand. She pushed Cloe down the corridor and closed the door with a wave. Cloe looked down the corridor and took off running. She had seven city blocks to go before she reached 7th street. She ran at a steady pace, a little faster than a jog. It didn't her no time to travel to the seventh block. When she got there she looked up at the manhole. She climbed the ladder and when she got to the top to lift it off, it came up swiftly and Cloe saw Jamar standing above her. He offered her his hand and helped pull her up out of the street.

She looked around as Jamar put the cover back on. He had a pick in his hand that was shaped like a L that fit through the manhole cover. He used it to replace it also. It saved his fingers she was sure. She took the keys from him and thanked him, he told her to be careful and he walked toward home. She drove to Rose's.

She went in the door without knocking. Rose was on the couch with Dewayne watching movies. When she came through the door they both jumped. Rose was on her feet when she saw Cloe's bloody shirt. "What happened? You got attacked gain?" Cloe nodded her head and shrugged. "By a bunch of birds and bugs."

"Huh?"

Cloe told her what happened when she decided to go to Madam's. She told her of the things Papa Whitney knew. Rose listened as she cleaned Cloe's hand off. Dewayne stood against the door frame of the bathroom listening to the girls. When they noticed that he was standing there Rose said "Oh, sorry Dewayne. Cloe this is Dewayne. Dewayne this is Cloe." Cloe and Dewayne waved at each other. Cloe turned and looked at Rose and smiled. Rose giggled. They moved into the living room when Rose said she was done.

When they got done cleaning her hand Cloe said she could go if she was interrupting anything. Dewayne said for Cloe to stay. He wanted to her story. Cloe told them about the painting and that she had found the figures around the picture of another scene. That was when she decided to see Madam on the next day. Cloe figured that they were guarding the building waiting for her to show up and if she did, then they were to attack till the death. Cloe told them how there was a tunnel underneath the building that reached beyond seventh street.

Dewayne said he had heard that story but everyone that it was just a fable. Cloe said it was really there. Rose thought maybe she would take Dewayne through it one time if she could. He said "I'd like that." Cloe thought that was weird how calm Dewayne was with all of this. She asked Rose "Does he know everything?"

"Ya, I've filled him on everything, and everything to come yet."

"It sounds like you've got quite a fight on your hands." Dewayne said.

"I guess. Maybe I can do this after all."

"You've had doubts." Rose asked.

"Sure, I've taken on one fallen before. And that wasn't very hard as far as physically." Cloe shrugged.

You can't go into a fight with a fallen with doubts. It just won't work." Rose said and threw a pillow at Cloe.

"I know. I don't mean too. But I don't think I can trick Lilith."

"God will help you with it. He always does." Rose said.

"I know."

"So when is the big showdown?" Dewayne asked.

"I don't know. Lance said that the ritual to bring her is in three weeks. I think I would have to call her in before they do."

"Who's Lilith?" Dewayne asked.

So Cloe told him the story of Lance, Cory and Lilith. Dewayne said that his religion also taught that the fallen were imprisoned with Satan and they were to be loosed with him when Michael lets them loose. Cloe said that was what she thought Lilith was for. She was somehow trying to set free the fallen and Satan.

"But that would bring about Armageddon." He said.

"Exactly."

"But how do you know that your trying to stop something that's suppose to take place? How do you know if God wants you to stop it?"

"Because Michael told me."

"Oh. Well good luck with that."

"Thanks." Cloe said.

Dewayne told the girls it was getting late and said he had to go. Rose walked him out to his car before coming back in all excited. "Its official." she exclaimed.

"What is?"

"We're a couple." she said as she excitedly jumped up and down.

"Really? That's great!" Cloe said and they jumped up and down together giggling.

After that they sat down, they talked about the whole thing. Cloe said the most important thing right now was where and when to bring Lilith in. She knew she would have to beat the fallen to the punch. Rose said "So the thing is, how do we trap her? She could just escape and then she'd be here because you brought her here. She'll go help them anyways."

"So we need something strong enough to contain her. Then we need to do something with her so they can't find her. Kind of like what we did with Botis."

"Ya but she'll be human form when she comes. What can she be when she's not human form?" Rose said, scratching her head.

"What did your notes say?" Cloe asked.

Rose went to her desk and dug out her notes that they collected from the library. She scanned several pages before she came across a note and she read it out loud "It says here that she turns into an owl."

"So that s what we have to put her into to keep her."

"Okay, but where are we going to bring her?" They thought on that. Neither one came up with a good spot. It would have to be a big area that Cloe would have to stay in also until one was defeated. They had two weeks to come up with something. Rose said Cloe needed to stay the night. Cloe reminded Rose of Buddy being home alone. Since it was a work day Cloe wanted to go home. Rose followed her.

Rose ended up spending the night instead and they got up early to go to work the next morning. Cloe got to work and Chris was there with some more men. They didn't belong to Lance's group. They were just regular men. Chris was taking them around the floor. They stopped at the drawing table in which Chris called Cloe over. Cloe got up from her desk and walked over. Chris introduced them to her and vise versa. They shook her hands and they all discussed the blueprints of the mall they were Redoing. When they were done at the drafting table, Chris walked off with some of the men while the others stayed and was drawing. Cloe watched the men with her talk about certain drawing. There was one with a mark under his eye like someone had punched him that left with Chris's group. Cloe wondered what that could have been about as she turned to watch Chris walk away. Cloe eyes grew big when she saw the same one with a black eye with casual shoes on. The shoes had blue powder on the bottoms.

Cloe caught up and followed Chris's group. When Chris went to help one of his own employees with something, Cloe took the men on tour some more. When she had a chance she asked the man with blue on his shoes "I don't believe I caught your name?"

"Oh, my name is Anthony." he said and held out his hand to Cloe.

She shook it "Do you live around here?"

"Uh, no, I live out in the country." he nodded.

"On a farm?" Cloe questioned.

"No. It's a private estate." He said with a shrug.

"You make pretty good money I imagine, but hey, who wouldn't need ten thousand dollars? Especially when you live in a estate. They are pretty expensive to maintain. I know I could use the money."

He nervously looked around and ran his fingers through his hair "What are you talking about?" he said with a false laugh.

"Oh you know what I'm talking about." she said softly "Did you notice that you had blue on your shoes?" He looked at her quizzically, then down at his shoe "Ya, I noticed, what's that gotta do with money?"

She got up next to him shoulder to shoulder and faced the same way as he was. To someone else they looked like they were having a pleasant conversation. "Because I know that's the bounty on my head that you tried to collect when you went through my window. That blue stuff? That's the stuff you walked through when you were at my house." She smiled and nodded at someone passing by.

"You're mistaken, that's not what's on my shoes." he said as he tried to give her the brush off.

"Whatever. I'm just gonna warn ya. Don't come back or you may not be so lucky to be standing here next time. Have a good day." She said the latter over her shoulder as she went to her desk. Anthony watched her walk away as he cleared his throat. When she got to her desk she sat down and made eye contact with him one more time before he joined the group and went to work. Cloe did the same and she never saw him again that day or after.

She went home at six and thought about how she solved that little mystery. She got home and petted Buddy's head and sat down to memorize the words that Madam had written on a piece of paper. She said them over and over again. When she was done with that she worked out. She exhausted herself around eight and ate supper. Rose drove up with Gigi and honked the horn. Cloe went out and helped unload him. He was happy to see her. He had strange symbols all over his body and on his hoofs. Cloe petted him and fed him. He went around his corral snorting and trotting. If he could talk it looked like he would say, 'It's good to be home." Rose was happy with her drawing and gave Cloe the paint to redo it when it grew off. They hoped by the time Cloe faced Lilith it would still be on. Rose went back to town and Cloe watched Gigi prance around and come up to her to get petted, only to take off again prancing around with his tail up.

She went in the house and went to sleep on the couch. Just in case she had any more visitors. She had dreams of fighting all night.

The next morning Rose called and wanted to go shopping at some local shops down town. They usually had the nickel and dime shops that kept tourist coming to the downtown area. The city kept most of the old buildings up and had the cobblestone streets still. Rose and Cloe got around and made it by ten. It wasn't to busy but it was getting there fast. They stopped by several little trinket booths that had an umbrella covering. They had various things from tee shirts to jewelry. Cloe loved to read the tee shirts. Some of them could be down right hilarious.

Cloe was looking at some necklaces and earrings and Rose was looking over her shoulder when the man who was sitting close by the booth, who was blind, said "I think that necklace would look good on you." At first Cloe just agreed while she browsed but Rose looked at her suddenly and then both girls looked at the old man sitting in the chair. He had a hat on that kept his face out of the sun and black glasses on. He just sat there with no emotion on his face. Cloe stepped up to him and brought her hand over his face a few times, then looked at Rose. Rose shrugged.

They went back to the booth and were looking and pointing when the man said again "Don't but that one, buy the one you were looking at on the right." Cloe stopped talking and then both girls went back to the man. "How do you know what I'm looking at if you're blind?" Cloe asked.

"Why would you assume I'm blind?" said the man.

"Because you are sitting here with blind man glasses on." answered Rose.

"Looks can be deceiving." the man said coolly.

"So you are not blind?"

"You tell me." he said. Cloe shrugged and went to take his glasses off but he grabbed her hand suddenly.

He was very strong and Cloe sucked in a breath and whispered "Shit."

She tried to back up and loose her hand but he held it firm. Rose went to grab Cloe's arm but noticed that they were now surrounded by a bunch of demons and wanna be's. They were distracted long enough to get surrounded.

Cloe looked around and Rose said "I don't think we're in Kansas any more Toto."

"Rose, we're going to have to fight." Cloe said at almost a whisper.

"Can't we just call for help?" Rose said in a whimper.

"You could try." snickered the old man that still had Cloe's arm. Cloe looked at him and he removed his glasses to reveal almost white eyes and sharp toothy grin. Cloe looked at him as he smiled. She would wipe that grin off his face. In a fluid motion she dropped her purse off her shoulder and grabbed the water guns that had holy water in them and yelled at Rose "Take these and start shooting." while she tossed them both to Rose. Rose caught them and looked at them in disbelief, along with the demons and her eyes went wide as she looked down at them. "What in Gods name, am I suppose to do with water guns?" she said at Cloe annoyingly. The demons and human helpers were snickering also. Cloe was looking at the old man and said "Rose…they are full of holy water…point carefully." Then she brought her foot up and kicked the old man in the face. He didn't loose her hand but his head spun side ways. He carefully brought head back around and looked at her. Mean while Rose was squirting everything that came near her and was shouting "I don't wanna die!" If they got to close she would backhand them or kick them.

The old man took Cloe's arm and spun it around to put a hurtful twist on her arm. Cloe in return ran up behind where the old man was sitting along the wall and was suddenly sitting on his shoulders. She took his head and snapped his neck. When he slumped forward she landed on the ground on her feet and went after the group that surrounded them. The holy water only held off the demons but not the humans. Which two were fixing to grab Rose. Cloe slugged one and reached around Rose to kick the other. Rose was breathing hard and looked at Cloe with wild eyes.

"Relax Rose, we're winning." Cloe said and went after another human.

Rose looked around and said wildly "We're winning? You seriously need your eyes checked!" and moved to the side as a body flew past her. She squirted one between the eyes and watched it scream in horror as it dropped to the ground with smoke bellowing off its head. She looked at Cloe and one had Cloe around the throat while another delivered a punch to her gut. Rose saw a demon run at them and squirted it in the back. It fell before it had a chance to reach Cloe and the others.

"How you doing over there?" Rose asked Cloe. Cloe looked at Rose and gave her a thumb's up while receiving another blow to the gut. Rose saw a demon coming at her and went to squirt it but no water came out. As the demon froze she held up the other gun and pulled the plastic trigger but it was dry also. She was terrorized suddenly and went to run circles around Cloe saying "Cloe, the guns are empty… what's your plan now," as she dodged a demons hands as he tried to grab her. Cloe brought both feet up and kicked the human in the face as he came in for another punch to her gut. He flew backwards, taking the demon that was chasing Rose with him to the ground. She flipped the man holding her by her neck over her body and kicked him between the legs when he landed on the ground. Cloe yelled to Rose "Where's my purse!?"

Rose said sarcastically "Gee, I'm kind of busy right now!…" Cloe looked around the ground for it frantically while Rose was throwing chairs and knocking over tables to get away from some humans that were chasing her. She spotted it by the old mans dead body slumped over in the chair. She was just about to grab it when she was clotheslined by an arm. She landed on the ground with a thud and hit her head on the cement. She cradled her head for a second while she tried to get the stars she saw to disappear. She heard Rose's voice yell "This isn't a time to be laying around, get up and get that purse!"

She looked up and saw Rose beating a demon with a leg off a chair.

She got up and looked around for the one who made her fall. He was waiting with his fist up and going from one foot to the other in a boxing fashion. Cloe brought her hands up and they went at it. He went to slug her and she ducked. She brought herself up again and dodged another blow to her face.

She ran backwards and ran up the wall to flip over his head and land behind him. Before he could turn around she delivered a few blows to his back ribs. He went to hurl around with his fist out in mid air but she ducked and kicked out is knee. He landed on the ground and grabbed his knee howling in pain and Cloe went for her purse. She had her tazer gun in there and some daggers.

She looked around and found two targets with her daggers and got throwing stars out and whirled them at two more. That left four. Rose looked at her and said "About time!" and Cloe shot her a look. One went for Cloe and she took her tazer and shocked it. It landed on the ground and Cloe stomped it in the gut. She went after the other one and shocked it. When it landed on the ground she punched it in the face. The other two looked from Cloe to Rose and then took off down the road. Rose was breathless and Cloe put her hands on her knees to catch her breath. Her gut hurt from earlier. People were standing around watching them. Cloe didn't realize they had an audience. A cop came through and told everyone to get back. He searched around and told Cloe to get her hands up. Cloe did and Rose came from around him with his her hands up also. He looked around suddenly and made sure there were no others standing around that he didn't know about. There were several cops suddenly and they were going from one body to another. The dead bodies were checked but they didn't know what to say because they were already old dead carcasses from along time ago. A cop came up to Cloe and said "What is going on here?"

"We were attacked." Cloe said with her hands resting upon her head.

"By what, what are these things?" he asked as he pointed to the shriveled up leathery bodies on the ground. Cloe just looked at him and Rose said "Well, their not human, that's for sure." The cop took off his hat and scratched his head. One cop came over and said "How do you want the report to go?"

"I don't know." said the cop with the most authority. The ambulance was there for the wounded, and went to the big guy with his knee out. The chief showed up and came up to the police that was questioning Cloe and Rose and said "I'll handle it from here." the cops nodded and took off with one last look and Cloe and Rose. Rose waved with a smile and Cloe just looked back at them. The chief watched them walk off before turning to Cloe and said "Put your hands down."

Cloe and Rose dropped their hands and the chief grabbed Cloe and pulled her to walk with him away from everything else. "What in the hell do you think you're doing?" he said through clenched teeth. Cloe was getting tired of his attitude and pulled out of his grasp. "It wasn't my fault!" she said each word with clarity. "They came out and attacked me, not the other way around. We were minding our own business and doing a little shopping."

"Maybe you should do your shopping somewhere else." he said with his hands on his hips.

"I live here, I don't have to do my shopping somewhere else." She relied back.

"You brought this on your self. You need to watch what you're doing." He spat at her.

"You're just pissed because you can't pin me with anything." Cloe said back.

"That'll change." he said. "Now get out of here before I really get pissed!"

Cloe just looked at him and pulled down on her shirt before she walked off. She walked towards Rose and said "Come on, lets get out of here." and Rose followed her through the crowd. The other cops were looking like they had just let a killer walk. Cloe knew they wouldn't understand. She just kept walking.

They got into the jeep and drove away. Rose made her way to a restaurant and parked the jeep. They made their way in and went to the bathroom. Cloe washed the cut on her face and Rose washed her bloody lip. There was a bruise around the edge of her mouth. After they washed up they went out and waited to be seated. They didn't talk much and Cloe knew Rose needed time to process what went on before she would start asking questions herself. The waitress looked at them and tried not to stare. She lead them through the tables to a booth and gave them their menus. She left them with drink orders and they looked over the menus. They ordered shrimp scampi and wine and then the waitress left them to their selves.

Rose looked out the window and Cloe folded and refolded her napkin. Rose chuckled and Cloe looked up. Rose looked at Cloe and said "That was almost like being in a movie."

"Except for the pain." Cloe answered back.

"Ya, then there's that." Rose said and touched her lip.

"You alright?"

"I guess, that was just crazy. It won't get any better."

"Not until we do something about Lilith."

"I was thinking about that. That is going to be a hard fight for you, you know."

"Maybe, maybe not. I can't think about that now."

☙

"I know. I want it to go back to the way it used to be. I don't want to fight physically, I want to help you get over your wounds when you fight physically."

"Gee, thanks." Cloe said with a shake of her head.

"Well, you're used to it. I'm not. You work out for it. I don't. I can't wait till this is over."

"I know. Either can I." Cloe said and looked out the picture window. Their drinks came and they took some swallows and then Cloe said "I'll tell you what, if you want to go shopping, we'll go out of town until this is over okay?"

"Okay, that sounds good."

"Good." Cloe said with a nod.

"So what did the chief say to you?"

"That he was tired of me starting fights, basically."

"But you didn't start that!" she said loudly.

"I know, I know." Cloe said and made a lowering gesture with her hand at Rose while looking around. "He has to blame someone."

"Well then he should consider getting in touch with his own kind."

"It doesn't matter to him. He thinks because I got involved in the first place that it's my fault."

"A lot of people think that." Rose said while studying her fork.

"I know."

❦

Their food came and they ate mostly. They only talked a little. When they were done they ordered dessert. It was brownies covered with ice cream and hot fudge. It was so delicious. They scraped the bowls with their spoons. When they were done they paid and left. They went to Rose's house and sat down on the couch. Rose pulled her shoes off and rubbed her legs. The muscles were tense from the fight. "So have you come up with a meeting place for Lilith?"

"No, everywhere I think of is public, that's big enough."

"Oh. To bad you couldn't go to one of these churches that have those youth centers connected to it around here and have a duel there." Cloe thought about that and then a idea come to her. "Rose, you're a genius sometimes. The Catholic Church has a big basement and it doesn't have anything breakable in it or it isn't used for anything but storage. I wonder if they will let me use it for this."

"I thought they didn't support you much." Rose pointed out.

"They don't, but maybe they will say yes."

"It's worth a try I guess." Rose shrugged as Cloe pulled out her cell phone and dialed father Scovley's number. The phone rang on the other end two times before he picked up.

"Hello?"

"Father, its Cloe."

"Oh, hello Cloe."

"Say. I wanted to ask you a question." Cloe said quickly.

"Okay."

"I was wondering if I could use the church basement."

"For what?" he asked.

She was hoping he wouldn't ask. "Well for something along the lines of conjuration."

"Are you insane? You know the church would never go for that."

"But it's important. Please consider it. You could even watch for study purposes!" Cloe said suddenly, knowing that the Catholic priest would probably want to see so they could take notes. Father Scovley must have thought so to, because he paused over the phone as if he was turning the thought over. "You could be right about that. I know that the bishops would be very interested." They didn't believe in what Cloe did as far as demon banishing went. They didn't believe she had the power.

"So do you think you could ask and see and let me know?"

"I guess I could." he said slowly.

"Thanks father, it has to be done. I can do it out in public or I can do it in the privacy of the church. But it has to be done. Lilith will have knowledge to free Satan and the fallen from heaven and you know what that means."

"Yes, yes...well I'll let you know soon." he said.

"Okay then, good bye."

"Good bye Cloe." he said and hung up.

"How'd it go?" Rose asked.

"I don't know. He had to ask the others and he'll let me know."

"I hope they say yes."

"Me too, but they may want to watch according to Father Scovley."

"Would that be so bad? It seems like you may have back up."

"They wouldn't get involved. It may be more of an audience to check out what I can do instead of what she can do."

"Oh, oh well. Let them play judge. You know what God says about that."

"Yes, I sure do."

They sat there and talked a little more before they made their way home. She fed her animals and let herself in. She didn't notice one of the windows open and walked past it to the kitchen. She got to the fridge when she suddenly felt odd as her hair stood on end and the air felt stiff. She looked into the fridge door where there was sort of a reflection and saw two red dots coming at her. She quickly grabbed a knife and turned around and hurled it in the direction of movement. The knife quivered as it stuck out of a demons head. It hissed at her but it stopped. It wasn't a special blade so it didn't kill it. Cloe thought quickly and everything was in the living room by the couch.

She eyed the demon as it started to make its way to her. She looked around for something to throw but didn't come up with anything. The demon knew that she was unarmed and it smiled as it came closer to her like a cat catching mice. She had her back to the counter and couldn't inch away any further. The demon froze for a split second before launching at her. It came from over the island in one jump and was in front of Cloe. It raised its claw to swipe at her but Cloe jumped up and grabbed the cast iron pan off the hanger on top of the cabinets and came down on its head. The pan vibrated in her hand and she heard the 'thunk' of the demons head. She dropped the pan and ran around the demon to the door. It gathered its wits and shook off the pain. It followed her with its eyes and in one leap it was on her back. She dropped to the floor and it drew up to claw her in the back.

Cloe yelled in pain as she felt the claws rip at her skin. She was trapped as it sat on her back. The demon grabbed her hair and slammed her head into the floor. Cloe quickly put her arm up to stop her head before it actually hit the second time. She heard the demon scream in frustration and knew another blow was coming. She got up and carried it half way with her to her couch. She had holy water balloons in a cooler and grabbed one to pitch it directly behind her. It must have hit because she heard a scream of pain and the demon let go. She got up and got another one to hurl at it like a football. It splattered and covered the demon all over its head and chest. As it withered in pain Cloe grabbed it by the foot and dragged it out on the porch.

She watched it for a second and it hissed at her before it flopped around again. She went to get her flame thrower and finished dragging it on the ground and started the demons body on fire. No sense in letting it suffer. She wasn't like that, no matter what it was. When it was a pile of ashes she took a shop brush and scattered the ashes in the yard for the wind to blow away. It had a odor from it which stank real bad.

Cloe never could get used to the smell. As she worked she figured in her head that they must know that she is close to ruining their plans some how. The demon took a big chance on coming into a church. It probably didn't feel one hundred percent. But it couldn't disobey orders either. She would have hated to be anywhere else and fight, it probably would have got the best of her. It was one of the bigger demons she ever saw. She went back in and Buddy followed this time. When she got into the house she froze as Buddy was growling at the bedroom door. She grabbed her flame thrower and then thought about how that might burn down her house so she quickly set it down and grabbed her beanie gun instead. She also had a holy water balloon in the other hand.

"Come out now. You can live if you want to, just come on out of there." Cloe said into the darkness. Buddy growled towards the door once more. Cloe saw something move in the shadows. She wondered what it was doing in her bedroom. It knew it probably would have attacked her in her sleep. That would be a bummer she thought.

"There's no where for you to go. Come out now." She called once again. She saw movement and finally a demon came to the door and hissed at her. It was a littler demon but Cloe knew that sometimes the littler ones can fool you. Cloe stood there and watched it, it watched her back. The more intelligent ones have a different look to their eyes. Cloe noticed right away that this one kept her stare. "How come you can be in a church?" she asked it. The demon looked at Cloe with cat like eyes and didn't answer. It was hoping that Cloe didn't know it could speak. Cloe saw it a dozen times, they pretend that they are dumb to get out of questioning by her. She wasn't letting this one go without some kind of answer.

The demon's eyes moved to the door. Cloe knew it was figuring out an escape. Cloe sighed and said once more "Look at me." It did. "I know you understand me and can talk. Now I want you to start talking or I'll burn you to a crisp. Please don't think I don't know you are trying to get out of here either." Its eyes got wide for a second and it hissed at her. Cloe brought up her beanie gun and pointed it at the demon. "Do you want to die?" Cloe said.

"Dieing isn't so bad." said the demon.

"There now, was that so hard?" Cloe asked.

"We are not supposed to talk to you, its orders." said the demon.

"How is it that you are in a church."

"We can tolerate it for awhile, but not for very long. It is killing us slowly and it feels like bugs beneath our skin."

"So it makes you weaker the more you stay. I guess you better start answering fast then." Cloe said defiantly.

"What do you want to know. Either way I'm dead."

"Why?"

"Because, if I give you answers, then they'll kill me anyway."

Cloe thought about that. Boy, they play rough. Oh well. "Who keeps sending you to me?

"There are many."

"Do they all work together or are there separate orders coming through?"

"We are all together." The demon said.

"I guess I have no more questions. You are free to go." Cloe said and dropped her gun. Cloe stood there and looked at the demon. The demon stared at Cloe and slowly made its way to the door, never taking its eyes off of Cloe. When it got to the door it opened it and took off in a run. They were quick like snakes when they ran. Buddy ran after it but gave up when it disappeared. He came back through when Cloe yelled for him and shut the door. She went through her house with her balloon ready and checked in all closets and under and in anything that had space.

She locked all doors, even her bedroom. She'd sleep on the couch tonight she thought. She took a shower to clean off her back. It had a big cut down it but the tear was clean and the skin overlapped the worse part. It probably could have used stitches but Cloe wasn't going anywhere tonight. She was tired. She wrapped a big towel around her and lay on the couch on her stomach. She fell into a light sleep.

❧

The next morning she went to work. She wore a very loose blouse and walked slowly. She went into Chris's office and told Chris she had a doctor appointment to go to. Chris said that would be fine and Cloe went back through the doors. She needed to have her back looked at because it kept oozing blood everywhere. She called Rose and said she had an emergency and Rose stayed at her house waiting on her.

Cloe drove to Rose's and went inside. She took off her shirt and Rose told her she really needed stitches. Cloe said she knew and told her what happened. Rose got out her stitch gun and while Cloe was talking Rose would pull the skin together and up. The stitch gun was like a hole punch but it stitched instead. After it clicked and released there would be one stitch. Rose worked on Cloe for an half an hour.

When she was done Rose covered Cloe's cut with antibiotic ointment and covered it up. Then she wrapped Cloe's mid torso inn gauze bandage to keep everything stiff and tight. Cloe felt better about moving around. She thanked Rose and they both took off for work.

She came back to work and sat at her desk when Chris walked up and asked her how the doctor went. She said fine and told Chris she had to get stitches. Chris looked shocked and said "I didn't know you were that badly hurt or I'd taken you myself. What happened?"

"I fell off my horse. I guess I must have landed on a sharp rock or something."

"I told you horses were dangerous." Chris said.

"It's not their fault, they act on instinct."

"Well, are you going to be okay? Can I get you anything?"

"I'm okay, I'm just not moving around a lot today."

"Sure, I have a bunch of quotes for you to do anyways." Chris piled papers on top of her desk. He smiled a toothy smile and walked off. Cloe looked at the pile and groaned. She took the top one gingerly and got to work. She stayed at the shop for lunch and took a half hour to eat something out of the machine. Then she went back to work. Around three her phone rang and she answered it. "Hello?"

"Its Father Scovley."

"Father, I hope you have good news?"

"Well, I think the answer may be yes but they want to meet with you tonight."

"What time and where?"

"At the church in the office and be here by five thirty."

"I will, thanks Father."

"No problem." and he hung up.

Well that was good news to Cloe. Now if she could make the others believe in her cause. She didn't have any other choice, really. She wished there was another way. She wasn't looking forward to calling in a grand demon or fallen, which ever Lilith may be, just to fight her again and hide her away.

But if that's the way its gotta be then so be it.

She knew she was on her own. She needed to get an owl.

It was four thirty before Cloe quit and went to the church. She looked around but the bishops and priests were still behind closed doors. They were having a meeting she gathered and went to the sanctuary. She said a prayer and asked for help. God has always helped her before. If this didn't turn out then there must be another way. Cloe went back and stood outside the doors and waited, her belly was full of butterflies.

The door opened and Father Scovley came out to greet her. She shook his hand and went inside. Everyone was in there gowns and looked all holy that she felt like she was under a microscope. Father Scovley introduced her to them and let her have the floor. "Hello, it's nice to see you all again. I wish it was under different circumstances but its not. I came here tonight to ask for your permission to use the basement storage in order to conjure Lilith and…" that made them all talk at once to each other "…and banish her in her true form to an owl so we can hide her away from the fallen that are here." She said the last very loudly above the noise of the talking. She looked at Father Scovley, who was looking at her. He put up one finger at her as if to tell her to wait. She stood there in the middle of a semi circle of men and watched them debate. She sighed as it seemed like it would go on forever.

The man in the middle who sat directly in front of her held up his hand and eventually everyone quieted down. He looked at her and then said in a loud but direct tone. "We have heard of your work. How do you know how to conjure?"

Everyone was looking at her now, waiting for an answer. "Well." said Cloe thinking *here we go* "Someone showed me."

"How did you learn of it?"

"From an Cajun. It's an old Cajun conjure."

"Does it have a title or name to it?"

"Not that I'm aware of." Cloe said.

"How did they learn of this conjure."

"They didn't know, but they learned it here in this very church. I believe St. Michael taught it myself."

That got them hopping. They argued and debated even more loudly than before. She thought she even heard the word blasphemy spoken somewhere. Cloe stood and listened and watched. She didn't have a very good feeling about this at all. The man held up his hand again and it got quiet. "Why do you believe St Michael taught this?"

"Because of what the man described to me, and I too, have talked to Michael in this church." that got a few snickering out of them, but Cloe wasn't backing down now.

"What did this 'Michael' tell you when you saw him?"

"He taught me how to use Deaths Dagger." Cloe said.

That got them to sober up. They just stared at her, some had their jaws open. They where whispering in each others ears until someone whispered to the man in front of her. He nodded and looked at her again and said "Wait just one moment please." a man at the other end opposite Father Scovley went out of the door.

He came back moments later with a very fat book that looked very worn and had bookmarks of all kinds hanging out of the pages. They gathered around the man in the middle as he looked something up. They were reading and pointing and then they looked up at Cloe. Some took their seats again and one of the clergy asked her. "How were you instructed to use Deaths Dagger?"

"By putting a fist over the heart of the victim and saying there true name, which Michael had delved to me what that was at the time I needed to know."

As she spoke there were some that followed along in the book and some just watched her. When she finished speaking they once again began whispering and pointing. The man in the middle closed the book and everyone sat down. He looked at her some more before he spoke. "It seems you speak the truth, even though it's hard to say how you know of these things…"

Cloe just stared at him in disbelief. She just told them of how and they still doubted. She would have gotten smart if this wasn't so damn important. She let him go on "But what matters is that you want to use the basement for a conjure. Why do you want to conjure Lilith?"

"Because I learned that Lilith holds very important information on how to free Satan and fallen and that's what the fallen are working on here, in this city, even as we speak."

"Have you seen the fallen?" he asked nonchalantly

"Yes I have. I have seen a dozen or more. I have killed one using Deaths Dagger. I have countless demons after me all the time because of this very thing we are talking about." That got them talking again. Cloe waited. The man in the middle motioned to Father Scovley and he went to kneel beside the man who was in charge. He whispered in his ear, and Father Scovley nodded and stood up. He walked over to Cloe and said "Can you please step out into the hallway a while?"

"Sure." Cloe said. She made her way out and closed the door. She stayed there and listened for a bit before she rubbed her temples and walked into the sanctuary. She could imagine this debating of theirs may take awhile. She couldn't believe they didn't believe her.

"Its hard to believe something you've never seen yourself." She heard someone say. Cloe looked around and there stood a huge muscular man with long brown hair and outstanding blue eyes. She knew it was Michael.

"Now that's more like it." She said "You in your true form." He laughed and came towards her. "You did a good job in there."

"How come you never show yourself to them?"

"Because they never ask me too." he said sideways at her.

"Oh, I wonder why." she said more to herself

"Am I on the right path?" she asked him.

"Yes, you are." He said and touched her head. She could feel her back pain slowly going away.

"You are going to have to come around more often so that you can doctor me up."

"You need to wear protective armor like I do when I battle." he said.

Cloe imagined that and laughed. It reminded her of the Gladiator movie. She could see her walking around town in that.

"I wasn't being funny."

"I know. Are they going to say yes?" Cloe sobered up.

"Yes."

"Am I ready for this?"

"I don't know, are you?"

"I hope so." she said with a shrug.

"Metatron is going to be there, as well as I am, when you bring her here."

"Are you going to help?"

"Yes."

"Why can't you just do it?"

"Because it's your calling."

"But I'm just a human."

"We could do it but God wants you to handle it. You will show a lot of humans that through God all things are possible."

"Can't we prove that another way?" Cloe said with a whine.

"This is the time." Cloe closed her eyes and rubbed her temple. When she opened them again he was gone. Cloe wasn't surprised. She went back to the hallway and stood against the wall opposite the door. It sounded like they mellowed out a little. But they were still debating. After another fifteen minutes the door opened and Father Scovley motioned for her to come in. She went through the door and Father Scovley closed it behind him and sat down at the table. The bishop in the middle looked at Cloe again with a scrutinizing look. Cloe looked back at him.

"We have decided to let you use the basement. We want to see for ourselves what is going on exactly. You don't mind an audience do you?"

"Uh, I guess not." Cloe said. She never had an audience before.

"Fine then its settled. When do you suppose your going to do this ritual?"

"I don't know. I didn't plan on getting past this part."

"I see. You will let us know when that is then?"

"Yes. I'll call Father Scovley."

"That will be fine. That will be all." he said and dismissed Cloe just that fast. Father Scovley was on his feet and coming towards Cloe to escort her out. He had her by the arm and Cloe kept up with his brisk pace. He opened the door and led her out. He closed the door briefly and Cloe said quickly "I want to thank you."

"Just don't bail out or they will never help you again. This is the time to prove something to them." He said and nodded. He squeezed her arm and disappeared back through the door. It closed firmly in Cloe's face and she took it as a sign that she was done here. She went out the exit and got in her car. She sat there for awhile thinking. So this was it she thought. It's just a matter of calling Lilith in and somehow making her turn into an owl and trapping her there. *I guess that's how I would do it* she told herself.

She shook her head and called Rose to tell her that she had the okay at the church. Rose was excited but scared for Cloe. Cloe said she would call her later with the details and hung up. She went home and checked her windows to make sure there were none open. After she fed her animals she felt over both animals bodies to make sure she didn't miss anything. Everything seemed okay. She let herself in and locked up behind her. She checked every room and closet.

She checked under her bed and in the bathroom. After she was satisfied she sat on her couch and looked at her statue of Jesus. *I can do this* she told herself. Suddenly she went to her bookshelf and pulled out a book of spells that was handed down from somewhere on her moms side of the family.

She looked under banishing and breaking spells. She thumbed through and read one, then read something else. Finally after an hour of reading she found something that interested her. A group of women made a circle and banished the spirit. It sounded like something out of the movie Practical Magic. Cloe was sure there were several spells that involved a bunch of women. After all several women together when doing a spell was a powerful thing.

She wondered if she could talk her sisters into doing this. It would be a good thing if she could get them involved. There would be strength in numbers.

And seven or eight including Rose would be a good number.

Cloe closed the book after reading several spells and wondered if she should ask her sisters. She put her head in her hands and rubbed her face. She let out a yawn and got up to carry herself to her bed. One thing was sure she thought before she fell asleep, it sure was quiet tonight.

☙

The next morning she went to work and kept busy. She passed by a window on her way to get a cup of coffee out of the vending machine. The sun shone and the sky was the certain blue that seems to go on for ever. It was as if the atmosphere was so crystal clear. Cloe looked into the sky and wished, as she done so many times, that she could at least see heaven. Sometimes she wasn't sure if she was doing any good. There was so much evil in the world it didn't seem like there was a God or a heaven. She sighed and went to get coffee. Maybe at lunch she would sit outside and enjoy it.

She went to work and got around to lunch at one in the afternoon. She got some quick fix it foods out of the vending machine and sat outside at the picnic tables. She sat out there for an hour before she went back to work. She loved the fall time when it wasn't to hot and the leaves starting turning colors. She also loved Halloween.

After work she drove to Sue's house and Sue was cooking outside. Cloe opened the back gate to the backyard. Sue saw her and said "Well hello stranger."

"Hello." Cloe said and sat down.

"Just in time for supper." Sue teased her.

"I'm not really hungry."

"Really, you must be sick." She said with a grin.

Cloe looked at her and said "Actually I came here to ask a favor."

"Oh, what is it?"

"I was wondering if you care to be in a ritual?"

Sue finished putting the hamburgers on the grill and closed the lid. She wiped off her hands and sat down. She looked at Cloe and shrugged "If its anything you're involved in, its probably dangerous."

"It could be." Cloe nodded.

"What does it entail exactly." Sue asked.

"It's for when I call Lilith."

"You got to be crazy!" Sue said as she leaned forward.

"Well that may be the case but I have the go ahead in using the Catholic church basement and they want to watch, so even if I wanted to back out, I can't because I told them they could oversee it."

"Is that the only reason why you're doing it?"

"No, it's what I have to do."

"Why are you asking for help?"

"Because, there is strength in numbers." Cloe said, she didn't mean to sound so cliché.

"Oh. Do you know of a spell that uses more than one person?"

"There are several. But you know you don't have to do this Sue. I understand if you say no. I just wondered if maybe you and the others would be interested in saving the world."

"What others? You mean our sisters?" Sue got up to check the hamburgers and laughed at Cloe to think that the sisters would get involved.

"You don't think they would? It's a great opportunity."

"For what?, for themselves?, for heaven?"

"One or the other." Cloe shrugged.

"I don't know. I mean I would love to help, if it were just me. But then there's the kids and Greg. And the sisters have families to think about. I'm not sure what kind of danger we would face just being there. I think though, if I remember right from reading the books, that what ever brings it to banish it will be the main target. Which would be you. If we are there, there's no way we are going to stand idly by and watch you get hurt, which puts us in danger." Sue said and put her arms over her chest and kicked at a stick. Cloe knew that was right. If the shoe was on the other foot, she would feel the same way. She scratched at the surface of the picnic table with her thumb nail. She felt awkward. Maybe she shouldn't have asked she thought. "I really understand Sue. It's not a problem and I knew I would be alone on this anyways, I just thought…"

"I know, I'm not mad. I just don't think it's wise."

"Okay, you're right. So how's supper coming along?" Sue laughed and turned attention to the grill. She got a plate and took some burgers and hotdogs off the grill and Cloe told everyone supper was ready. They sat around the table and ate and visited. When it got dark Cloe said good bye to everyone and went home. She did her chores and checked everything out before settling down on the couch. She checked her machine. Rose was on the other end telling her to call her.

She dialed Rose's number and Rose picked up on the second ring. "Hey, what's up?" Cloe said.

"Nothing. I was bored and called but you weren't home."

"Yah. I went to Sues and asked her if she thought maybe her and the sisters could help in conjuring Lilith."

"How'd that go?" Rose asked.

"Like a turd in a punch bowl." They both laughed.

"Well can you blame her?" asked Rose.

"No, not really." and they talked some more about nothing and planned to spend lunch together the next day before they hung up.

She worked out on JuJitsu and Ti Chi before she went to bed. It was good enough to make her fall asleep but she didn't stay asleep for long. She heard a loud thunderous crack outside then Buddy was growling again at the front door. She crawled out of bed and stayed on the floor. She reached into her dresser for her daggers and throwing stars. She grabbed a few of each. The daggers she put between her teeth, the stars she carried between her fingers. She heard the front door open this time and she slid behind her bedroom door that was left open.

She heard footsteps and then she heard a mans voice say "Cloe, come out, come out, wherever you are?" Cloe's eyebrows come together and she tried to figure out who this stranger was. She peeked between the door and brace to see a tall man walking around her living room. "Seriously Cloe, come out. I just want to talk. I don't want to fight."

Cloe slid out from her door and put her daggers in the band of her pajama pants in her backside and had her stars ready for throwing. She walked out her door and there in her living room stood a fallen. He was tall with black leather pants and trench coat on. He wore black biker boots also. Cloe came out in the open and the fallen saw her and stopped. He smiled a white smile that made Cloe think of Cory. That same perfect white teeth model smile. He bopped his head a little and fell backwards on the couch. His feet came up to cross on her coffee table and his arms went out to each side of him along the back as he made himself comfortable. He motioned for her to sit also but she stood there looking at him.

"To what do I owe the pleasure of your company?" Cloe said tiredly.

"Well, there are a lot of reasons why I'm here. But first let me introduce myself. My name is Semiaza. You can put your weapons away, they won't do you much good anyway." he said while eyeballing her throwing stars and noisily chewed on gum with his mouth open.

"Unless I take out your eyes." Cloe replied.

"Think your that good?" He quipped.

"I know I am." She said quickly.

"Is that anyway to treat a guest?"

"I don't believe you were invited." She said with a short shake of her head.

"I don't have to be." He responded and squinted his eyes at her.

"So once again, why are you here?" Cloe asked and shrugged.

"Because I was sent." He said with a short laugh.

"And what is that to me?" Cloe asked as she watched his jaw chew quickly.

"I am one of the chiefs of the fallen." He said and picked up Cloe's spell book she was looking at earlier. He blew a bubble and started reading it as Cloe put her throwing stars on an end table and sat down on the chair. She watched him read a few pages with a 'humph' or a weird sort of hysterical giggle here or there. He nodded as if he understood what was going on and replied "There is some really good stuff in here." He looked up and around and eyed her bookshelf. Then he swiftly got up and went to it to pull out a book here or there, and read the titles. Some he even laughed at when he read it.

"So, are you on book patrol?, I promise I've returned all my books where they belong." Cloe said while watching him.

"Naw, I just want to see what kind of information you humans pass around. It all started with our information that we gave humans at the end of our war in heaven. But then the humans took it and made their own crap up. You can hardly find an ounce of truth for what we have shown so long ago anymore." he said and put the book he had in his hand back on the bookshelf. He passed by the Jesus statue and mockingly saluted it.

He went to the couch to plop down once again. He put his feet up and looked at her and smiled. Cloe's eyebrows drew together.

"I just wanted to come visit you. I have never got to meet you but I've heard so much about you." he said and touched where a heart was supposed to be. He said the latter sarcastically with a pucker to his lips.

Cloe sighed and shifted in her seat.

This was going to be a long night.

"So, word has it that you are ready." he quoted in mid air with a roll of his eyes "To bring Lilith."

"How would you know?"

"You don't listen much, do you?" Semiaza said as his face took on a more sinister look. "I said, word has it, you know what that means, right?"

"If you're going to be sarcastic, you can carry your sorry ass out of my home, you know what that means, right?" Cloe said through clenched teeth getting peeved.

Semiaza just looked at her like she had lost her mind, then he smiled and settled in a bit more on the couch. "No wonder Vetis had such a time with you. Fine, I apologize." he said with a wave of his hand.

What, does he think I'm stupid? Cloe wondered.

"Oh, I know you are smarter than most. I wanted to see for myself if you are everything I've heard about. So far you are holding up to expectations." he said with a nod and starting chewing frantically again. "How you have gotten this far is way beyond most of us Angels, fallen or not. We know you have had God's help in a lot of what you do, which has really shaken the grounds where we stand. I think the only ones who are one hundred percent sure of you are Michael, Gabriel, and Metatron. And with them on your side you'll have the hatred of most all others because of their support of a lowly human. But the three of them are closer to God than most others, and that is what saves you I think."

"And your here to tell me this?" Cloe said and stifled a yawn. Not believing his every word.

He looked at her and curled his lip to mock her. He got serious and said "No. I'm here because we want to know if you are really going to bring in Lilith?"

"Why." Cloe shook her head at his nerve.

"Because if you do then we won't have to. All we have to do is wait till she kicks your ass and then she'll come to us. You have already found the place." Cloe froze on the inside "Oh don't look surprised." he said as he tossed a pillow in the air and caught it "You are being watched all the time. So we know where and we know you know how to bring her, better than most of us, but we don't know when."

"And you want me to tell you when?" Cloe asked very slowly.

"Well, I was hoping to get that from you, yes."

It was Cloe's turn to laugh.

Why would they think she would give that away? She looked at him and he wore that look again of sheer hate as he chewed his gum. They don't like to be laughed at. "I really don't know myself when I'll call her in." she said. She wasn't going to lie. He didn't believe her. "I thought you'd say that." He said and stared hard at her.

"It's the truth. I really don't know." Cloe said again.

He studied her for awhile and Cloe guessed after trying to read her mind found she was telling the truth. He straightened up and asked "You really don't think you can win, do you?"

"Anything's possible." she said.

"But not probable." he countered back.

"With God on your side it is." she quickly said back. Knowing they hated to hear those words. As on cue his face turned a several shades redder as if he was holding his breath. He looked at her and Cloe pushed the issue, knowing it was dangerous. "You should have stayed there in heaven. Then you would know these things. I've told Vetis myself that you made a mistake following a damned angel and for what?"

"What would you know?" he hissed out between clenched lips

"So that you can perish at the end. I'm surprised that you are even wanting this war. It brings about the end for you faster."

"It can change." he said while looking down at the coffee table

"Ohhhh." Cloe said with understanding. "That must be some of Lucifer's lies. You can't tell the difference by now?"

Suddenly his hand was around her throat and his face was close to hers as he smelled her skin. "I could kill you right here and now and then we wouldn't have to worry about it anymore." he hissed and looked into her eyes.

"True." she wheezed "But then I'll be in heaven and be with the others and plan against you anyway. God could always choose another to take my place. I'll be in the right spot to help."

As if he weighed her words out he let her go in a second and was on his feet. He straightened out his coat and combed back his hair with his hands. He went to the door and turned to her one more time "I'll see you around." and vanished.

Cloe sat there and looked at the closed door. He didn't go through it, he just vanished. Lucifer is telling them something different all this time and they still believe him? Maybe some do, some don't. It wouldn't make a difference. The fallen didn't have anything to lose now. Maybe Lucifer played on their hopes for living longer than what God promised.

She just couldn't understand how they would not know the end. How could they not know how it would play out?

She went back to bed knowing that nobody else was going to show up. She was almost sure she was done fighting with demons for now. Everyone was waiting for the big showdown. And if she was being watched by unseen demons or spirits that convey information then she had to careful of what she said to anyone as to not give anything away. That was going to be hard.

The next morning she went to work and when lunch came she met Rose at the local taco place after a short phone call telling her to be there. Cloe sat down and said "I have to be careful of what I say to you because I'm being watched. I want to tell you of when the day will be but I don't want to say it out loud. How can I do this?"

"How do you know you're being watched?"

"Because I had a visitor last night. A fallen named Semiaza who is a chief of the fallen. They know about using the Catholic Church and he wanted to know when."

"Why would he think you would tell him?" Rose asked.

"I have no idea. But they're going to let me because then they don't have to worry about it."

"Let you do all the dirty work."

"Right."

"Huh, well, let me think about this for a minute." She said and bit into a taco. Cloe followed and bit into hers. This was another favorite. She ate noisily as the taco crunched as she bit into it. She was thinking of how to talk code. Rose asked when she got done chewing. "Do you have a day planned?" Cloe crossed her eyes. Rose smiled and shook her head. She grabbed her soda and took a drink through the straw.

"If you said yes." which Rose knew she did, "What day were you planning on?"

Cloe thought about how to put it. She wondered if they knew pig Latin. Well even if they didn't it would be easy to figure out. She said "Seven." Rose looked at her and had a screwed up look on her face. Seven, Cloe thought and looked at Rose eye to eye. They were pretty equal in their thoughts and had the same ideas. She knew Rose would catch on. Rose thought about that. Seven is a number so it would be a number but the seventh of this month has already passed. Today was the twenty third. Rose's eyes got big and she nodded. "Seven." she said. Seven really meant the twenty fifth. Which when adding the two numbers together, it equals seven.

The twenty fifth was the up coming Wednesday.

Rose nodded and Cloe nodded and they both smiled. Rose smiled because she loved riddles and solving them, Cloe smiled because she knew she was driving the enemy crazy trying to figure it out. Rose asked "What time?" and raised her eyebrows up and down. Cloe laughed and followed the same rule. "Twenty three." she said. Rose nodded, Cloe would start at five. Cloe slid Father Scovley's number on a napkin in Rose's hand and Rose knew that she was to call the Father. They wouldn't watch her much. She would have to drive to the church to tell him. Either way Rose got the message.

They talked about others things that they didn't have to code. They finished their tacos and went back to work. After work Cloe went home and worked out until she possibly couldn't lift another set of weights or anything else. For the next two days she did that until Wednesday came. All day at work she was nervous and prayed a lot. The work day cruised by and before she knew it, it was time to go to the church.

At four she left work and got there at four thirty. She had her books with her that contained the rituals and the paper Madam Agnes wrote Papa's words on.

Cloe went in the door and found the steps to the basement. *If her sisters could be here this would be easy!* she thought. The more women in a circle the better the chances are to banish a demon or whatever. But they said they didn't want to be involved and she understood that. She followed a corridor and came into a big empty room large enough to park forty cars in. To the very back was chairs and a table. She imagined that was where they were going to sit to watch. She set her things down and got busy drawing a circle around the area that she would conjure in. She hoped the setting of the church was enough to hide her actions from the outside world and the fallen wasn't on to her yet.

As she worked the clergy started filing in and while watching her, took their seats carefully. Rose came in sometime later carrying a caged owl and set it down. Cloe told her where she was at in the book and Rose helped draw some symbols around the very large circle. Cloe had brought a lot of chalk, it was the best thing to use. And salt where ever she could use it that was readable. Salt was very good to use.

They worked diligently and soon it was done. Cloe looked at Rose and nodded her head and Rose stepped out of the circle. Cloe took out the paper that Madam gave her and said as she looked it over, she put her hands together liked Papa showed her and started chanting "Three times I call your holy name, Lilith." and repeated it two more times before she said "Make her come, humiliating and repenting, to me by the most holy of holy."

Nothing happened and Cloe looked at Rose, Rose put her hands out as if to say 'its not my fault' and Cloe took a deep breath and said it with a lot of force again "Make her come, humiliating and repenting, to me by the most holy of holy." while she held her hands and fingers together. She could feel the ground tremble and the lights swayed. She held her ground as she could feel a force push against her. She braced herself with her legs and held her hands up with the symbol.

All of the sudden a white light burst into the room and everybody but Cloe shielded their eyes from the brightness. The light died down and there was smoke. *Cloe* focused on the smoke until it cleared and there was a figure that was like the one in the painting that she had seen and studied. The figure was lying on the ground like she was unconscious. As Cloe studied her Lilith's eyes flew open. She sucked in a hard breath as if she was holding her breath and looked around wildly. Cloe was afraid at first that she had made a mistake.

Did I get the right one? She thought.

But Lilith got up and while looking around came to Cloe's face and let out a high pitched scream like a banshee.

She wasn't happy.

"Yep, I got the right one." said Cloe out loud, more to herself than anybody else.

She got that reaction a lot when she pissed them off. Cloe looked around as everyone was taking their hands off their ears. Lilith was moving for her but stopped as she noticed that she had an audience.

Then she noticed that she was in a circle.

That really got her hopping mad.

All at once everyone was ducking as fireballs where flying through the air.

Moments later when the fire show stopped Cloe came out from behind a pillar that held the ceiling up in the basement and came out to see Lilith breathing heavily as if she was trying to calm herself. She looked like a caged wild cat as her slits in her wide oval eyes darted around the room once more as she eyed the priests and bishops.

She looked really awesome.

No wonder man can't resist her.

She had a beautiful body that was model perfect with white looking skin, she had arms and legs but her hands and feet were flames. She was naked but her long hair covered a lot of her body, it was full and black, and hung down to her waist and around her buttocks in waves and curls. She could make a man see anything they wanted to see.

Cloe looked around to make sure nobody was hurt by the burst of fireballs. One of the priests had a fire extinguisher and was putting out anything that had caught on fire.

"Why did you call me here?" she demanded in a husky voice mingled with a high pitch.

Cloe licked her lips and looked at Lilith and Lilith looked at her. "I brought you here so that you wouldn't help the fallen. I know of the plan of the war in heaven and to free your brethren and Satan. You can't do this Lilith."

As if she was going to talk any sense into her.

"Why can't I?"

"Because it would end time as we know it."

"Maybe It's time to see who is to reign supreme." she said with a triumphant voice.

"We don't need to find out. It's known everywhere." Cloe said.

"Your faith is astounding."

"So is your ego."

"You plan to stop me?" she asked with a laugh.

"I hope so." Cloe said more to herself than Lilith.

Lilith began to square off and Cloe took a stance. Lilith began to glow and suddenly fire balls were flying everywhere. Cloe screamed out to everyone and people scattered or ducked down. Cloe ran and slid behind the pillars again. The fireballs were hitting the pillar with such a force it was bumping Cloe forward from her back. When it became quiet Cloe peeked out from behind her cover and Lilith floated in mid air. Lilith saw Cloe peek out and let out a joyful laugh. She had white fangs that where long. Cloe slowly came out from the pillar and stood up. She looked at Rose and nodded. Rose uncovered the owl in a cage. The plan was to make Lilith her true form and send her essence into the owl. Cloe looked back at Lilith and watched her watch Rose. She saw the owl and her face became studious. She didn't turn her head but her eyes went to Cloe and Cloe stood there waiting.

Lilith looked back at the owl and Rose began to chant a sacred chant to transform Lilith. Lilith began to glow again and aimed everything towards Rose. Rose's eyes got big as she realized what was happening and ran and leaped over a table, tilting it with her as she landed on the floor. The table acted as a shield and the fire hit it and fanned out to disappear. Cloe took that opportunity to run around Lilith and grab a blanket that was damp with holy water sitting by the priest. She unfolded it as she ran and jumped into the air with the blanket wide open. She came behind Lilith and covered her with the blanket. Cloe hung on with everything she had to bring the figure down to the ground.

Lilith was screaming and flailing wildly as Cloe hung on. Cloe felt tremendous heat all of the sudden and had to let go. Lilith had started the blanket on fire and Cloe quickly scrambled to her feet to run behind the pillar again. Cloe looked up at the ceiling and wished she had thought of other ways to stop Lilith. She was totally unprepared. She wished the sisters would have been here, She looked out from behind the pillar to see Lilith come up from the flames of the fire like a jack in the box. She was looking for Cloe. She came after the pillar that Cloe was hiding behind.

Rose saw her coming for Cloe and screamed at Cloe to get out of there. Cloe looked frantically around and saw the water pipes above her. She ran and jumped and barely grabbed a pipe overhead. She lunged again and got the other hand on the pipe and brought her feet up to bend over the pipe to bring her body up on top of it. She saw Lilith come around the pillar at that time and got up to crawl down the water pipes away from Lilith.

Lilith screamed and looked around. There were several pillars within the circle. She went looking for Cloe but couldn't get out of the protection circle the girls had made. Lilith didn't know that Cloe couldn't either, or she might have figured out that Cloe was directly on top of her on the water pipe. Cloe was trying to slow her breathing down so she wouldn't make any noise. She was running out of options.

Suddenly the basement door came open and in came five figures in different colored robes. They were coming in single file. The first color was blue, then came red, then came white, then came black and last came green. You couldn't see there faces but Cloe knew who they were. She smiled as she realized her sisters had came just in time.

Lilith whirled around and Rose came up from behind the table. Cloe jumped down and told Rose "Rose, it's the sister's. Put on the robe they will give you then we'll space out around the circle and chant. They will help us!" and Cloe took her place and caught the purple robe that was thrown to her. She put it on and watched Lilith as she looked around at the visitors. Rose was thrown a yellow robe and put it on. The women came around the circle chanting a chant of protection so that Lilith couldn't attack them.

Lilith didn't know that the robes would protect them from any onslaught she could bring. She looked like a caged animal ready to attack. She looked at each one like she couldn't decide who to go against first. Finally she lit up like a small sun and fireballs came out of her sphere like fireworks. They shot in every direction but stopped short of the women and the protection spell. Sue looked at Cloe and said "I hope you have a plan." Cloe looked at Lilith and then she knew what to do.

Someone had said to her once that they would be there to help with Lilith. She had to call Michael. Once again she laced her fingers together like Papa Whitney had showed her and called Michael this time. The sisters helped her and chanted the same thing with their fingers laced together like hers.

Michael showed up in a rainbow of lights. It was like someone had busted a prism and the shards were floating around. When it cleared there stood Michael. Lilith looked at him and hissed. She didn't have a mean look on her face anymore. It was more of a worried look. Michael told Cloe to get the owl and Cloe moved quickly to bring the birdcage into the middle of the circle. Michael put his sword toward Lilith and after shouting the same words over and over again, the sword began to glow. Lilith screamed and went to cover her face with her hands. Then a lightening bolt came out of the sword and hit Lilith. It transformed her into the owl.

When the lightening died down and disappeared, all that was left was the owl in the cage. Michael had disappeared also. Everyone looked around at each other and it was deafly quiet in the basement. Cloe realized that they did it and she told everyone "We did it!" Everyone was now patting each other on the back and talking about how Michael showed up when the clergy behind them made a noise. The sisters and Rose stopped talking and turned around to look at them. Father Scovley waved to Cloe and smiled. Cloe nodded back. They took off their robes and went to gather around the owl. It changed colors. Its body was white but went to a blood red at the ends of the wings and talons. Cloe went to pick up the bird but she suddenly heard from behind her "I think that is our bird now."

Cloe turned around and went to the group of clergy standing behind them. She nodded and lifted up the cage to bring it to one of the clergy members who had his hand outreached. The clergy took the birdcage and the owl let out a piercing screech. Cloe said "Make sure nothing happens to that owl. They will be looking for it and even might attack you all for it."

"We understand." One said. And with that they took the bird and filed out of the basement door. Father Scovley came up and squeezed her shoulder and nodded. Cloe patted his hand. He walked off with the others. Cloe and the sisters picked everything up and cleaned up before leaving themselves. They made their way to a local tavern and celebrated. They were all amazed at the events that took place that night. Sometimes they were quiet and thinking. Then someone would say something and they all began to talk and drink at their drinks.

Cloe was thinking about the night's event and she figured out that they all needed to be there to make Michael appear in the circle. Not only to help but to make the others believe. She thought that she probably couldn't have done it by herself, that it did take a full circle of female energy to win. And is she did fight on her own, it probably would have taken a long time.

"What made you guys change your mind?" Cloe asked the sisters. After looking around at each other Cheryl said "We all couldn't sleep. We all had this feeling" and the other sisters nodded to each other.

"And I called Sue." Cindy said. "And she told me what was happening."

"And I called Lisa." Sue said "And she told me she felt the same thing that I felt."

"Then I called Cindy." Billie Jo said "And she told me what was happening."

"So we all met at my house and decided to come and help." Sue said.

Cloe stood up and gave a speech to thank them for showing up. She knew that they risked a lot to show up to help. She was glad they did. Rose said "Amen to that." and everyone laughed. Cloe raised her glass and said "To God and

Michael." and everyone followed and drank up on last time before heading home.

On her way home she thought about the future. She knew it wasn't over between her and the fallen or demons. She imagined her life was still in danger as before. But at least they wouldn't take her lightly either. One thing was for sure, she couldn't wait to see what was in store for her now. She was glad this night was over, or was it?

Her cell phone rang. She looked at the caller ID. It was Father Scovley.